Soaring Eagle

D1021476

3 1853 01298 9708

SOARING EAGLE

Stephanie Grace Whitson

THOMAS NELSON PUBLISHERS
Nashville • Atlanta • London • Vancouver

Published in Nashville, Tennessee, by Thomas Nelson, Inc.

Scripture quotations are from:

The Holy Bible, KING JAMES VERSION.

The NEW KING JAMES VERSION of the Bible. Copyright © 1979, 1980, 1982, 1990, 1994,
Thomas Nelson, Inc., Publishers.

Scripture quotations noted NASB are from the NEW AMERICAN STANDARD BIBLE, Copyright © 1960, 1962, 1963, 1968, 1971, 1972, 1973, 1975, 1977 by The Lockman Foundation and
are used by permission.

Library of Congress Cataloging-in-Publication Data

Whitson, Stephanie Grace.
    Soaring Eagle : a novel / Stephanie Grace Whitson.
        p.   cm. — (Prairie winds : bk. 2)
    ISBN 0-7852-7617-3
    1. Frontier and pioneer life—West (U. S.)—Fiction. 2. Indians of North America—West
(U. S.)—Fiction. 3. Women pioneers—West (U. S.)—Fiction. I. Title. II. Series: Whitson,
Stephanie Grace. Prairie winds ; bk. 2.
PS3573.H555S6 1996
813'.54—dc20
                                                    95–39368
                                                      CIP

Printed in the United States of America
13 14 15 PHX 04 03 02

FOR BOB

My leader, my example,
my beloved, my friend

Acknowledgments

Now thanks be to God who always leads us in triumph in Christ, and through us diffuses the fragrance of His knowledge in every place. . . . Thanks be to God for His indescribable gift!

2 Corinthians 2:14, 9:15†

- Thank you, Bob and Shannon and Max, for hugs and love and willingness to help.
- Thank you, everyone, for your kind words and encouragement.
- Thank you, Pastor Gil, for allowing me to put your words in Pastor Thundercloud's mouth.
- Thank you, Lonnie, for your continued encouragement.

In a world where parents and teenagers are expected to disagree, battle, and generally dislike one another, I have been blessed with two teenagers who are just that—a blessing. During the writing of this book, they have been especially precious, and I want to say a special thank you to Brooke and Zachary for:

- challenging me to be more godly
- willingly using your talents and abilities to serve our family
- making faces
- doing chores
- reading what I write and saying you like it.

You are both treasures, and you have no idea how very much I love you and how often I thank God for what He is doing in and through you.

I have one wish for every reader: "May the God of peace Himself sanctify you completely; and may your whole spirit, soul, and body be preserved blameless at the coming of our Lord Jesus Christ. He who calls you is faithful, who also will do it (1 Thess. 5:23-24†).

PROLOGUE

The battlefield was quiet. Only an occasional shot was still being fired somewhere in the woods about a mile down the valley. Here, an eerie silence prevailed, broken only by the occasional low chant of a victory song as the warriors collected souvenirs from the dead.

Soaring Eagle stood surveying the battlefield. At his feet lay the body of one of the soldiers. The stench of death filled the air. Soaring Eagle closed his eyes and inhaled deeply, reminding himself to remember this victory.

Taking up his knife he crouched down and grasped the soldier's thick black hair in one hand. The glint of gold stopped the knife in midair. Soaring Eagle tore the bit of gold from around the soldier's neck, examining it carefully. As he turned it over, it fell open, revealing the likeness of a young woman. Soaring Eagle caught his breath and stared in wonder, not at the young woman, but at the other one—the one whose gray eyes stared back at him from beside the younger woman's face.

She was older, but the mouth was set in a serious straight line. Soaring Eagle remembered. The hair was held back in the way of the whites, but waves and curls that could not be tamed still framed the face. Soaring Eagle remembered. Looking into the eyes, Soaring Eagle knew. Here, looking back at him, was Walks the Fire . . . his mother.

He had broken the chain pulling it from the white soldier's neck. Now he reached into the pouch at his side and drew out a buffalo sinew. Shutting the locket, he threaded it onto the sinew, tied a strong knot, and drew it over his head. As he pulled it down, his fingers traced the other bit of gold that had hung about his neck for many years . . . never taken off . . . cherished as the last remnant of his mother's existence.

A shout from one of the other warriors who scavenged the hillside interrupted his memories. Soaring Eagle stood up and replaced his knife in its scabbard, raising his hand to again feel the outline of the cross that hung at his neck. Then, touching the locket to be certain that it was secure, he leaped onto his pony and raced back to the village.

The battlefield was quiet. Distant shots were all that remained of the encounter. Long Hair and his men lay dead. It would take ten days for the news to reach Lincoln, Nebraska, where Walks the Fire would hear of it and fear for the life of her new son-in-law and wonder about the fate of her adopted son. It would be even longer before the truth was known.

The son-in-law, MacKenzie Baird, lay dead on the Little Big Horn, while the adopted son, a Lakota brave, rode away with a locket in place of a scalp.

CHAPTER 1

 Our persecutors are swifter than the eagles of the heaven: they pursued us upon the mountains, they laid wait for us in the wilderness.

Lamentations 4:19

A re they all killed?" Sitting Bull asked.

Soaring Eagle dismounted and approached the chief. "*Wicunkasotapelo!* (We killed them all!)"

Sitting Bull nodded and turned away. "Then let's go back to camp."

Soaring Eagle held in his dancing pony and followed Sitting Bull to where the women scurried about treating their wounded and erecting scaffolds for their dead.

A small cry came from one group of women as Soaring Eagle rode by. A young squaw rushed to his pony. "You are wounded," she said, reaching up to touch the fresh flow of blood on his arm.

Soaring Eagle sharply withdrew from her touch. Still, his voice was gentle as he answered. "It is nothing."

The squaw drew in a deep breath and made a face. "Death is in the air here."

Soaring Eagle nodded and turned to look back at the hill dotted with bodies dressed in blue. "We will need to move the camp." He urged his pony forward. The young squaw reached out once again. This time she put her hand on his knee and whispered, "I will cook tonight, Soaring Eagle. Perhaps you would like to come to my father's fire to share the tales of this great victory." Her eyes shone as she looked up at him. "You have gained many new feathers today. I heard Walking Bear and Lone Wolf talk of you. You counted coup no less than four times."

He wanted to end the conversation abruptly, but he knew that the group of young women Winona had been talking to were watching. Graciously Soaring Eagle smiled at her as he sought an answer. When it came, it was not what she wanted to hear. "I will not be sharing victory songs tonight." Gunfire in the distance gave him an excuse. "There are still soldiers up on that bluff. I want to get a shot at them." Soaring Eagle turned his pony sharply and urged him away, leaving Winona standing in the dust.

"Will he be coming to your campfire tonight?" called out one of the young squaws insolently. "He has a bit of gold from the soldiers. He did not offer it to *you*." The voice taunted Winona. "He is too old for you, anyway. You should be hoping for a younger man."

The taunt had its desired effect. Winona bustled over to the group of young women and hissed back, "Soaring Eagle is the best hunter in our band. He is the bravest warrior—and there is not a man in the village who would *dare* race his ponies!" As Winona listed Soaring Eagle's virtues to her friends, a middle-aged woman approached the group.

Prairie Flower scolded the young women. "Hush, now, gossips! What a time is this to be telling silly girl's tales! There is work to be done here!" She shooed the group away and, putting her arm about Winona's shoulders, drew her aside.

"You know they say these things only to make you angry."

Winona kicked at the dust. "They are such children!"

Prairie Flower smiled and patted the young girl's arm. "They are *your* age, I believe." Pausing for a moment, she said in a voice warm with kindness, "Soaring Eagle is a good man. But he *is* much older than you."

Winona shook Prairie Flower's arm off her shoulders and answered defiantly, "The braves my age are fools. They make war to prove their bravery. They make war to bring honor to their families. They make war to win horses. They make war to win hearts. I am sick of war. I want to go where there is no more war."

Prairie Flower considered the outburst before replying softly, "I do not think there is such a place. We are becoming like the mound of earth that rises from the waters of the Moonshell. All around us the white men swirl, taking more and more of the small mound of earth on which we live."

Shots rang out in the distance. The small group of soldiers had taken shelter on one of the high bluffs. In the distance the women could see their warriors' ponies darting back and forth at the foot of the bluff.

Prairie Flower muttered, "I heard them say that they would leave a way open to the east in case the soldiers wanted to get away."

"Good!" came the response. "I hope they go away. I hope they will leave us alone!" Winona's face brightened. "Perhaps then Soaring Eagle will come to my father's campfire—"

Prairie Flower interrupted her,"Perhaps then he will wrap you in his buffalo robe?"

Winona smiled as Prairie Flower hugged her and then pushed her toward her father's tepee. "Go! There is much work to be done. Soaring Eagle said the camp would have to be moved, and I think he is right. Your mother will be expecting you to help her." The two women scurried off and made ready to move amid the sounds of the distant skirmish.

All that day and into the evening, shots continued to be fired. Sitting Bull, Soaring Eagle, and many others charged to and fro, daring the bullets from the soldiers on the bluff, while the eerie sound of mourning songs and shrieks of grief from those in camp who had lost loved ones in the battle rang out. The soldiers on the bluff were unnerved by what they thought were the sounds of victory dances. But the Sioux did not rejoice. Too many of their own had been lost that day.

When Sitting Bull returned to camp, he called his young warriors to him, noting with satisfaction that they had obeyed his warning. He had had a vision of a great victory less than two weeks before they had camped here on the Greasy Grass.

When he shared the vision, he had warned his people: "The victory will be a gift from Wakan Tanka. Kill the soldiers, but do not take the spoils. If you set your heart on the goods of the white man, it will prove a curse to this nation."

Sitting Bull stared around the campfire at his young followers, and he was glad. "You have done well. But my heart is filled with sadness at what I have seen around us. Guns, Army horses, and white men's clothing are everywhere." Sitting Bull pointed an accusing finger at Soaring Eagle who had just approached the group crouched about the campfire. The gold locket shone in the light of the fire. "You have taken the spoils. Now you will be at the mercy of the white man. You will starve at his hands. And the soldiers will crush you."

Soaring Eagle answered harshly, "I believed your warning, Sitting Bull. It seemed right to me. I have taken this because it was something very dear to me. The soldier who wore it seems close to me, now, and I am sorry for his death." As he spoke Soaring Eagle removed the locket to open it. While he fumbled with it, two of the younger braves nudged one another and snickered.

Finally, Soaring Eagle managed to open the locket. "I do not know its meaning, but this is the one we called Walks the Fire when she was among us. It has been many moons since she was among us, but I called her *Ina* then. I think this other one must be the sister Prairie Flower told me of when she came back from the fort."

Soaring Eagle paused. It had become very quiet about the fire. Every eye was on him as he held the locket out to Sitting Bull. The chief took it and examined it carefully, turning it over and over in his palm. He looked from the faces in the photos to Soaring Eagle and back again many times. At last Sitting Bull snapped the locket shut and returned it to Soaring Eagle. "Perhaps Wakan Tanka will consider this truth and save you from the punishment that will come upon our people."

After the brief council around the fire, the Lakota hurried to complete their burials. The next morning, the newly armed warriors gathered and made a last charge against the entrenched survivors of the battle. With many new guns and much ammunition scavenged from the dead, they grew hungry for more blood. But the women of the village were striking the last of the tepees, and Sitting Bull had his way. Charging up and down the long line of young warriors he shouted, "It is enough! They came against us. We have killed most of them. If we kill them all, they will only send a bigger army to punish us."

Soaring Eagle reined in his pony and followed Sitting Bull back toward the village. Prairie Flower had already struck the tepee and waited only for the appearance of her adopted son before heading toward the Big Horn Mountains. When Soaring Eagle rode by her and took his usual place at the head of the long procession, she shouted encouragement, "It was a great battle, my son. Tonight we will have a victory dance." Winona walked by her side, and as Soaring Eagle glanced their way, her face lit up with a hopeful smile.

But Soaring Eagle did not join the victory dance that night. While his friends rejoiced, he withdrew to the tepee he once shared with Walks the Fire, his widowed mother; Old One, his grandmother; and Prairie Flower, their good friend. His mother had been abducted by Howling Wolf many moons ago. Howling Wolf had died in the same blizzard that had wiped out any hope of ever finding Walks the Fire. Old One had gone on to the next life not long after that. Now there were only Soaring Eagle and Prairie Flower. Prairie Flower had joined the circle of women dancing about the fire.

As the shadows of dancers played on the skins of the village tepees, Soaring Eagle sat alone, staring at the faces in the locket.

CHAPTER 2

O my God, my soul is cast down within me.

Psalm 42:6

Mama's room was dark. Her favorite quilt still covered the bed, and a small pine table at the side of the bed still held her Bible. The dresser was nearly bare, just as it had always been, except for the wedding photo of MacKenzie Baird and his new bride LisBeth. In the dusky light, LisBeth moved across the room and picked up the photo. Tears welled in her eyes as she cradled it in one hand, tracing the pattern of roses that trailed down the side of the gilded frame. LisBeth walked to the window and pushed back the heavy curtains. Afternoon light flooded the room.

Footsteps sounded in the hall. Joseph hesitated at the door, a worn carpetbag in hand. LisBeth turned quickly and smiled through her tears. Looking down at the photo in her hand, she found no words to say. Joseph set the carpetbag down just inside the door and retreated down the hall, returning a few moments later with the rest of LisBeth's baggage.

LisBeth stared out the window of Mama's room and said in a half-whisper, "Thank you, Joseph. You've always been such a good friend."

Joseph took a step toward the door. "You need anything else right now, LisBeth?"

LisBeth shook her head. Silence filled the room, pressing in on the two friends, creating an awkward breach between them. LisBeth tried to close it. "I don't know quite what to say, Joseph, . . ." Her voice trailed off, and she took a deep breath before continuing. "All I could think about was coming home,

home to the Hathaway House Hotel. Mama would be here working, and she'd bring me here to her room, and . . ." LisBeth barely controlled her sobs.

His usually booming voice was gentle and quiet as he tried to ease her pain. "That's all right, LisBeth. That's all right. Nothin' you *need* to say or do right now. Jus' unpack and rest up. I'm still here for you. Just over at the livery. And Augusta—she's not your mama, LisBeth, but she loves you like you was her own child. They's plenty of time to think through it all. The Lord'll help you."

LisBeth cast a glance at her mother's Bible. She answered miserably, "Oh, Joseph, I *want* to believe that. Really, I do. But there seems to be such a great *space* between the Lord and me. I don't know how to get across it. When I was little and there was trouble, Mama always took up that book—she always knew just what to read, just what to say. When they told me Mac was dead, all I could think was, *I'll go home now, and Mama will know what to say. She'll know what to do.* Then I got off that train, and she wasn't there. You brought me home and Aunt Augusta told me that Mama *died* last week. . . . " LisBeth stopped and bit her lip. She looked up at Joseph. "It's hard, Joseph," she whispered. "It's real hard."

As she talked, LisBeth's hands gripped the edges of the photograph. Tighter and tighter she gripped until her whole body was trembling with the effort to control her emotions. Just at the moment Joseph prepared to run for help, Augusta entered the room.

Augusta Hathaway described herself as "all prickles and quills." But the woman who quickly crossed the room to comfort the late Jesse King's daughter showed none of that. Augusta took the photo from the trembling hands and placed it on the dresser. Settling LisBeth on the edge of the bed, Augusta said gently, "Now, honey, you just sit here while I get you a glass of water. Then I'll help you take down your hair and you can rest."

LisBeth gratefully allowed herself to be mothered. She obediently drank the water and sat still while Augusta unpinned and brushed her abundant dark hair. She watched numbly as Augusta unpacked the carpetbag and arranged its contents in the empty dresser drawers.

Where are Mama's things? LisBeth wondered. But she was too weary to ask. Augusta spread LisBeth's nightgown across the bed and patted LisBeth's hand as she said, "Now, honey, I know you're a grown woman. I'll not be bossing you around like you was a child. But right now what you need is to rest. You've had a terrible shock, I know. You rest, and when you're ready, Joseph and I will be here to tell you everything."

While Augusta talked, she retrieved a button hook, undid LisBeth's shoes, set them side by side near the rocker, and retreated toward the door. Joseph had long since disappeared. "Now you take a little rest, and when you waken, we'll have a long, long talk." Augusta's blue eyes sparkled with love as she gave LisBeth one last encouraging smile. Before she closed the door, Augusta added, "LisBeth, honey, if you could have just *seen* your mama's face when we found her. I don't know what it was that carried her to heaven, but it surely was something that made her happy. I've never seen such a look of peace and love on a woman's face."

Augusta's firm footsteps retreated down the hall toward the kitchen. LisBeth sat on the edge of the bed for a long while, fingering her dark hair, trying to sort through things. *I came all this way . . . I just knew Mama could help me know what to do.* Lifting her eyes to her wedding photo, LisBeth gave in to grief. She buried her face in her pillow and cried fiercely.

The Lord is my shepherd; I shall not want. The words echoed in her mind, and it was Mama's voice saying them. Mama had read those words over and over again. Whenever they had faced a problem, she had read or recited those words. But now they brought LisBeth little comfort. *But Mama . . . I do want,* she thought bitterly. *I want my husband back. . . . I want the life we were planning . . . and I want you!* Angry tears stained the pillow as LisBeth spent the emotions she had stored up through the long train ride home from the west.

When the tears were finished, something replaced them. She did not realize it, but in rejecting the words that had always comforted her mother, LisBeth made way for a tiny root of bitterness in her young life.

CHAPTER 3

 As thou knowest not what is the way of the spirit . . . even so thou knowest not the works of God who maketh all.

Ecclesiastes 11:5

LisBeth woke from her afternoon rest feeling weary. Dragging herself out of bed, she settled into the rocker by the window and stared through the glass, remembering the empty, flat expanse of land that she and her mother had come to only a few years ago. Then, Lincoln, Nebraska, had been little more than a few dugouts and cabins, among them a small boardinghouse run by Augusta Hathaway. Augusta had taken in Jesse King and her daughter, LisBeth, had grown to love them as her own family, had included them in her plans to transform the boardinghouse into a prosperous hotel. Now the Centennial Opera House was just about completed. Beyond the Centennial several new houses dotted the landscape. A white picket fence had sprung from the prairie to protect a two-story abode from errant wildlife. *I remember when Mama wouldn't let me walk to Miss Griswall's school alone for fear a coyote'd cross my path!* She smiled briefly at the memory, but then fresh grief set in and she stood up abruptly, pulling the curtains across the window to shut out the view of the growing city.

LisBeth finished unpacking the large valise Augusta had left untouched. Familiar sounds filtered down the short hallway. Dinner was being readied for the hotel boarders. Taking a deep breath, LisBeth opened the door and headed for the kitchen. She hesitated at the door, watching as fifteen-year-old Sarah Biddle and her nine-year-old brother

Tom moved about. They worked as a team, Tom limping about beside Sarah, often knowing what she needed without her having to say a word.

Sarah and Tom looked up from the open oven and quickly set aside the trays of fresh biscuits. Sarah took the lead. Wiping her hands on her muslin apron, she crossed the kitchen quickly and held out her hand to LisBeth.

"I'm awful sorry about your husband, Miz Baird. And your ma too."

Tom added. "I'm sorry, too, Miz Baird."

LisBeth had had almost too much sympathy that day. Controlling the urge to weep, she took the offered hand and grasped it momentarily before saying, "Yes. Well. Thank you." There was an awkward silence until Augusta came in. Taking LisBeth by the hand she led her to the table where the July 12 edition of the *Nebraska State Journal* lay open.

"I thought you'd like to see it, LisBeth," Augusta said. "Charles Gere did right by your ma."

LisBeth read:

Born into the Spirit world at the Hathaway House Hotel in Lincoln on Sunday, July 10, Mrs. Jesse King, after a sojourn on this earth of 54 years.

She was born into the earth life in St. Clair County, Illinois, in 1822, was married in 1841 to her husband, Homer King, who predeceased her, was the mother of one daughter, Lis-Beth, who grew to womanhood, and one son, Jacob, who passed as an infant to that life where she has now joined him.

Mrs. King was a consistent Christian, having been baptized as a young woman and a faithful member of the Congregational Church until summoned by the Death Angel to enter on the enjoyment of the future life.

Mrs. King lived a full life of goodness and beauty, affording her child and friends an example well worthy of their imitation. Sustained by her confidence in God's love and her expectation of a happy life to come, she calmly fell asleep to wake in that home where there are no more separations.

On Tuesday her body was laid in the earth, the services conducted by Rev. W. E. Copeland.

As LisBeth read, Sarah and Tom returned to work. Joseph came in with another stash of firewood for the stove. Exchanging a concerned expression with Augusta, he helped himself to a cup of coffee and took an inordinate amount of time to stack the wood. When a log fell off the pile and hit the floor, LisBeth jumped. She wiped her tears and blew her nose and looked up at Augusta. Everyone in the kitchen appeared to be working furiously. In reality they were doing nothing, waiting for LisBeth to get through her mother's obituary.

"I want to go to Wyuka, Augusta." LisBeth took a deep breath. "I remember all the fuss when they chose those rolling hills so far from town. I thought it was all so silly, bothering over a cemetery. But then, I never thought about someone *I* loved being buried there. I wish Mac had a place like that—nearby—"

Joseph tried to rescue LisBeth from a new bout of tears. "You just say when, LisBeth. I'll hitch up the carriage and take you out there any time you say."

Augusta mumbled something about there being plenty of time for that, but LisBeth rose and said, "I think I'd like to go now, Joseph. Maybe," her throat tightened, "maybe it will help."

Joseph was already out the door.

LisBeth retreated to Jesse's room. As she tied on her black bonnet, she studied her reflection in the dresser mirror. Her dark eyes were red and puffy, and thin lines had appeared at the corners of each eye. Once a warm, golden brown, her skin now looked almost sallow. She had lost weight, and her high cheekbones were more prominent, the slight dimple in her cheek more pronounced.

LisBeth remembered an evening less than a year ago when her mother Jesse had said wistfully, "You got that dimple from your pa, Rides the Wind, LisBeth. He was a handsome brave—at least *I* always thought so." Then Jesse had laid her own fair-skinned hand next to LisBeth's. "Fact is, LisBeth, you look mostly like your pa. His skin. His eyes." She had sighed and added softly, "I sure wish you could have known him, LisBeth."

LisBeth had reached out to take her mother's hands in her own. "Do you wish we still lived among the Lakota, Mama?"

Jesse had thought carefully before answering. "No, LisBeth. The Lord brought us here. At least that's how I've come to view it. With your pa dead, it would have been harder for us. I was Walks the Fire to the Lakota, but I wasn't really Lakota. Except for Prairie Flower, I didn't have many friends." Smiling again, Jesse had said, "We're where we belong now. I still wish sometimes for you to know Soaring Eagle. I'll just leave that in God's hands. He always does what's best. If it's to be, it will be."

The memory of Jesse faded and was replaced by a feeling of aloneness so complete that it caused a physical hurt deep inside LisBeth. A soft knock sounded at the door. Sarah stood in the doorway, hands clasped tightly, her earnest blue eyes blinking rapidly.

"Miz Baird, I feel so bad about what's happened to you. You don't know me, ma'am, but your ma—"

Eager to block out the painful memories, LisBeth begged, "Sarah, please, come in. Sit here, in Mama's rocker."

Sarah settled nervously on the edge of the rocker while LisBeth talked. "Mama wrote all about you and Tom, Sarah. She went on and on about how hard you work and about how smart Tom is. She had great plans for Tom."

"Yes, ma'am, Tom has always been the smart one." Sarah said it proudly, but then she returned to her subject. "What I wanted to say, Miz Baird, was, I feel kinda bad about bein' in your room, now that you're back and all. I don't *have* to be so near the living quarters. Maybe Miz Hathaway could give us another room—"

LisBeth interrupted. "Don't be silly, Sarah." Her next words won Sarah's allegiance and something approaching love. LisBeth reached out and took both of Sarah's hands. "Mama loved you and Tom, Sarah. I've always wanted a sister. I've lost two brothers in my life. Little Jacob died long before I was born, when he was only a baby, and the other brother—well, circumstances just tore us apart. I've never even met him—" LisBeth stopped short. "Please, Sarah, let's be friends. And don't even think about the room a second longer. It's not *my* room anymore, Sarah. It's *your* room."

Sarah squeezed LisBeth's hands, gratitude shining in her eyes. A year of living with Augusta Hathaway and Jesse King had prepared Sarah Biddle to open the door of friendship when the opportunity arose. Now, she quickly turned the handle and fairly flung it open as she began to share a bit of herself. "LisBeth, I know how it feels—to have people you love taken away. I know it's awful for you right now. But it'll get better. You'll get through it."

Something told LisBeth to let Sarah Biddle talk. "I had a sister once. Her name was Emma." Sarah withdrew her hands from LisBeth's and twisted the edge of her apron. She studied the floor as she continued. "Ma got sick and Pa wouldn't bring the doctor. He just said, 'We got no money to pay for a doctor.' Well, one day, I was rockin' by the wood stove, trying to soothe Baby Emma. Then Pa brought in some lady. Said she could help Baby Emma. Said she'd get her some milk, and that Tom and me could come see her whenever we wanted. Said when Ma got better, Emma could come home."

Sarah looked desperately into LisBeth's eyes. "So I let that lady take her. She said we could have her back just as soon as Ma got better. But Ma didn't get better, LisBeth. Ma died the next day. Then Pa took Tom and me to the Home for the Friendless. He said he'd come back for us. But he never did."

Sarah took a deep breath before concluding, "But what was even worse, LisBeth, was our Baby Emma was *gone*. Somebody rich just took her to be theirs."

LisBeth listened, breathing as soundlessly as possible, hoping that Sarah would stop, but knowing that she needed to go on.

Sarah smiled a tight, bitter smile. "'Course, nobody ever wanted Tom and me. I figured, I let go of Baby Emma, and they took her. I never let go of Tom. Plenty of folks wanted me to come work for them. But they wouldn't take Tom. So we just stayed at the Home. Then we got put on that train. Nobody wanted us then, either—not in all the towns we stopped at. They'd look at Tom's limp and just turn away. We'd get back on the train and ride to the next town. Tom and me finally ran away. I figured we could do better on our own. Nobody wanted us until your ma found us and took us in."

Sarah stopped abruptly. She flushed with embarrassment. "Goodness—I rattled on and on. As if you don't have enough troubles of your own." Sarah was flustered. "What I wanted to say was I *know* how it hurts. But it gets better. It does. You'll be all right. You got Joseph. You got Aunt Augusta. You got your Ma's love inside you—and Mr. Baird's love too. And, if you want, you got me for a friend," Sarah's voice lowered slightly as she timidly said the word *friend*. She was surprised to realize that sharing her past with LisBeth had come so easily. She felt strangely refreshed, as if the telling of the hurt had somehow cleaned out the last remnant of bitterness she had been nursing.

Impulsively, LisBeth reached out and stepped through the door of friendship that Sarah had opened so willingly. As she hugged Sarah, Lisbeth's eyes filled with tears. Augusta's voice rang down the hall and into the room. "LisBeth! Joseph has the carriage ready. . . ."

Joseph had been waiting patiently with his finest team and carriage for quite a few minutes when LisBeth finally stepped outside the hotel and climbed up beside him. As he urged the horses to a swift trot, the wind came up. It was a hot, dry wind, and before they had traveled a mile, LisBeth felt sweat trickle down her back and wished she had minded Augusta's suggestion to make the journey early the next morning, before the afternoon sun had launched its assault.

Shading her eyes with one hand, LisBeth gripped the side of the carriage seat and stared to the northeast, along the banks of the Salt Creek. A few clumps of elms and cottonwood flourished along the creek beds, but no shade gave respite to the two travelers heading out O Street to the "place of rest" chosen by the legislature.

"Why'd they have to pick a spot so far away?" LisBeth wondered aloud.

"They's bad air around a cemetery, LisBeth. Leastways, white folks thinks they is," Joseph offered. "They wanted it far out from the city."

"Well, they certainly accomplished that," LisBeth snapped.

"You want to turn back? We can do this in the mornin' when it's cooler."

LisBeth shook her head. "No, Joseph. I need to do it now. I've been dreading it something awful. I just need to get it done." LisBeth interrupted herself. "Stop, Joseph. Just a moment—see those flowers? Mama loved those. Just wait a minute." She was already jumping down from the carriage and hurrying to a clump of bushes covered with bright orange blossoms. LisBeth shooed away several butterflies and gathered an enormous bouquet before climbing back up beside Joseph.

"I recollect your Mama did like those—"

"Remember that time those men came in from Omaha, and Augusta was so worried about impressing them with Lincoln's fare—and Mama ended up cooking a whole meal with wild things?"

Joseph smiled at the memory. "And them Omaha gents was surprised as could be. Your Mama had fun, too, teasin' 'em about them eatin' dog meat stew."

LisBeth chuckled briefly before sighing, "We made soup from the roots of this plant and—" Her throat tightened. She stopped in midsentence. They had arrived at the entrance to Wyuka Cemetery.

Joseph eased the moment, "They gonna have winding lanes here, they said, jus' like in a big city park. Got lots of plans for trees and flowers too. They gonna make it a real nice buryin' place, LisBeth. It's a good place to be laid to rest."

LisBeth looked about as she asked, "Where?"

Joseph didn't have to answer. They had turned left inside the entrance and wound around the base of a low hill. A few small headstones shone in the afternoon sun, and there was one new grave. LisBeth had to shade her eyes from the brilliant white to find the name. It was carved under a simple design of palm fronds.

Jesse King
Born January 26, 1822
Died July 10, 1876
Aged 54 years, 5 mos., 14 days.
Gone home

Joseph helped LisBeth down and then led the team to a small brook that ran along one edge of the cemetery grounds. LisBeth stood staring at the tombstone for a long while before bending over to place her bouquet at its base.

"You were only fifty-four years old, Mama," LisBeth whispered. "I thought I'd have you forever. I thought you'd always be here, at home. I thought you'd always be here." The young voice quavered, and LisBeth cried freely before going on. "Mac's gone, too, Mama. My dear, beautiful Mac is gone. How did you *do* it, Mama? How did you *bear* it when Papa died?" LisBeth sniffed loudly and blew her nose. Then she sat down on the prairie and ran her fingers through the coarse, dry grass. She looked around her at the barren hills.

"I wonder every day about what it must have been like for you, Mama. You loved a Lakota man, and then he died. You raised his son, and then you were forced to leave him behind. You had so much pain. But when I remember you, I remember you smiling. How did you do it?

"I'm going to plant a tree here for you, Mama. You know what kind? A pine tree. I remember you told me that Papa once cut down the tallest lodgepole pine you'd ever seen, just so that you could have the biggest tepee in the village. Well, now you'll be able to rest in the shade of a pine tree again, Mama."

In only a few moments in the sun, the brilliant bouquet had

begun to wilt. "I miss you, Mama. Without you and Mac, I'm not sure where I fit in the world. When I was Jesse King's daughter and MacKenzie Baird's wife, it didn't matter much that I was half-Lakota and half-white. But now I'm all alone. I'm not sure *how* or *who* I should be." LisBeth stood up wearily and brushed off her black skirt. The wind tugged at her clothes. Reaching up to straighten her bonnet, LisBeth whispered, "There are so many things I don't understand, Mama. I wish you were still here. You'd know what I should do about—everything."

Staring down at the new grave, LisBeth waited a few moments longer before turning abruptly and hurrying away. On the way back to Lincoln, both LisBeth and Joseph made several attempts at conversation, but each attempt failed. Finally, they rode along listening to the hot, dry wind blowing across the open prairie.

When they drove up to the kitchen door, LisBeth climbed down from the carriage before Joseph could get around to her side to help her. Her eyes thanked him, but her voice failed her. She went inside, crossed the kitchen without a word to Sarah or Augusta, and retreated to her mother's room where she lay staring at the ceiling with no tears left to cry and an unquenched thirst for comfort.

When she finally fell asleep, Lakota warriors and the U.S. Army crowded into the darkened room. They engaged in mortal combat until only one soldier and one brave remained. As the two faced one another, LisBeth realized that the Lakota warrior looked just like her.

LisBeth woke from the dream and sat up. Shakily she got out of bed and made her way to the washstand to dash water on her face. When she returned to bed, she turned onto her side with her back to the one thing that could have brought her greater comfort than even Mac's or her mother's loving arms. On the small table at the bedside, within easy reach, lay Jesse's Bible, and in it were all the words that Jesse would have shared had she been able to meet her grieving young daughter at the train station. But the Bible remained unopened, and the grieving young heart was not comforted.

CHAPTER 4

 There is no soundness in my flesh . . . neither is there any rest in my bones because of my sin. For mine iniquities are gone over mine head: as an heavy burden they are too heavy for me. . . . I am troubled; I am bowed down greatly; I go mourning all the day long.

Psalm 38:3–4, 6

In the end, it was the children who did it. Walking miles in 105-degree heat didn't do it. Slogging through knee-deep mire for mile upon mile didn't do it. Even when his favorite mount gave out and was butchered and served for supper, he'd held up. Other men sat down in the muck and cried like babes. But not Jim. Corporal James Callaway didn't break. He didn't give out. He was born to a soldier's life, and it was a life he loved. He'd done everything he'd been asked, including learning the language of the enemy. Until he saw the children.

He was ordered forward to negotiate the Indian warriors' surrender. Gripping his pistol tightly, he slipped into the ravine and was astounded when a wet, shivering woman grabbed at him, yammering hysterically, pleading for her life. With his free hand Jim grabbed her and pulled her out. When he didn't shoot, other women came eagerly, grasping Jim's hand, begging his protection. One clutched a lifeless infant to her breast as she screamed out, "We are not warriors. We have no guns. Why do you kill us?"

Then the children came. They filed out of the ravine and settled into the dust and waited. Some had horrific wounds. They stared at the white men. It seemed to Jim that they were all staring at him. Their eyes had questions he couldn't answer.

And all the while, they were bleeding, and no one seemed to care, no one moved to help them.

One young private picked up a knife and grabbed a squaw. A child, perhaps four years old, screamed and ran to her side, pulling at the soldier's hand, pleading. That did it. That broke Jim Callaway, sent him right over the edge of sanity into a bleak world where there were no reasonable answers.

Suddenly, the warriors who had told their women to surrender and plead for mercy charged out of the ravine. Vastly outnumbered, they cried out their death songs and stepped into eternity. In the confusion, Jim slipped into the ravine. Following the southwesterly twists and turns, he ran away. He briefly wondered whether he would be followed, but a glance back convinced him that he would probably be assumed to have fallen into the enemy's hands.

Jim Callaway had, indeed, fallen into enemy hands. Broken in spirit, outraged by the things he had been called upon to do, Jim fell to the dark enemy within himself. He stumbled along for miles. The battle sounds receded, but the vision of the children did not. In his mind, the children swirled and danced, muddling his thoughts until he grabbed his head in his hands and shouted for them to stop. Then, sobbing, he begged aloud, "I didn't know. . . . I thought I was fighting grown men. I didn't know there were women—mothers—your mothers. I didn't know."

Jim Callaway had been born to the military, had grown up at Fort Kearny, Nebraska, watching his father be promoted, growing prouder as each day passed, eager to serve his country. When Jim was only a child, two Lakota prisoners were sent to the fort. Instead of being locked up, they were given the run of the fort. Sometimes they even went on scouting expeditions with the soldiers. Eventually the two were given the run of the fort, and Jim could still remember them wrestling with him. Jim had discovered that there were both good and bad Lakota, just as there were good and bad men among the soldiers.

He had enlisted as soon as he could and had begun a career that gave him intense satisfaction. The world of polished boots and parades, a fine mount, and defending his country was all he had ever wanted. It had been glorious—for a few years.

But then, the "Indian problem" became a daily reality. Jim's father retired and settled near Kearny, Nebraska. Jim was transferred north, to the Dakotas. Settlers began encroaching on lands that had always belonged to the Indian. When gold was discovered in the Black Hills, Jim sensed the beginning of the end for the Lakota.

With the arrival of settlers in Dakota, the role of the military took a direction Jim didn't like. At Fort Kearny he had been a friend to the emigrants who were "passing through," helping them find their way safely, providing a haven where tired travelers could raise their eyes to see the flag flying and feel comforted. But settling the land to the north—that meant inevitable conflict.

Jim had remained loyal to the oath he had taken when he was only eighteen years old. For six years he walked the tightrope of conscience, watching earnest farmers and equally earnest Lakota in a struggle that Jim knew would have to end badly for the Lakota. He had continued to follow orders, even when he hated what they demanded of him.

But he hadn't counted on killing women and children. Sitting in a ravine, going over and over the images from his past, Jim tried to sort things out and found that he could not. He blinked back tears and stood up abruptly.

He pulled at the five brass eagle buttons holding the front of his dark wool blouse together and threw them as far as he could. He ripped the insignia off his hat and stomped it into the dust, putting the hat back on and pulling it far down over his eyes. He wanted to rid himself of every vestige of the military, but the Colt revolver had to stay. He would need it to hunt for food. Reaching down to the looped belt around his waist he counted twenty-four unspent cartridges. If his luck held, he could eat once a day for nearly a month until . . . until what?

Jim smiled grimly. No one would be coming after him. They would all be too caught up in sorting out their new prisoners and the dead bodies to worry about one missing infantryman. If Charlie Blake were still alive, Jim might have something to worry about. Charlie had been a friend. But Charlie had died two days earlier in a senseless argument over rations. Jim had withdrawn weeks ago from the others in his company. Caught up in the inner struggle about this mission and his part in the war with the Indians, he'd become increasingly morose and withdrawn. A few men had tried to draw him out, finally giving up and allowing him to retreat further and further into himself.

He'd eventually be reported missing, but no one would care much what had happened to him. As for his folks, it would be better for them if they believed he had died in the line of "duty." The word left a bitter taste in his mouth. He stumbled on southward until nightfall, falling into an exhausted, troubled sleep out on the open prairie.

Days passed before Jim realized that the screws holding the top and bottom of his boots together had worn through the soles and begun to gouge his feet. He examined the blisters with disinterest, finally kicking off the remnants of his cavalry boots and stumbling on, barefoot. His trousers split at the knees as he knelt to drink at a slow-moving, muddy creek one day. His auburn hair bleached out in the sun and his beard came in pure white.

Hunting with the revolver proved fruitless. Finally, hunger drove him to gnaw on tree bark and what berries he could find just to stay alive. At last, his body gave out. He mumbled to himself, trying to make the children's faces disappear, but they would not go. They stared at him, day and night. It did not matter where he ran. It did not matter how loudly he screamed at them, nor how he wept and begged them to forgive him. Still, they stared at him.

Finally, with a little smile, Jim Callaway decided to die. He lay on his side, clutching his knees to his chin, waiting. He waited a long time, until the dark eyes of the children finally melted away. In his madness, Jim thought they had accepted his death as sufficient. They had all gone, save one. It was good that they were gone. With only one watching, he would die.

But the one who stayed to watch talked to him, grabbed him, shook him roughly. Jim pushed the hand away. He turned his face to the earth. The hand jerked him upright.

Drawn from his delirium, Jim saw that the dream-children were gone. In their place, live, adult Indians had come. But they were not the bedraggled, defeated lot at Slim Buttes. These were warriors in all their finery. They sat astride their ponies like the lords of the plains they believed themselves to be. They discussed their find in low tones, not deigning to look at Jim, unaware that he understood their mutterings.

Jim listened dully. He had assumed they would kill him—slowly. The prospect bothered him, but not unduly. He wanted to die. He deserved to die for the sins he had committed in the name of duty.

"That man has on a blue shirt," Soaring Eagle argued, "the gun and the belt are a soldier's. Until we know more, we had better not kill him. His friends may be looking for him."

"Let them come!" Thunder cried out. "We will fight them! We will fight them all! Do we not wear the white man's treasures even now? Even you, Soaring Eagle—you have gold around your neck taken from our last victory."

Soaring Eagle glanced down at Jim. "This one has nothing worth killing him for. There is no honor in killing this way. I say we take him back to camp. Feed him. Let him drink. Let him rest. Let him tell us what he can. Then," Soaring Eagle jumped up on his pony, "we can kill him."

The warriors reluctantly agreed. They knew that Sitting Bull would want a chance to learn directly from a soldier. There would be plenty of time for killing.

"He can't walk," sneered one of the braves, "I won't weary my best war pony hauling a half-dead soldier."

Soaring Eagle dismounted once more. Tying Jim's wrists and ankles together, he threw the soldier over his pony's haunches like a deer carcass and leaped up in front of him. "My father's ponies are strong. It will do them no harm to bear a carcass along with their friend Soaring Eagle." With a side-long glance at the dissenter, Soaring Eagle urged his pony to a canter and lead the war party toward the distant buttes where Sitting Bull's camp was nestled in a canyon.

CHAPTER 5

Give instruction to a wise man, and
he will be yet wiser: teach a just man,
and he will increase in learning.

Proverbs 9:9

When Soaring Eagle rode into camp with Jim Callaway in tow, a large group of Lakota assembled, staring curiously at the wild-looking white man. When Soaring Eagle untied his prisoner and threw water in his face, Jim regained consciousness, sputtering and coughing. He looked about him and saw only Lakota faces. Then he unwittingly did the right thing. Standing upright, he faced Soaring Eagle with a cold stare and waited to be killed.

Had he cowered in the dust, Jim Callaway would no doubt have been beaten to death. The entire village would have taken out its rage against the whites on this one prisoner. But when he stood up with what appeared to be bravery and faced Soaring Eagle with a cold stare, they hesitated. It saved Jim's life, because it gave Soaring Eagle time to drag his prisoner across the few feet to the council tepee. Once Sitting Bull had arrived and expressed his pleasure at the prospect of interviewing a captive soldier, none dared kill the prisoner.

Jim tried to continue standing before Sitting Bull, but his weakened body would not. He went down like a felled tree in the midst of the council and could not be revived. Soaring Eagle dragged the prisoner to his own tepee.

Prairie Flower did what she could to revive the white man physically, but she was helpless to heal his mind. The sickness that was there became evident after dark when he awoke the entire village, screaming out meaningless words at the unknown images in his dreams.

In disgust, Soaring Eagle slapped the man's face and yelled at him, "Silence! We will not harm you—we only want to know where the soldiers are going now!" Even as Soaring Eagle cursed himself for the uselessness of speaking Lakota to a white man, he heard a response. It came as a moan. "I want you to kill me. Kill me and let me pass on where there may be some peace."

Soaring Eagle grasped the red hair in one hand and forced his prisoner to sit up. Jerking the head back, Soaring Eagle looked into the gray-green eyes. The two men stared at one another for a moment before Soaring Eagle hissed, "You speak Lakota, then you know what we want. We want to know where the soldiers are. Tomorrow you will tell us. Then Sitting Bull has said that we will let you go."

Jim smiled an ugly smile. "I don't know about the soldiers. I have nowhere to go."

Soaring Eagle settled back on the dust to question the prisoner. Jim shook his head to bring himself fully awake and sat up, facing Soaring Eagle.

"Why did you leave the soldiers?"

Jim shook his head and didn't answer.

Soaring Eagle shoved Jim's shoulder and demanded again. "Why did you leave them?"

In the flickering firelight a glint of gold at the Indian's throat caught Jim's attention. He saw that it was a cross and wondered. The brave's broad forehead and well-defined jaw, a slightly cleft chin and a mouth that turned down at the edges all formed a handsome face. A long scar formed a crescent that began underneath one eye and curved across the cheekbone and down the side of the face. *How old are you,* Jim wondered, *and what horrors have the likes of me inflicted on your family?* Jim grimaced at the thought.

The brave was growing impatient. "Why did you leave them?"

But Jim didn't answer right away. He considered the question. Then, from somewhere else in the camp a dog barked. He realized that it didn't matter what he said. They would undoubtedly kill him as soon as they learned what they wanted to know. He focused on the golden cross and, in a rush of words, hastened to give his confession.

"I was a good warrior. I meant to protect my people. Then my people began to ask me to do things I did not want to do. I saw them taking land they promised to leave for the Lakota. Still, I said nothing. I continued to fight. I was a good warrior. But," Jim shuddered suddenly. He bowed his head and mumbled, "I killed women and children. . . ." Putting his hands over his head, Jim moaned, "I killed women—and children. I didn't *know* they were in that ravine when I was ordered to fire. I thought I was fighting warriors. But then they started screaming. And I saw what I had done."

Jim stopped talking. The dog outside had stopped barking. Soaring Eagle sat listening. With a deep breath, Jim looked up at Soaring Eagle. The handsome face showed no trace of emotion, but the anger had gone out of the eyes. Jim finished his confession. "I'm not killing any more. I'm done killing. I'm done with it. You can do what you want with me. I don't care anymore. I don't care. I can't tell you what you want to know. I don't know where the soldiers are. I spent the last days running *away* from the soldiers. I was just waiting to die when you found me."

When it appeared that Jim was finished, Soaring Eagle rose and went back to his own buffalo skin to ponder the revelations concerning the white captive. In the quiet, he heard the man breathing deeply and knew that he was sleeping again. His mutterings continued, but there were no more screams.

When the sun rose, Jim found that he had been untied and was free to move about the tepee. The woman named Prairie Flower offered him a thin gruel to assuage his hunger. As he ate, they watched one another curiously. The woman appeared to be past middle age. A bad scar across the bridge of her nose marred what had undoubtedly been a beautiful face.

Kindness shone in her eyes and sounded in her voice when she spoke. "There is water not far from here. I will show you."

Jim nodded and followed the woman to a slow-flowing creek. For all her years, she walked gracefully and quickly. Jim sank into the water and tried to wash the grime from his hands. Pushing up his tattered sleeves, he scrubbed at his arms, too, then his face. He was still squatting in the middle of the shallow creek when Soaring Eagle came for him. Together, they walked to the center of the camp where Sitting Bull waited to talk.

When Jim entered the council circle and was shoved into the center, he stumbled and fell headlong in the dust. His wet clothing was caked with mud. There were jeers from a few of the younger braves, but Sitting Bull quickly motioned for them to be quiet. Jim looked up and was amazed to see something that looked like kindness in the chief's face. He wore no paint. His thick braids reached almost to his waist in front. One lone eagle feather adorned the scalp lock in back.

Jim scooted back and sat cross-legged across from the chief, waiting. Sitting Bull looked his captive over carefully before speaking. When he finally spoke, he asked no questions of Jim.

"I have never thought I was against the white man," he said. "Any white man who comes to my land to trade is welcome. I don't like to start a fight, but the whites have come into *He Sapa*. The soldiers have built their forts where the treaties said they would not. All I want is to see how and where I can find meat for my people. Still, the soldiers line up to kill us."

Sitting Bull stopped abruptly. "Tell me, soldier, what do they call you?"

"Jim Callaway."

"Jim Callaway. Do you see this land?" The chief gestured toward the horizon dramatically. "Before your people came, I could ride my fastest pony for a week and still not come to the end of the land where my people could hunt and live. Now the whites have come, and they want me to go to the agency where I will have to tell the Grandfather when I am hungry."

Rumbles of anger sounded in the throats of the men around

him. Sitting Bull continued, "When the white men first came among us, all they wanted was a place to build their tepees. Now, nothing is enough. They want all of our hunting grounds, from the rising to the setting sun. They want to kill our warriors. They even kill our women and children. They will not leave us in peace. So we take up our weapons. My warriors are brave, but the white men are too many for us. They have made a spider's web around us, and we cannot escape. Still, we will not die without a fight. So, Jim Callaway, you must tell me. Where will the soldiers come to fight again? I want to meet them."

Throughout the long speech, Jim had watched Sitting Bull's face become animated with the conviction of what he said. When he asked the inevitable question, Jim reluctantly shook his head. "I cannot tell you where the soldiers are. They will come to fight, but I do not know where. Your men found me like this," Jim indicated his tattered clothes. "I was waiting to die. The sun has risen and set many times since I saw any soldiers."

"We will have to kill you if you do not tell us what we must know." The words came from behind Jim, and he recognized the voice of Soaring Eagle.

Jim answered tersely, without looking around, "I told you last night that I'm done with the soldiers. I want nothing more to do with them. Kill me. I know nothing to help you."

Sitting Bull and Soaring Eagle held a brief conversation as if Jim were not present. Soaring Eagle told of their nocturnal conversation bluntly. Other braves held council with one another. The younger men were eager to kill the white intruder.

After considering Soaring Eagle's information, Sitting Bull concluded the council simply. "He has nothing worth killing him for—no horse, no rifle. He was leaving our country. We will let him go. But first," Sitting Bull suggested, displaying his legendary generosity, "we will feed him and give him a horse."

Soaring Eagle had dragged Jim Callaway into camp as a prisoner, but Sitting Bull's decision transformed him from prisoner to a stranger in need of help. Soaring Eagle grasped the chance to show hospitality. "Prairie Flower has stew cooking. We will feed him. When he is ready to travel, I will give him one of my ponies."

Sitting Bull nodded with satisfaction at Soaring Eagle's generosity. "Good. You will be a great leader one day, Soaring Eagle."

None of the younger braves murmured against Sitting Bull. They knew that his hospitality was meant as a sign of strength, not weakness. Some among them regretted not having stepped out more quickly than Soaring Eagle to show their own goodness.

Soaring Eagle was surprised to feel a sense of relief at not having to kill Jim Callaway. Killing wounded animals had never brought him pleasure.

When Soaring Eagle brought Jim Callaway back to his tepee as a guest rather than a prisoner, Prairie Flower welcomed the stranger warmly and began to chatter happily.

"I knew they would not kill you," she assured Jim. "He hides it well, but in his heart Soaring Eagle is a kind man." Being allowed to live by the very people he felt he had persecuted brought Jim a measure of peace. He listened with interest as Prairie Flower boasted about Soaring Eagle.

"Your son saved my life," Jim finally said. He didn't express any gratitude, he just said it, hoping that the woman would continue to talk.

"Son?" Prairie Flower said. "No, he's not my son. His first mother died. Then there was another woman from among your people." Prairie Flower's voice softened as she went on. "She was my friend. Did you know her? Did you know the one called Jess-e-King?"

The name sounded a familiar note from the past, but Jim shook his head, not wanting to remember.

"She was a good woman," Prairie Flower went on, barely acknowledging Jim's presence. "She came among us and took

Soaring Eagle to her heart when he was still in his cradle board. She was with us for many years. After she was taken from us, Soaring Eagle became as my son. But he still carries Walks the Fire with him, near his heart."

Standing just outside the tepee, Soaring Eagle listened intently, angered by Prairie Flower's easy acceptance and casual sharing of his background with a stranger. He lurched inside and barked at Prairie Flower. "We will not kill him, but we will not be his friends. Feed him and get him ready to travel. That is all."

Hurt shone on the kind, scarred face. Soaring Eagle's voice softened with regret. "They are not all like Walks the Fire, *Unci.*"

It was Prairie Flower's turn to be angry. "And you think *I* do not know that! I was with you when we walked through the camp where the soldiers had been. *I* helped pick up the bodies! *I* helped find lodges to take in the orphans!" As she spoke, she grew more animated, until finally she stood before Soaring Eagle, shaking her finger in his face. "I know they are not all like Walks the Fire! But this one," Prairie Flower shook her finger in Jim's direction. "This one has been mad with grief for what he has done. You said you found him waiting to die. I say he has suffered enough. I say here is a good man who must live. And if he is to live in *my* tepee, I will talk to him as I please!"

Prairie Flower snatched down the waterskin from the lodge-pole and shook it at Soaring Eagle. "I am going to get water," she announced angrily, "and when I get back, if Jim Callaway wants to know about the Lakota, *I will tell him!*"

Prairie Flower stormed out of the tepee. After she left, Soaring Eagle stood still for a moment, pondering her speech. Then he squatted by the fire and, without looking at Jim, said casually, "You are a hard people to understand, Jim Callaway."

"You are a hard people to understand, Soaring Eagle," came the echo.

For the first time, the two looked at one another as men.

CHAPTER 6

 For I know the thoughts that I think toward you, says the LORD, thoughts of peace and not of evil, to give you a future and a hope.

Jeremiah 29:11†

There were just two of them. He had stumbled over them in the dark, feeling his way along the cold stone edges, shivering and withdrawing his hands. Now, in the daylight, he inspected them more closely. Grass had grown up around the graves. As he leaned over the tombstones, Jim's attention was drawn to a huge yellow and black spider that had spun a lace hammock between them. Dangling in the breeze, the spider waited for dinner to be caught in its web. Jim watched for a long moment, studying the web. He reached out impulsively to brush it away but stopped his hand in midair and denied the impulse.

The two stones were little more than huge red rocks, probably hauled from one of the fields that surrounded the abandoned farmhouse. Their inscriptions said only "Ma" and "Pa," the words crudely chipped away from the center of each rock. "Ma" had apparently died before "Pa," for the cedar seedling planted behind her stone was taller than Pa's by a foot.

Jim stood up and walked to the well. By unwinding and mending the rope at several places, he made it long enough to reach the water below. In the barn he had found a bucket. Letting it down, he drew up water and gave both trees a thorough drenching. Drops splashed from the bucket onto the spider's web, and the creature sought refuge in the tall grass growing around the graves.

Having watered the trees, Jim set to work pulling the weeds that had sprung up around the graves. After only a couple of hours' work, the plot appeared well cared for. Jim stood back and grunted with satisfaction.

He turned his attention to the house and barn. *Why had such a good start been abandoned?* he wondered. The house was modest but seemed well built. On the north, a low porch sheltered the front door. Wrapping around one side, the porch also covered another entrance toward the back of the house. This door faced east and looked out toward the barn. The door facing the barn had blown loose and hung flapping on its hinges. The place had obviously been empty for a while. The roof seemed tight and the siding was in place, but an attempt at paint had long since worn off the exposed wood, showing only under the porch in a few faded splotches.

Jim inspected the massive barn. The owner had had big plans, all right. Inside there were eight box stalls, and on the wall opposite the stalls, elaborate harnesses hung covered with cobwebs and dust. Beyond the box stalls were two other large stalls, big enough to hold several sheep or goats. A ladder, ascending the far wall, gave access up to the hayloft.

Jim climbed the ladder. In one corner of the loft a pitchfork stuck out of the hay, as if its owner had just heard the supper bell and left his work. Jim ran his rough hands along the posts and beams of the barn, admiring the workmanship. Whatever had happened, the man who built this barn had had plans to stay for a long time.

A mouse skittered across the floor, and Jim hopped aside as a yellow cat shot by in hot pursuit. In a moment, the cat reappeared atop the huge pile of hay, his prize dangling from his mouth. Jim turned his back on the scene and retreated down the ladder. He walked to the far end of the barn again, outside and around the back, stepping over a fallen fence post and into the corral. Deliberately he opened every stall door, letting light pour into the stalls.

They needed mucking out. Jim retrieved the pitchfork from the hayloft and began clearing out each stall. In a corner of the barn, he found a hinged box half-hidden under a rotting saddle blanket. Inside was an array of tools that had obviously been cared for by loving hands. Taking up the hammer, Jim extracted a few nails and repaired a broken corral rail.

There was no reason for doing the work, and yet restoring the broken things in this abandoned farmstead brought an odd type of peace. Jim had weeded the burial plot and cleaned out the barn. Night was fast approaching. With it came a gnawing hunger. It would not be the first night Jim Callaway had bedded down without eating. Pulling a clear bucket of water up from the well, Jim drank deeply, climbed the ladder to the barn loft, and fell asleep.

Jim woke at dawn and sat upright with the sudden realization that last night, for the first night since Slim Buttes, the eyes of the Indian children had not come to haunt his sleep. He had slept fully and deeply, and the first moments of his waking had been curiously peaceful. Something about this place had seemed to welcome him. He was in no hurry to move on. But the pangs of hunger in his belly reminded him that he had to do something about eating, and soon.

From outside, the sound of a wagon rattling into the farmyard interrupted his plans to try fishing in the creek out back. Lying flat on his belly, Jim slithered to the edge of the loft and peered out the haymow at the intruder who had climbed from the wagon and stood by the graves, scratching his head in wonderment.

The intruder looked about him, hands on hips, and began to speak to the sky. "My, my, won't you look at that! Now who'd be comin' out here cleanin' up them graves?" Joseph's eyes scanned the farmyard for signs of life. Only the open door of the barn gave a hint of human habitation.

Jim was just about to believe that he would escape detection when a little gray dog shot out from under the wagon seat, into the barn, and to the ladder, yapping furiously. The man clamped his hat back on his head, drew a rifle from under his wagon seat, and followed the dog to the ladder.

"Whoever you are, you'd better come down outta that loft right now," a deep voice boomed.

Jim Callaway stood up and brushed the hay from his clothes. He called from the loft, "Calm down, mister. I mean no harm. I came into the farmyard late and just spent the night up here in the loft, that's all."

"You got nothin' to hide, then you quit yer hidin' up in that loft." Joseph silenced the little dog and carefully aimed his rifle at the broad back that descended the ladder. As the young man turned around, Joseph noticed the tattered clothes, the unkempt beard, the long hair. He wondered at the whiteness of the beard, the redness of the hair. He had seen that happen before—once. Joseph had been called on to help sift through the remains of a fire. A young wife and her two children had died in the fire, and her young husband had stood by, helpless to rescue his family. His beard had come in white, too, even though the hair on his head was black as a raven. This boy had been through something horrible. Even with the military buttons removed, Joseph recognized the tattered Army uniform. He squinted his eyes and muttered, "Suppose you just tell me what you been doin' here on the Baird place, anyhow? And if I believe yer story, maybe I'll lower this rifle, and we'll talk some more."

Jim Callaway met the hard stare of Joseph Freeman calmly. He stood up straight and answered honestly. "I've been wandering for quite a while, mister. I just stumbled into the farmyard last night. Everything was dark. I figured the folks was asleep and wouldn't mind if I slept in their loft. I planned on offering to work for the night's board this morning." Jim glanced out at the graves, "But it doesn't seem there's anybody around."

"Why you been wandering?" came the demand.

Jim looked away and blinked several times. Swallowing hard he said quietly, "Look, mister, I'd tell you if I could. Fact is, I can't tell you. . . . I'm not a criminal or anything like that. . . . I just can't. . . ."

"You're a military man." Joseph stated it as fact, and Jim flinched and swallowed hard. His gray-green eyes met Joseph's hard brown stare and looked away. But before he looked away, Joseph saw it. He knew the look, because he'd seen it in dozens of eyes before. Every slave he'd ever met who was running away from the past had that look about him. This boy—and to Joseph he was just a boy—was running away from a past too awful to talk about. Something in the straight shoulders, the square chin, the attempt at an honest answer touched Joseph. The stare said, "I've got a story to tell, but don't you ask it because it's buried too deep. I'm trying to be an honest man. I'm looking for a new start. Just don't ask about *that thing* in my past, and I'll be all right."

"I'll be going if you'll just lower that rifle." Jim said it as calmly as he could, but his eyes pleaded kindness.

Slowly, the rifle was lowered. "Why'd you fix up those graves?"

The broad shoulders shrugged. "It just seemed to need doing."

"Why'd you clean out these stalls—mend that fence?"

At the look of surprise on Jim's face, Joseph said, "Yes, I know every board and every rock on this place. I been watchin' it for years. So why'd you clean out these stalls—mend that fence?"

Jim repeated, "I really don't know. It just seemed to need doing."

The stillness that arose between the two men was broken by a voracious growl from Jim's long-neglected stomach. Joseph Freeman suddenly laughed, a deep, booming laugh that filled every corner of the barn.

"Well, while I figure out what kind of varmint you are, guess you'd better come out here and eat some of Miz Hathaway's biscuits. I don't want no *dead* varmint on my hands!"

Jim sat in the shade of Joseph's wagon and wolfed down three huge biscuits before Joseph questioned him again.

"Now, listen here, young man, you don't need to tell me your whole life story if you don't want to, but you got to tell me a few things. You're thin as a rail, and you need a good pair of duds. Are you running from the law?" Joseph looked into the gray-green eyes and demanded, "And don't you be lying to me, either. You runnin' from the law, that's your business, and I'll let you run on. But I want to know the truth."

Jim looked squarely into the kind face. "No, sir, I'm not running from the law."

"Where you headed?"

Jim pondered the question before answering, "I don't know, sir. Anywhere away from," the voice lowered, "where I been."

"You far enough away from where you been to stop runnin'?"

Jim considered the question before slowly nodding, "I guess so."

Joseph stood up and put his rifle back under the wagon seat. "Then climb on up here and we'll get back to town. Miz' Hathaway will fill you up with more than just biscuits, we'll get you some decent clothes, and . . ."

At the mention of "town," Jim jumped up and stepped away from the wagon. "No!" he almost shouted. Then, embarrassed, he said more steadily, "No, sir, thank you, sir, but I've got no need to go to town. I—I just want to be left alone, sir." He stammered and grabbed the side of the wagon to steady his shaking legs.

Compassion filled Joseph's voice. He used the soothing tone he had always used to quiet a nervous colt. "Now, settle down, son. Ain't nobody hauling you to town against your will. You want to stay on your own, that's all right. Every man needs time to hisself now and then. . . . " An idea came and Joseph spilled it out before having time really to consider it. "You was right about this place. Folks that worked it is all gone. Their son asked me to keep a watch over it. I been watchin' it for two years now. The son didn't want it. He's gone now, too, God rest his soul. His widow don't care what happens to the place.

So it just sits here, like this, falling apart." Joseph sighed. "An it's a real shame too. It could be a fine place."

As Joseph talked, Jim stopped trembling. Joseph talked until the boy was visibly calm before he said, "I like the way you cleaned up the folks' graves. Shows respect. You cleaned out the barn real good too. Why don't you just stay here while I go into town, get you some clothes, some food, and bring them on back here?"

Jim considered the offer for help from a stranger suspiciously. "I've no money to pay for new clothes or food, mister."

Joseph pointed to the graves and the barn. "Seems to me you already earned something for your work on the place."

Joseph tried to lay a broad hand on the young man's shoulder, but Jim flinched and moved away, staring at Joseph out of the corner of his eyes, squinting against the sunlight.

Joseph stretched out his open hand, "You can trust me, son. I'll bring you out some fresh clothes and some supper. You just stay here long enough to eat a decent meal. Then, what you do is up to you. Shake on it."

Jim looked at the outstretched hand. Wiping his own grimy palm on his pants leg, he slowly reached out to grasp it. Joseph felt the firm handshake with satisfaction. The stranger was young and scared, but he had a strong hand and a steady eye. As he climbed up into the wagon and clucked to his team, Joseph smiled. He shouted over his shoulder, "Side door on the house is getting mighty loose on its hinges. You find a way to fix 'er, I'll make it good."

The wagon rattled down the road and Jim retreated from the hot sun to the barn. He looked over his shoulder at the house. Instead of attending to the loose door, he pulled down a harness. The tool box yielded everything he needed. Jim spent the afternoon cleaning and oiling the harness until it shone.

A gentle wind blew in the barn door and through the stalls, stirring up the faintest aroma of hay and horses. Jim sat absorbed in the work of the harness until the setting sun began shooting darts of pinking light in the door of the barn. With a start, Jim heard the rattling of the returning wagon. Joseph jumped down and came to the barn, leaning against the doorway and watching as Jim rearranged the harness on its pegs.

Jim smiled sheepishly. "I didn't get to the door."

Joseph shrugged. "No matter. You can always do it in the morning—uh, before you go. I got to get headed back. Here's some new rags for you. And some supper." Joseph returned to the wagon and reached under the seat. "Figured you could use these too." He handed Jim a box of shells for his pistol, waving aside the young man's protests.

Jim grasped the man's hand in gratitude. "I've got no way to say thank you, sir."

Joseph smiled warmly, "You fix that door before you leave in the mornin', and that'll be thanks enough. Good-bye." He climbed back into the wagon seat before adding, "I'll be praying for you, young man."

Jim nodded once and raised his hand as the wagon pulled out.

"I didn't get his name, LisBeth," Joseph said quietly, "but I know he'd do right by you and MacKenzie if you was to give him a chance on the homestead. You should see the way he's cleaned up around the place. And just to pay for a night in the hayloft!"

LisBeth frowned. "You don't even know his name, and yet you want me to agree to asking him to work on the place?"

Joseph nodded and added the very thing he knew would secure "the young man's" place on the homestead—if he wanted it. "I know it's a mite out of the ordinary, LisBeth, but, fact is, the years are catching me up . . . and I don't have the energy I once had, and I just thought . . ."

LisBeth's frown was replaced with concern, "Oh, Joseph! I'm sorry—I didn't think. I *have* expected a lot from you. We didn't have time to make the proper arrangements before Mac left with his regiment—and then," LisBeth sighed, "I came back all alone. I just hadn't *thought* about all you've been doing. Joseph, I'm sorry. Of course, if you need the help, do ask this fellow to stay on. Just ask him to come into town tomorrow, and we'll work something out."

Joseph bargained, "Does he have to come into town, Lis-Beth? A ride out to the place would do you good, and I'd be glad to take you out there myself on Sunday."

LisBeth flinched. "Oh, no, Joseph! I don't want to go to the homestead, not yet."

Joseph rushed to excuse her, "That's all right, LisBeth. . . . I understand. Some things is pretty hard so soon after a loss. No need for you to go at all. I'll take care of the arrangements."

LisBeth was visibly relieved. "Thank you, Joseph. I don't know what I'll do about the homestead, but until I decide, there's no use in its falling apart."

Joseph retreated quickly before LisBeth could repeat a request for the young man to come into Lincoln. He climbed into his wagon, humming to himself, and made his way south again, toward the Baird homestead. In the wagon were provisions for at least a week for the young man he was hoping to convince to stay on.

When Joseph drew aside the cover that had hidden the provisions, Jim grinned and agreed to stay. "But just for the week. I'll have things repaired by then, and I'll be ready to move on."

Joseph agreed that a week would be more than enough. But somehow, the next week came, and there were more chores that needed to be done, and Joseph's rheumatism was acting up. Jim agreed to stay another week. On the seventh day, Joseph's wagon rumbled onto the place with a bay gelding tied to the back of the wagon.

"Been nothing but trouble since I bought him," Joseph recited carefully. "Nips and bites at everything I put in the stall next to him, and won't have a thing to do with a saddle. I sure got taken when that horse trader come through town last week.

So I thought if I was to bring him out here where he's all by hisself, maybe you could gentle him for me—I just hate to lose my investment in him."

When Jim started to protest, Joseph held up his hand, "I know you was fixin' to leave tomorrow morning. But I just need a little more help with this here gelding, and then you can be on your way. Don't need no fancy horseman. Just need somebody with the time to talk to the old duff and settle him down a bit. What d'ya say?"

"Jim" was the answer.

Joseph had been untying the perfectly well-mannered gelding while he talked. When the young man offered his name, he stopped and looked up in amazement.

"Jim, that's my name, sir. Jim Callaway. And I'll help you with the horse. I'm pretty good with horses. It won't take long to solve this one's problems," a slow grin crept over the sunburned face, "seeing as how he's perfectly well-mannered already."

Joseph's rumbling laughter filled the air, and he slapped the gelding's neck. "Caught me, didn't ya! Well, I just thought you needed company out here, and if you did decide to leave, you've more than earned a better way to travel than those two feet. So, Jim Callaway, will you stay on the place? I brought you a horse I don't really need help with, but the fact is Miz Baird *does* need help with this here place until she decides whether to keep it or sell it. Her husband was killed at the Little Big Horn, and she ain't got over it yet. Came home to find she'd just lost her Mama too. She said she'd like to have you stay on and keep the place up, if you want the job."

"She won't need to pay me," came the curt reply. "It's a place to stay, something to do. Something worthwhile—bringing a place back to life. I'll like it." He took a deep breath and his eyes met Joseph's. "I'd be obliged to Mrs. Baird if she lets me stay on here and bring her place back to life. Maybe it'll help—" Jim snapped the door shut on his past before finishing the sentence.

Joseph was satisfied. He nodded gravely, "I know, son. I

know. I been in places like you been. Just don't get bitter, Jim. Bitterness will kill your spirit quick as anything. Just let it go. Count your blessings and move on, Jim."

Once again, the bay gelding brought Jim back to reality. The rubbing had stopped, and the gelding shoved his big head at Jim again, nearly pushing him over. Joseph laughed and Jim smiled slowly. "Real mean horse, Joseph. Don't know how I'll ever calm him down, but I'll do my best."

Joseph swung onto the wagon box again, laughing all the while. "Thank you, Jim. I shorely do appreciate it. Now, I'll be out again in a couple a days and you make me a list of what you'll be needing to get the place going again. Miz Baird'll be right happy to know her husband's home place is going to be taken care of."

CHAPTER 7

Be ye kind one to another, tenderhearted, forgiving one another.
Ephesians 4:32

A few days later LisBeth made her pilgrimage to
Mac's homestead. Thinking of Jim's plea to be
"left alone," Joseph protested mildly, but in the end LisBeth
had her way. Secretly rejoicing in a day of freedom away from
sympathetic eyes, LisBeth climbed up beside Joseph and settled back for the supply run to "Mac's place."

"I've never seen the place, Joseph," LisBeth reminded him.
"Seems like I ought to at least *see* it before I decide what to do
with it. Heaven knows I'm no homesteader." Her voice softened, "But there's no grave to visit, and I like the idea of being
able to visit the place where Mac was a boy." LisBeth turned
her head away, straightening her shoulders and lifting her
chin.

"I recollect how your mama used to do just that when she
was fixin' to take on a chore," Joseph said.

"Do what?"

"Used to pull her shoulders back and lift her head up and
face things straight on."

"Is that what she did that night we stumbled across your
campfire outside Fort Kearny?"

Joseph smiled at the memory. "Well, now, it was mighty dark
that night. But, I shore recollect she faced the next day head
on." Joseph began to chuckle. "You was a feisty little gal,
LisBeth."

LisBeth smiled ruefully. "Hope I still am, Joseph. Life hasn't been too good lately, but I'm going to pull through, whatever it takes. Mama always said to just trust the Lord and go ahead. Well, I'm trying to go ahead."

"Don't forget the other part," Joseph interjected. "The part about trustin' the Lord."

LisBeth changed the subject. "May I drive the team, Joseph?"

Joseph shook his head. "This team just needs the man's touch, LisBeth."

LisBeth begged. "Please, Joseph. It would be fun!" She put on such a pathetic face that Joseph burst out laughing.

"My, my, LisBeth. You look just like you did that day you begged your mama to let you sit up beside me on the wagon. And me a stranger and all! Shame on you, girl, you do know how to get your way!"

Joseph handed the reins to LisBeth, keeping his foot near the wagon brake and keeping his voice low and gentle as he instructed the new driver. The horses flicked their ears suspiciously. The voice was the same, but there were new hands on the reins. It required all LisBeth's young strength to manage them. She welcomed the challenge. After the first few miles, she relaxed a little and began to look beyond the team's ears to the landscape about her.

Sunflowers were everywhere. They ran along the road, giving way here and there to tangles of low-growing wild roses and butterfly weed. On one side of the road, a thicket of chokecherries had attracted several meadowlarks. They flitted among the small trees, snatching the deep red fruit greedily, then rising to higher tree branches to fill the air with song. With youthful willfulness, LisBeth refused the memories that tried to crowd in. *No*, she thought, *it's a lovely day, and I'm going to enjoy the sunshine.*

She studied every detail of the scenery as the team jogged along. Joseph pointed out the place where the drive to the homestead met the main road, and LisBeth urged the team to a canter. Joseph's voice lost its gentle flow as he urged LisBeth to slow down. They clattered into the farmyard, and LisBeth found herself standing up and pulling back with all her strength to stop the team and prevent their running past the barn and into the field beyond.

As they rattled to a halt, Jim Callaway rounded the corner of the barn. LisBeth was out of breath, and her hair had come down on one side from jouncing along the last bit of the road. For a moment she was LisBeth King again—unaffected and natural, enjoying a lovely day in the country with no thoughts of the tragedies in her life. The sun shone in her dark eyes, and she squinted into the barn with a smile playing about her mouth. *There,* she thought, *I've done it. Joseph didn't think I could, but I've done it.*

Jim only got to see LisBeth King for a fraction of a moment. Even as Joseph called out a hello and introduced her, LisBeth's eyelids drooped to cover her sparkling brown eyes. She sat down and hastily pushed her hair back into a tight bun at the back of her head. Climbing down stiffly, LisBeth became the widow LisBeth Baird.

Accepting Jim's hand as she climbed down from the wagon, LisBeth offered an explanation. "Joseph didn't want me to come, but I thought I should. We brought your supplies." She turned to look about the farmyard. The freshly painted house fairly gleamed in the sun. "You've been working hard."

"Yes, ma'am. My folks always said, 'If a man's taken the trouble to paint the house and the barn, then he's got a good crop in the ground and success on the way.' I figure if you're going to sell the place, you'll get a better price this way."

"Yes—well." LisBeth stood uncertainly, then walked toward the back of the wagon and helped Joseph pull the canvas cover off. "I didn't really give Joseph much chance to check the supplies before we left. I hope we remembered everything you need."

"I'm sure it'll all be fine, ma'am," Jim said, twirling his hat round in his hands awkwardly.

Joseph rescued him. "I'll water the team, Jim. You go ahead and unload your supplies."

Jim turned to LisBeth. "There's shade up on the porch. Can

I—" Jim cleared his throat nervously. "Can I bring you a drink of water?"

With a quick "No, thank you," LisBeth crossed the farmyard and took shelter at the edge of the porch. She sat in the shade and watched the quiet, tall, redheaded man haul bundle after bundle into the side door of the house. Something about the way he moved and held himself was oddly familiar.

Finally, she stepped into the sun. "This is ridiculous. I can help you with those."

"Oh, no, ma'am," Jim protested. "I'm nearly done. There's only that barrel of flour and then it's done." He hastened to hoist the barrel up on his shoulder.

LisBeth sat back. That voice—that sounded familiar too. When Jim came out of the house, he checked the harness. LisBeth watched him carefully, wondering. Stepping around the team, he carefully inspected the team's hooves for stones. Finally, he turned back to LisBeth. "Thank you for bringing the supplies out. I don't want to be any trouble."

"Oh, it's no trouble," LisBeth answered. "I enjoyed the drive out." She sighed. "Sometimes, in Lincoln, where everyone knows me and everyone knew Mac, well, sometimes it's hard. I enjoyed driving out here."

The team was watered and Joseph checked the harness as LisBeth climbed up onto the wagon seat. A small package caught her attention. "This must be yours, Mr. . . ." LisBeth smiled. "I just realized that Joseph has never told me your full name." She paused, expecting a reply. But Jim didn't answer. He reached for the package, and as he did it came undone and fell to the ground. It held a tiny plant, much the worse for the long journey it had taken.

As Jim stooped to pick it up, he smiled sheepishly. "My mother had one of these growing up the side of the porch. I thought I'd build a trellis and see if I could make it grow here. They're mighty pretty when they bloom."

"What is it?"

"Roses—but not the kind that grow along the road. I saw this one in town last week." He hastened to explain, "Joseph and I went hunting and it was too late to get back here, so I rode into town with Joseph and bunked in the livery until sunrise. But I saw this rose, just the same color my mother loved." He was embarrassed, and his face glowed red. "I guess Joseph must have asked for a slip."

LisBeth looked at the scrawny root. "I hope it grows," she said softly. "Mac would love to see this place brought back to life. I just know he'd be pleased."

Jim set his future rose bush in the shade of the porch. "Oh, it'll grow, ma'am. I'm good at making things grow." He reached up to scratch the back of his neck. "Not much good for anything else—but I can make things grow."

Joseph had been watching the two carefully. He climbed up beside LisBeth and took up the reins while introducing them. "LisBeth, seems I've forgotten my manners. I forgot to introduce you two. This here's my friend, Jim Callaway. Jim, meet LisBeth Baird. Guess she's your landlord now, Jim."

Jim Callaway! The name hung in the air while LisBeth stared, disbelieving. It couldn't be! Not Jimmy Callaway from Fort Kearny. Jimmy Callaway had been a fat little brat who had made LisBeth's life miserable, pulling her braids, boasting of his future as a soldier, and constantly reminding LisBeth that *his* father was an officer while she didn't even *have* a father. Once, Jimmy Callaway had even called her that name. The word had made her cry, but she had run quickly away before he could see the effect of his taunting.

LisBeth stared at Jim in disbelief. He had taken his hat off to reveal a thick shock of unruly auburn hair. Even sun-bleached, the red in his hair stood out in stark contrast to the snow-white beard. The eyes were solemn, and they seemed to hold a question. They looked directly at you, but never rested long on one thing, as if not wanting to intrude for very long. Surely this couldn't be *that* Jim Callaway. No, *that* Jimmy Callaway couldn't have grown up to be so—so distant!

Jim nodded and said mechanically, "Pleased to meet you, ma'am." He paused, searching for more words. "And . . . and thank you for hiring me on."

"Pleased to meet *you,* Mr. Callaway." The humor in the coincidence won over childish hurts, and LisBeth added with a mischievous grin, "Joseph left out part of my name, Mr. Callaway. I'm LisBeth *King* Baird. I believe we may have met before—at Fort Kearny?" She watched carefully for a reaction. When it came, it was not what she had expected. Jim frowned slightly and stepped away from the wagon. He looked quickly about the farmyard and cleared his throat, but said nothing.

Finally, Jim cleared his throat again and almost whispered, "Your ma was Mrs. King, Mrs. Jesse King? Joseph said she just passed on, ma'am. I'm real sorry." He looked up at LisBeth and squinted his eyes. "I remember meeting her. She was always real kind to me," Jim's voice faltered, "even when I didn't deserve kindness." He paused again, and LisBeth began to regret having broached the topic of their childhood acquaintance. It seemed to be causing him so much difficulty.

LisBeth hurried to fill the silence. With a forced chuckle she tried to lighten the discussion. "I remember you as a chubby redheaded officer's son who teased me mercilessly."

The man standing before her held little resemblance to the Jimmy Callaway who had so tormented her as a child. Jim Callaway, the adult, shuffled his feet in the dust and looked over her head to the fields beyond as he said quietly, "I'm sorry about that, Mrs. Baird. I truly am. I was a mean little cuss." LisBeth was beginning to feel embarrassed by the earnest tone in his voice. "Please, ma'am—I never meant any harm. Guess I just didn't think how it must have hurt to be made fun of. Sure hope you don't hold it against me."

LisBeth held up a hand and interrupted him. "Heavens, no, Mr. Callaway. I was just enjoying teasing you a bit, that's all. Please don't go on about it. It's just odd, meeting up with someone from Fort Kearny after all this time. . . . I always thought you'd be a military man too. You were sure set on it back then, as I recall."

Jim looked at Joseph and pleaded without words. Joseph answered the plea, interrupting the conversation. "Well, now, it's high time we started back to town—think I smell rain in the air. I'll be back next week with some garden seeds, Jim," Joseph added quickly. "You can try that fall garden you was talkin' about."

With relief Jim nodded a reply and headed for the barn as Joseph pulled the team out of the farmyard. LisBeth was unusually quiet for several miles of the ride. At last, she asked Joseph, "What do you think of him, Joseph? He sure didn't want to talk much about his past, and when I mentioned the military—"

Joseph shook his head. "Don't know, LisBeth. But I'm sure it ain't nothin' that we need to be worried about. That boy's had plenty of chances to steal you blind and run for it since he come. He's honest and a hard worker. I guess I'm content to leave him alone about things he don't want us pryin' into."

Joseph's comments prevented any further speculation from LisBeth. The two rode back to Lincoln in comfortable silence, LisBeth wanting to know more about Jim Callaway, and Joseph wanting to comfort the boy for whatever horrible thing he had endured in the military.

One thing sure, Joseph pondered, *whatever it was, it's still with him. He's got to learn to put it behind him and get on with life.* The faces of his own lost family interrupted his concerns. Joseph burst into song so abruptly that LisBeth jumped. Together they rode along the road to Lincoln, singing words that carried them both to their own hurts.

"We'll meet again"—how sweet the word! How soothing is its sound!
Like strains of far-off music heard on some enchanted ground.
We'll meet again. We'll meet on "the evergreen shore."
We'll meet again, yes, meet to part no more.

One voice abandoned itself to the words and found healing in the anticipation of a wife and two lost children he would someday meet again. But the younger voice quavered uncertainly and found little comfort in the song, for questions crowded in to drown out the message of hope.

CHAPTER 8

. . . her own works praise her in the gates.

Proverbs 31:31

The moment Jacob Winslow disembarked from the dinner table at Hathaway House and waddled up the stairs to the room "with windows that open to the north please—I always sleep better when my head is pointing north," Augusta swooped down on the table and loaded every dish onto her tray. She balanced her load carefully, barely making it to the sink before LisBeth rescued the glass that was rolling off one edge of the tray.

"Thank you, dearie!" Augusta smiled.

LisBeth teased, "Aunt Augusta! 'Take two trips if necessary, dear. We can't afford new china every week'!"

Augusta smiled again. "Goodness, did I make that speech that much?"

Sarah called out, "You still do, ma'am."

Grabbing the evening paper, Augusta settled into her rocker. "Shame on you two young girls, ganging up on me like that! All right, all right—I confess. I broke my own rule. But, listen to this, ladies!

For Centennial tickets, address or call on R. P. Miller, O Street Union Block, sign of Buffalo head, and get a 'Centennial Guide' now ready for free distribution, giving map and detailed statement in relation to route, rates, etc., to the Great Centennial Exhibition. Bear in mind that by this route, you reach Philadelphia hours in advance of any other lines, and

that there is but one change of cars from Lincoln, and that is
at the Union Depot in St. Louis, where you simply step from
one train to another. . . .

Augusta stopped reading abruptly. "LisBeth, we've simply
got to go. John Cadman took out a huge ad in the paper—here
it is—fully three columns wide. All it says is: 'John Cadman has
gone to the Centennial. He will return September 1.' Just like
a man—he has to let the whole world know he's rich enough
to stay all summer in Philadelphia. And he's so secure about
his hotel that he can leave it, and it'll run itself. It just rankles
me to think of him being there to see all the new inventions.
Why, who knows what ideas he'll come home with to imple-
ment over at Cadman House. And besides," Augusta rattled
the paper for emphasis, "if Lincoln is going to grow into the
twentieth century—" Augusta interrupted herself, "Oh, I
know, I know, *I'll* probably not see the twentieth century, but
you will," Augusta called out over her shoulder, "and so will
you, Sarah Biddle. We must know the newest and best ideas
around. There's no better place to do it than Philadelphia!
What do you say, LisBeth—will you go with me?" Then, in
characteristic fashion, Augusta talked on without giving Lis-
Beth a chance to respond.

"Oh, I'm an old one to have as a traveling companion, I
know. . . ."

I'll no doubt have trouble keeping up, LisBeth thought.

". . . and Philadelphia is a long way off . . ."

I'd love to get away from here, LisBeth thought.

". . . and, of course, it will be more work for Sarah . . ."

*She already knows more about running a hotel than I'll ever
know. . . .*

". . . but I feel it my civic duty to keep up on things."

Finally, Augusta paused long enough for LisBeth to inter-
ject, "I'd love to go, Aunt Augusta."

Augusta didn't hear at first, and went on, "It certainly won't
hurt to look into accommodations, then if we just can't get
away, we'll just—" Augusta looked up at LisBeth.

"Did you say something, dear?"

LisBeth grinned. "I'd love to go."

"You would?"

"I would."

"But the hotel—"

"Sarah could run this hotel without either one of us, and you know it, Aunt Augusta."

Sarah turned to look at LisBeth with a grateful smile, and LisBeth winked at her. "What do you think, Sarah. Can you get along without us?"

"I'd ask Alma Dodge to come stay. The two Cortland sisters just finished school and are looking for extra work. If Joseph will keep me in firewood, I can handle the cooking."

Augusta was doubtful. "Don't you want to see the Exposition?"

"No, ma'am!" Sarah blurted out. "I seen all the big cities I ever want to see in my life. You go on and have yourselves a high time. I like it just fine here in Lincoln."

"Well, we'll go then," Augusta said. "But only if you'll agree to take a vacation when we get back."

Sarah protested. "I got nowhere I want to go, Aunt Augusta. I don't need no vacation." Thus only *two* travelers represented the Hathaway House Hotel at the Centennial in Philadelphia, Pennsylvania.

"See here, young man," Augusta announced loudly. "I don't know what kind of establishment you think you are running here, but a hotel simply does *not* fail to accommodate those with reservations—"

"But, ma'am, you were late."

"The *train* was late, young man. I could hardly be expected to control that, now could I? We have paid for two adjoining rooms, and I expect to get two adjoining rooms!" Augusta punctuated her demand by thumping the tip of her parasol on the highly polished floor of the elegant Philadelphia hotel.

The desk clerk bobbed his head sympathetically and turned

red. "Yes, ma'am, I understand, but Mr. Braddock himself demanded these rooms, ma'am, and when you didn't come—"

Augusta interrupted him. "And just *who* is Mr. Braddock, that he thinks himself so important as to throw two women traveling alone out into the street for his own comfort?"

The desk clerk looked over Augusta's head and blushed even more fiercely. His head bobbed up and down rapidly as a rich bass voice called out, "*I* am Mr. Braddock, madame." Augusta turned to face her adversary as he added smoothly, "And you may be assured that *my* hotel will not turn you out in the street."

Even with his silk top hat removed, Mr. Braddock towered over Augusta and LisBeth, who had been doing her best to become part of the wallpaper during Augusta's outburst. The tall stranger continued to talk to Augusta, but he looked only at LisBeth.

"Hanley," he began, as the desk clerk snapped to attention and peeped, "Yes sir!"

"Hanley, there's been a misunderstanding. Kindly send a note across town to my mother." His eyes never left LisBeth's. "Tell her I'll be staying at home, after all. Send Thompson up to remove my trunk from those rooms I requested, and," he finally turned his gaze to Augusta and offered a winning smile, "order fresh flowers for our guests with apologies from David Braddock for failing to live up to the name of our 'city of brotherly love.'"

David Braddock doffed his hat, bowed gracefully to the two women, and was gone before Augusta could sputter her thanks. LisBeth took a deep breath and watched the broad shoulders exit the hotel lobby and climb into a carriage outside. She was brought back to the moment by Augusta's satisfied voice, "Now, LisBeth, you see what I mean. Just let me do the talking and we'll get along fine. I mean to see that we have a lovely time at the Exposition!"

The two women were led up the grand winding staircase that swept guests from the lobby to the rooms above. Just as they arrived at their rooms, Thompson exited with a gentleman's trunk in tow, and someone else entered with a massive bouquet of fresh flowers.

LisBeth peeked into her own room and took in a sharp breath. It was small but elegantly furnished with a massive carved walnut bed and matching marble-topped washstand and dresser. A small writing desk stood in an alcove created by tall bay windows along one wall. The sun streamed through the windows and reflected off the silk drapes and bed coverings, bathing the room in rosy light. It was a cool day, and a fresh breeze came in through the transom at the top of each window.

"I know why that Mr. Braddock wanted these rooms for himself," Augusta called from the next room. "They're facing just the right direction to catch the cool breeze."

Augusta was in the middle of a favorable critique of their meal when she noticed that LisBeth had flushed and developed an unusual interest in the details of the china pattern used by the hotel.

"What is it, dearie?"

"I beg your pardon, madame," interrupted a familiar voice. David Braddock bowed and introduced himself. "Please forgive my forwardness, but lacking a mutual acquaintance, I have elected to breach custom and introduce myself. I am David Braddock, the owner of this establishment. I sincerely regret the manner in which you made my acquaintance. May I enquire as to whether your accommodations are satisfactory?"

Augusta sipped her tea before responding. "The accommodations are quite satisfactory, thank you," she said coldly.

LisBeth felt the color rising in her face. Finally, she could stand it no longer. "Aunt Augusta! That's not like you at all." Looking up at Braddock, she said quietly, "Aunt Augusta is all prickles and quills—by her own admission, Mr. Braddock. But, really, she's harmless. The rooms are lovely, thank you. I hope we haven't inconvenienced you."

Braddock interrupted her. "Not at all, Miss—?"

Augusta replied for LisBeth. "*Mrs.* LisBeth King Baird, Mr. Braddock."

LisBeth rose from the table and offered her hand, repeating "Thank you, Mr. Braddock, for giving up your rooms for us."

"I assure you, Mrs. Baird, it was a pleasure." With a masterful bow, David Braddock smoothed down Augusta's prickles and quills by bending low to brush the back of LisBeth's offered hand with a continental kiss. Augusta stood up, reached for LisBeth, and literally herded her out of the dining room. Braddock smiled to himself and returned to his own table, finishing off an entire roast hen while completing the details of his plan to learn more about Mrs. Hathaway and Mrs. Baird—with the emphasis on Mrs. Baird.

Both LisBeth and Augusta were awake at dawn the next morning, reading over their Centennial guidebook and planning how best to attack the massive Exposition. As they planned, a small envelope was slipped under the door. LisBeth stooped to retrieve the envelope and read the note with evident pleasure. Augusta smiled too and congratulated herself on coming up with the trip. It was good to see LisBeth happy and smiling, her mind diverted from her troubles.

LisBeth read, "Mr. David Braddock requests the honor of supplying a carriage to transport the ladies from Nebraska to the Exposition. Reply to Hanley at the front desk."

Augusta bristled. "It appears to me that Mr. David Braddock has done quite enough for the ladies from Nebraska. And he's been snooping about, or he wouldn't know we're from Nebraska! We can catch a streetcar right around the corner and make the run in less than an hour, with only eighteen cents spent. Although . . . a carriage would be more comfortable."

LisBeth smiled hopefully. Augusta saw the smile and changed her mind. "But it's best not to be beholden to strangers."

"Mr. Braddock seemed harmless enough, Aunt Augusta."

"Mr. Braddock is very interested in *you*, Mrs. Baird."

LisBeth protested. "Nonsense! He's a gentleman, that's all."

"With the emphasis on the *man* part, LisBeth. And, just like any man, he'll be expecting us to fall all over ourselves thanking him for helping us poor, defenseless creatures, and while we're doing that, he'll be stealing his way into your affections and—"

"Aunt Augusta!" LisBeth was angry. Her eyes blazed. "What do you *take* me for? My husband has been dead less than a month." Her eyes filled with tears, and Augusta retreated, flustered.

"Oh, my dear—I'm sorry. I didn't mean *you* would ever do anything to blight dear MacKenzie's memory. I just don't think we should—"

LisBeth snapped back, "Then tell Hanley that we won't require Mr. Braddock's carriage, and be done with it." She handed the note to Augusta and walked briskly into her room, closing the door behind her just a bit too firmly.

Augusta scribbled a reply. A soft knock sounded at the door, and when she opened it, she was astonished to see a bellboy waiting patiently in the hallway. He tipped his hat respectfully before asking, "Will there be a reply, madame?"

"Goodness! Have you been waiting all this time?"

"Mr. Braddock gave orders to wait for a response, ma'am."

Augusta handed him the note and abruptly closed the door, wondering how much of her exchange with LisBeth the bellboy had heard and how much would be repeated word for word to Mr. Braddock.

When LisBeth emerged from her room a few moments later, her efforts were not wasted on Augusta. She wore her most simple mourning gown and had drawn her hair back into a tight bun that allowed no tendrils to escape to soften her profile. No jewelry adorned the gown, and her face reflected the fact that grief had once again arisen to dominate her life.

Augusta reached out to her imploringly, "LisBeth, please forgive me. I didn't mean to imply—"

LisBeth shook her head. "I know. I suppose I was feeling

guilty. I think I did flirt a little with Mr. Braddock." She sat down before continuing. "I was really appalled at my own behavior yesterday. I noticed a handsome man." She looked up at Augusta seriously." And when I noticed, I felt guilty—like I'd *betrayed* Mac somehow." Tears welled up in her eyes again, and she looked away.

Augusta interrupted, "Come, come, LisBeth. You're a very normal young woman. I know you loved MacKenzie Baird as surely as I know that we are in Philadelphia at this moment."

LisBeth swallowed hard before answering. "Sometimes I can't quite remember Mac's face." She looked out the window before continuing. "It's only been a few weeks, and I'm losing him." Her shoulders slumped as she added miserably, "How can I forget so quickly?"

Augusta settled beside LisBeth and took her hand. "It happens to everyone, LisBeth. Our loved ones slip away from us, but that doesn't mean we love them any less. It's *human* to forget. And it's part of the way the good Lord helps heal the hurt."

"But I don't *want* to forget. I don't want to forget *anything*. Not until . . ."

"Until what, dear?"

"Until I can understand it, find my way, where I belong now, what I should do."

Augusta patted LisBeth's arm. "It takes time, dear. You must give it time. I know everyone has said that to you, and you must be weary of hearing it, but it's true. In time, you will be able to bear the memories. You'll find the ones that comfort you, and keep them close. The others will fall away."

Augusta stood up and pulled LisBeth up beside her, bantering gently. "Now, as to forgetting, I hope you never forget what a handsome man looks like, dearie. And if you hadn't noticed that Mr. David Braddock is one handsome young man, I'd have had the doctor up today to check you over! I'm an old woman, LisBeth, but I'm not dead. I noticed." When LisBeth opened her mouth to protest, Augusta interrupted her. "Yes, you're a widow. But you're also a very young woman, with a life ahead of her. You don't need to feel one moment of guilt. MacKenzie Baird was a fine man. But he's gone now, and he would want you fill your life with another husband someday."

LisBeth shuddered. "I'll never—"

"Oh, yes you will, dearie, yes you will." Augusta insisted. "But not yet. It's too soon. Give it time and keep your life full. Now let's get going! There's a lifetime worth of progress to look over at that Exposition, and I for one can't *wait* to see it."

LisBeth retrieved her bonnet, and Augusta hustled her out the door, chattering away, "Can you believe it? They actually found a woman who could run a steam engine. They had to go all the way to Canada to find her, but not one man has a thing to do with the Women's Pavilion!"

They hurried through the lobby and around the corner and were just in time to crowd onto a streetcar. As they crossed the Girard Street bridge, the two women caught their first view of the twin towers of the largest building in the world, the Exhibition's main building. The streetcar continued from Girard down Elm to Belmont, where they passed row upon row of buildings that had sprung into being solely to serve the masses of people attending the Exposition. There were hotels and restaurants, saloons and beer gardens.

"Well, I declare!" was all Augusta could muster when confronted with the main building. It was a mountain of glass, ironwork, and red-painted wood and ran for a third of a mile along Elm Street. Inside, row upon row of elaborate walnut and glass display cases touted the ingenuity and success of the United States of America.

"Bringing fresh water to Lincoln would be no problem at all, if we had one of *these* powering our waterworks!" Augusta exclaimed. She was standing before the massive Corliss engine in Machinery Hall. Lincoln had had its share of water woes, due to the saline content of much of the well water in town. The Corliss engine towered above them, producing enough power to operate thirteen acres of machines that accomplished dozens of feats from pumping water to sawing logs.

Augusta nudged LisBeth. The engineer who operated the

behemoth had laid aside his newspaper and clambered up a stairway to oil a gear. His task done, he returned to his chair and continued reading. "Just like a man. They always find a way to do things faster and better—for themselves. Why don't they ever try to harness that power to make a woman's work easier, I'd like to know! LisBeth, just think of it. One man, assisted by one engine, doing the work of eight thousand men! We're on the verge of a new era in America; I can feel it with every step I take through this exhibition hall."

LisBeth responded with a noncommittal "um-hum" and whispered, "Aunt Augusta, isn't that Mr. Braddock?" indicating a tall figure quite a distance away, intently examining the contents of a display case.

"Well, now, my eyes aren't what they used to be. Can't say for sure." Augusta opened her Exhibition guidebook. "Come along, dearie. We've miles to go before the end of the day!"

Augusta was a mountain of energy all morning, pushing and prodding their way through the main building and Machinery Hall, then past Agricultural Hall and Horticultural Hall, to seek out the twenty-four respective state buildings arranged along a strip named State Avenue. Near noon, Augusta fairly collapsed on a shaded bench and announced, "Goodness, LisBeth. I'm plumb tuckered! And we haven't even begun to see the state buildings."

"We can always take the tour on the West End Railway," LisBeth replied absentmindedly. Once again, she had spotted a now-familiar gray silk top hat in the distance. *Is it my imagination,* she wondered, *or has he been following us all morning?*

"Never!" came the reply. "I don't care if they *have* put up signal bells and hired flagmen. That train is being run entirely too fast to be scooting about crowded grounds. Just like a man—everything for speed and no consideration for the safety of women and children!"

"But, Aunt Augusta," LisBeth teased. "I thought you wanted to experience all the things that could bring progress back home. Why not try it out? It might be the forerunner of an automated streetcar system for Lincoln!" *I wonder if he'd follow us even then.*

The challenge was too much for Augusta. "You're right, LisBeth. Let's give her a try!" Holding on as if her life might be left at the next crossing, Augusta boarded the railway, and they were whisked across the grounds at the alarming rate of eight miles per hour. LisBeth watched carefully as the gray silk top hat got in two cars behind, and followed at a respectful distance as the two women made their way for the Women's Pavilion.

The gray silk top hat was not in view as Augusta and LisBeth walked through a doorway with the inscription, "Her works do praise her in the gates." LisBeth felt a tinge of disappointment, but then her interest was won by the Exhibition Hall. Decorated in soft light blues, the one-acre hall had been built in the shape of a cross. At the center, a fountain sent its sprays of water toward a chandelier that hung from the cupola. The walls were lined with paintings, carved wood, and every aspect of endeavor from the hands of women.

"Now, *there's* the woman I want to meet!" urged Augusta, as they approached the engine that ran every machine in the pavilion.

"Miss Allison, if I may ask," began Augusta, "do you run this engine all by yourself?"

The lady in question turned to Augusta with a warm smile. "Everything from lighting the fire in the morning to blowing off the steam at closing."

LisBeth noticed that the gray silk top hat was studying a marble bust across the hall. Its owner had just been greeted by someone else, and as he turned to reply, he cast a glance in her direction. It was David Braddock. He flashed a smile at LisBeth and hurried across the hall to join her and the small group that had collected to hear what Miss Allison had to say.

A rather stout gentleman beside Augusta drew a huge puff of smoke from a cigar before asking, somewhat skeptically, "Seems a bit of a huge job for a slip of a woman, if you don't mind my saying so."

"Oh, no, sir, I don't mind your saying so. Tell me, sir," asked Miss Allison. "Do you have the joy of children in your home?"

The lady on the gentleman's arm smiled, "Why, yes, Miss Allison. We have five precious little ones."

Miss Allison looked directly into the man's face and said sweetly, "Why, then, sir, your wife could certainly operate this engine herself. It's not nearly as exhausting as tending a cookstove, and it's far less complicated than raising children!" The wife in question smiled appreciatively and the gentleman took the opportunity to take a few more puffs on his cigar and extricate himself from the conversation.

A chuckle sounded from behind LisBeth, and David Braddock said, "Ladies, I see we meet again. May I escort you to lunch?"

CHAPTER 9

. . . there is a friend that sticketh
closer than a brother.

Proverbs 18:24

Two days after LisBeth and Augusta departed for
Philadelphia, Jim Callaway began his journey
back. He had been near insanity once. Weeks on the homestead had begun to heal the darkness inside, but there were
still long nights of passionate struggle and days of grief when
the enemy within threatened to realize a final victory. The
winning of Jim's internal war came as Joseph Freeman nearly
lost his life.

While Jim was in the barn rubbing down the bay gelding,
he heard the wagon coming. The sound was too harsh, the
pace too fast, and Jim hurried outside just as the lathered team
came to a grinding stop in the farmyard. Joseph was not in the
wagon seat, which had broken and pitched him forward between the horses. Though tangled in the reins, he had somehow managed to lock his brawny forearms around the tongue
of the wagon that separated the team. They had half-drug him
along, and pieces of his clothing had been ripped away first,
followed by pieces of skin.

Brighty, the dependable bay, stood stock still, trembling,
blowing hard as Jim approached. But Brighty's usual partner
had been replaced be a rangy chestnut. At Jim's approach the
chestnut tossed his head, rolled his eyes and snorted, spraying
Jim with foam and kicking at the unconscious body hopelessly
trapped between the two horses.

Jim grabbed the chestnut's halter and shook it ferociously.

"Settle down!" he ordered. "Settle down!" The horse rolled its eyes again, but recognized the authority in the voice and began to quiet. As quickly as possible, Jim unharnessed the chestnut and trotted him into the barn, shutting him in a stall. Then he began to work on freeing Joseph.

"Joseph, I can't cut you out. I'm gonna need this harness to get you to a doctor. Hang on, Joseph, hang on." As he talked, Jim untangled the broken body from the web of leather, and lowered him to the ground. "Your leg's broken, Joseph, I'm sure of it." As he laid the still form in the dust, he was sickened by the sight of a hoof-shaped indentation on the left side of Joseph's head.

"You've been kicked hard. But you're still breathing. That's somethin'." Jim continued to talk, both to calm himself and in the hope that Joseph would make an effort to hear him and not die.

"I'm putting you in the wagon now, Joseph. You just lie still. I'll get a blanket from the house—be right back." Jim ran for the house and came back with two tattered quilts. One he rolled up under Joseph's head, the other he used to cover the still form.

"I'm getting Buck now, Joseph. That chestnut's finished for today. Does Buck know how to pull? If not, I guess he'll learn." Jim ran into the barn to harness the horse. "Well, Buck, do you know how to pull? Let's see how you do."

The gelding nodded its head kindly and followed Jim to the wagon. He patiently let himself be harnessed in place, but when Jim took up the reins, it was obvious the Buck hadn't pulled a wagon before. "Come on, boy, you're a good horse. Just let Brighty lead, and you follow. We've got to get to Lincoln—fast!" Jim pulled to Brighty's side, ordered "Git-up," and was greatly relieved to see Buck follow Brighty's lead, if not smoothly, at least willingly.

"Thank God you're a kind hearted old boy," Jim said out loud. He forced himself to walk the horses out of the farmyard, giving Buck a chance to feel the harness. A moan from the bed of the wagon ended Buck's initiation. "Hold on, Joseph, we're on our way to help. Just hold on." Jim urged the horses to a trot. Buck jerked and bumped Brighty, but Brighty took it in stride, and soon the horses were working together. "Brighty, I'm sorry. I know you're worn out. But you've got to keep going," Jim urged. Brighty seemed to get his second wind. He picked up the pace, and Jim talked to Joseph for the rest of the trip to Lincoln, urging him to "hold on," promising "we're almost there," and "we'll be at the doctor's soon, Joseph." He kept his voice level, but his heart was racing and when he pounded on the kitchen door of the hotel, Sarah Biddle saw desperation on his face.

"Doctor!" he croaked. "Joseph's hurt! Where's the doctor live?!"

"Doctor Bain is closest—down O Street, second left, upstairs."

Jim was in the wagon seat and gone before Sarah could get back inside to grab her bonnet. Breathlessly, she shouted for Tom. "Tom! Tom! It's Joseph. He's hurt real bad. I'm going to Dr. Bain's to see about him." She was out the door in time to see the wagon disappear around the corner two blocks ahead.

Jim had already charged upstairs to the doctor's office when Sarah caught up. Clambering up into the wagon box and kneeling beside Joseph, she did her best to shade his face from the blazing sun while she waited for the doctor to come out. Moments passed, and Sarah finally climbed the stairs that carried patients from the sidewalk up to the doctor's second-story office. She heard a voice raised in anger.

"What do you *mean* you won't treat him?"

"Those people have their own healers."

"Joseph has no time for me to look up someone else." Through the window in the door, Sarah could see Jim clamp a huge hand on the doctor's shoulder.

"You'll treat him. Now."

The doctor winced from the iron grip on his shoulder but still resisted. "I don't treat those people!"

Jim slammed a coin onto the desk. "Get downstairs and take care of him."

The doctor looked at the coin. The grip on his shoulder grew tighter. He tried to shake off the hand, but Jim didn't let go. Finally, the doctor whispered, "All right. All right. Let go of me. I'll see what I can do."

The two men brushed past Sarah and descended to the wagon. The doctor pulled back the quilt covering Joseph and pursed his lips. He felt the side of Joseph's neck and said, half-amazed, "There's a pulse. He's alive."

"Thank God," said Sarah. The doctor looked up. "You know this man?"

"Know him?" Sarah responded. "He's Joseph Freeman. Owns the livery next to Augusta Hathaway's hotel. He's one of the first settlers of Lincoln." Sarah thought quickly and managed to say the right thing. Added to the threatening physical presence of Jim Callaway, it assured that Joseph would receive Bain's best—if reluctant—care. "Joseph is one of Aunt Augusta's dearest friends. She's away, but I know she'd be extremely grateful to you if you can help Joseph."

Cornelius Bain was new in Lincoln, Nebraska. His practice wasn't proving to be as successful as he would have liked, and the good will of a prominent citizen like Augusta Hathaway would prove helpful. "Let's get him upstairs. Be careful when you lift him. He's lost a lot of blood. I'll hold his leg still. You," he added, nodding at Sarah, "hold the door. Then I'll need water. Lots of water."

Jim and Dr. Bain carried Joseph up the stairs. As soon as he was placed on the hard examining table, he began to jerk uncontrollably.

Dr. Bain announced without feeling, "Brain seizure. Caused by that skull fracture. I'll have to treat that first, or he'll die for sure." The doctor raised his eyes to look at Sarah. "You got a weak stomach, girl? I could use some help, but I got no use for you if you're going to be fainting away halfway through the procedure."

Sarah's face grew red. "I'm no weakling, mister. You tell me what to do. I'll do it. And there'll be no fainting. Unless it's him!" Sarah nodded toward Jim.

"I'm staying," Jim said matter-of-factly, and the doctor didn't argue. He was already at work, shaving Joseph's head.

"Here," he finally said, handing the razor to Sarah, "you finish this while I wash up and get my surgical tools. And you," he said, turning to Jim, "You hold him down if he begins flailing around again. If he does any more damage to that leg of his, he'll likely lose it. But I got to fix the head first."

The doctor was gone only a few moments. Jim watched Sarah shave the last of the graying hair away, worried over how still Joseph had become. His breathing seemed to be growing more and more shallow.

When the doctor returned, he had a small tray of ominous-looking instruments, which he handed to Sarah. After a quick incision along Joseph's hairline, he began removing fragments of skull. The doctor used one of his instruments to lift the indentation in the skull. Miraculously, Joseph's head regained its normal shape. Sarah looked away from the doctor's hands only once, to stare wide-eyed at Jim. He returned her look momentarily, then they both went back to watching the doctor.

Cutting away a pant leg, the doctor ordered curtly, "Wash his leg." Sarah complied, gently pressing a clean muslin bandage over the worst wounds. The doctor set the broken bone and bound it between two boards. Jim watched every move the doctor made as if Joseph's life depended on his watchfulness.

When at last every wound had been cleaned, the doctor checked Joseph's pulse. "Well, he's still alive." The doctor arched his back and stretched wearily. "He'll need round the clock care. And he can't stay here."

Jim answered, "Don't worry, Doc. I wouldn't leave a horse I hated with you any longer than necessary. Can I move him now?"

"I've a stretcher in the back room."

"I'll get Asa Green from the livery. We'll take him ourselves." Jim turned to Sarah. "Can you stay with him till I get back?"

"Of course," Sarah answered. She pulled up the doctor's chair next to Joseph and sat down, laying her small hand over Joseph's.

When Jim returned, a frightened Asa Green was at his side, exclaiming nervously, "Jus' look at him. He looks dead already."

"Oh, hush, Asa!" Sarah ordered. "Joseph's going to be just fine. He needs rest and lots of good care. And we're going to give him both. Now let's get him out of here." Jim and Asa held the stretcher while the doctor and Sarah moved Joseph as gently as possible.

As they went out the door and maneuvered the stairs to the ground floor, the doctor saw that a small crowd of townspeople had gathered. He took the opportunity to advertise, calling down, "You have any questions at all about his care, you just call. Day or night. I'm always available to help in any emergency."

Jim answered grimly, "Sure thing, Doc. We all know just how ready to help you are." His eyes met Sarah's and neither one smiled.

"Let's walk him home," Jim suggested. "I don't think jostling him any more in that wagon is a good idea."

Jim and Asa carried Joseph to his small room behind the livery. Sarah plumped his pillow and smoothed his sheets. After the still form was tucked in and a candle lit, the trio stood outside the door, talking in low tones.

Asa urged, "Better telegraph Miz Hathaway to come home."

Sarah shook her head. "No, Asa. Joseph would never forgive us for ruining her and LisBeth's holiday. By the time they could get home, we'll know if Joseph—" her voice quavered slightly. "We'll know. Either way, their coming home won't make any difference."

Jim agreed. "Can you run the livery, Asa?"

Asa smiled confidently. "Joseph been teachin' me everything he knows 'bout horses and all. I can do it all."

"I'll take care of Joseph," Jim said.

Sarah looked up at Jim admiringly. "You're the man Joseph

told us about. You're Jim Callaway. Joseph said you were doing wonderful things for the homestead. He likes you a lot, you know."

Jim was uncomfortable. He cleared his throat and addressed Asa again. "Asa, can you ride out to the place and bring that chestnut back into town?"

"That wild so-and-so," Asa muttered. "Joseph can gentle anything with four legs. But that chestnut, he's been trouble since day one. He ain't worth bringin' back."

"Maybe so, but he belongs to Joseph, and we need to see that he's cared for until Joseph can make a decision about him."

Asa nodded agreement. "I'll bring him in."

"He's probably mad with thirst. I didn't do a thing but leave him standing in that stall, heaving and snorting."

Asa reassured Jim. "I'll take care of it, Mr. Callaway."

Jim jerked his head from side to side. "None of that, Asa. I'm just plain Jim Callaway. Just Jim'll do."

Sarah peeked in at Joseph. "I'll bring you water, and some supper. I'll be back soon." She hurried out the back door of the livery and across the yard to the kitchen. Worrying over Joseph Freeman and preparing supper for the hotel guests kept her young mind and hands busy for the next few hours. But when she had washed the last supper dish and sent Tom across the yard with a bedroll for Jim, she sat in Augusta's rocker with half-closed eyes, thinking about Jim—"just plain Jim Callaway."

Jim spent the night listening for Joseph's breathing. Just after midnight it took on an unsteady, gravelly sound. Jim bolted up and was at the bedside immediately, lighting a lamp and peering anxiously into his friend's face.

"You *live*, Joseph Freeman," Jim whispered earnestly. "You hear me? You *live*." Joseph complied. His breathing regained its restful rhythm, and Jim sank back down onto his pallet, not yet realizing that in that moment he had taken his first step back to humanity. Joseph Freeman had reached across the darkness of Jim's past and pulled him back to caring.

CHAPTER 10

If any man thirst, let him come unto me, and drink.

John 7:37

Winona sat in Prairie Flower's tent, tears coursing down her cheeks. "Tell me what to do, Prairie Flower," the young girl begged. "I do not want to go to the Grandmother's Land. I want to be with Soaring Eagle. Always I have wanted to be with him." She wiped away the tears and continued, "But my father and mother say they will go with Sitting Bull. Soaring Eagle says nothing. He hunts and works his ponies. He walks through camp like a man asleep." Winona bowed her head and hugged her knees. "He won't even look at me."

Prairie Flower sat across from the young woman and listened sympathetically. With a sigh she reached over and covered Winona's young hands with her own gnarled ones. "You are a fine young woman. Any of the braves would find a good wife in you. But," Prairie Flower sighed again, "I fear that this is not to be."

Prairie Flower continued. "It is not *you*, Winona. It is *him*. Soaring Eagle knows that because of what happened at the Greasy Grass, the whites will never rest until we are all at the agency. They want what they call the Black Hills. They will never rest until they get them. That Jim Callaway told him there are more soldiers than we can ever fight. He said that there are enough soldiers to kill us all. He said they will not stop until they have what they want." Prairie Flower's voice grew sadder as she spoke. She stopped speaking for a moment to gather her thoughts, but she continued to hold Winona's hands in her own.

At last she continued. "Winona, you should go with your parents to the Grandmother's Land."

Winona interrupted her defiantly, "I want to be where Soaring Eagle is! I want to go with him. I will cook for him and take care of his tepee—and you. And when he dies, I will die with him!"

It was the brash speech of youth, but Prairie Flower considered the words as if they came from the wisest woman in the village. Slowly she replied. "Winona, I do not think you want to watch someone you love die."

Winona began to cry again. "Better that than to never see him again!"

Just at that moment, Soaring Eagle entered the tepee. It was evident by the way he looked from woman to woman that he had heard their conversation. He settled on the earth beside Winona and took her hand in his. Her young heart beat quickly.

"Winona," he began. "My sister. You must go north with Sitting Bull. Perhaps you will find peace there."

She tried to interrupt him, but he held up his hand to silence her. "Hear me now. Of all the young women in this village, if I were to choose one to wrap in my buffalo robe, it would be you." Winona held her breath, collecting every word.

"But this is not a time for beginning a family. This is a time of dying for our people. There was a victory dance after the Greasy Grass, but inside each dancer there was the knowledge that the victory would be a short one. Jim Callaway said that the victory on the Greasy Grass would be our destruction. I hated hearing those words, but I believe he is right. Winona," Soaring Eagle said bitterly, "I see a beautiful young woman before me, but in my heart I wonder when the soldiers will come and take her for themselves. I see children playing in the village, but in my heart I wonder when the soldiers will come to kill them. I see the buffalo on the prairie, and I wonder when the hunters will succeed in killing them all so that we starve."

He took a deep breath and continued. "Our ways are ending. I will not run away from death when it comes to find me. And," he looked deep into her tear-filled eyes, "I will not take you with me to find death."

Soaring Eagle stood up and left abruptly. He stayed away from the tepee until late that night. When he finally returned, Prairie Flower sat alone by the fire. He joined her, and she looked up, smiling kindly. He reached for a stick and stirred the fire. "Some of the others are leaving for the south tomorrow. I will go with them." As if it were an afterthought, he added, "You have been a mother to me, Prairie Flower. But I would not take Winona with me, and I will not ask you to go if you wish to find peace in the Grandmother's Land."

Prairie Flower stretched out her hands toward the fire. "These hands wrapped you in clean fawn skin when you were a baby." She pointed to his scarred cheek. "These hands cleansed that wound. These hands did the beadwork on your moccasins. They helped to bury your father. These hands signed 'love' to Walks the Fire one night when she gave me the cross that you wear. When the time comes, these hands will be there to wrap your body in your buffalo robe and raise it on a scaffold." Prairie Flower flexed her fingers and folded her hands in her lap. Then she said simply, "Bring the dun-colored pony to me in the morning. I will strike the tepee."

The next morning, Sitting Bull's ever-shrinking band headed north for the Medicine Road in search of peace. As they walked, Sitting Bull sang the song he said he had learned from a wolf:

> I am a lonely wolf, wandering pretty nearly all over the world.
>   He, he, he!
> What is the matter? I am having a hard time, Friend.
> This is what I tell you: you will have to do also.
> Whatever I want, I always get it.
> You name will be big, as mine is big. Hiu! Hiu!

As the band topped a rise, Winona turned to look behind her. It was too late. Soaring Eagle and the others had already disappeared behind a ridge to the southeast.

To his surprise, Soaring Eagle did not meet up with soldiers. His small band wandered the vast prairie for weeks, living in the old way, enjoying peace. No one mentioned the fact that they seemed to be heading ever closer to the agencies. Game was scarce, and winter's approach was ominously near. It would be another starving time.

Rising early one morning, Soaring Eagle rode out alone to seek the spirits' guidance. He had gone only a short distance when the sight of a thin plume of smoke curling into the morning sky piqued his curiosity. He urged his pony to a canter, covering the few miles between him and the campsite quickly. At the foot of the last rise, he dismounted and crawled cautiously up the mound of earth to peer over the top. Below him was a lone tepee made of old skins that hung stiffly from a few short poles. Dozens of strips of meat hung from drying racks around the campfire.

Springing onto his pony's back, he rode forward cautiously. When the tepee's owner signed a friendly greeting, Soaring Eagle relaxed.

The stranger called out, "Welcome, my brother. Come and eat. The hunt has been good."

Soaring Eagle dismounted and replied, "The whites have spoiled the land for hunting. In all of my village there is not this much meat. What spirits helped you find so much?"

The stranger was tall and lean. He was Indian, but his hair was cropped short. At Soaring Eagle's question, he sat on the ground, motioning for Soaring Eagle to join him. The two attacked the pot of stew bubbling over the campfire before the stranger responded.

"I am called John Thundercloud. There is only one Spirit, my friend. He is the Spirit of the One who made all that we see around us." Thundercloud licked his fingers before continuing. "It is true that there is much less game now. I am sad to see things change. God has made me swift, like the deer. He has made me good with a gun. Once, I got twelve ducks in only three shots."

Soaring Eagle looked doubtful but didn't want to insult his host. The stew was too good. "My father was a great hunter," he ventured, nodding toward the rifle that leaned against the tepee, "but he never had one of those sticks to help him."

John Thundercloud smiled. "That is one of the good things that came with the white men."

Soaring Eagle spat angrily. "The price we pay for easier hunting is too high."

Thundercloud shrugged. "You are one of the wild Lakota. Tell me, how is your life?"

Between bites, Soaring Eagle described the fruitless hunt for food and his band's lack of readiness for winter, ending with, "It will be another starving time."

"It does not have to be that way," the stranger said quietly. "Come with me. You will have food."

"Come with you to some agency?" Soaring Eagle shook his head. "Give up my ponies? I have a fine herd. They belonged to my father, who gentled his stallion when we were free men."

Thundercloud changed the subject. "What is the meaning of this?" he asked, pointing to the locket and the gold cross. "These are from whites."

Soaring Eagle answered simply. "This," he touched the cross, "was worn by my mother." He opened the locket, motioning to Jesse's likeness. "She was taken from us. I think this other one is my sister. She was born after my mother left us. They walk with the whites now."

John Thundercloud didn't ask any more questions. Instead, he began talking softly. "My brother, I hear bitterness and hatred in your voice. A man cannot live long with such feelings. I have told you that one Spirit helped me hunt this meat. You tell me that your people are hungry. I want to give you this meat. When you go, we will pack it onto the back of that dark pony over there. It will be my gift to you so that you will not have a starving time this winter."

Soaring Eagle looked about him in disbelief. "I have nothing to give you in return."

"Give me your ears while I tell you about the Spirit who led you to me today." Thundercloud smiled. "But first, let us hunt together."

They finished the stew, and Thundercloud unfolded himself and stretched. Disappearing inside the tepee, he emerged with an old bow and arrows in hand. "I think I would like to hunt in the old way today."

When they returned from the hunt, they had a pony laden with fresh meat. It took the better part of the day to skin and clean the carcasses. Another rack had to be built for drying, and by sundown the two were sitting by a dying campfire and Soaring Eagle found himself telling John Thundercloud stories from his own youth. Living in the past, Soaring Eagle relaxed. The bitter lines around his mouth faded. His eyes softened as he told of his parents sitting around the campfire reading from what they called the "God-book." Thundercloud's eyes shone with interest. He interrupted Soaring Eagle. "And what did you think when they read that book?"

Soaring Eagle shrugged. "I liked hearing the stories." Soaring Eagle sighed with regret. "Those were good days. They are gone now."

"Is that all it was for you, stories from a strange people?"

Soaring Eagle pondered his response. The question hung between them and Thundercloud waited patiently. Finally, Soaring Eagle said, "I still have the book they read. Sometimes I wish for someone to read the stories to me again. Now that I am a man, perhaps I could understand why it meant so much to Rides the Wind and Walks the Fire."

John Thundercloud took the conversation over. "My brother, earlier today I told you that you could pay me for the meat if you would give me your ears to listen. I was not always called John Thundercloud. In the days of my youth, I was Kills

Two. I killed the first two whites I ever saw. I hated them for what I saw them doing to our people."

"And now you live where they tell you to live and eat what they give you."

Thundercloud ignored the sarcasm in the voice. "Now I live on the Santee Agency. I have eighty acres that I am learning to farm so I can feed myself in a way that will not make war. I want to live at peace. I want to grow old with my wife and see my children have children. At the agency, there is a mission with a school and a church. I am what they call pastor of the church. That means I teach those who come about God." As he spoke, Thundercloud watched Soaring Eagle carefully.

"My brother, I cannot set you free to hunt the hills as we did in our youth. I cannot pay to buy back the land that the whites have stolen from you. But I can tell you of One who set me free to know peace even though these things have happened."

Soaring Eagle spat in the dust. "You have been fooled by some white man to believe in his god."

John Thundercloud refused to be insulted. "I thought as you once, my brother. But I learned that this God is not just the white man's God. He often lived as we do—beneath the sky, cooking His food over an open fire—traveling with a small band of friends. And He was not white when He walked the earth. He was dark—more like the Lakota than the whites."

Soaring Eagle made a low sound of derision. "Even the Lakota know that the Great Mystery that created all things is not a man."

"You are right, my brother. The God who made us all is not a man. And He is holy. We are not. We cannot be His people when we are covered with the wrong things we do. So His Son became one of us. He walked the earth. He did no wrong. Then He died to pay for the wrongs of others.

"We spend our lives trying to walk in harmony with the spirits, trying to do more good than evil so that God will be pleased with us. But we cannot please God because God says we must be holy, and we cannot be holy. The Son of God did for us what we cannot do. He was holy. Then He paid for our wrongs. We do not have to pay for them."

Thundercloud's eyes shone with quiet joy. "When I first heard of this, my heart was made glad. I asked the Son of God to take my sin. When I did this, a great weight was lifted from me." He paused a moment and then continued. "Times are bad for our people. My heart breaks for the wrongs that are done. But my heart is glad when I think that I live in peace. Whatever happens, I am at peace with God. This peace is in here," Thundercloud thumped his chest, "and it is always here, no matter what men do to me."

Finally, Thundercloud concluded, "Since the day that I came to be at peace with God, I have tried to tell those I meet about Him and how to be at peace with Him. That is why I am no longer Kills Two. The people call me John Thundercloud after a man in the Bible. He had a brother named James. Together they were called 'Sons of Thunder.' Someone thought I was like them. So I am called John Thundercloud. I live at Santee on the Big Muddy."

Soaring Eagle said, "They wanted Sitting Bull to go to what they call the Standing Rock Agency. I know that place."

"Santee is toward the rising sun from there and below the Big Muddy. If your people come with me, they will have food. We have a school to teach the children. We have a place where we learn about God. You could learn to read the book your parents read.

"I have been away from there for several weeks. My people sent me for a rest. I think the Spirit of God sent me here to tell you about Him. If you come with me, I can teach you the words in your mother's book. Then you can decide about God for yourself."

Soaring Eagle shook his head then stood up. "When I was a youth, the country was beautiful. When I hunted, I could see the trails of many kinds of animals. But now the land is changed and sad. The living creatures are gone. I see the land desolate. I see my people dying. I see them running away from the soldiers. I wish that white people had never come into my country."

John Thundercloud pondered Soaring Eagle's speech before he said, "There are good whites and bad ones, Soaring Eagle, just as there are good Lakota and bad Lakota. The good whites want to help us. They cannot change the evil that is done. They come to help us learn to live a new way."

Soaring Eagle stared into the dying campfire. Loneliness pressed upon him. "I do not want a new way. I want the old ways."

When the sun rose the next morning, Thundercloud insisted that Soaring Eagle take all the meat that hung on the drying racks. "But it will take two of your ponies to carry all this meat—and you only have three ponies," Soaring Eagle protested.

Thundercloud insisted. "God has brought us together, my brother. You gave me the gift of listening so that I could share the truth of His love with you. Now I give you a gift of meat. I am glad to see these old ponies go to someone who will care for them. When they are too old to help you, set them free to roam the prairie."

When the camp was struck and the last slab of meat tied securely on the last pony, Thundercloud grasped Soaring Eagle's arm in friendship. "When you are ready, my brother, come to the Santee Mission and ask for John Thundercloud. I will pray for you. I will pray that God will help you to see His way for you. Only when you go His way will the hole in your heart be filled."

As Soaring Eagle turned to go, Thundercloud called out *"Hancan kin nicipi un nunwe* (The Lord be with you)." As Soaring Eagle led the pack train away to the west, John Thundercloud stood watching and praying.

CHAPTER 11

A man's heart deviseth his way: but
the LORD directeth his steps.

Proverbs 16:9

Augusta had almost declined when David Braddock offered the invitation to lunch. But when he presented an elegant note written by his mother, Augusta softened and accepted his arm. "After all," she whispered to LisBeth, "it's his *mother* who extended the invitation. Any boy who takes two new acquaintances to meet his mother can't be a villain."

David led the women through the maze of Exposition buildings to his carriage. A uniformed driver doffed his cap and helped the women up into the carriage.

From the seat across from them, David Braddock smiled politely. "May I ask, Mrs. Hathaway, what has interested you most at the Exposition thus far?"

That was all Augusta Hathaway needed. The rest of the drive to Abigail Braddock's was filled by Augusta's soliloquy on progress and the inventions that would be needed if the West were to prosper. "Now, mind you, Mr. Braddock. I know what you easterners think. You think it's a vast desert out there. But just give us a few years. I'm convinced that Nebraska will one day be a rich farmland. All we need is an efficient way to tap the water supply and irrigate the land. Mark my words, Mr. Braddock. One day Nebraska will help feed the world."

LisBeth expected David Braddock to smile wisely, pat Augusta on the shoulder, and placate her. Instead, he seemed genuinely interested in her ideas. He listened carefully to everything she said and asked pointed questions about the west.

"I've never been west, myself, Mrs. Hathaway. But," he looked at LisBeth, "there's a first time for everything."

Had LisBeth and Augusta known how sought after a luncheon invitation from Abigail Braddock was to residents of Philadelphia in 1876, they would have climbed the stairs to the elegant mansion with quaking knees. As it was, both women were blissfully ignorant of the fact that they were about to be entertained by the dowager empress of Philadelphia society. Indeed, preceding Augusta Hathaway and LisBeth King Baird as luncheon guests in the manse were none other than the Emperor Dom Pedro of Brazil; Prince of the Houses of Bourbon, Braganza, and Hapsburg; and his wife, the Empress Theresa.

The Braddock mansion was set back off the street in the middle of a park of tall trees. A wide porch completely surrounded the house, ending at the portico where the carriage pulled up to let the guests out. Entering the manse, both Augusta and LisBeth gaped at the grandeur before them. Two vast staircases swept up the sides of the entryway, meeting at the top to form a balcony. Abigail Braddock stood on the balcony, smiling warmly before gliding down the stairs to meet her guests.

"Welcome!" Her voice was mellow and sincere. "Welcome to Philadelphia. I hope we've been treating you well. Things have been a bit hectic since the Centennial opened. People aren't always what they should be. . . ."

Abigail shook Augusta's hand seriously, and then turned to LisBeth. "LisBeth King Baird. I have heard about you," LisBeth blushed, "and I see it's all true." The woman was friendly without being overbearing. "Come, let's have some refreshment on the porch."

LisBeth and Augusta followed Abigail through the arched doorway under the balcony, and into a sitting room that fairly glowed with golden light. The chairs were covered with gold damask, and a floral rug caught the golden tones and accented them with deep blue. At the far end of the room stood a harp and a piano. Above the piano was a massive portrait of a young mother and two children. It was unmistakably Abigail. Dressed in heavily embroidered and beaded black silk, the woman held her aristocratic head on a long, slender neck. Her hair was swept up and held in place with jeweled combs. At one side sat an infant with sparkling brown eyes, his hair pomaded, his long gown elaborately trimmed in elegant lace.

"Is that you, Mrs. Braddock?" LisBeth asked, nodding at the portrait.

Abigail smiled. "Yes, Mrs. Baird, it is. David is six months old there," the smile faded a bit, "and his father had been dead for only four months. The portrait had been begun shortly after David's birth, but then his father became ill and I just couldn't bear to sit for the artist. So we had it put in storage. One of the last things David's father demanded of us was that we promise to finish the portrait. It was to have been the crowning piece, the last thing to finish the house he'd had built for us." Abigail sighed. "Sadly, he never lived to see it all finished."

"I'm so sorry, Mrs. Braddock," LisBeth apologized, but Abigail Braddock smiled kindly.

"You don't need to apologize, dear. Time heals the bitterest of wounds. And now I enjoy remembering. William and I had a wonderful few years together, and I enjoy talking about him."

LisBeth realized that she had just heard Augusta's words of the previous day repeated. She grew quiet and studied her gloved hands.

Abigail reached out and took LisBeth's hands in her own. "Forgive me, my dear, for being so forward, but since you know my story, perhaps you'll allow me to venture beyond our brief acquaintance. David has informed me of the tragic loss of your husband at the Little Big Horn. I extend my heartfelt sympathies." The older woman squeezed LisBeth's hands. "I know that doesn't help much, dear, but take the word of a woman who's been where you now stand. The pain will get better. It won't ever be completely gone, but you'll be able to bear it, with time."

LisBeth stared dry-eyed at Abigail Braddock for a moment. She lifted her chin and pressed her lips together firmly. Then, her lower lip began to quiver and her eyes filled with tears. Embarrassed, she tried to gather herself, but Abigail wouldn't let her pull away. Impulsively she pulled LisBeth into her arms, "There, there, dear. Don't be embarrassed. All this Victorian nonsense about hiding one's true feelings is a blasted inconvenience."

When David joined them, LisBeth was wiping her eyes with his mother's lace-edged handkerchief, and Augusta was smiling approvingly at both of them. It was Augusta who broke the silence. "David Braddock, thank you for bringing us here. Your mother's a charming woman, and if half of Philadelphia is as nice as she is, then we'll certainly enjoy the rest of our stay here."

"Perhaps we'll even persuade you to extend your visit?" David asked hopefully.

Augusta boomed, "Not on your life, young man! I've a schedule to keep and a hotel to run. LisBeth has a life to get on with—in Nebraska."

LisBeth added, "And Nebraska wouldn't last long without Aunt Augusta looking out for her."

Abigail showed them to a corner of the porch shaded by bittersweet vines. She waved away a young servant girl who stepped out onto the porch. "Never mind, Betsy. I'll do the serving myself." Betsy curtsied and hurried off. Abigail served lemonade while they talked, then guided them through an elegant lunch served in a small dining room on the opposite side of the house.

Settling into her place at the table, LisBeth observed the array of china, crystal, and silver. Finally, she leaned over to say to Augusta in a stage whisper, "Good thing you had me work the dining room, Aunt Augusta. I've set enough tables to know which fork is for what!"

Abigail Braddock enjoyed the comment immensely, following it with an anecdote about her own first encounter with a properly set table. "David's father took me home to meet his parents. I thought I'd die when I saw all the china they used—for *one* meal. I don't remember a thing that was said at that entire two-hour ordeal. I spent the entire time watching every move William's mother made. She'd pick up a fork; I'd pick up a fork. She took a drink; I took a drink. I thought, *Even if she does it wrong, she'll do it with class, and I'll be safe!*" Abigail laughed at the memory. "I'd been brought up on the *other* side of town and didn't even have my own fork until I was two years old! I'm sure William's mother was horrified. How he ever convinced her to let *me* into the family, I'll never know!"

It was a warm, cheery lunch, and when the carriage was brought around to return LisBeth and Augusta to the hotel, all of Augusta's suspicions about David Braddock had been laid to rest. As she and LisBeth settled into the Braddocks' carriage, Augusta informed LisBeth that David and Abigail Braddock were obviously honest, God-fearing people, and she considered it a blessing that they had been nearly kicked out of their hotel rooms if it meant meeting the Braddocks. LisBeth was inclined to agree.

As the carriage departed, David inquired as to his mother's opinion of the two women from Nebraska. Abigail answered without hesitation. "I like them both, David. Augusta—as she insists on my calling her—is brusque, but she's got a heart of gold. Anyone can see that. And LisBeth is lovely. She's deeply shaken by the loss of her husband and mother, but she's young. She'll be all right." Abigail reached over to pat the back of her son's hand. "I'm *glad* you brought them home for lunch, David."

David Braddock pursed his lips and nodded gravely at his mother. "I'm glad you approve, Mother. For *that*," he said, nodding toward the carriage, "is the woman I am going to marry."

CHAPTER 12

Draw nigh to God, and he will draw nigh to you.... Humble yourselves in the sight of the Lord, and he shall lift you up.

James 4:8, 10

J oseph was going to live. When Dr. Bain called the day after the accident, Jim dismissed him with a curt, "I got Dr. Gilbert coming now. Want to make sure he gets the best care." Dr. Bain had blanched with anger at the rude dismissal, but Jim didn't care.

Nearly three days after the accident, late in the night, Joseph moaned. It was barely audible, but Jim, who had kept constant vigil, was at his side immediately, talking in low tones. "That's it, Joseph. You just take it easy. We got the doctor coming in the morning. You rest till then." Jim poured a glass of water and gently lifted Joseph off his pillow. "Here, now, you take a swallow of this." When his patient complied, Jim smiled with satisfaction. Another low moan brought more talk. "You're back home in your room back of the stable. I'm here, and I'm not leaving, so if you need anything, you just let me know. Asa's taking care of the horses and the business. Nothing to worry about, there. Try to rest, now, Joseph." There were no more sounds of life from the still form, and Jim soon returned to his cot.

When dawn broke, Jim sent Asa for the doctor. As he waited, he heard Joseph take a deep breath. There was a pause, and then another deep breath and a sound, not really a moan, but a grunt that ended high, as if Joseph wanted to ask a question. Jim drew up a chair and sat by the bed. At last, without opening his eyes, Joseph muttered, "Ow," and reached up to feel the left side of his head.

Jim answered the unasked question. "It's all right, Joseph. Doctor Bain fixed it."

There was a long silence before Joseph made another sound. Then he croaked, "Don't remember nothin' after that fool gelding kicked me in the head."

"The team brought you to the homestead," Jim explained. "I brought you to town. Got you sewed up."

One eye opened and Joseph searched for the voice. When he could focus on Jim's face, he managed a half-smile, then closed the eye again. "How long you been here, son?"

"Since the accident three days ago."

Joseph sighed. "Thanks. I'm fearful tired." He fell asleep. When the doctor arrived, he looked Joseph over thoroughly and changed his bandages.

"No change in what you need to do, son," the elderly doctor said, patting Jim on the shoulder. "Just keep the wounds clean and wait. If he wakes up again, offer him soup. I'll stop in next door and ask Miss Biddle to put some chicken stock on so it'll be ready."

"Doc," Jim broached the subject awkwardly. "I gave Dr. Bain all the cash I had. I don't know about Joseph's situation. But I'll find work and see that you get paid."

Dr. Gilbert snapped his medical bag shut and said crisply, "Young man, I've known Joseph Freeman since I first came to Lincoln. Many's the night he got out of a warm bed to saddle a fresh horse for me to make a crazy ride to some home-steader's cabin when my own mare was wore out or had thrown a shoe. And *that*," Dr. Gilbert said with emphasis, "is all that needs to be said about my fee!"

Hours later, Joseph opened both eyes and managed a weak grin when Jim helped him take another drink of water. "Oo-*ee!*" he exclaimed, "that hoss packs a wallop in his hind foot!" Slowly, Joseph raised his hand to try to take the glass Jim held, but he couldn't quite manage it.

"Easy does it, Joseph," Jim chided. "You've been unconscious for three days. Don't rush things."

Joseph twitched one finger back and forth and muttered, "You waitin' on me, son?"

"I'm waitin' on you till you can wait on yourself, Joseph."

Joseph smiled slowly. "I recollect Doc sayin' he'd ask Miss Biddle to fire up the stove and put some soup on. Think it's ready yet?"

Jim was out the door and back almost immediately with a bowl of soup. Joseph managed to swallow several spoonfuls before falling asleep again. Jim settled back with satisfaction to watch Joseph sleep.

It was several days before Joseph did much more than wake, swallow a bit of soup, and sleep. But slowly his waking hours lengthened until he grew restive and began to ask questions about Asa, the livery, the hotel, the homestead.

"Quit worrying, Joseph," Jim chided. "Asa's doing a fine job. Sarah Biddle seems to be doing okay with the hotel too. At least things always seem to be going smooth in the kitchen. I get away when you're sleeping and split wood now and then. I've nothing much left to do at the homestead before winter. The fall garden isn't important, so there's no need to be shooing me out the door." Jim sat down and leaned his chair back against the wall, stretching his long legs out before him. "Just rest and get better. Mrs. Baird and Mrs. Hathaway'll be home soon."

There was a long pause before Jim added, "There's something I been wantin' to ask you, Joseph."

The patient looked keenly at Jim and waited.

"You said Mrs. Baird wanted to sell that homestead. Think there's any chance she'd sell it to me?" Jim rushed ahead, "Oh, I know, I don't have money. But I'd work on the place, pay her as I could." His voice took on a hint of doubt. "Of course, it'd take a long time." The chair he'd been leaning back in plopped back onto the floor. Jim answered his own question.

"She probably wouldn't want to wait for me to pay; it'd take too long. Forget it, Joseph. It was a dumb idea."

"Now hold on, Jim. Don't talk yourself out of it if it's what you want. I don't know what she'll say, but you ought to ask her, if it's what you want."

Jim looked down at his worn boots while he talked. "Don't quite know *what* I want, Joseph. But I sure do like the idea of making things grow. That rose you brought out started to grow up the side of the porch. Those fields are just waiting for a plow. I'd like to plow that ground up and make it yield a crop. Seems like maybe I could make a life out there."

Joseph interrupted him. "Glad to hear you talkin' about makin' a life for yourself."

Jim looked up and grinned ruefully. "Guess that's a change, isn't it?"

"Guess it is. Glad to hear you thinkin' about stayin' around here. You're a good man, Jim Callaway."

Jim stood up abruptly. "No, I'm not, Joseph. I'm not a good man at all."

"All I know is you work hard. You're honest. You saved my life. That's all I need to know. What's past is past. When a man proves his worth like you have, then all that's left is forgive and forget the past."

Jim picked up Joseph's water glass and pitcher and moved toward the door. "Some things aren't to be forgiven."

"If the good Lord could forgive the ones that killed him, then who's to say we can't all be forgiven?"

"It's not the Lord's forgiveness I'm talking about, Joseph," Jim said quietly. "It's mine. Some things a man just can't forgive *himself* for." Jim left before Joseph could answer.

Joseph had taken a nap and was sitting up, leaning back on the plump pillows behind him, thinking, when Jim returned with supper. The two men ate in silence, but as soon as Jim had taken the tray off his lap, Joseph reached under his pillow and retrieved a book.

"I asked Asa to get this outta the trunk there at the foot of my bed while you was gone, Jim. I can't read myself, but I got this book from a peddler that came through town a while back. I was wonderin' would you read to me?"

Jim reached for the book. It was a Bible. Opening it, Jim asked, "You aiming to convert me, Joseph? I already had a good dose of religion growing up. Went to church every Sunday with my parents."

"I'm not an educated man," came the response, "but I'll tell you somethin'. Goin' to church on Sunday and gettin' a dose of religion's not the same thing as knowin' the Lord. You get to *know* the Lord, you'll know what I mean."

"Well, suppose I try to get to know the Lord and find out the Lord don't want to get to know me?" Jim asked.

Joseph shook his head from side to side. "Ain't no such thing as a man the Lord don't want to know."

"You sure of that?"

"Well, it says so in that book you got in your hand. I can't read it myself or I'd show you, but I recollect it's in there." Joseph smiled. "Suppose you just start readin' it to me, and we'll see if it don't say so."

"You win, Joseph," Jim answered. "You win." Opening the book, Jim asked, "So where should I start?"

"Anywhere you want."

Jim turned a few pages until he came to one titled The Names and Order of the Books of the Old and New Testament. He scanned down the page and grinned. "Hey, Joseph, there's a book in here called James."

"Well, read that, then, James Callaway. *You* may not believe it, but *I* do, and it'll sure bring comfort to hear it." Joseph settled back comfortably while Jim found the book of James in the Bible and began to read. He hadn't gone far before he stopped abruptly.

"You read real nice," Joseph said.

"I was just thinking. I could teach you to read it for yourself, you know."

Joseph looked suspicious. "You goin' somewhere?"

"No, I don't mean that. It's just that you're gonna be laid up for a while. And you're not used to that. I need to be thinking of things to keep you down so you heal up good. Wouldn't you like to read it for yourself?"

Joseph considered. "Naw, I'm too old. You can't teach an old dog like me."

"You're *not* too old, either," Jim argued. "You want to learn, I can teach you."

A soft knock on the door made Jim snap the Bible shut abruptly. Tom Biddle opened the door and said in a stage whisper, "Is Joseph all *right?* Is he *asleep?*"

Joseph called out, "I'm doin' fine, Tom. Come on in here!"

Tom pushed the door open and limped over to Jim. "Sarah said to bring this right to you, Mr. Jim. Said you'd know what to do."

The telegram was a perfect reflection of Augusta Hathaway—brusque and to the point. All it said was, *Arriving noon Friday. Joseph please meet train.*

Jim read it aloud. "Guess they'll have to take me instead."

Joseph was doubtful. "You don't like crowds, Jim. Asa can meet the train."

"They're gonna be all worked up when you're not there and they hear why, Joseph. I can settle 'em quick, let 'em know you're okay. Asa's great with the horses, but . . ." Jim hesitated.

Joseph finished the sentence with a broad smile, "With people he ain't so good. You're right. I just didn't want to ask you to do it if it would bother you. I recollect how the first time I mentioned town—" He didn't finish.

"I'm still not interested in any church socials," Jim said, "but I can meet the train and see that Mrs. Hathaway and Mrs. Baird know you're all right."

So it was Jim Callaway who stood at the train station as the train rolled in. He leaned against the corner of the station building, away from the crowd, his hat pulled down over his eyes, going over in his mind what he would say. LisBeth's foot had barely hit the boardwalk when he was at her side, hat in hand, giving his rehearsed speech. Augusta hadn't heard, and when she descended from the train, he hastily introduced himself and repeated his speech.

"Joseph isn't here because he's been laid up. He'll be fine, but the doctor says it will take some time. Asa is running the livery, and I'm taking care of Joseph until he's better." Jim clapped his hat back on his head. "Wagon's over there." He pointed in the general direction of the wagon and headed off toward the baggage car before retracing his steps.

"Uh, forgot to ask you. How many trunks?" He stood uncertainly on the boardwalk. Other passengers crowded past and looked curiously at the tall stranger come to meet Augusta Hathaway and LisBeth King Baird. One passenger sidled up to Augusta. It was Agnes Bond.

"Augusta! LisBeth! Welcome home! How was the Centennial? Charity and I just got back from visiting Mother Bond in Omaha. Now who is this handsome stranger?" Jim blanched and looked uncomfortable. LisBeth rescued him. Taking the arm he had not offered, she said gaily, "Augusta, you wait in the wagon. I'll point out the trunks to Mr. Callaway. We'll be along directly. And Agnes," LisBeth added, "you tell the women at the sewing circle hello. I just can't *wait* to tell them all about our trip!" She literally pulled Jim toward the luggage car before Agnes could say anymore.

They walked down the boardwalk together until LisBeth pointed out one of the trunks and released Jim's arm. Just as he hoisted the trunk on his shoulder LisBeth pointed out another one. "That one, the dark one that has Augusta's initials." Jim nodded curtly and strode towards the wagon where Augusta waited, trying to rid herself of Agnes Bond, who stood beside the wagon chattering about nothing, trying to learn something about Jim Callaway.

Jim loaded one trunk and went to retrieve another. To avoid crowding between Augusta's ample form and Jim Callaway, LisBeth climbed up into the bed of the wagon and perched herself on her trunk. Having learned nothing from Augusta, Agnes turned to LisBeth.

"And who's the handsome stranger?"

"Jim Callaway. I've hired him to take care of the homestead until I can sell it in the spring."

"Is he from around here?"

"You'd have to ask Joseph about that, Mrs. Bond," LisBeth answered. "He located Mr. Callaway for me, thank God. He's done wonders for the place."

Just then Jim returned with Augusta's trunk. Ignoring Agnes Bond, he walked around her and climbed up beside Augusta. Jim slapped the team a bit too briskly and they lurched off, nearly unseating LisBeth from her perch and leaving Agnes Bond standing in a cloud of dust, a frown on her face and a determination to learn more about Jim Callaway well *before* the sewing circle.

As fall came and went, Joseph's body healed. He was finally able to stand on his mended leg and hobble about with the help of a cane. His first meal at the hotel's kitchen table was a celebration. LisBeth's eyes shone warmly as she held out a chair for Joseph. They seated him at the head of the table for that meal, and the honor was not lost on the faithful friend.

"I recollect as your ma used to sit here," Joseph said as he scooted the chair up to the table.

LisBeth's smile wavered and she said earnestly, "Joseph, I'm so *glad* you're going to be all right. I don't think any of us could take another loss. It would just be too much."

There was an awkward silence before Sarah plopped a huge bowl of mashed potatoes onto the table. Augusta said heartily, "Well, praise the Lord and pass the potatoes! We're all here and we're healthy. Eat up!"

Jim sat at the table, yet he was outside the circle of friends who laughed and reminisced. When the meal ended and everyone settled into their routine of cleaning up, Jim stood up and said quietly, "I'll be getting to that harness you wanted cleaned now, Joseph." He was out the door before Sarah could invite him to stay for the second piece of pie she had been saving for him.

After he left, the women discussed him thoroughly while Joseph listened. Finally, Augusta turned to Joseph. "He seems nice enough. Lord knows he tends to you like a faithful sheep dog. There's just something—"

Joseph interrupted her. "Something's missing. I know, Miz Hathaway. Whatever turned that boy's beard white—he carries it with him. It weighs him down. He survived it, but it still owns him." Joseph sighed. "He's better than he was when I found him, but he's still not *living* life. He's just *enduring* it."

LisBeth said softly, "I think I know how he feels." She was sitting at the table with her head bowed. She fingered her wedding ring, twisting it round and round, then she stopped abruptly. "I promised to go to the sewing circle tomorrow— Lord knows why—so I'd better turn in." She scooted out her chair and took her empty coffee cup to the sink to rinse it. Then, impulsively, she crossed over to where Joseph sat and threw her arms around his neck. He was so startled that he sat speechless while she said in a choked whisper, "Don't you *dare* try to tame any more wild horses, Joseph Freeman. I need you!" Embarrassed by her show of emotion, LisBeth fled to her room, leaving Joseph and Augusta to cluck their tongues and wonder how to help the young people in their midst who seemed to be nearly drowning in grief over the past.

Joseph limped slowly back to his room in the livery stable where Jim sat reading the Bible with what seemed like more than his usual interest.

Augusta Hathaway retired to her own rooms with a heavy heart. Her prayers that night were particularly earnest. "Lord, I *know* you know what you're doing. I *know* you're God, but forgive me, Lord—are you *sure* you haven't put too much on those children?"

It was deep into winter before forgiveness flooded into Jim Callaway's life. Snow lay ten inches deep outside and the odor of straw and horses permeated the tightly closed livery. The night was still and the kerosene lamp burned brightly. Jim had long since finished reading the book of the Bible that carried his name, and Joseph's own ability to read had progressed steadily. Still, Joseph insisted that Jim read aloud every evening. Being unfamiliar with the Bible, Jim had simply continued to read whatever came after James.

They had progressed through the books named for Peter and were now ready for the one called The First Epistle of John. Jim read steadily through the beginning of chapter 1, *"That which was from the beginning, . . . This then is the message which we have heard of him, and declare unto you, that God is light, and in him is no darkness at all. If we say that we have fellowship with him, and walk in darkness, we lie, and do not the truth."*

Jim's voice quavered. He stopped reading.

"What's wrong, Jim?" Joseph asked gently.

Jim cleared his throat. "Nothing."

"*Nothing* don't make a man quit reading."

Jim scooted the chair back against the wall and fidgeted. "If I'm understanding this, Joseph, it says that men who walk in darkness don't have fellowship with God."

"That's what I'm hearing, too, son."

Jim took a deep breath. "I always thought I was a child of God. But I've walked in a lot of darkness—done a lot of dark things."

Joseph urged Jim. "Keep reading, boy."

Reluctantly, Jim obeyed. *"But if we walk in the light, as he is in the light, we have fellowship one with another, and the blood of Jesus Christ his Son cleanseth us from all sin."*

Cleansed from sin. That's it, Jim thought. *That's what I want. I want to be cleansed from what I've done.* The hint that this might be possible made him tremble.

Joseph urged again, "Keep reading."

"If we say that we have no sin, we deceive ourselves, and the truth is not in us."

Then he read it. They were only words on a page, but they seemed alive. They washed over him in such a wave that he was physically shaken. *"If we confess our sins, he is faithful and just to forgive us our sins, and to cleanse us from all unrighteousness. . . . And if any man sin, we have an advocate with the Father, Jesus Christ the righteous: and he is the propitiation for our sins: and not for ours only, but also for the sins of the whole world."*

Jim's voice trembled and he cleared his throat. He tried to continue, but found he couldn't. Instead he sat, his head bowed, his hands shaking as he drank in the words on the page. Over and over he read them, while Joseph watched and waited.

"Joseph." Jim finally raised his head. "Am I getting this right? Does this mean that a man could be forgiven? No matter what he's done, he could be *forgiven?*" The gray-green eyes were hungry.

"That's the way I understand it."

Jim refused it. "That's too easy. It can't be." He tossed the book aside and buried his face in his hands. As Joseph quietly waited, a groan sounded from the agonized young man. "I wish to God it was that easy, Joseph."

"Wasn't nothin' easy about it," Joseph said. "I recollect it cost Jesus an awful price."

Jim listened to Joseph's calm, soothing voice. Then, before he could stop them, the words spilled out. Jim went back to Slim Buttes and relived the nightmare. Joseph listened as Jim retold every detail in an agonized voice that nearly broke Joseph's heart. He wanted to reach out to comfort the boy, but he was afraid to move, afraid to interrupt Jim's agonized retelling of his past. When Jim finally finished, his work shirt was drenched with sweat and he sat, his head bowed, whispering bitterly, "I wish to God I could be forgiven for that. I wish to God I could be forgiven."

Joseph reached out and put his hand on Jim's shoulder. "Why don't you just try asking him to forgive you?"

It seemed too simple. He shook his head. "He won't. Some things are not to be forgiven."

"Seems to me you got to try, boy," Joseph urged. "You got to try or this thing is going to destroy your life."

Another groan and Jim reached up to grab Joseph's hand. He clenched it tightly and waited. He didn't really know why he waited, but then something happened. The words he had read seemed to leap off the page and into his life. He didn't mouth intelligible words, but he threw his past up to the heavens, wondering if God could possibly forgive even that. He let go of Joseph's hand and grabbed the Bible again. He reread 1 John, desperate for comfort. Slowly, the message of what he read poured into his heart, became part of him. Then it happened. *"If we confess our sins, he is faithful and just to forgive us our sins, and to cleanse us from all unrighteousness."* He could be forgiven! Even Slim Buttes could be forgiven!

Jim read eagerly, drinking in the words. *"Whosoever believeth that Jesus is the Christ is born of God."* It seemed too simple, and yet the promise was there. *"These things have I written unto you that believe on the name of the Son of God; that ye may know that ye have eternal life, and that ye may believe on the name of the Son of God."*

When he had finished reading, he closed the book tenderly and looked up at Joseph with shining eyes. "Joseph, I need to take a walk."

He walked out into the stable. The hay smelled sweeter than he had ever remembered. Clear moonlight sifted in through the cracks in the walls, dappling the floor of the stable. Buck heard Jim and whickered low. Jim crossed the stable and rubbed the gelding's ears. When he returned to his cot, Joseph had turned down the lamp and fallen asleep. Jim picked up the Bible. He wanted to read it again, to make sure he had not misunderstood. *"These things write we unto you, that your joy may be full. . . ."* Maybe that's what it is, Jim thought. *Maybe it's joy.* Whatever it was, something had replaced the agony of guilt he had carried for so long. Search as he would, he could not find the guilt to take it up again.

CHAPTER 13

 He that trusteth in his riches shall fall; but the righteous shall flourish as a branch.

Proverbs 11:28

It was a hard winter of deep snows and bitter cold. Few travelers ventured out through the worst months, and the hotel generated less labor than usual. The women sewed, read to one another, and helped Tom with his school assignments. LisBeth and Sarah's friendship deepened, and Augusta smiled with satisfaction as she watched the two lean over young Tom to help him with his lessons or entertain him with games.

One evening, the women lowered Jesse's unfinished quilt from the rafters. The protective sheet that lay over the top was pulled away to reveal an elaborate green and red appliqué. LisBeth's eyes grew wistful. "It's the same colors as the Princess Feather Mama made for me."

Augusta sniffed back tears and cleared her throat before explaining. "She called it the Whig Rose, LisBeth." Looking across the quilt at Sarah who was running one hand lovingly over its surface, Augusta added, "Jesse said it was going to be for Sarah's hope chest."

Sarah looked up, wide-eyed. Then she tucked her chin to her chest and said with wonder, "For me? Oh, I never dreamed—"

LisBeth prevented the moment from becoming too maudlin with a quick laugh, "Mama! As if she needed an excuse to quilt!" Then, stroking the quilt's surface, she added, "Mama said quilting always helped her think, sort things out. She said stitching brought her comfort." Looking at Sarah she decided quickly. "We ought to finish it, Sarah."

Augusta agreed. "It would have made Jesse happy, girls. That's for certain. Although heaven knows it won't be as pretty as if she'd stitched it herself!"

"One thing's sure," LisBeth said, "Mama would much rather have *us* do it than take it over to the ladies at the church and give it over to *Agnes Bond.*"

With that, the three laughed and began their nightly quilting bee. They stitched all through the winter, filling every open space of the Whig Rose with feathers and ferns. LisBeth stitched hopefully, waiting for the comfort her mother had experienced. On New Year's Day, as they took the quilt from its frame, LisBeth realized that the hoped-for comfort had not come.

It took only one evening to bind the quilt. The next evening, Jim Callaway knocked at the kitchen door and hoisted in a huge trunk Augusta had selected at Miller's store. The quilt was carefully folded and laid at the bottom of the trunk with almost religious reverence.

Sarah closed the lid carefully and looked up at LisBeth, her eyes sparkling with joy. "I never had hope of any kind of future before we came here. Now I have a hope chest, and a dream." She blushed and stopped talking, but her eyes sought out the retreating figure of Jim Callaway.

February 1, 1877

We believe the entire country is on the verge of a boom—in which the Braddocks would like to participate. To that end, Mother and I have planned a trip west in search of investment opportunities, in particular, the purchase of land that will no doubt rise in value as the next decade advances. We would hope to presume on the hospitality of the Hathaway House during the month of April. Adjoining rooms would be preferable. We look forward to your response and to visiting your fair city. Kindest regards to both you and Mrs. Baird.

Your servant,
David Braddock

Augusta read the letter enthusiastically the evening it arrived and immediately began making plans. "Finally, girls," she crowed to Sarah and LisBeth, who were up to their elbows in dishwater, "someone influential has seen the promise here. Abigail Braddock and I have been writing back and forth all winter, and *finally*, I've gotten someone to listen! The Braddocks believe in the future of Lincoln. They believe that we are on the verge of a boom—and they are right!"

Sarah and LisBeth looked at one another with knowing smiles and waited for the other shoe to drop. It took only seconds.

"In fact, I think we need to move ahead with my plans for a face-lift for the Hathaway House. Girls, *we* are going to build a new wing—and it won't be clapboard siding, either. I'm riding out to Yankee Hill tomorrow and put in my order for brick! When Abigail and her son arrive, they'll see progress in action!"

The next day, Augusta had Jim drive her the few miles to the new foundry at Yankee Hill where she arranged to receive the first few firings of brick in the spring. When they pulled up to the livery door, Augusta climbed stiffly down and walked briskly through the stable to check on Joseph. He was sitting on an inverted barrel at the back of the livery, oiling a harness, his crutch leaning against a stall door. When Augusta launched into her new plans for the livery stable's expansion, he leaned over to rub his leg and began shaking his head from side to side.

"What, Joseph?" Augusta demanded. "What's wrong with the plan?"

"Ain't nothin' wrong with the *plan*, Miz Hathaway—just somethin' wrong with the *man*, that's all. My leg ain't mendin' as quick as it should, and no way am I gonna be able to handle the horseflesh you're gonna need to serve that many new rooms full of folks."

Augusta snorted, "Nonsense, Joseph! You'll be fit as a fiddle by spring."

While they talked, Jim led in the team and began rubbing

them down. The horses' breath filled their stalls with clouds of steam, and they tossed their heads and snorted appreciatively as Jim offered them buckets of hot mash and molasses.

Augusta added, "What about Jim Callaway? You said he's a good worker. Take him on as a partner."

"With all due respect, ma'am," Jim broke in, hanging a curry comb on a nail and closing a stall door behind him, "I'm not fit to be a partner in a business." He pushed his hat back on his head. "At least not in town. I've stayed on to see that Joseph mends well, but as soon as he's fit, I'll be moving on."

Augusta wheedled, "No need to move on. Lincoln is a fine town to start a life in, and with my hotel feeding this livery business, it'll easy support—"

Jim interrupted, "Sorry, Mrs. Hathaway, but I'm not cut out for city life. Fact is," he said, looking earnestly at Augusta, "I've been trying to work up courage to ask Mrs. Baird if she'd consider selling her homestead to me. I'd have to work for it, of course. I've got no cash. But I could pay her a little at a time."

Augusta countered, "Farming's no way to make a way in the world, Jim Callaway. The city is where a man who wants to make a name for himself wants to be."

Jim answered quietly, "I don't care much about making a name for myself, ma'am. But I would like farming that homestead."

"That's not a dream—working and sweating all your days and hanging on by a thread at the mercy of the weather! It's a hard life. You deserve better."

Jim looked at Augusta soberly. "Time was when I didn't think I deserved to live, ma'am. Guess I've come a long way to have any dream at all. It's a small dream, but it suits me." He paused for a moment before adding, "Do you think Mrs. Baird will sell?"

Augusta didn't hesitate. "She'll sell, all right. When I read her that letter from David Braddock, she mentioned it right away—selling the homestead."

Jim frowned. "David Braddock?"

"The hosteler we met at the Centennial. He and his mother are coming to Lincoln, looking for investment property."

"She's already decided to sell to Braddock, then?"

Augusta shivered, "Land sakes, no, young man! She hasn't decided a thing. She just mentioned it, that's all. If you want the place, just speak your mind. I'm freezing to death out here. You two coming in for dinner or not?"

She hurried off muttering to herself, "Just like a man—can't make up his mind and when he does can't *speak* it." From the doorway she almost shouted back to Jim, "Well, are you coming or not? You'd better get LisBeth's ear today before she sells that homestead out from under you, young man!"

She closed the door firmly. As the sound of her footsteps retreated along the board sidewalk, Joseph chuckled. "Guess she told you, Jim Callaway! Speak your mind or lose your dream!"

Jim grinned sheepishly. "I've been walking around in a fog for so long, Joseph. I half surprised myself, talking to her like that about buying the homestead." He took a deep breath and whistled low, "But I've been wanting it for a long time. I've been praying on it for a long time too. Talked to some folks. Made some plans. Guess it's time to go find out if my *dream* for me and the Lord's *plan* for me agree."

LisBeth stared in amazement at Jim and stammered, "Why, of course, Mr. Callaway, I'd be happy to have you walk me to the sewing circle." She pushed away from the table and added, "Just let me get my cape."

Augusta grinned at Joseph and nodded her head knowingly while Jim offered his arm to LisBeth and led her out the door and up the street toward the church. Neither Augusta nor Joseph noticed Sarah frown and take an almost frantic interest in clearing the table.

Jim walked beside LisBeth easily. He appeared relaxed, but he didn't say anything for the first few moments of their walk. LisBeth held his arm lightly and prayed that Agnes Bond was nowhere in sight. It was far too soon for a widow to be escorted by a man, even on a walk to the sewing circle.

Finally Jim began. "I know I'm a stranger to you, Mrs. Baird."

LisBeth interrupted him. "Hardly a stranger, Mr. Callaway. You've been our guest for meals for weeks now, and please, call me LisBeth. Every time I hear someone say 'Mrs. Baird,' I feel like I should reach for a cane!" LisBeth smiled brightly and looked up into Jim's gray-green eyes.

"Then you call me Jim."

"Fair enough, Jim."

They were almost at the church steps, but Jim found that he could not muster the courage to speak his mind. They had walked up the narrow steps and he reached to help LisBeth off with her cape before he could begin his carefully prepared speech. "Mrs. Baird—uh—LisBeth." She turned and looked up at him.

"Yes, Jim?"

Jim hesitated. "I'd like to buy the homestead. On shares. I've got no cash, but I'm a hard worker and I'd take good care of the place. The soil's rich. It'll give a good crop. I could make the first payment as soon as a crop came in. The equipment's already there. Joseph said he'd loan me a good team if I'd break a few yearlings for him. All I'd need would be enough to live on—and seed. I talked to Mr. Miller over at the general store last week. He's not much for granting credit, but when I offered to paint his store for him this spring, he said it'd be a fair trade—seed for the painting job. At fifteen dollars an acre, I figure I could have you paid in a few years. If you could see your way to wait, ma'am. I'd do my best by you."

Jim had spent weeks praying for the Lord's will, but as he stood sharing his dream with the woman who could either make it come true or kill it, he couldn't help clenching his hands nervously as he waited for her answer.

LisBeth asked innocently, "Fifteen dollars an acre. Is that a fair price?"

Jim looked confused. "I talked to the land agent, ma'am. He said—"

LisBeth interrupted him. "He said the place is only worth ten dollars an acre. You're not the only one who's been talking to the land agents."

Jim felt the back of his neck grow hot. With dismay he realized that he was blushing. He looked down at his boots uncomfortably. "Well, ma'am—I guess it's worth more to someone like me."

LisBeth put her hand on his arm impulsively and asked, "What's someone like you see in an abandoned homestead that makes you willing to pay five dollars an acre more than it's worth?"

Jim gathered his thoughts and looked at her squarely. "Well, ma'am, it's like this. Time was I didn't think life had anything left for me. But then I started working on the place, fixing things. Then Joseph taught me some things. He showed me how the Lord loves us even when we don't think we deserve to be loved." Jim heard himself talking, opening up to LisBeth, and he felt his neck heat up again. *She must think me a fool,* he thought, *blabbering all over the place about myself.*

But LisBeth didn't give any hint of thinking Jim Callaway a fool. She stood in the vestibule of the church and listened attentively to every word he said, her dark eyes soft with understanding and friendship. Jim noticed for the first time that LisBeth King Baird was a mighty attractive woman. Then he cleared his throat and continued talking, suddenly very aware of her hand on his arm.

"So, ma'am, I'd like to stay on the place, if you'll sell it to me. I can make something of it. Make things grow. That would be worth more than I can say, ma'am. Worth more than I can say."

LisBeth listened carefully to the earnest voice, and when he had finished, she didn't hesitate an instant. Smiling warmly, she removed her hand from his sleeve as she said the words that handed Jim Callaway his dream. "Jim, I can't think of a man that I would rather have taking on Mac's homestead than you." She lowered her voice and added. "The homestead has seen a lot of unhappiness. It holds bitter memories for me. Make some new memories out there. Make it a happy place."

She stood back and shook her finger at him, breaking the seriousness of the moment with a laugh. "And you'll not pay one cent more than ten dollars an acre, either. Now let's shake on it."

LisBeth held out her gloved hand, and Jim clasped it in his own as he offered his thanks. Just then the door opened and Agnes Bond came in. LisBeth backed away from Jim as she said quietly, "Don't thank me, Jim. You've taken a great weight off my shoulders. I was hoping to talk David Braddock into buying the place. I'm glad not to have to wait two months to have the matter settled."

Jim Callaway barely nodded at Agnes Bond before going outside. He bounded down the steps to the church and ran to Miller's where he ordered seed on credit and arranged to paint the store as soon as the weather broke. LisBeth followed Agnes downstairs to the sewing circle where she took her usual place at the quilting frame in an unusual state of mind.

Agnes Bond was ready. She picked up a needle and thread and settled herself directly across from LisBeth at the quilting frame. Then she carefully steered the conversation of the small group of women to her advantage so that she could ask the question innocently, "Now tell us all about that nice young man who walked you to circle today, LisBeth. Isn't he the young vagabond who's been taking such good care of our dear Joseph Freeman since that horrible accident?"

LisBeth studied her quilting and took a bit too long formulating an answer for the women who raised their eyebrows and exchanged telling glances.

Charity Bond was not nearly as tactful as her mother. "Lis-Beth!" she exclaimed, "are you giving up your mourning—*already?*"

LisBeth looked up from the quilt with fire in her eyes. She silenced Charity with one look and then lifted her chin and straightened her shoulders as she looked around the quilting frame at each pair of eyes. She ignored Charity's remark in her crisp answer. "*Mr.* James Callaway is the man Joseph hired for me to take care of Mac's homestead. When Joseph was nearly trampled to death, Mr. Callaway showed himself to be a true and faithful friend. He has given up his own interests to care for Joseph, and he has assured us that he will continue to put his own interests aside until Joseph is able to resume his work. However, Mr. Callaway requested a chance to speak with me about a business arrangement. To that end, *I* suggested he walk with me to the sewing circle. Mr. Callaway has suggested very generous terms for buying my husband's homestead. I'm very grateful to him for taking the burden of the homestead off of my mind.

"As to telling you anything more about him, I haven't been so rude as to ask him questions of a personal nature over the dinner table at the hotel, which is the only opportunity I've had to see him. He is very devoted to Joseph and spends nearly every waking hour attending to the duties required to keep the livery stable operating. I have no reason to think anything but good of him. In fact, I'm proud to call him a friend. Just today—as I'm sure you heard, Agnes—we began addressing one another by our Christian names. I'll be sure and keep you all informed of every little detail of Jim's life that I'm able to pry out of him, now that I've won his confidence."

LisBeth's final sentence dripped with sarcasm and not only silenced Agnes Bond, but also prevented her next fishing expedition, which was to be to discover the identity of the David Braddock LisBeth had mentioned, for Agnes Bond had been standing outside the church door listening closely to every bit of the conversation between LisBeth and Jim.

LisBeth's biting reply put a damper on conversation for the rest of the afternoon. The women all wished heartily that LisBeth would have been angry enough to leave so that they could talk. When she did not, Charity retrieved her copy of Mr. Dickens's *Great Expectations* and read aloud while the women stitched. LisBeth paid little heed to the book, for while Pip was enjoying life as a gentleman, LisBeth was wondering why social standing held no allure for Jim Callaway.

CHAPTER 14

 Now my days are swifter than a runner: they flee away, they see no good. They pass by like swift ships: like an eagle swooping on its prey.

Job 9:25–26 (NKJV)

Soaring Eagle was wrong about the winter of 1876. It was not a starving time for his tiny band. Although the winter was hard, with more than the usual snow and many days of bitter cold, thanks to the generosity of John Thundercloud, they had plenty to eat. Huddled about their fires, they wondered what spring would bring. One family at a time they came to Soaring Eagle, dejected but firm in their resolve to turn themselves in to the agency. They went, a few at a time, until there was only one lonely tepee tended by an aging woman and a small group of fine ponies tended by a confused, bitter young man.

As they watched the last of their band leave, Soaring Eagle turned to Prairie Flower. "If you want to go with them, I will understand."

She put a wrinkled hand on his shoulder and shook her head firmly. "I go where you go, Soaring Eagle."

When the winds howled around their lone tepee, they stayed indoors, huddled about a small fire, waiting. Soaring Eagle retold the story of his strange encounter with John Thundercloud until Prairie Flower had it memorized. They discussed going to the Santee Agency, but they did nothing. They wandered the prairie in indecision, enduring the winter and telling stories of the past.

The years had been kind to Prairie Flower. She had aged gracefully and remained healthy, but as winter wore on, a persistent cough grew worse until she began to lose strength. She grumbled against it but finally had to rest each afternoon.

Soaring Eagle sought out the fruits and leaves of cedar trees, boiled them, and fed her the resulting liquid. The time-honored remedy did little good. Prairie Flower continued to cough and to lose strength until Soaring Eagle cared for her full time. She managed to sit up and eat with great effort, then finally lost her appetite.

"You must fight," Soaring Eagle demanded. "The spring will come soon. Think of how the land comes alive then! The sun will warm your bones, and I will set you on my finest pony, and we will find a new band and return to the old ways."

With shaking hands, Prairie Flower pointed to the cross and chain that she had given him years ago. She pressed his hand and said, "Go. Remember that you have known a good white. Remember that I have loved you as a son. Leave me. I am old. I have had a good life. Go. I will die here and be at peace knowing that you have gone to meet tomorrow like the brave man you are."

Soaring Eagle insisted, "I will take you with me, my mother."

"I am not strong enough to make the journey," Prairie Flower softly replied. "I am not strong enough to learn the new ways. I am part of the old ways. I am part of what you must leave behind in order to have a life."

Prairie Flower's eyes filled with tears. "There is a new enemy in our land, Soaring Eagle. But this enemy cannot be beaten back. The white man is here, and he will stay. He is too powerful for us to fight if we wish to live. There will be many among our people who will not be able to stand what is happening, but there will be some who run to meet this new enemy bravely—just as our bravest warriors always ran to be the first to meet the enemy in the old battles." She patted Soaring Eagle's hand. "I want you to be one who runs to meet this new enemy."

"There are too many of them, Prairie Flower."

"There are many ways to have victory, my son. Perhaps you will have victory by making this new enemy your friend. Perhaps you will have victory by learning from him and making a better life for yourself in the new world."

Soaring Eagle protested. "The whites offer our people *their* world. They tell the Lakota to farm the land. The Great Spirit did not mean us to farm. He gave us the hills and covered them with buffalo. He made us to hunt and fish. I don't want anything to do with a people who tell an Indian warrior to carry water on his shoulder and dig in the earth like a woman!"

Prairie Flower was growing more and more weary, but she forced herself to contend with Soaring Eagle. "Soaring Eagle, there was a time when our people did not have horses. When the horses came, there were those who were afraid of them. There were those who worshiped them. But the wisest among our people caught the horse and tamed him. And with the horse, they conquered this land.

"Now the white men have come. Some Lakota are afraid of them. But the wisest will find a way to have victory. I don't know what the new world holds for you, but I want you to go forward to meet it. Do not be like the others, always fighting to keep the old ways. Thundercloud told you of good whites who want to help our people. If we keep to the old ways, we will be beaten and bad whites will have victory. You must go *forward*, Soaring Eagle. Find that man who wants to help you. Learn the new ways. Show them all that the Lakota are real men!"

The long speech had exhausted her. Prairie Flower lay back on her buffalo robe, her eyes shining with the challenge she had thrown at Soaring Eagle. Seeing her fatigue, he stood up abruptly. "I will go to check on the ponies." As he reached the opening of the tepee he turned back to say gently, "You have spoken in wisdom, my mother. Rest. Then we will talk more." He pulled a thin buffalo robe over his shoulders and went outside to check on his small herd.

When he returned, he saw that Prairie Flower had curled up and fallen asleep. Before falling asleep, she had managed to open the brittle parfleche that she had kept from the old days. Her arms were wrapped about a white blanket that had belonged to Walks the Fire. Prairie Flower had kept it safe for years, wrapping it about her only on special occasions.

Soaring Eagle stood over Prairie Flower's form, and as he looked down at her, he said quietly, "Many winters ago, I returned from the hunt to find that Walks the Fire had been taken from us. It was a dark time." He squatted beside Prairie Flower and pulled the buffalo robe around her shoulders. "It was you who put the light back into the world for me. In all the winters since that time, I have had a tepee to come to that was warm and clean and filled with mother-love."

As he covered her with a buffalo robe, Soaring Eagle realized that the still form was no longer breathing. His howl of grief split the night.

Soaring Eagle sat by Prairie Flower's body through the next few hours of darkness, waiting for dawn when he would lay her to rest. Painting her face red, he dressed her body in her white wedding dress. She had kept it in the parfleche, along with a pair of heavily beaded moccasins made years ago by Walks the Fire. Pressing Prairie Flower's knife and sewing case into her hands, Soaring Eagle wrapped her body in buffalo robes secured with rawhide straps. When the body had been prepared, he went outside and searched the edge of the creek that ran by their campsite until he found a tree with four strong branches. Then he carried the body out and placed it high in the tree. Seating himself at the base of the tree, Soaring Eagle crossed his legs and leaned against the trunk, weeping and singing a death song,

> *Prairie Flower, you saw me and took pity on me.*
> *You wish me to survive among the people.*
> *Great Mystery, help me, do help me!*
> *I love my country so;*
> *In losing it I am having a hard time.*

Soaring Eagle remained camped near the tree for four days

of agonizing self-searching and grieving. On the morning of the fifth day, he rounded up his ponies and led them to the base of the tree where Prairie Flower's body lay. Patting their backs and running his hands through their thick winter coats, he said, "You have been my friends. I must run to meet the future. If I take you there, the soldiers will take you from me. But I am setting you free to go into the next land. Find my father, Rides the Wind. He will welcome you to his herd and lead you to green grass and fresh water. Tell him that his son, Soaring Eagle, has gone to meet the enemy. Tell him that Soaring Eagle will not stand and be defeated. He will find a way to be a man in the new world." Slowly, deliberately, Soaring Eagle killed each pony until there was a ring of ponies about the foot of the tree. Returning to the tepee, he removed the brittle parfleche that carried mementos of the past and tied it to the one aged pony he had saved to ride. Then he gathered wood to build a huge fire around the base of the tepee.

He lit the fire and mounted the pony. Heading southeast, he turned to look back at the old campsite. It was consumed in flames. Looking up at the sky, he muttered, "Rest well, Prairie Flower. I am doing what you asked. I am going to meet the future. I will look for those men who want to help us. I will learn the new ways. I will show them that the Lakota are men!"

The sun rose and set seven times before Soaring Eagle topped a rise and looked down on the little cluster of buildings that made up the Santee mission founded by Alfred and Mary Riggs seven years earlier. What had begun as little more than a rough log cabin and a few tents was now a cluster of frame buildings. Seeing a plume of smoke rise from a pile of stones that went up the side of one building, Soaring Eagle circled about until he found the door and waited uncertainly, his heart pounding.

From behind him he heard the approach of a horse, and wheeling his pony about he saw a Dakota man and woman coming up the road. They approached cautiously. When they were only a few feet away, the man signed "peace." Soaring Eagle returned the friendly greeting, and the stranger slid off his pony, handed the reins to the woman, and came closer on foot.

"You come in peace. You are welcome here. How far have you come?"

"Seven sunrises—from there." Soaring Eagle pointed west before adding, "I met one called John Thundercloud. He said to come to the white buildings made from trees on the Big Muddy. He said I would be welcome here." Soaring Eagle stayed astride his pony. He was tense, and the pony danced nervously as he spoke.

The man looked about and asked, "Where are your people?"

"I come alone."

"My name is James Red Wing," the stranger said. Nodding toward the woman he added, "This is my wife, Martha. We help teach here. This is the girls' home. We call it Birds' Nest." John Thundercloud comes to help us worship God." James Red Wing pointed across the compound to a small white building with a cross on the top. "John Thundercloud comes there to help us worship God. His house is there—not far." James Red Wing pointed toward a line of trees to the south. "Are you hungry?"

Soaring Eagle nodded.

"Then come with me to eat. Then we will go to John Thundercloud."

Looking from James Red Wing to his wife, Martha, and back, Soaring Eagle saw kindness. He relaxed imperceptibly. Months of wandering, days of mourning Prairie Flower, and a week of traveling into the unknown had taken its toll. For the moment, his desire to fight was gone. Wearily, Soaring Eagle slid from his pony's back. He reached out to grasp the hand of friendship that James Red Wing offered.

"Please, come with us. Mr. Riggs will help you. He is the one who built this place of learning. He cares for our people." As James Red Wing talked to Soaring Eagle a door opened slightly. Soaring Eagle turned to see enormous blue eyes peeking curiously out of a white child's face. The door swung open wide. Behind the child stood a ring of whispering Indian girls and a white woman.

The white child didn't seem to care that he was one of the wild Sioux everyone feared. Meeting Soaring Eagle's stony gaze with equally unblinking icy blue eyes, she marched across the porch of the house, reached up to grasp the gold locket that hung about his neck, and demanded, "Can I see?"

The woman standing behind the group clustered in the door gasped.

Soaring Eagle bent down to bring his own eyes level with the child's. She had hair the color of Walks the Fire's. Her eyes sparkled with a color that his own mother's had lacked. Still, the memory of Walks the Fire softened his features. He didn't smile, but he did reach up and open the locket to show the demanding child what was inside.

"It's a pretty lady, Mama. And *another* lady too. Come look, Mama!" she sang out, smiling and giggling. She was still pointing at the faces in the locket when her mother grabbed her and swept her up and away from the wild Indian. As she half-carried, half-dragged the child away, she grunted, "Carrie Brown! What do you *think* you are *doing?*" As the woman retreated to the safety of the house, Soaring Eagle saw that one side of her mouth turned down severely. The bones around that eye were malformed. Her expression was drawn into a perpetual squint and a permanent frown.

James Red Wing called out, "It's all right, Mrs. Brown. He looks fearsome, but he says he has come in peace. He knows Pastor Thundercloud, so I believe him. I'm just going to take him over to meet Reverend Riggs. Then we'll ride out to Thundercloud's."

With Martha Red Wing's help, Rachel Brown shooed the girls away from the door and closed it firmly. Soaring Eagle and James Red Wing turned to walk the short distance to the Riggs's cottage. As they walked, Soaring Eagle turned to look back at the Birds' Nest. A pair of bright blue eyes watched him from a front window.

CHAPTER 15

He saved them for his name's sake.
Psalm 106:8

S oaring Eagle leaned against the wall of the church
building. Crossing his legs, he settled back to
listen to the sounds that floated through the window above
him. It had become a familiar routine in the few weeks he had
been at the agency. Every seventh sunrise, James and Martha
Red Wing invited Soaring Eagle to accompany them to the
church service. Every seventh sunrise Soaring Eagle declined.
Then, as the Red Wings's wagon rumbled out of sight, Soaring
Eagle trotted on foot the four miles to the church. He always
arrived just as the choir of Indian men were concluding their
singing, and he listened with disgust at the rich voices that
blended together, not in the familiar cadence of Lakota song,
but in foreign harmonies and strange words.

> *Jesus Christ nitowashte kin*
> *Woptecashni mayaqu—*
> *(Jesus Christ, thy loving kindness*
> *Boundlessly thou givest me.)*

He didn't understand all the words. Still, something kept
him sitting there in the dust, listening to the service. Something made him strain to hear the words spoken by John
Thundercloud.

Thundercloud preached in a different dialect than Soaring
Eagle had grown up speaking. But Soaring Eagle had been

studying both the new dialect and the white man's tongue for weeks. Unlike many whites, Reverend Alfred Riggs believed that even the wild Indians were intelligent and could learn. He offered instruction for both children and adults.

Soaring Eagle refused to let them cut his hair. He refused to abandon his native dress. Still, he appeared each day to open the simple readers and learn the words being taught.

The white man's tongue was oddly familiar. Sometimes Soaring Eagle felt that he was not really learning it but only remembering it. He didn't consciously remember that Walks the Fire had spoken to him in this tongue when he toddled about the campfire in the days before she was fluent in Lakota. He didn't remember that he had, for a time, babbled in Lakota to his father and in English to his adopted mother. The words had been forgotten long ago. Still, the patterns remained and aided his learning.

When Thundercloud preached, Soaring Eagle strained to hear every sound. Occasionally he heard a familiar word or phrase. He sat listening carefully, not moving, until the usual distraction came along to call his attention away from the nonsensical sermon.

Just when Soaring Eagle's brain grew weary of the strain of listening for familiar words, Carrie Brown peeked around the corner of the church building. Just as he had every Sunday since coming to the mission, Soaring Eagle pretended not to see her. Just as she had every Sunday since he had come to the mission, Carrie marched up to where he sat and waited impatiently for him to look up. As soon as he did, she pointed to the locket and settled in the dust at his side, waiting expectantly. Soaring Eagle obediently removed the locket and opened it, whereupon the child repeated the soft cadence, "Such a pretty lady."

He didn't understand what she said, but the sweetness in her voice spoke to some longing in him, and he grew to enjoy her company. This particular Sunday morning, Carrie had come with her corncob doll strapped across her back. Snapping the locket shut, she stood up and impulsively put the cord over Soaring Eagle's head. Then, she pulled on one of his dark braids to get his attention and, pointing to the doll, said proudly, "Papoose."

Soaring Eagle smiled. Carrie didn't see it, for he kept the smile inside. What Carrie saw was a reluctant nod that said that he had understood her. She felt a childish pride that she had, at last, elicited a response from the stoic wild Indian. She decided to try for another conquest. Pointing to herself she said, "Carrie."

Soaring Eagle looked into the wide blue eyes and repeated quietly, "Carrie."

The blue eyes sparkled and a radiant smile revealed two missing front teeth. A long, slender finger poked his chest and a question appeared in the blue eyes. Soaring Eagle took a deep breath and said his name slowly.

Carrie was elated. Clapping her hands with delight, she triumphantly repeated his name, and when he nodded, she bent over and whispered, "We're friends now."

Soaring Eagle shook his head to show that he didn't understand. The church service was ending. He had come to recognize the sound of the closing prayer. Although he had no idea what the change in tone meant, he knew that it signaled that the people inside would soon be coming outside and that meant he must get away. Standing up abruptly, he patted Carrie on the head and trotted away, darting behind the first hill before James and Martha Red Wing emerged from the service.

Martha looked expectantly at Carrie and was pleased to see her nod at the unspoken question. Then, Martha leaned toward her husband. "He came again today, James. Do you think he will ever come *inside* and really listen?"

James shook his head. "Hard to say, Martha."

Their conversation was interrupted by the arrival of Pastor Thundercloud. "You are speaking of our brother Soaring Eagle?" When James and Martha nodded, the pastor sighed.

James offered, "He refuses to learn to farm, but he works hard at the languages each day. He cares for the livestock. He's amazing with the horses. But he never talks. He just watches everything carefully. He's done everything we've asked, except work in the field. When we mention anything to do with the garden or farming, he just looks at us and shakes his head from side to side. Then he goes hunting."

"*I* think he's *lonesome*," a childish voice offered. Carrie Brown skipped across the porch, stopping abruptly to rescue her corncob baby when it fell from the ragged bit of cloth she had used to tie it to her back.

Martha Red Wing shivered, "Well, lonesome or not, I wish he'd at least try to talk to us. When he looks at me, I wonder if he's trying to learn or plotting something."

Rachel Brown joined the group. "When he first came and Carrie just walked up to him, I was terrified. But then I watched him. I decided he was just as terrified as I was, only he had the good sense not to show it. He must feel so desperately lonely. I think he's grasping for some way to go on living." Rachel stroked her crooked jaw and looked lovingly at Carrie. "He may even be looking for some *reason* to go on living."

There was an awkward silence before Carrie sang out, "Well, if he's lonesome, he can come visit us *anytime*. I told him we're friends now." Her face puckered into a frown. "Just don't know if he *understood* me."

Pastor Thundercloud smiled down at Carrie. "The next time you see Soaring Eagle, Carrie, do this." He held his right hand in front of him, palm out, his first and second fingers extended. Carrie shifted her corncob doll from her right to her left hand and with some difficulty imitated the sign.

"That's it. Now raise your hand until the tips of your fingers are as high as your head. There. Just like that. That means 'friend' in a language Soaring Eagle will understand."

Carrie looked to her mother for approval and saw that she was practicing the sign as well. Rachel said softly, "Carrie and I came to the mission to be of help. Soaring Eagle seems to be taken with Carrie. The Scriptures say that a little child shall lead them. Perhaps the Lord will use Carrie to save another lost sheep."

Sooner than they expected, part of Rachel Brown's prophecy was fulfilled. The Lord did use Carrie in Soaring Eagle's life, but it was Carrie who was the sheep that was nearly lost and Soaring Eagle who did the saving.

The following Sunday morning when Soaring Eagle left the church building, he walked for hours before making his way to the shady ravine that marked the halfway point between the school and the agency. In this land where the wind often blew dust and grit for days at a time, such a spot was a favorite. Several large cottonwood trees lined the banks of the creek that flowed strong and clear. Unlike most creeks in the region, this one had a white sandy bottom.

Soaring Eagle slipped down into the ravine and settled onto a flat rock, intending to stay until the sun set behind the cottonwoods. He had been there for only a few moments when the intense murmur of a familiar, mellow voice made him crouch down and listen carefully.

"Carrie, be still. Just be very still. It will probably move away if you don't scare it."

"But, Mama, it's raising its head up at me. I don't like it, Mama—I'm scared, Mama. . . . " The young voice was making every effort to stay quiet, but terror laced the last few words.

"Carrie, you must be still. Now, I'm going to pray with you, and we'll ask God to make it go away. If you are very still, it will go away. Now, pray with me. Let's say it in Dakota. That will make us think harder, and it will keep us calm."

Rachel's voice began, *"Wonmakiye cin Jehowa hee: Takudan imakakije kte sni."*

When Carrie did not join her, Rachel asked quietly, "What comes next, Carrie? Do you remember what comes next?"

A moment and a whimper, and Soaring Eagle heard Carrie begin to recite, *"Peji toto en iwanke maye kta; Wicoozi mini kin icahada yhus amaye kta."*

"That's right. Now what is the snake doing, Carrie?"

"It put its head down, Mama, but it's not moving. It's not going away."

"Let's go on with our prayer. *Minagi yuccetu kte; Woowotanna canku kin ohna amay kta; Iye caje kin on.*"

Rachel urged Carrie again. "It's working, Carrie. The snake will go to sleep and then we can get away. Say the next verse. Sit very still and say the next verse."

As the childish voice obediently began to recite, Soaring Eagle stealthily crept along the creek bed and peered over a huge boulder. Below him, on a blanket, sat Rachel Brown, her bare feet dangling in the water. At her side was Carrie, but the two sat rigidly, not daring to move. Not three feet from Carrie, a huge rattlesnake had emerged from under a rock and was eyeing the two suspiciously, coiling up and waving its head back and forth.

Rachel was holding Carrie's left hand tightly, trying to remain calm as they recited. They had finished the Dakota rendition of Psalm 23 and begun in English when Rachel saw movement across the creek. Soaring Eagle raised one finger to his lips as he bent to pick up a huge stone with his right hand. Then, before Rachel could say a word to Carrie, he had flung the stone with a mighty force that crushed the snake's head and left it writhing in harmless death throes.

Carrie screeched and jumped up. Rachel sat trembling, her face white. When Carrie saw who had thrown the rock, she splashed across the creek and flung her arms around Soaring Eagle's waist. Rachel wiped away tears of relief and quickly drew her bare feet under her skirts as she rose, weak-kneed, and tried to thank Soaring Eagle.

Finally, Carrie recovered enough to remember her lesson from Pastor Thundercloud. Tugging on one of Soaring Eagle's braids to get his attention, she carefully made a fist, extended two fingers, and signed "friend." Soaring Eagle smiled, and this time he let Carrie Brown see the smile.

"Thank you, thank you, Soaring Eagle," Carrie chanted happily, hugging him again.

Soaring Eagle looked across the creek at Rachel and saw

with amazement that she, too, was signing "friend." One side of her mouth was turned up in an attempt at a smile. Ruefully, she rubbed the part of her mouth that would not smile.

Soaring Eagle stroked Carrie's long red mane and, pointing to her, said, "Carrie—Red Bird." Then, looking at Rachel he said firmly, "Good Bird." Rachel blushed and bent over to pick up the quilt they had been sitting on.

"Thank you, Mr. Soaring Eagle. I don't know how much of this you understand, but thank you."

Soaring Eagle nodded soberly before turning away. Quickly he ascended the steep side of the ravine and trotted out of sight before Rachel could make any more attempt at communication. As Rachel and her daughter walked carefully up the pathway that led from the creek to where their team of horses had been tethered, Rachel began to tremble again with the realization of the danger they had been in and at the unlikely savior that God had sent to answer their prayers for help.

CHAPTER 16

Love one another: for love is of God.

1 John 4:7

He decided to go in. John Thundercloud looked up from the text for his sermon in surprise and smiled at him. Two blue eyes peered around the edge of the rough-hewn front pew. Before her mother could stop her, Carrie Brown trotted down the aisle, took Soaring Eagle's hand, and led him up to the front. Rachel Brown smiled primly and scooted toward the open window, making room for Carrie's guest.

Soaring Eagle had dressed for the occasion, wrapping his thick braids in strips of colored cloth, pulling on his ceremonial scalp-shirt and beaded leggings, and adorning his scalp lock with the five eagle feathers he had earned in battle. The congregation of Dakota men and women tried not to stare impolitely, but the sight of a wild Sioux in full battle regalia walking calmly down the aisle of their church caused quite a stir.

John Thundercloud nodded to Soaring Eagle and returned to his sermon. He spoke in English. Soaring Eagle was pleased to find that much of what Thundercloud said made sense— linguistically.

Pastor Thundercloud had called his sermon that day "The Dying That Gives Us Life." Soaring Eagle understood the words. He listened to the pastor read the text from 2 Corinthians.

We are troubled on every side, yet not distressed; we are perplexed, but not in despair; persecuted, but not forsaken; cast down, but not destroyed.

Soaring Eagle wondered at Thundercloud's ability to read these words and apply them personally. He thought how good it would be to say those words and mean them. They were the words of a man who had fought a great battle and refused to be defeated. But how could a man who had been taken from his homeland and imprisoned be saying these things? Soaring Eagle grew angry as the pastor talked of loving and forgiving. He decided not to listen any more. But just when he was about to get up and leave in disgust, Carrie Brown's small white hand found its way into the battle-hardened hand of the Lakota warrior.

Soaring Eagle looked down at Carrie. The child was beaming with satisfaction. He couldn't help himself. He smiled back.

John Thundercloud gave a sermon that challenged his congregation that day. Soaring Eagle was not ready to hear those words. Still, God used a child to give the sermon that Soaring Eagle needed. It didn't require words, but it had a title. Carrie put her hand in Soaring Eagle's and spoke the sermon called "Love."

On the day that followed Soaring Eagle's first true attendance at the Santee Church, Rachel Brown stepped out her front door and nearly tripped over a piece of bark holding a huge, fresh trout. The next day, there was a prairie chicken. Mary Riggs reported the arrival of mystery game on her doorstep one morning—as did Martha Red Wing and John Thundercloud's wife, Gray Dawn.

When Carrie tumbled out the school door for recess that morning, she noticed that Soaring Eagle walked beside James Red Wing as he prodded the mission's two white oxen to pull the water wagon up a steep incline. The water wagon had made its daily trip to the nearby river, and when it neared the Riggs's cabin, Soaring Eagle hoisted a barrel out of the back of the wagon and carried it in.

When school was over that day, Carrie skipped to the building site for a workshop that was to open soon. Soaring Eagle was helping James Red Wing skin the bark off a felled log. Every day thereafter, Carrie saw Soaring Eagle helping at chores and taking part in mission life. He was still very quiet, but he worked diligently alongside the other men.

The next Sunday, when Rachel and Carrie Brown entered the tiny church building, Soaring Eagle was already there, sitting on the back pew, waiting for the service to start. Carrie looked slyly out of the corner of her eye at him as they walked past and grinned. Soaring Eagle pretended not to see her. Still, he turned one palm up and clasped his two hands together. Carrie understood. He was thanking her for last Sunday.

After the sermon, Carrie hurried outside to look for Soaring Eagle. "Your friend has gone hunting, Carrie," James Red Wing said.

Carrie pursed her lips with disappointment. After bolting down her lunch, she ran outside to play, wandering ever closer to the far-off grove of cottonwoods and the sand-bottomed creek where she and her mother had last picnicked. With a careful look about her and under every rocky ledge, she settled onto the bank of the creek and dangled her bare feet in the clear water, singing softly to Ida May, the corncob doll. A shadow fell across the water and, before she had a chance to look up, Soaring Eagle had settled beside her.

"Can I see the pretty ladies in there again?" Carrie pointed to the locket.

Soaring Eagle took off the locket and handed it to her. As she looked at the women, Soaring Eagle pointed to Walks the Fire. "My mother." Before Carrie could ask the question, Soaring Eagle explained her presence among his tribe, ending with, "she had hair like the setting sun, the color of Red Bird's hair."

Carrie smiled with pleasure before asking, "Who is the other one?"

"I think she is my sister. She came after Walks the Fire was taken from my village." Soaring Eagle changed the subject. He pointed to the horizon and said, "My father hunted buffalo here."

Carrie looked up at the somber face. Pointing to the scar on his left cheek, she asked about it, and Soaring Eagle told her the story of how he earned his name. Carrie gasped, "You just stepped off a cliff? Just like that?" She pointed to the top of the ravine. Soaring Eagle looked up and shook his head. "No, much higher."

"I think you must have had an *angel* watching over you!"

Soaring Eagle frowned. "Angel. What is angel?"

"*You* know—an *angel*—with wings! God says we have *angels* watching us, taking care of us."

Soaring Eagle laughed. "I do not think your God would have sent angels to help a frightened Lakota boy so many years ago."

Carrie shook her head. "He would too! He cares about *every*body. My mama said so."

Soaring Eagle deferred. "If Good Bird has taught you this, then you must believe it."

"Did you believe what your mama taught you?"

Soaring Eagle shook his head. "She believed." The memory of the old Bible folded up carefully in his parfleche rose up to accuse him. "Even though I did not believe, I still remember."

The afternoon passed with Carrie asking questions and more questions. Each one took Soaring Eagle back to his people—back to his childhood—and back to a time when the Lakota were the hunters, not the hunted.

"Why are you so sad, Mr. Soaring Eagle?"

"I am not sad, Red Bird. The Lakota learn silence to hide from our enemies and to catch the best game. We learn to wait so that we will not rush into battle foolishly."

"How come you're so strong?"

"A man among my people must be able to go without food or water for two or three of your days and not complain. He must be able to run a day and a night without rest."

"That's how you ran so far to get help when your father was hurt on the cliff!"

"That is how I ran so far."

"What do those feathers mean?"

"They mean that I have 'counted coup' five times on my enemy. In battle, we run to strike the enemy with our hand or with a stick, without killing him. To run at a man who shoots at you with his gun and to strike him with your open hand, that is a brave thing. When my friends saw that I had done this, they said it around the campfire, and I was allowed to wear one eagle feather for each coup."

"Then you must be *real* brave!"

Soaring Eagle smiled. "There are many among my people who have more than five eagle feathers, little one. Five is not so many."

"Would you like to find your sister?"

Soaring Eagle thought for a moment. Then he shrugged his shoulders. "My sister would not be pleased to meet her brother."

"Why not? If *I* had a brave brother, *I'd* want to meet *him*."

"Because, little one," Soaring Eagle rose. "I think that I killed her husband."

Carrie tried to absorb the meaning of the words, but Soaring Eagle gave her no time to ask further questions. "The sun is getting low in the sky. You must return to the Bird's Nest. Good Bird will think that a bad spirit has come to steal you away."

Carrie scrambled up the steep side of the ravine. From behind her, an owl hooted. She whirled around at the top of the hill and looked back. The owl hooted again. It was Soaring Eagle.

"Do it again! Do it again!"

Soaring Eagle complied, calling up, "That is *Hinkaya*. What do you call that bird?"

"Owl," Carrie answered.

"Owl says that you must hurry home now, little one. I will follow to guard you from the night."

CHAPTER 17

 And he said, This will I do: I will pull down my barns, and build greater; and there will I bestow all my fruits and my goods.

Luke 12:18

D avid, be reasonable. We've been traveling for thirty-five solid hours; we haven't had a decent meal since we left Chicago," Abigail Braddock peered out the door of the Lincoln railway station and exclaimed, "and we've landed in the middle of a *lake*, for heaven's sake! We'll be in Lincoln for a month, dear, you don't need to rent a carriage this afternoon and flounder through the mud. Let's find the Hathaway House, greet Augusta and Mrs. Baird, and settle in for an evening reading the paper and getting reacquainted with our friends."

David Braddock paced up and down the railway platform, muttering at the inclement weather. It did, indeed, appear that the railway station had been built on an island. Water surrounded the station and separated railway passengers from the boardwalks of the city of Lincoln.

"I imagined something a bit more—"

Abigail raised her eyebrows and finished her son's sentence, "Cosmopolitan? They've only *existed* for ten years, dear." Abigail squinted and peered across the lake at the fledgling city. "I'd say they've gotten a good start. And besides, didn't you say you wanted to *precede* other investors? If everyone back home in Philadelphia were looking to Lincoln, Nebraska, you wouldn't be finding any bargains. Don't let a little rain discourage you. Where's your pioneer spirit?"

David bent to pick up his mother's traveling bag as he said, "Any number of our friends would take one look at this bog and get back on the train for home."

Abigail smiled wisely and pulled on her gloves. "I dare say you're right." She patted his back and teased, "But then *they* aren't being met by a lovely widow who is at this moment riding in a wagon that's headed directly toward us."

David stood up abruptly and looked across the bog. Indeed, there was LisBeth, perched next to a disturbingly handsome man who urged a smart pair of bay geldings to step high as they sloshed their way toward the train station.

Abigail and David stepped out to the edge of the platform and LisBeth motioned to the driver. The wagon pulled up and LisBeth bounded down, apologizing for being late, asking the man, Jim, to help David with the luggage, and explaining why Augusta hadn't come herself—all at once. "I told her you'd understand." Thrusting out her hand she concluded, "Welcome to Lincoln, Mrs. Braddock."

Abigail smiled warmly. Motioning to the wagon, LisBeth apologized again. "I'm afraid this is the best we could do. It's a scandal, and Augusta nearly had an attack of apoplexy when Joseph told her the carriage's wheel broke just this morning." Looking at Abigail's fine silk dress and the rough wagon, LisBeth suddenly frowned. "I guess Augusta was right. It *is* a scandal."

Abigail shook her head, "Not to worry Mrs. Baird. Remember, I'm *new* money, as they say. I remember riding in one of these when Mr. Braddock was just getting started." With one quick step, Abigail grabbed the wagon seat and hoisted herself up. She laughed lightly and arranged her skirts primly, looking down at LisBeth with a grin. "I'm old, but I'm spry!" She raised her parasol with a snap just as David and Jim emerged from the train station hauling two huge trunks.

"I'll ride in the back, LisBeth," Jim offered. "The gentleman can drive, if he likes. If Mrs. Braddock doesn't mind being crowded a bit, you can all three fit on the wagon seat. It's not that far to the hotel." Without waiting for a reply, Jim grabbed the side of the wagon and leaped into the back.

David offered, "That's a fine set of bays, Mr.—"

"Callaway. Jim Callaway, Mr. Braddock."

LisBeth climbed up beside Abigail, and David slogged through the mud to climb aboard and take up the reins. As he settled on the wagon seat, he felt moisture oozing under the soles of his new boots. Looking down he noted with dismay that he was covered with mud nearly to his ankles. Abigail looked down at the mess and stifled a grin. "Welcome to the frontier, son," she whispered gleefully, "I think it's going to do us both good."

In Lincoln, Nebraska, in 1877, it was the custom of the daily newspaper to list who was registered at what hotel. Augusta Hathaway and John Cadman, owner of the Cadman Hotel, kept careful notes regarding their competitor's guest list and waged a friendly war to end each year with a total greater than the neighbor's. The land agents Walsh & Putnam and A. J. Cropsey took note of newcomers and were careful to "drop by" the hotel dining room to invite prospective customers to visit their respective offices. Agnes Bond read the list religiously— with an irreligious motive. The morning after David and Abigail Braddock registered at Hathaway House, Agnes scanned the list and rushed outside to where Charity was hoeing their spring garden.

"*David Braddock,* Charity—where have we heard that name before?"

Charity straightened up and leaned against the handle of her hoe before answering. "Can't say as I recall, Mother."

"Well, think, girl! David and Abigail Braddock are listed here as registering at the Hathaway House Hotel just yesterday. Oh, and listen to this:" Agnes read,

We understand that there are several capitalists in the city, among them Mr. David and Mrs. Abigail Braddock of Philadelphia. The report is that, if things suit them, they will invest largely in Nebraska real estate. We hope they will be pleased with what they see.

"Now," continued Agnes, "I know I've heard—" Agnes stopped in mid-sentence. "I've got it! I remember now. Last fall when I overheard LisBeth Baird—" Charity smiled knowingly and her smile brought Agnes up short.

"I mean, last fall when I just *happened* to come in and accidentally heard LisBeth Baird arrange to sell MacKenzie's homestead to that Callaway fellow, LisBeth said—I remember now—LisBeth said, 'I was hoping to talk David Braddock into buying the place.' Now David Braddock has turned up in Lincoln. I bet she met him at the Centennial. Now, the question is, who's Abigail? His mother or wife?"

"Mother!" Charity had been less patient with her mother's gossip of late. She chided, "I've got to get this garden hoed and the carrots in before it rains again. If you want to know who David Braddock is, why don't you call on Mrs. Hathaway and ask her?"

"Charity!" Agnes insisted. "I could *never* do that! It wouldn't be polite!"

Charity adjusted her bonnet and bent to her work. "Then think of a *polite* way to learn what you want to know. Heaven knows you won't be able to do a thing until you do." Meaning to joke, she added, "Invite them to church. That's innocent enough."

Agnes crowed with delight, "Perfect, Charity! Perfect. I'll invite them to church." Agnes was already folding up the newspaper and heading for the house to do her Christian duty. Charity realized with a faint tinge of bitterness that she would, once again, be left to do the morning chores while her mother flitted off to learn some new bit of gossip. Sighing, Charity said a quick prayer for patience, which she punctuated with wicked attacks on imaginary weeds.

Abigail Braddock was relishing her morning coffee when, over David's shoulder, she saw that LisBeth had been cornered by a large woman wearing an outmoded hat decorated with ridiculously long ostrich feathers. With every nod of her head, the feathers whirled and shook. Abigail's eyes lit up in amusement as she watched the woman. The amusement faded when she noticed that LisBeth's face was flushed and she was vociferously shaking her head from side to side and trying to guide the woman out of the dining room as discreetly as possible. But the woman was not to be guided. Forcefully removing her elbow from LisBeth's guiding hand, she turned her head toward the Braddocks' table and said, just loudly enough to be heard, "But of *course* they must be properly welcomed to Lincoln, LisBeth. I simply want to invite them to our social Saturday evening. Certainly that can't do any harm."

Agnes stepped briskly toward the table and a very uncomfortable LisBeth followed her. Agnes's ample bustle swished through the dining room and brushed the open newspaper that David had been scanning. He looked up in surprise, and then hopped up to greet LisBeth with a warm smile.

Agnes held out her hand and LisBeth capitulated. "Mr. Braddock, Mrs. Braddock, this is Mrs. Agnes Bond. Few who come to Lincoln escape Mrs. Bond's notice, and those who meet her, never forget her." Turning to Agnes, LisBeth said, "Mrs. Bond, may I introduce Mr. David Braddock and his mother, Mrs. Abigail Braddock, of Philadelphia."

"Mr. Braddock, Mrs. Braddock," the ostrich plumes bobbed up and down energetically, "welcome to Lincoln!" David stood up and bowed.

Abigail set down her coffee cup and Abigail replied remotely, "Thank you, Mrs. Bond. We've had a fine welcome from Augusta and LisBeth."

Ah, they're on a first name basis. "LisBeth has told us so much about her trip to Philadelphia."

"Really." Abigail turned to David. "David, dear, please don't let us keep you from your business. I know you had that appointment with Mr. Gere to see the newspaper office. Really, dear, do go on."

David bowed and left the dining room without a word.

Agnes noted, *He didn't say a word to LisBeth.* "Young people!" she exclaimed. "They always have important business to rush off to."

Abigail changed the subject. "Thank you for taking the trouble to come meet us, Mrs. Bond. I'm sure we'll meet again." She stood up.

"I came to invite you and your son to our church social this Saturday night. It's a small church, surely nothing like what you're used to in Philadelphia." *Do they go to church?* Agnes watched Abigail for a clue, but the older woman's eyes were somber and she gave no response other than to say graciously, "Thank you, Mrs. Bond. I'll be sure to let David know of your kind invitation. Of course, we just arrived in town yesterday, and since it's so *early* on our *first* day here, we haven't had time to discuss our schedule. Now, if you'll excuse me." Abigail sailed gracefully past Agnes and swept up the stairs to her second floor room.

Agnes turned to watch her go, bobbing her head uncertainly and turning her attentions to LisBeth. "What a lovely woman," she said sweetly. "Certainly upper-class Philadelphia. You can tell that right off."

LisBeth began to clear the table, noisily rattling the dishes as she said through clenched teeth, "The Hathaway House prides itself on giving its guests good meals in *privacy,* Agnes." Hoisting a tray full of dishes, LisBeth headed for the kitchen. As Agnes turned to go, she noticed that David Braddock had left the newspaper he had been reading rolled up on his chair. She bent to retrieve it and carried it home, where she was delighted to learn that the Braddocks of Philadelphia had indeed come to Lincoln looking for land, for both A. J. Cropsey's and J. P. Lantz's advertisements had been circled.

"I'm sorry, David," LisBeth said as she spread the last dining table with a clean linen cloth, "but I can't tomorrow. We do laundry in the morning, and in the afternoon I have my sewing circle."

"The next day, then?" David reached for a stack of napkins and began to help LisBeth set the table.

"Stop that!" she exclaimed, taking the napkins from him. "Augusta would never forgive me for letting a guest set his own table!"

David looked at LisBeth seriously. "I suspect that Augusta and Mother are deep in some serious discussion and we won't hear from either of them again this evening. *And*," he added with emphasis, "I have a feeling that Augusta would understand my wanting to be here—and my *not* wanting to sit lazily by while you work."

LisBeth laid the last of the napkins at the table and began with flatware. David tried again. "Well, then, what about Wednesday?"

"No, that won't do, either. Wednesday morning we iron the linens, and then the Ladies' Missionary Society is meeting."

"Thursday?"

"I have to prepare to teach Sunday school."

David placed both hands on the table before him and said slowly, "Mrs. Baird, Mother and I have been in Lincoln for nearly two weeks now, and aside from being served by you in this dining room, I have not succeeded in spending a moment with you. I have the distinct impression that you are trying to avoid me."

LisBeth flushed. "I am not! I'm just busy, that's all."

"You weren't too busy to go driving with Jim Callaway on Monday."

Her back was turned to him, but David saw her shoulders slump slightly before she answered him. "Jim drove me out to my mother's grave. It was hardly a social afternoon."

"I'm sorry, LisBeth. I didn't know."

"I thought you came to Lincoln to invest in property."

"I—we did. But," it was David's turn to be ill at ease, "forgive me for being so forward, but there are many western cities where investing would be even more promising than Lincoln, Nebraska. However, there is only *one* western city where a certain lovely widow resides."

Carefully, LisBeth finished setting the table before she turned to look at David. Her eyes were large and solemn. "David, you are a very kind and attractive man. I have grown to love your mother—sincerely, I have. But," LisBeth's chin trembled, and she pressed her lips together firmly and cleared her throat before continuing, "this time last year, I was a newlywed." She had to stop again. One hand came up to her throat. Her eyes filled with tears.

"I'm sorry." David reached out to take her hand, but she shook her head and moved away from him. Stomping her foot she regained control. "It's odd, but sometimes I get so *angry* about it all I could scream. It isn't fair. I loved MacKenzie so *much.* I get angry at General Custer for leading him to his death and angry at the Sioux who killed him, and then I get angry at myself for hating them when they were only trying to defend what used to be theirs. In the end, I end up angry with God, because he could have prevented the whole mess, and he didn't. And when I'm angry at God, I can't exactly *pray,* which is what my mother would have told me to do."

She smiled ruefully as she wiped errant tears. "And *then* I get really crazy because I get angry at my mother because she isn't here to help me."

David hastened to draw the subject away from MacKenzie. "Augusta and Sarah Biddle have nothing but kind words for your mother. She must have been an amazing woman."

LisBeth looked at the ceiling and blinked her eyes before she sighed and said wearily, "No, there was nothing particularly unique about Mother. You would have walked right by her on the street and never noticed her. She cleaned and cooked and then got up to do it all over again. Other than her quilts and a nice obituary in the paper, there's nothing left to even mark that she lived."

"I'd have to disagree with that, LisBeth. There's *you.*"

"Yes, there's me." *And there's a Lakota brave somewhere—if he hasn't been killed yet,* LisBeth thought, but she didn't mention Soaring Eagle. "I guess it remains to be seen what will become of me."

"I'll wait," David said quietly.

An evening breeze rustled the muslin curtains, and LisBeth shook off her dark mood and smiled. "Well, I'm keeping busy. Augusta says 'Time heals all wounds.' I hope she's right." She was serious again. "David, I enjoy your *friendship*. But I'm not sure I'm fit to be a very good friend right now."

David interrupted her. "Well, then, as one *friend* to another, may I take you for a carriage ride on—Saturday? I'll ask Augusta and Mother too. Augusta has a superb knowledge of the area, and I'm interested in acquiring more land."

"*More* land?"

David smiled. "Well, yes. I signed papers this morning at Cropsey's land office for a few city blocks."

"A *few* city *blocks?*"

"Just a few. Now I want to add some agricultural acres to the portfolio. Do you know any good farmers who need fast cash?"

It was Saturday afternoon and LisBeth and David, Augusta, and Abigail were making their way south on 9th Street, around the old Market Square to J. P. Lantz's Land Office, where David was to pick up information regarding some available farms.

"'Fifty miles from anywhere,'" Augusta snorted. "That's what they used to say about us. 'On the edge of the Great American Desert. No navigable river. Missed by all the early explorers. Bypassed by the great trails to the west. Nothing but sunflowers and salt.' The salt is what brought the first ones here. Thought they'd make it a great industry. Can't say as I blame them, but it didn't work out. No matter. We stuck. We've got the railroad now, and we're growing fast. One of these days I'm going to have a big dinner at Hathaway House and invite those uppity-ups that said we'd never make it. Serve them a free meal—with crow as the main course!"

Augusta chuckled when LisBeth interrupted, "You'd better ask some questions soon, Mrs. Braddock, or you'll have to hear Aunt Augusta's *entire* monologue."

The wagon pulled up sharply at the door of 1110 O Street.

A false front had given the building the appearance of a much more imposing two story office. Over the door, the address was painted on the transom. Gold lettering on the window announced the J. P. Lantz Land Office. David jumped from the carriage and went inside, reemerging in just a few minutes with several sheets of paper that he handed to Augusta.

"May I impose upon you, Mrs. Hathaway, to look these over and tell me what you think? If there's anything worthwhile, perhaps we could take our drive in the direction of the property." As he spoke, David urged the horses east down O Street. Coming to 17th, he made a sharp right turn and passed the state Capitol building on the right and the mansion belonging to former Secretary of State Thomas Kennard. He pulled the horses up abruptly at the west side of the Kennard mansion and gestured lazily to the south. "That's one of the blocks we've purchased, Mother."

Augusta interjected, "Close to the Capitol, David. Good thinking. You'll make a good return on your investment here in no time. In fact, I know of someone who might be interested in it in just a few months."

"Oh, I'll not be selling this property, Mrs. Hathaway. I'm going to improve it first."

Abigail took her cue and spoke up, "Well, Augusta, I've wanted a pet project for some time, now, and David and I have decided we might like a little vacation home in the 'wild west.' We're thinking of building on the property—if you think you could put up with having us about now and then."

Augusta crowed, "*Put up* with you? I'm delighted! Lincoln will be *honored* to have such fine people added to our city directory, won't we, LisBeth?"

Seated next to David, LisBeth nodded and turned to look back at Abigail. "Mrs. Braddock, it will be *wonderful* to have you nearby."

David's face flushed with pleasure as Abigail explained happily, "We'll be leaving by the end of next week to go home to find an architect, and furniture, and a gardener."

David added, "And a housekeeper."

"No, David, I've found the proper housekeeper. That is, if I can convince her to come. But first, I have to make certain I won't be losing a good friend if I hire her away. Augusta," Abigail turned to face her friend. "Would you be terribly offended if I asked Sarah Biddle to be our housekeeper?" Abigail rushed to explain. "I know she's devoted to you. I wouldn't dream of asking her if you feel at all negative about it. I don't know what your plans are for her future. But if she'd come to stay with us, I'd see that she had every advantage. As for Tom, I agree with you that that boy has great potential. I'd like to see him continue in his schooling and maybe go to the university some day. I could help with that, but only if I won't be overstepping my bounds. If you have any hesitation at all, please say so, and I'll look for a housekeeper elsewhere."

Augusta remained quiet for a very long time, surveying the site of what she knew would be a fine mansion. Finally, she spoke quietly. "I hate to admit it, Abigail, but I can't offer Sarah much more than a steady job. I'm not poor, but I'm not wealthy, either, and I promised Jesse King years ago that whatever I have in this world would someday belong to LisBeth."

Embarrassed, LisBeth interrupted, "Aunt Augusta, please!"

"Now, don't 'Aunt Augusta' me, LisBeth. I won't have a lot. But I do have the hotel. You've worked so hard all these years; I'm glad I've been able to hire more help in the past few months. It's meant less labor for you. But in some ways it's meant harder work for Sarah. She oversees so much for me these days. Bless her, she hasn't complained a bit. But I know it's hard for her. A young girl like that ought to have dreams— and a way to see them come true. Being a housekeeper for a rich lady is quite a step up from working in the kitchen at the Hathaway House Hotel. What's fair is fair, and I wouldn't think of standing in Sarah's way. And, Abigail," Augusta reached over to pat Abigail's hand, "God bless you for understanding that where Sarah goes, there goes Tom. It'll break my heart to lose them, but my heart will mend. You ask Sarah. I'll see that she gets past any silly loyalty to me. She'll say yes. And she'll be the best housekeeper you ever had."

Augusta blinked rapidly and rustled the papers in her hand, scanning them quickly and barking out, rather too loudly, "Here, David! Here! This one's just south of town a few miles and right next to MacKenzie—I mean, LisBeth's place."

LisBeth interrupted. "It's Jim Callaway's place now, Aunt Augusta. We signed all the papers two days ago. He's paying me ten dollars an acre over ten years."

David frowned. "Pretty generous terms, LisBeth. A lot can happen in ten years."

"I didn't sell the place to get the money. I sold the place because MacKenzie wouldn't like it rotting away and Jim Callaway seems to have a sincere love for the land out there." LisBeth turned to look back at Abigail and Augusta. "He's even planted a rose arbor by the house. Said his mother always had roses. Mac's ma and pa are buried there, and he cleaned up their graves and planted roses there too."

Abigail understood. Gently, she said, "It sounds like Mac-Kenzie would be proud of the place, LisBeth. I'm sure he'd approve of your selling to Jim Callaway."

David was quiet, and Augusta continued with the history of the area. "When I settled in Lancaster, there were just a few scattered homesteads out this way. Five years ago, the Keys and the Meyers got together and laid the town out, but it wasn't organized until just last year. Now this place you're looking at, it's far enough from Salt Creek that it shouldn't give you any trouble. It gives some folks fits flooding. There's talk of building a school. There's a Methodist Church. Plenty of potential for grain and livestock. A farm down that way would be a good buy."

As they drove farther from Lincoln and closer to Roca, the wind began to blow hotter. Abigail and Augusta put up their parasols, but LisBeth tilted her head back and breathed in the warm air, reveling in the sunshine. The older women turned their talk to plans for Sarah and Tom, and Abigail began to describe her vision for the new house to Augusta.

David clucked occasionally to the team, but otherwise seemed lost in his own thoughts. LisBeth listened to the meadowlarks and noted the greening of the fields with pleasure. Finally, Augusta, called out, "Here, David, turn west here. The old Ellis place should be just over this hill—if the land office has the directions right."

They drove up a winding path and into the farmyard. LisBeth hopped down while David helped his mother and Augusta out of the carriage. One massive cottonwood towering over the tiny abandoned stone house afforded the only shade in sight.

"Doesn't look very promising, does it?" David muttered to LisBeth. But LisBeth was enthusiastic.

"I think it's wonderful!" she exclaimed. "Let's go inside."

"You go ahead, children," Abigail called out. "We'll get the sandwiches and spread a blanket here under this tree. I'm famished!" At sight of the premier hostess of Philadelphia preparing a picnic on the Nebraska prairie, David Braddock chuckled.

"Remember asking me where my 'pioneer spirit' was, Mother? I think I know—you have it all!" He followed LisBeth into the tiny house. Old clothing and broken dishes littered the floor. A broken chair leaned against one wall.

"Look, David," LisBeth called out. On the west wall of the room hung a framed piece of needlework. The glass was broken, and a leak in the roof above had stained the threads. Still, the words "Remember Me" stood out in deep rose and blue embroidery. LisBeth shivered and looked around her at the littered floor.

David murmured, "I wonder what made them leave everything like this. It's as if a storm came through and tossed it all in a heap."

"There *was* a storm," LisBeth explained. "Grasshoppers. They came again and again. I remember the faces of the people that wandered into town that summer. Broken, haunted. Everything lost." LisBeth looked about her and added, "That was how I met Mac. The grasshoppers drove his father to—to take his own life. Mac couldn't stay on then. He had to get out. He came to Lincoln." Suddenly LisBeth fled outside, shaking off the memories, hurrying over to where Augusta and Abigail had spread out lunch.

Augusta pointed to the well. "There's water on this place. That's a good sign. They found water not too far down. You should have Jim Callaway look the land over. LisBeth says he's got a great sense for good farmland."

David was quick to reply. "I've already decided to buy this place. I won't be needing Mr. Callaway's help."

The brusque tone was not lost to Augusta, but LisBeth was not quite so observant. She suggested, "On the way back to Lincoln, we should stop in and see him."

"We should be getting back. I want to get the papers signed."

LisBeth added, "And I'd love you to see Mac's place."

"Of course, I can always sign papers first thing in the morning." David changed his mind midsentence. In no time the party had eaten lunch, climbed back in the carriage and begun the short drive to Mac's place. When they turned up the drive to the house, LisBeth noted with satisfaction that a row of cottonwoods had been planted up either side. Someday there would be a shaded archway to welcome visitors to the place.

As the carriage pulled into the farmyard, Jim Callaway stepped out of the barn, a scowl on his face. Seeing LisBeth and Augusta, he smiled and waved. David climbed down and the two men shook hands.

"David's buying the old Ellis place, Jim," LisBeth explained. "You'll be neighbors."

Jim forced another smile and said coolly, "Didn't know you had an interest in farming, Mr. Braddock."

"I don't. Just in good land. Bought the place as an investment."

The two men had no more to say to one another. Jim turned abruptly to the women in the carriage and took off his hat. "Excuse my manners, ladies. Can I offer you a drink of water?"

Abigail Braddock answered, "Oh, no thank you, Mr. Callaway. We must be getting back to Lincoln. We just thought we'd stop by and say hello. LisBeth told us what a wonderful job you'd done with her husband's homestead." Abigail looked about her with appreciation. "And she was certainly right. I can see why she was glad to see you buy it."

Jim smiled warmly. "Thank you, ma'am."

They said their good-byes, and David climbed back into the carriage. As he turned it around, LisBeth called out, "David, wait. What? Someone's added—"

Jim, who had been heading back to the barn, turned around and saw what LisBeth was looking at. He walked quickly over to the carriage and looked up at her. "Hope you don't mind, LisBeth. I remembered what you said—about not having a grave. I hope I didn't overstep."

LisBeth choked back tears and smiled warmly at Jim. "Oh, Jim—it's—I'm so—" She looked down at her hands and said quietly, "Thank you."

"I wanted to get the fence built before I showed you. Thought a picket fence would be nice, then more flowers."

Augusta broke in. "Jim Callaway, Joseph Freeman said from the first day he met you he knew you were a good man. I never doubted it, but if I ever could, this prevents it."

They were all looking at the small plot of graves. Beside the two red stones that said "Ma" and "Pa," Jim had placed a third stone that said "Mac."

"I'm sorry it isn't fancier, LisBeth. I wanted it to say his whole name and the dates."

LisBeth reached over the edge of the open carriage and put her hand on Jim's shoulder. "It's perfect. I wouldn't have it any other way." She looked at him, her eyes shining. "Could I—could I come out and plant the flowers with you?"

"Any time you want. I'll have the fence ready in about a week."

As the carriage rolled down the drive, Abigail Braddock commented, "What a dear thing to do." She turned to LisBeth. "Thank you for insisting we stop by, LisBeth. You've enabled us to see the most beautiful part of Nebraska—its people."

CHAPTER 18

I will say unto God . . . Why hast
thou forgotten me? Why go I
mourning?

Psalm 42:9

N ow, Asa, stop fussing and hitch up the carriage
for me. Joseph's taught me plenty about driving,
and I want to get out of town *early* before anyone invites
himsel—uh—themselves along."

As LisBeth talked, Asa Green took his hands out of his
pockets and led one of the older horses out of its stall and
began to harness it to the carriage. He shook his head from
side to side. "Now what am I goin' to say to Joseph when he
gets back from fishin' and finds out I let you go out alone?"

"Just tell Joseph I put my mind to it and there was no
changing it," LisBeth said as she climbed into the carriage and
picked up the reins. "He'll know you didn't stand a chance,
Asa, and he won't have any reason to be angry with *you*."

"Where you headed, in case he asks?"

"*Out of town*, Asa. Just *out* and *away*. I've got to have some
time to *think*. I need to be alone for a while. Just tell Joseph I
needed some time alone. He'll understand."

"When you comin' back? In case Miz Augusta asks."

"When I've figured out what I need to figure." LisBeth
flicked the reins and was gone, leaving Asa standing in the
doorway of the livery. As she headed west on Q Street toward
the Burlington depot, LisBeth heard Asa calling after her, but
she pretended not to hear, urging the mare to a trot.

The air was fresh and clean, and for once no wind blew to
stir up the dust from the road. After tossing a brief, cold snow

at Lincoln, nature had just as exuberantly flung spring at the land, spreading brilliant green over the dormant prairie. In recent days, thousands of migrating birds had soared over town, making so much noise that LisBeth and Sarah found themselves running outside several times a day to watch the great flocks make their way north.

LisBeth felt as if she had been driving for only a few moments, but she had already reached the turnoff that led to the homestead. As she guided the carriage between the row of cottonwood seedlings, she smiled, imagining the shaded drive that would one day welcome visitors to the prim, white farmhouse.

There was no sign of life about the farm. LisBeth looked about nervously. The dog Jim had befriended in Lincoln was nowhere to be seen. *Odd*, LisBeth thought, *Jack usually bounds right out from the barn to say hello.* Suddenly the dog tore around the side of the barn, a black ball of urgency, barking at LisBeth, running back around the corner of the barn, then back to the carriage.

LisBeth leaped down from the carriage and ran after Jack. He led her along the lone furrow that led from the edge of the corral up a small rise to the east.

"Jim!" LisBeth called, "Jim Callaway! Are you all right?!" No answer came, and when she got to the top of the hill, LisBeth saw why. He was lying unconscious on the ground, a trickle of dark blood oozing from his left temple and running into his auburn hair.

Kneeling at his side, LisBeth put her hand on his forehead. At the cool touch of her hand, Jim moaned.

"Jim, you stay put. It's LisBeth. I'll be right back." LisBeth was on her feet again, hurrying back to the barn, calling over her shoulder, "You stay put!"

But Jim Callaway didn't stay put. By the time LisBeth had managed to haul a bucket of water out of the well, run to the house for a rag, and head back across the field, Jim was sitting up, his elbows on his bent knees, his head in his hands.

As LisBeth struggled through the tall prairie grasses, water from the bucket sloshed over her skirts. Jim called out, "Take your time, Lizzie, it ain't so bad. I'm not *dyin'.*" *Now you've done it,* Jim thought. *You've no right to call her Lizzie to her face—not yet.*

LisBeth hurried anyway, kneeling beside him and wringing out the rag as she taunted back, "I know you're not *dying,* Jim Callaway, but your brain's addled. Whoever you knew named Lizzie, I'm not her." Reaching up to touch the wet cloth to Jim's temple, she added, "You've had quite a wallop to the head! You're going to have *some* headache and maybe a black eye to boot."

Jim leaned his head away from LisBeth and took the rag from her hand. "I'll be fine, Liz—uh—LisBeth. I must have hit a stump." He smiled sheepishly and shook his head. "Sorry about that Lizzie business. Guess that plow whacked me harder than I thought. It appears soldiers don't make natural farmers." He stopped abruptly, dabbing gingerly at his temple. "Now I'll have you thinking you sold the place to the wrong man, to some fool who doesn't even know how to plow." With a grunt, Jim stood, steadying his wobbly legs by laying one arm across Buck's sturdy back.

"Soldier? So, you *were* a soldier." LisBeth stood up, too, brushing the dust off her skirt.

Jim sighed. He closed his eyes briefly and reached up to tug at his beard. "I don't like to remember it. Rather not talk about it."

Stepping beside him she laid her hand lightly on his sleeve and asked, "Can you make it back to the house? You ought to rest, you know. Maybe I should drive you back to town to let Dr. Gilbert take a look at that."

"No need to go back to Lincoln, LisBeth. I may be new at farming, but I'm *old* at taking knocks to the head. It'll take more than a little wallop with a plow to do much damage. Sure am glad you came along, though. The buzzards would have been circling before much longer! The Lord surely does look out for his own."

"How long have you been out there?" LisBeth asked.

Jim squinted at the sun. "I'm not sure—a long time."

"Seems like the Lord could have maybe had someone come along a little sooner."

As they talked, Jim was unhitching his gelding. He put Buck in the corral and watered the little mare LisBeth had driven out to the farm. Then they walked to the side porch and sat on the steps. LisBeth began presenting her idea. He listened carefully. She finished with, "So I thought, David doesn't want to *live* on the place. He only wants to *own* it. And he'll be looking for someone to rent it from him, to improve it. I know you've got all you can handle as far as actually farming, right here. But what if you were to sort of oversee the other place? Make sure the tenant, whoever it turns out to be, does a good job, is honest about the yields, that sort of thing? I know David would pay well for the right person to look after things for him. He might as well pay *you*, and then you could have this place free and clear—faster." *And be able to marry Sarah*, she thought.

As LisBeth talked, her animated dark eyes glowed with interest in her plans for Jim's—and Sarah's—prosperity. The morning sun put red highlights in her hair, and Jim suddenly realized that LisBeth had stopped talking. Apparently she had asked a question, which she repeated, "Well, what do you think?"

Jim stared at her blankly. "About what?"

"About overseeing David Braddock's farm. What do you *think*?"

"Not interested."

"But, Jim—"

"Not interested." Jim motioned to the little green plant at the side of the porch. "My rose is coming up, LisBeth. Bet I get some blooms this year."

LisBeth blinked several times and asked again, "Just like that? *No?* Just like that? Don't you even want to *think* about it?"

"Nope."

"But—"

"LisBeth," Jim said with a sigh. "Do you need the money for this place right away?"

LisBeth shook her head. "No, it's not that."

"You sure?"

"I'm sure. I just wanted to help."

"Thanks."

"But I just don't understand why you wouldn't want to take the opportunity to—"

Jim pulled at his beard. "LisBeth. I told you I don't like to remember it, but I'll say this much. I spent most of my adult life having to take orders from someone else." He bowed his head and rubbed the back of his neck. "Taking orders from someone else, I ended up doing some . . . terrible things." The words caught in his throat.

"I got it all settled with the Lord. But I don't want to have to take orders from anybody *but* the Lord ever again. Not if I can help it." Jim looked at LisBeth soberly. "I don't know David Braddock. I've no reason to think he's anything but an honest man. But I don't want to put myself where I have to take orders again. There's plenty of men in town can check on the place for Braddock if he rents it out. I just can't do it. Thank you, but no."

Looking down at the tiny rose bush, LisBeth asked softly, "Mind if I ask you something?"

"Anything you want."

"You said you had things settled with God." She looked up at him. "How'd you do that? Get things settled?"

"Well, I just *asked* him, I guess. Joseph said to just ask him to help me settle things. It sounds crazy, I guess, but I did. I just asked him."

"Then what?"

"Well, I asked, and somehow I just knew things were okay between us. I read it in Joseph's Bible, in First John."

"That's it?" LisBeth demanded.

"Well, no, it wasn't so simple. It took some time." Jim corrected himself. "No, that's not quite right. It took a *lot* of time and reading and praying too." Jim turned to LisBeth. "He'll take care of you, LisBeth. You just ask him and trust him. Give it some time."

"You sound just like my mother. She always said almost exactly those same words."

"Well, she said them because they're true."

LisBeth sighed. "They *were* true—for her. She loved God and He took care of her." LisBeth's voice was wistful as she added frankly, "Trouble is, I *don't* love him—not after what he's let happen to me, to Mac. I can't love him anymore. And if I don't love him, there's not much reason for him to take care of me, is there?"

Not knowing what to say, Jim did the right thing. He listened. LisBeth poured out some of the bitterness she had been keeping inside and then stood up abruptly. "I'd better get back to town. Augusta and Joseph will be worried. I left Sarah shorthanded too."

"She can handle it."

"Indeed, she can. That young woman's going to make some man a fine wife." LisBeth watched Jim carefully as she spoke. When he didn't react, she added, "Well, you take care of that hard head of yours, Jim Callaway. I expect to see crops growing in that field the next time I come out here."

Jim's gray-green eyes twinkled happily as he answered her. "Next time you come I'll have the fence up around the graves. We can plant flowers then if you like. And I'll show you the whole place and tell you all about how it's going to look someday. It's going to be the showplace of Lancaster County. You'll see."

CHAPTER 19

 He found him in a desert land and in the wasteland, a howling wilderness; He encircled him, He instructed him, He kept him as the apple of His eye. As an eagle stirs up its nest, hovers over its young, spreading out its wings, taking them up, carrying them on its wings.

Deuteronomy 32:10–11†

I don't know what to do," Agent Janson said. "After all, the Indian is by birth and by natural disposition out of sympathy with our American institutions." The agent had ridden to Santee for his weekly meeting with the school's headmaster. As usual, the two had become embroiled in an intense discussion about what Janson called "the Indian problem."

Reverend Alfred Riggs smiled grimly. "I suspect any group of people that had been dispossessed in the violent manner taken by our government would be inclined to be 'out of sympathy,' as you so tactfully put it."

Janson leaned forward in his chair. "But they have to be *civilized*, and I'm at my wit's end trying to do it. Only last week, we gave out some of the cash they were to be paid for their land, and a group of the young men were seen down at the river, skipping their gold coins across the water like stones! Now, civilized people have to know how to use money. But what can we do if all they do is take it and use it as a toy? They'll never learn, and I don't know what can be done about it!"

Alfred replied, "You know, Thomas, this 'Indian problem'

you talk about—some of the native pastors here call it 'the white man's problem.' I've found that if I show a fraternal spirit—rather than act as if I'm the master and they are the servants—it goes a long way in getting hold of their hearts."

Seeing Janson's jaw harden with anger, Alfred hurried to finish his argument. "The Indian is repelled by a proud and dominating spirit, as are most men of any race. We can force a boy to wash his face and attend school, but if we do not get hold of his heart, the moment he gets out of school and returns to his home, he will be a wild Indian still. Here at the school, we have found that much is overcome by kind and sympathetic treatment."

Janson blurted out, "It's hard to be sympathetic with a bunch of lazy tramps."

It was Alfred's turn to be angry. His hands clenched the arms of his chair tightly as he answered, "Oh, yes, I forgot, the Indians are lazy and the whites are industrious, so industrious that they are filling up penitentiaries and poor houses everywhere! There are lazy people in every community, Thomas. And I wonder if, under the same conditions as created at the agency, whites would not behave the same as our Indian brethren. A man tends not to value what he is given freely. I believe that the intention of our agency system was intended as a benevolent one, but in *giving* the Indians everything they need to live, we have removed the one thing that motivates manliness and character—the pride of accomplishment, the knowledge that one is supporting one's family and doing well. That is why we expect our children to work and why we expect the parents of our students to contribute in some way to support the school."

"And what good is it doing, may I ask?" Janson argued. "Are they any more civilized this year than they were when you came back in 1870?"

"Keep an open mind, Thomas. Don't believe everything you've been told. The Sioux are not sphinxlike, unfeeling savages. I've seen them collapse with peals of laughter when one among them successfully mimics—" Alfred stopped abruptly, realizing that it was Janson who had been the subject of the recent mimicry that had so amused the Dakota.

Janson calmed down a bit. "All right, Alfred, all right. I'll grant you that I've a lot to learn. I'll agree that the Indian is *human*. I've seen that they *can* learn, in spite of what I was told by some of the zealots back east. But are you having any *success* in changing their lives for the better? I just don't see it happening at the agency. I don't love them like you do, but I'd like to do a decent job and see them live more useful lives. It'd be better for everyone."

Alfred pondered the questions. "Well, Thomas, our converts rise and fall just like those in any congregation would. They hold fast and quit; they lag and start ahead; they mature and they stand still, just like Christians everywhere. We haven't had many graduates as yet, but I did receive one letter from a graduate who has made his way out to Montana to serve. He wrote back to say, 'Santee Normal Training School sows good seed. May her deeds shine as the stars.' In all the failures we've had—and there have been many—one success like that makes the work worthwhile."

"What about this wild Indian I heard about that showed up on your doorstep? Will he be coming Saturday to collect provisions? He'll have to register, you know."

Alfred answered skeptically. "Do you think you could wait on the regulation about registering, Thomas? He's stayed on, but underneath the cooperation there's a very rebellious spirit still."

"We don't need any more troublemakers. If he's going to cause trouble, I'll have to send him out to Standing Rock. That's where the Lakota belong, anyway."

Alfred answered quickly, "Oh, no, it's nothing like that. I don't think he'll cause any trouble; he's just slow to adjust. But he met Pastor Thundercloud when we sent him on vacation last fall, and John seems to think he'll come around. Soaring Eagle is a willing worker, and he's also worked hard at language study."

Janson relented. "All right, Alfred. You're the Indian expert—as you've reminded me. I'll not make a stir about it for now. Just you see that you keep him busy. Get him a civilized name too. And keep him *here* if at all possible. I don't need the agency all stirred up about the arrival of some wild Lakota."

When James and Martha Red Wing invited Soaring Eagle to accompany them to the agency for their annual issue, Soaring Eagle demanded, "What is 'issue'?"

"*Issue* is when we all receive things from the government. Things they give us to help us get by. Things we cannot grow. Things we used to trade for. It's a day of celebration. We take our fastest horses and have races. There will be visiting and feasting, like the old days when the traders came."

Soaring Eagle helped James lead his fastest pony out of the corral and tie it to the back of the wagon before responding. "I know of this. I did not know it was called 'issue.' The government always gives things to our people when we meet for talks. Then they take whatever they want from us."

James countered, "No, they will not be *taking* from us this time, Soaring Eagle. I have my eighty-acre farm. It is mine. I have a paper that says it belongs to me. But there are things we need to get started. The government gives us these things."

Soaring Eagle jumped into the back of the wagon and sat down, his back to the wagon seat. As James slapped his team and the wagon lurched along, Soaring Eagle said to no one in particular, "Giving things will make some lazy. When I was young, there was a lazy brave in our village. Those who tried to help by giving him things only made him worse. He stopped trying to hunt. He started to make trouble for everyone. That is what will happen on the reservation if everything is given to these Indians."

James looked at Martha and smiled. "I think he's been listening in on Reverend Riggs."

Soaring Eagle heard and said soberly, "If Reverend Riggs said this, he is right."

As they bumped along, James took the opportunity to share some of his own story with Soaring Eagle. "Soaring Eagle, my brother, in times past I walked over a dark road. I hated all the whites, and I fought them when I could. I was in misery, in the midst of many fears. My people were dying, and there was no man on earth to save me, so I fought. But the soldiers came and I was taken far from home and put into prison in a place called Davenport. Alfred Riggs came to that place and told me of the Good Shepherd, he who never tires; he who walks bravely in difficult places and in desert lands, ever seeking the lost.

"The Good Shepherd—Christ, the Son of God—delivered me from the valley of death and from the place of torment of the Evil Spirit. He caused me to live. He is the Savior of both body and soul. It is he who even now adds night and day to my life. I am going to get the things at the agency, but I do not trust the government to make me live. I will work on my farm, and I will trust Christ. His Word alone I obey. I am trying to live his life, and I am grateful to God for his servant Alfred Riggs. I will take his help, and I will take the government's help, and I will live for Christ."

James Red Wing spoke quietly, but there was a passion in his voice that Soaring Eagle had not heard before. When they reached the agency, Soaring Eagle jumped out of the wagon and helped James unload the large wooden box they had brought for the government provisions.

Dozens of families had come to the agency. As the Red Wings's wagon trundled up and stopped in line, dozens of eyes saw the new face riding in their wagon. Dozens of voices whispered. James and Martha greeted friends and introduced Soaring Eagle, who nodded solemnly to each new acquaintance. When he had grown tired of introductions, he took refuge in the back of the wagon and pretended not to see or hear anyone around him.

On the porch of the agency sat a clerk, reading names from

a list. Soaring Eagle heard the name James Red Wing and watched as James stepped forward to have his ration ticket stamped. The box from the wagon was dragged up to the porch. Then, Agent Janson read from a list while an assistant tossed things into the box. "Four blankets. Eleven yards dark blue flannel. Three and one-third yards red flannel. Ten yards linsey. Twelve yards cotton flannel. Twenty yards gingham. Two shirts. One shawl. Two pair socks. Two pair stockings. One hood. One pair boots. One pair shoes. Six skeins yarn. One man's overcoat. One man's jeans suit. Six spools thread. One man's hat. One pair gloves. One mattress."

As the stained pillow tick that passed for a mattress was stuffed into the box, James and Martha stepped off the porch, dragging the box with them. Soaring Eagle watched in disbelief. As they loaded the box into the wagon, James explained, "We get this once every twelve moons." Looking over the top of the wagon box, Soaring Eagle frowned. "This is for *twelve* moons?" He fingered the calico. "This will not last twelve moons. You should have hides."

James smiled patiently. "Hides made good clothes for the old ways. Now Mary makes our clothes from this cloth."

James pointed east of the agency building to a corral full of livestock. "Now we'll have some fun." Several braves had painted their faces and were circling the corral, raising their guns in the air. Once again, a family name was called out. This time, a steer from the corral was driven down a chute and let loose. Immediately one of the braves on horseback chased it across the prairie. It bellowed and charged momentarily before dying at the hands of the Indian who chased it. The afternoon was spent in this pursuit, and with each family busy butchering its own beef, it was late afternoon before the promised races could begin.

James Red Wing got up stiffly from cutting the last hunk of meat from the carcass and pointed at Soaring Eagle. "You should ride Little Star in the race."

Soaring Eagle shook his head. "She is your mare."

"But you are a better rider than I. And I would like to prove that she is the fastest mare. I want to build a good herd of ponies. If the others know that Little Star is fast, they will want her blood in their own ponies' veins." James drew Soaring Eagle to the back of the wagon. "Look." He pointed to a huge cottonwood tree in the distance. "It is only to that tree, then toward the sun to the creek, then back again. You can win easily. If you win, I will give you Little Star's sister. You need another pony."

Already the other men were lining up to race. Friendly shouts rang out, bets were placed, and the ponies snorted and pawed. Soaring Eagle looked each one over and knew that Little Star could easily win. The temptation was too much. Pulling off his shirt and stripping to only a breechclout, he leaped on the pony's back and urged her to the line, just in time for someone to shoot off a pistol. The line of ponies stretched out across the short course, their hooves pounding the dirt and raising a cloud of dust. Approaching the cottonwood, Soaring Eagle slipped to Little Star's off side and made such a sharp turn that her hide nearly scraped the bark of the tree. James let out a whoop of delight. Little Star tore across the remainder of the course to the creek, and when she neared the tree the second time, Soaring Eagle once again slipped to her side. She won easily.

"Some race, James!" called one of his rivals. "That wild friend of yours knows how to ride! I'll be over tomorrow to talk to you about breeding her to my stallion. We'll have some fine horses from those two!"

Soaring Eagle trotted up on Little Star, smiling with the joy of the race in spite of himself. Seeing that he was the center of attention, he immediately dropped to the ground, tossed the reins at James, and retreated to the wagon, where he pulled his shirt and leggings back on. He sat at the back of the wagon, catching his breath. James came leading Little Star and slapped Soaring Eagle on the back. "Thank you, my brother! Already I have the promise of a fine stallion to breed to Little Star."

Soaring Eagle looked up soberly. "I thank you, James Red

Wing." At the question in James' eyes, Soaring Eagle laid his hand over his chest and explained. "Today, when Little Star and I were running over the prairie, there was joy here. It is good to know that my heart remembers happiness. I had begun to believe that the hurt would be forever."

CHAPTER 20

 She looketh well to the ways of her household, and eateth not the bread of idleness.

Proverbs 31:27

Sarah Biddle sighed as she looked out the window of her small upstairs room in the Braddock mansion in Philadelphia. Sarah's room was tucked under the eaves at the back of the mansion, and while it was tiny, with a slanting roof and only one small window, from her vantage point Sarah could see the garden. Roses were blooming in profusion in the formal rose garden, and beyond that shone a riot of color from dozens of other flowers. Sarah watched as the gardener bent over his roses, pruning and fussing his way along the last row, gathering a basket full of blossoms that Sarah knew would grace the dinner table that evening.

From behind her, Tom said, "I can't help it, Sarah. I'm homesick. Mrs. Braddock is a nice lady, and David's swell, but I want to go *home*."

Sarah's rather thin lips turned up in a wistful smile as she turned and said softly, "Me, too, Tom. I want to go home, too, but our new home isn't finished yet, and we have to wait just a little bit longer."

"Why do we need a new home anyhow, Sarah? I liked Aunt Augusta's just fine. And I just *know* I'm not going to like living in some big fancy house! I don't like it much here."

"Oh, it'll be different in Lincoln," reassured Sarah.

"How can you be so sure?"

"Well, when we get to Lincoln, you'll get to go back to Miss Griswall's school, and all your friends will be there. They'll be *very* impressed to hear about your trip to Philadelphia. Besides that, in Lincoln, *I'll* be in charge of the house."

Sarah winked at Tom, who climbed up on his bed and rubbed at his leg before saying, "Thank goodness! No crabby gardeners. No high and mighty housekeepers shaking their fingers in my face."

"Now, Tom," Sarah remonstrated gently. "Mrs. Titus is a good housekeeper. She's not really high and mighty, not the way you mean. She just—"

"—wants to make sure things are just the way Mrs. Braddock likes 'em," Tom finished Sarah's sentence for her. "I know. Mrs. Titus ain't so bad. I'm just sick to death of big cities and big city folks."

Sarah was inclined to agree with Tom although she didn't say so out loud. The past eight weeks had been full of cleaning and cooking and gardening. Sarah's mind whirled with the myriad things she was expected to learn.

The first week, Mrs. Titus confined Sarah to the kitchen and sent Tom outside to amuse himself. Fondants and marshmallows, butterscotch, and pastils took up every morning ("Mr. David just loves candy").

Having learned that Sarah was an adequate cook, Mrs. Titus concentrated on attractive presentation and serving. "You can't go in there with raspberry stains all over your hands," Mrs. Titus grumbled one day. "Here. You take oxalic acid and cream of tartar in equal proportions. I keep ours in this box in the pantry. Be certain to mark it 'poison' so that brother of yours doesn't think it's powdered sugar and eat it! Anyway, wet your hands and sprinkle them with this. That's it—rub some more. See?" Sarah obediently scrubbed until the raspberry stains disappeared and dutifully wrote down the "receipt" in her notebook.

During week two, Sarah was inundated with cleaning solutions and routines.

"Now, some use jeweler's sawdust, but I think the secret is in the rinsing. Put a few drops of aqua ammonia in the rinse water, and the cut glass will sparkle. Dry with old silk handkerchiefs.

"You'll need to polish the silver once a week. I do that on Friday so that any weekend guests will see only gleaming silver. Use a velveteen rag and cream of tartar. If you do it once a week, that should suffice to keep the silver shining. If a piece gets really tarnished, you can boil it. Use one teaspoonful each of cream of tartar, salt, and alum to one pint of water." Mrs. Titus raised her eyebrows, "But I certainly hope you don't have to resort to that."

Sarah followed Mrs. Titus through her routine and scribbled notes until her head ached. "I declare, Tom," she said wearily one evening, "I'm beginning to think I don't have sense enough to even clean house for Mrs. Braddock, let alone run the whole place."

"Aw, Sarah, you can do it. You practically runned the hotel back in Lincoln."

Sarah sighed. "I'm afraid the standards of our hotel guests weren't quite what they are here in Philadelphia. I can't believe what Mrs. Titus does every day. Start a fire, cook breakfast, empty the cinders, wash off the stove, heat water for dishes, wash the dishes, then it's upstairs to air the beds, make the beds, empty the bedpans, clean the bedware, clean and fill the lamps, trim the wicks." Sarah arched her back and stretched, turning her head from side to side and groaning. "In the hotel we have help. At the Braddocks' it'll be up to me to see that it all gets done."

"It won't be so bad. It's only Mrs. Braddock and Mr. David. They can't be so messy."

Sarah laughed. "You're probably right. And it *is* a good opportunity."

Just when Sarah thought she had begun to understand running the house, Mrs. Braddock called her in to the library and added another task—grammar lessons from a private tutor.

Sarah balked. "Since when does a housekeeper need fancy

grammar, Miz Braddock? I missed out on schoolin', but I'll be a first-rate cook."

Abigail Braddock smiled wisely. "Sarah, you'll be receiving my guests, and I don't want them to think you're a country bumpkin. I want them to be amazed at what a lovely and graceful girl you are. You never know what opportunities might walk in the front door for a lovely young girl with proper diction!" Abigail winked playfully and Sarah blushed.

"Aw, Mrs. Braddock, I know what yer gettin' at. I got no interest in gettin' married off to some rich guy. I wouldn't know how to act."

"But you *will* know how to act when Mrs. Titus and the tutor get through with you, Sarah. And, like I said, you never know."

Sarah looked away and pictured Jim Callaway riding up to the Braddocks' door. "The only man who'd maybe call on me would come to the *back* door, Miz Braddock. No disrespect intended, but that'd be just fine with me."

Abigail teased, "It sounds like you have someone in mind already. Am I having Mrs. Titus teach you only to lose you?"

Sarah blushed. "No, ma'am. Ain't nobody showed no interest in me."

"Well, if you won't take the help for yourself, then I'll appeal to you for Tom's sake. As you know, Augusta and I have great hopes for Tom. He's bright."

Sarah nodded energetically, "Yes, ma'am. Tom's real smart. He's gonna go far. Now that we got ourselves a good home, and he can go to school and all, he's gonna be *something*. I'm saving up so he can go to the University."

Abigail wheedled. "Well, then, we both agree on that. And Tom needs to see his sister setting a good example. So why don't you attend the grammar lessons with Tom—as a good example. He'll improve quickly, I know, and when he gets back to Miss Griswall's school in the fall, she'll be astounded."

Sarah grinned. "You just don't take no for an answer when you set yer mind to a thing, do ya?"

Abigail shook her head, "No, Sarah, I don't. I'm a spoiled old rich lady used to getting her way. Will you humor me?"

"When you put it that way, ma'am, I can't say no again. I'll go along with the grammar lessons." And she had, proving quickly that Tom was not the only good student named Biddle. Now, as Sarah and Tom talked about returning to Lincoln, she spoke with nearly flawless grammar.

"I think I've about learned all Mrs. Titus can teach me, Tom. My head's so full of cleaning solutions and routines, I think it may burst. And if it does, I just know a bottle of carbolic acid will fall out! Maybe Mrs. Braddock would let the two of us go back home before the house is finished—"

Tom jumped off the bed. "You think she *would*, Sarah, really? I can't *wait* to—"

Sarah laughed, "Hold on, Tom — I said *maybe*. I'll ask Mrs. Braddock tomorrow. Tonight she's having guests in for dinner, and I'm to help serve. If I do that well, then I'll feel justified in asking about going home a little early. The fact is, I could probably be of more help there. Mrs. Braddock says the house will be finished soon, and I could be there when the furnishings begin arriving to unpack and arrange and have things all set up when the Braddocks come in the fall."

Tom headed for the door. "I'm going to bed early. Then tomorrow will come sooner and you can ask about us going home." Tom closed the door firmly, and Sarah sat down to write home.

Dear Aunt Augusta and LisBeth,

It's been eight weeks now, and Tom and I are more homesick than ever. Neither Tom nor I care much for the big city of Philadelphia. On Saturdays Mr. Braddock has been kind enough to drive us about town. He showed us where the Centennial was held last year.

But we miss Lincoln—Joseph, and Asa, and even Jim Callaway. Have you seen much of him lately? I guess he's busy on the homestead, and I hope he does right by you, LisBeth.

Mrs. Braddock insisted that both Tom and I take diction lessons while we were here. I guess a fine lady even needs maids that talk fancy. Now, that wasn't proper grammar, was it? Please don't tell on me!

Anyway, I'm going to ask tomorrow if we can come home. I've learned all the cleaning and cooking a girl should have to know.

Your faithful servant,
Sarah Biddle

When Augusta read Sarah's letter, she couldn't help commenting, "Seems like every letter we've received has said something about Jim Callaway."

LisBeth, once again up to her elbows in dishwater, chuckled. "I think she's set her hopes on Jim."

Augusta looked up surprised. "Nonsense! He's way too old for Sarah. She's getting herself into a wonderful position—a fine career. There's no need to go tying herself to a dirt poor farmer."

LisBeth scolded. "Aunt Augusta, Jim Callaway is a fine man, you've said so yourself. And as to his occupation, he told me this spring that someday that place will be the showplace of the county, and I believe he'll do it."

Augusta was not to be deterred. "Yes, he'll do it, no doubt, after years of scraping and sweating and wearing himself down. And whoever hitches up to him will be old before her time."

LisBeth disagreed. "Oh, I don't know as it would be all that horrible."

"LisBeth Baird! I've heard you talk about the sodbusters headed west. You've seen your share of broken dreams come in that hotel door and ask for a room."

"True, but there's something about Jim's dream—" LisBeth set the dutch oven she'd been scrubbing up on the counter to dry and turned to face Augusta as she dried her hands. "Jim has a passion for the land. The last time Joseph and I rode out to visit, Jim took us on a walk. He's planted nearly one hundred apple trees in that field just west of the house. He talks about his plans, and I can't help but see it the way he plans it: mature orchards, fields laden with ripe grain, a barn full of fine stock—"

Augusta burst the bubble. "Posh, LisBeth. Castles in the air. Two summers of drought, and he'll go under."

"I don't think so," LisBeth disagreed gently. "Something about Jim Callaway makes me think he'll stay. Even in the tough times. I think he'll just dig in and stay put."

Augusta took a moment to consider, and then did an about face. "Well, if our Sarah *is* taken with him, if she has her heart set on him," Augusta looked up at LisBeth, "he could certainly do worse!"

LisBeth grinned. "Yes, he could, Aunt Augusta, much, much worse. But, goodness, Sarah hasn't even begun to work for the Braddocks yet, and we're planning for her to leave! We'd better not let Abigail and David find out about that!"

"Well, I hope Sarah talks Abigail into letting her come home. She sounds really sick of Philadelphia."

"That she does." LisBeth smiled. "I wonder if she still carries that pouch with her."

"What pouch?" Augusta wanted to know.

"Oh, when she was packing to go, she had a little pouch tied around her neck. When I asked her about it, she said, 'I got train fare for Tom and me. Anything happens, I always know we can get back home to Lincoln.'"

Augusta laughed, "That girl! Nobody will ever outsmart her." She was suddenly serious. "I'm glad to know she finally feels that she *has* a home. There was a time when I didn't think Sarah or Tom would ever trust anyone again."

"You've done wonders for them," LisBeth said.

Augusta rustled the paper and refused the compliment. "Me?! Nope, wasn't me that took them both off the street and made them stay until they felt loved. That was your mama, LisBeth."

LisBeth smiled warmly. "And another kindness done by Jesse King rises up to bless her memory." LisBeth stood up abruptly. "Which reminds me, Jim Callaway promised to help me set out another cedar tree at Mama's grave tomorrow. That storm last week tore the top out of the one I set out last spring. Guess I'll be turning in."

LisBeth retreated to her room. Lighting a lamp in the dark, she accidentally knocked Jesse's Bible to the floor. As she picked it up, she noticed that the open pages were filled with notes and underlinings. Out of curiosity, LisBeth settled into the rocker with Jesse's worn quilt across her knees. As she began to read, Lisbeth's eyes were drawn to the verses her mother had underlined, but her heart was drawn to the author of the book.

CHAPTER 21

. . . be swift to hear, slow to speak, slow to wrath.

James 1:19

Soaring Eagle, you speak English and Dakota very well now. But in order to progress in society, you really do need to learn other things. Please. Take this history book and just read it aloud." The two men were sitting at the Red Wings's kitchen table, a kerosene lamp and a stack of books between them. James Red Wing was leaning forward earnestly, while Soaring Eagle leaned back in his chair, his jaw set.

James tried another strategy. "The boys have all begun to look up to you. They see you ride in the races at the agency and win. They watch as you help build the shops and haul water. You are very strong, and they admire that. But they also see when you refuse to learn something that Reverend Riggs has included in the school. They see when you fold your arms in church. They see that you do not pray to thank God for your meals. Now, in the matter of religion, I cannot ask that you pretend to believe what you do not believe. But I *can* ask that you study history and geography as do all of our other adult students. The boys will try harder if they know that you, too, are studying these things."

Soaring Eagle reached across the table and took up the top history book. Opening it, he pointed to the first drawing in the text. A farmer stood on a huge rock in the center of the drawing, his seed bag at his side, his arms outstretched to the skies. Below him stretched a huge body of water on the opposite side of which could be seen a tiny village. The sun peeked over the horizon in the distance.

"This," Soaring Eagle said bitterly, "is not a history that I want to learn about. The white man stands high up and stretches out his arms and says 'All that I see is mine.' Then he takes it."

James Red Wing tried to interrupt, but Soaring Eagle held up his hand to silence him and tapped the open book with a finger as he continued, "The white man sees the sun in this drawing, and says that it rises to shine on the village and on all that he possesses." Soaring Eagle laid his open hand over the drawing. "But the Lakota sees this drawing, and he knows that the sun is sinking behind the hills, and that all that has been Lakota will be no more." He closed the book carefully and laid it back on the table. "Why should I want to learn more of this?"

James Red Wing agreed. "What you say has happened. It *is* happening. I cannot stop it. You cannot stop it. But you *can* refuse to be defeated by the changes that are coming. You can learn. You can help the boys here to learn to live in the changed world. I know it is hard to give up the old ways when a man had only to hunt well and fight well to live. Now a man must do more. A man must *learn* more." James paused briefly before continuing. "Did you know, Soaring Eagle, that there are many whites who think that the Indian *cannot* learn?"

Soaring Eagle retorted, "We learn as well as the whites. We have muscles, brains, and eyes just the same as the whites. If we cultivate our brains and muscles and eyes we can do just the same as they."

"Of course that is true," said James. "That is why Reverend Riggs began the English edition of our newspaper—so the white Christians who send money for the school will see that the Indian can learn. Reverend Riggs understands better than any other white man that it is not that we *cannot* learn, it is just difficult for us to change. Here we have the school and teachers. We have farmers and blacksmiths to teach us how to travel on the corn road. If these boys in our mission school can learn and help their brothers to learn, if they can learn to live and work in the white man's world, then we will have done something just as important as your father did when he taught you to hunt. We will have given them a *life*, Soaring Eagle. When everything they have known is dying, we can help them have a *life*."

"I wish the white man had never come to this country."

"Don't look back, Soaring Eagle. The road that our fathers walked is gone. This was once our country. Our pale brothers told us to move a little farther, and a little farther. Now the white people are all about us. There is no use in the Indian thinking of the old ways. He must now go to work as the white man does.

"Here at the Mission we have everything to learn about the white man's road. We have to learn to live by farming instead of by hunting and trading. We have to learn to cut our hair short and to wear close-fitting clothes and to live in houses. We have to learn to harness a work horse and turn a furrow in a field and cut and store hay."

James Red Wing took a deep breath and finished. "The government has given each family on this reservation eighty acres. This is our last stepping ground. The only way to hold that is to get educated ourselves. Our only chance is to become as the white man. We must get civilized."

"This *get civilized*, it means 'Be like the white man.'" Soaring Eagle said. When James Red Wing nodded in agreement, Soaring Eagle added, "And if the boys in this school become like the white man, you think they will have a better life."

James Red Wing nodded.

Soaring Eagle leaned forward again. "When I was young, I was not hostile to the whites. A white woman cared for me from the days I was first wrapped in a cradle board. When I remember the old ways, I see a white woman cooking for me. A white woman cried when I won my eagle feathers. A white woman mourned when my father died. We had buffalo for food and their hides for clothing and our tepees. All we wanted was peace and to be left alone. It was a good life."

Soaring Eagle paused and looked hard at his friend before

going on. "Then one day we came through the Buffalo Gap and there were white men looking for gold in our sacred hills. We told them they must leave, but they would not. The government promised they would have to leave, but then the soldiers were sent out in the winter and destroyed *our* villages. Then Long Hair came. They say we massacred him, but he would have done the same to us had we not defended ourselves and fought to the last. After that, I went up to the Shining Mountains with Sitting Bull. When Sitting Bull went to the Grandmother's Land, I did not want to go from the land. Many of my people went to the agency, but I did not want a life of idleness on the reservation. That is when I met John Thundercloud. I hunted and camped through the winter. When the last of my people were gone, I came here."

Martha came into the room, but neither of the men noticed her. Without making a sound, she sat down and listened to Soaring Eagle's anguished voice as he broke his long silence about himself.

"Sometimes I find it hard to believe that I ever lived our old Indian ways. I have gone to the white man's school. I have read books. I no longer live in a tepee. I live in a house with chimneys. I am helping to teach the boys to follow the white man's road. But I cannot forget our old ways. Often as the sun sets, I go to the Big Muddy and watch as the shadows come over the water. In the shadows I seem again to see my village, with smoke curling upward from the tepees. In the river's roar, I hear my father's voice. I hear my mother's laughter as she calls back to him. It is a dream. I see only shadows. I hear only the roar of the river, and tears come to my eyes."

Soaring Eagle swallowed hard and cleared his throat. He glanced at Martha Red Wing, who was wiping tears from her cheeks. Wearily he stood up and walked to the door of the small house. He reached up to put one hand on the door frame, where he leaned for a moment with bowed shoulders. Then he threw back his shoulders and turned around. Regaining his proud bearing, he said earnestly to James Red Wing, "I can learn to raise wheat and corn. I can learn to follow what you have called the corn road. I can learn the white man's history and geography. I will do these things. I will help the young boys at the mission to learn these things. But I do not believe Indian ways are wrong. You cannot make a white man of me. That is one thing you cannot do."

Soaring Eagle was true to his word. He kept his long braids and his Lakota dress, but all that summer he studied history and geography and every other subject required by Reverend Riggs. Even when the school was closed for the summer break and the students who were supposedly following his example returned to their homes on the reservation, Soaring Eagle studied. When he had completed the elementary courses, he began high school work, so that when the boys returned in the fall, their idol had surpassed them and challenged them to catch up.

When he wasn't studying, Soaring Eagle worked. His natural ability with horses made him the logical choice to tend the mission livestock. He hated the pigs and chickens, tolerated the oxen and cattle, and pampered the two old draft horses used to plow the fields. When work at the mission was done, he returned to the Red Wings' home where he helped James and Martha.

Plowing presented a challenge he would gladly have foregone. He hit stumps and rocks and repeatedly fell on his knees as he tried to keep up with the lurching plow and the unruly draft horses who had immediately discerned that the man at the reins was a novice. But he had determined to learn everything, and he did, even the things that set him to muttering under his breath.

During the summer break, the empty residence halls required a thorough cleaning and many repairs. James Red Wing was a good carpenter, and together, he and Soaring Eagle spent weeks hammering and whitewashing, building and scrubbing. What would have been "women's work" in the Lakota village often fell to James and Soaring Eagle.

Scrubbing down the church's rough board floor one day,

Soaring Eagle called to James Red Wing, "The white women here should be very happy. They would never bear the work in a Lakota village. This would be women's work there."

Rachel Brown's voice called from the doorway, "And tell me, Mr. Soaring Eagle, just which tepees in your village had board floors?"

Soaring Eagle turned away to hide his embarrassed smile as Rachel made her way up the center aisle with a bucket of water. Behind Rachel came Carrie, skipping along with a basket full of prairie flowers. The two arranged the flowers in the bucket and placed the bouquet in front of the altar. When Rachel left, Carrie stayed behind, scooting along a pew and watching Soaring Eagle work.

"I saw the bees, Soaring Eagle. Lots of bees."

James Red Wing looked up. "That could be the swarm that got out of one of the hives yesterday. Where did you see them?"

"In a tree by the ravine, where Soaring Eagle killed the snake."

Soaring Eagle laid down his brush and looked at Carrie. "Can you show us?"

Carrie took Soaring Eagle's hand. James Red Wing retrieved the empty hive and a saw. Together, the three walked toward the ravine. Stopping abruptly, Carrie pointed up at a tall cottonwood. The end of one branch was entirely covered with swarming bees.

Soaring Eagle bent down and said to Carrie, "Red Bird, you must go back now. We will get the bees to come back to live in our hive. Then you can have honey again whenever you want it. But I do not want you to get stung. Go back to the church."

Soaring Eagle took the saw from James and, tying it to his waist with a strip of leather, began to climb the tree. When he reached the branch where the bees were swarming, he sat with his back to the tree trunk and straddled the branch. Then he reached out as far as he could to tie a string around the branch and began to saw. The branch began to bow toward the ground. Carrie slipped behind another tree to watch.

"Get ready!" Soaring Eagle shouted to James, who waited below, beehive in hand.

A few more strokes with the saw, and the branch was cut through. Soaring Eagle lowered it slowly and dropped to the ground just as James clamped the box over the swarm. Both men began beating on the box to draw the bees up into the hive.

Just as James Red Wing bent down to make certain that all the bees had followed the queen into the hive, Carrie Brown let out a shriek. Soaring Eagle called her name and ran to where she stood, beating the air with her arms, trying to ward off the bees that swarmed angrily about her head.

Quickly, he carried her off and plunged her into the nearby creek. Her entire body except for her face was submerged. Soaring Eagle crouched over her prone body, enduring the stings. When at last the bees were gone, Soaring Eagle picked Carrie up and, with a groan, staggered out of the creek and back toward the mission. Carrie sobbed and called for her mother. Hearing her, Rachel came running from the church. Upon seeing her child soaking wet with several red bumps on her pale face, Rachel turned angry eyes on Soaring Eagle and raged, "What have you *done?!*"

Through her tears, Carrie protested, but Rachel didn't hear her. Angrily she railed at Soaring Eagle, who stood, dripping wet, until Rachel had swept Carrie inside to tend to the bee stings.

James Red Wing hurried up the path from the ravine with the full beehive in his arms just in time to see Soaring Eagle hurry away.

When Carrie had finally changed into dry clothing and explained what had happened, Rachel was mortified. She found Soaring Eagle in the church, solemnly scrubbing the floor. A loose shirt covered his back, and he moved very carefully.

As she stepped inside, he looked up and said, "I would never hurt Red Bird."

"I know that, Soaring Eagle. How can I tell you how sorry I am?"

Rachel sat down in a pew, her crooked face miserable. "Come to the Birds' Nest. We can put something on the bee stings."

"It will be well." Soaring Eagle bent to his work.

When a dejected Rachel got up to go, Soaring Eagle took the locket from around his neck and held it out to her. "Tell Red Bird that I am sorry about the bees. Tell her she may keep this until she is better. Perhaps it will help her to forget the bees if she tells you the stories about the pictures inside."

Rachel turned to go, then she looked back at Soaring Eagle and apologized again. "Mr. Soaring Eagle, the Bible teaches that Christians should be quick to hear, slow to speak, and slow to wrath. I am ashamed to say that today, I was *slow* to hear, and *quick* to speak, and *quick* to wrath. You, on the other hand, behaved like any Christian gentleman would. I hope you can forgive me."

Soaring Eagle quoted from Ephesians, "Be ye kind one to another, tenderhearted, forgiving one another." As Rachel's crooked jaw dropped open in amazement, he added, "I am not a Christian, Rachel Brown, but I am not what the whites call a savage Indian. I listen to Pastor Thundercloud, and I hear much wisdom in what he teaches. I forgive you."

CHAPTER 22

Go ye therefore, and teach all nations.

Matthew 28:19

L isBeth!" Augusta called from Sarah's room.
"Someone's knocking at the back door like there's
a fire in the barn. Could you see who it is? I'm trying to get
Sarah's bed made."

LisBeth peeked out the window. "It's all right. It's only
Agnes Bond. I'll take care of her." With a sigh, LisBeth headed
for the door. The moment the latch was turned, Agnes
launched herself into the room, her bonnet askew, a rolled up
newspaper in one hand.

"Did *you* put her up to this, LisBeth?" she demanded, pacing
back and forth. Not waiting for an answer, Agnes added. "I
declare, I'll have someone's head for this nonsense! Where's
Augusta?" She paced back to the door where LisBeth stood.
"The very idea! *Charity,* of all people!" She paced across the
room again.

LisBeth interrupted. "I'll get Aunt Augusta, Mrs. Bond.
Please, sit down." LisBeth fled down the hall and summoned
Augusta. "She's in quite a state. You'd better come quick."

Augusta continued to smooth the sheets on Sarah's bed.
"Agnes is always in a state about something, LisBeth. I'll just
finish the bed and—"

Agnes stood in the doorway, her eyes blazing, thumping her
open palm with the rolled up newspaper. "That may well be,
Augusta. I happen to be one of those people who feels things
more than others. But this—this—outrageous notion of Char-

ity's. Well, someone's got to talk her out of this foolishness. She won't listen to a word I say." Agnes glared at LisBeth. "*Someone's* put it in her head, and *someone's* going to take it right back *out* of her head, or there's going to be serious trouble around here!"

Augusta smoothed the last quilt over Sarah's bed and took Agnes's arm, piloting her down the hall. "Now, Agnes, sit in my rocker and have a cup of tea and tell me what the fuss is all about."

Agnes sat on the edge of the rocker. "No tea, thank you, Augusta. I'm not here to relax. I'm here to put a stop to it!"

"Put a stop to *what*, Mrs. Bond?" LisBeth wanted to know.

"This fool idea that Charity has of becoming a missionary— to the *Indians,* of all things!"

LisBeth and Augusta both sat down with a thud, staring speechless at one another. Agnes's voice lost its accusatory tone. "So, you didn't know about it either?"

LisBeth said, "No, Mrs. Bond. Charity never said anything. She's been, well, *different* lately, but I had no idea—"

Agnes's chin began to quiver, and a tear trickled down her cheek and dripped off her ample chin. "Here it is, all in this dreadful newspaper. Charity says she's going. Well, she can't. I won't let her."

Agnes handed the newspaper to LisBeth and began groping for a handkerchief. To the accompaniment of her sniffing, LisBeth opened the paper and read to Augusta,

I left my place at Santee just for a time, but now I must stay here at Oahe Mission, and no one has made her appearance there to take up that work. What am I to do? Strange as it may seem, one person cannot work in two places at once. Truly there ought to be someone, somewhere, who would be a very real mother to these twenty girls, who would be willing to stay with them, year after year.

The duties of the field matron include:
— care of a house: cleanliness, ventilation, warmth, furnishings, refuse disposal

- preparation and serving of meals
- mending
- laundry
- adornment of the home: selection of pictures, curtains, rugs, planting of flowers and grass
- care of domestic animals with necessary milking, butter making, beekeeping
- care of the sick
- organization of games and sports for the children
- teaching Christian Endeavor Society meetings on Sundays and Sunday school when required
- religious improvement of the children in your care.

The students are expected to assist their field matron. At least eight hours a day is considered necessary for five days a week to fulfill the tasks required.

Augusta stifled a smile as LisBeth read the last sentence. "Yes, I should think so."

Agnes sobbed, "Oh, it's not funny! Charity broods over every issue of that mission paper. Now she insists she's going to *fill* that position, for heaven's sake. She won't listen to *me*. *Someone* has to talk some sense into her!" Turning to LisBeth Agnes pleaded, "LisBeth, you've got to talk her out of this. It's ridiculous. Why, Charity doesn't know the first thing about missionary work."

"It doesn't sound like they expect any special training, Mrs. Bond. Charity's been doing all of your housework," Agnes pursed her lips and glared at LisBeth, "I mean, you've certainly trained her well in domestic duties, Mrs. Bond. So I think she could do the job."

"Of *course* she could *do* it, LisBeth. That's not the point." Agnes began to cry again. "I can't imagine why *anyone* would want to go to that place!"

Augusta asked, "I know *you* can't imagine it, Agnes. We're not talking about *you*. What has *Charity* said about it?"

Agnes sniffed again before blurting out, "She's been mooning about for weeks. Ever since that Reverend Oakley held the revival last year, she's been different."

As Agnes Bond talked, describing the change that had come over her daughter in the past year, LisBeth was thinking, remembering the little things that she had noticed about Charity. First, there was the slow withdrawal from the gossip that went round the quilt at the sewing circle. Then Charity had taken a new interest in the missionary society, volunteering to be the recording secretary, and corresponding regularly with Priscilla Nicholson, a Lincoln girl who was serving in Eastern Turkey. Finally, Charity had recommended the Ladies' Missionary Society sponsor two Dakota children at the Santee Normal Training School, subscribing to the *Word Carrier,* the mission newspaper, with her own money and reporting on its contents at each meeting. LisBeth had been jealous of Charity's newfound zeal, especially when it spread to the Sioux.

Agnes was finishing. "I *told* her she doesn't need to throw her life away like that. I told her some man'll come along to marry her and give her a family."

Augusta repeated her question. "And what did Charity say to that?"

Agnes sniffed, "She said that she didn't care about that, that God's called her to serve him and she'd go where he called her." Agnes looked up at Augusta. "Now I ask you, Augusta, where'd she get a fool idea like that? Since when does God need beautiful young women to throw their lives away like that. And what, I ask you, am *I* to do without Charity about? With Mr. Bond gone on before, I'll be all alone."

Agnes begged, "Please, LisBeth. You've got to talk to her. I know I'm not exactly your favorite person. I've been . . . difficult sometimes, but surely you must care something for Charity. Please, LisBeth, talk to her. Maybe she'll listen to you."

LisBeth looked from Agnes to Augusta, the latter of whom nodded encouragement and raised her eyebrows in sympathy, then she answered, "All right, Mrs. Bond. I'll speak to Charity."

Agnes bounded from her chair. "I'll send her right over!"

As Agnes bustled to the door, LisBeth called out, "Mrs. Bond, here's the paper you brought."

"Burn it!" Agnes shot back over her shoulder as she hurried out the door.

In only a few moments a soft knock came at the kitchen door. Charity stepped quietly into the room and removed her bonnet, trying to tame her unruly curls as she waited for LisBeth or Augusta to speak. When neither woman said anything, Charity started, "Well, mother ordered me to come have you talk some sense into me. I suppose I should warn you that I am, I believe, completely sensible—perhaps for the first time in my life." She smiled confidently at the two women and sat in the same rocker her mother had recently occupied.

The *Word Carrier* lay open on the table, and LisBeth picked it up and read the advertisement aloud again. "Charity, this article describes an incredible amount of labor. Are you certain you know what you're committing to?"

"I'm not afraid of hard work, LisBeth," Charity answered confidently. "When Father died, Mother pretty much turned over the running of the house to me. I was only twelve at the time. But I'm twenty-three now. I've had many years to perfect housekeeping. I think I know what's involved—although," she laughed a low, pleasant laugh, "the twenty children will no doubt provide some interesting challenges."

Augusta took over the discussion. "What do you know about the Santee Normal Training School, Charity?"

"I've read every issue of the *Word Carrier* for the past few months. I've talked to Miss Abbott, who used to be a matron there."

"And why did she leave?"

"Her health just didn't hold up. It *is* a prodigious amount of work. But I'm as healthy as a horse. There's no reason why that should be a problem for me."

"What do you know about the Sioux, Charity?"

"Nothing, really. Except what I've learned from the *Word Carrier*."

Augusta settled back, a look of doubt on her face. Charity went on, "But what did Philip know about Ethiopians when he shared with the Ethiopian eunuch, Mrs. Hathaway? What did he know about Macedonians before God called him to Macedonia? What did Miss Nicholson know about Turks before she left for Eastern Turkey? I don't really see that that's an issue."

"Go on, dear," Augusta invited.

Charity smoothed her soft brown hair with a trembling hand and looked boldly into Augusta's eyes as she shared. "All my life, I've been a selfish, sinful girl. When Dr. Oakley preached last year at the revival, I only went because I thought that Jim Callaway might show up, and I wanted to—well—I wanted to flirt with him." Turning to LisBeth, she blurted out, "LisBeth, I've been dying of guilt over the way I treated you at the church social that time—with MacKenzie. I was so rude to you both. I'm ashamed of myself." Charity's eyes grew moist as she earnestly pleaded, "I hope you'll forgive me. I'm sorry for the way I behaved."

LisBeth blinked rapidly a few times before answering mechanically, "Of course I forgive you, Charity. It was a long time ago."

Charity went on, "When I think of the way I behaved. . . I was so hateful, and then what happened later. . . I wanted to come and offer my condolences, LisBeth. Really, I did—I was just so ashamed of myself. And, you know," Charity lowered her head, "I've been so insincere all my life, doing what's expected, scheming of how it might help me. Then, when I felt honest sympathy, I didn't think you'd believe me. I didn't think you'd want me."

You're right, LisBeth thought. *I wouldn't have wanted you here.* But even as she thought it, Charity continued. "Well, there I was at the revival, and Jim Callaway didn't come. So I was stuck. Thank God for that. I had sat near the front so everyone would see my new hairdo and my new bonnet. But something funny happened that night. It just seemed like Dr. Oakley was talking right to me. It seemed like he knew all about my schemes, and I can't exactly explain it, but something changed inside me. I decided I wanted to be different. But I knew I couldn't do it on my own. So I asked God to help me change."

Charity sat back in the rocker and sighed. "And he did. Not all at once, of course. Little by little. I began to feel ashamed of the gossip at the sewing circle. So I tried to stop. Then I began to care about other people—people far away, who don't have all the advantages I've had. When I started to read the *Word Carrier,* I remembered how your mother," Charity turned to look at LisBeth, "used to get so mad when folks would rage about the 'savages.' I started to read the Bible, and it changed how I felt about things. I've tried to change."

LisBeth spoke first. "You *have* changed, Charity. And it's all been for the good. What do you hope to do at the mission?"

"I want to make a difference. Working there would be a chance to make a difference. I prayed that I would have a burning faith, LisBeth. I'm not just spouting youthful enthusiasm. When I talked to Miss Abbott, she dispelled any romantic notions I might have. She told me all about the flooded cellars, the bedbugs, the mice that perch on the edge of the cream cans, the rats in the corncrib, the lazy students who don't want to work and don't want to learn. She made it sound awful."

"And what did you think about those things, Charity?" Augusta asked.

"I thought," Charity said firmly, "that if the Lord Jesus could suffer death for me, then I can suffer a few rats and bedbugs for him."

Augusta Hathaway and LisBeth Baird walked Charity home that evening. When Agnes opened the door, Charity kissed each of the women on the cheek and went inside. Agnes stepped out on the porch where Augusta said, "Agnes, your daughter has been called by God to serve him. The gifts and the calling of God are irrevocable. My advice to you is to accept that call and make the best of it. Charity will not be dissuaded, and if you fight her, you may do irreparable damage to your future relationship. Besides that, if you fight her, you are fighting God, and *that* is not a position any human should willingly assume."

"Well!" Agnes huffed. "Fine friends you two turned out to be. I'll thank you to stay *away* from Charity. I'll see to this myself. She is *not* going to Santee."

Two weeks after the late-night session in the Hathaway House kitchen, a news item appeared in the *Daily State Journal:*

Miss Charity Bond left today for service at the Santee Normal Training School in the northern region of the state, where she will take up duties as house matron at the Bird's Nest, a residence hall for Dakota Sioux girls. Those wishing to correspond with Miss Bond may address her in care of The Santee Normal Training School, Santee, Nebraska. At Miss Bond's request, we remind our readers that the Ladies' Missionary Society of the Congregational Church will be accepting donations of clothing to be distributed at the school. Donations may be left at the Hathaway House Hotel where Mrs. LisBeth Baird will oversee the proper cleaning and mending of used items. Overcoats and shoes are especially needed. Ladies are encouraged to join the Society on Wednesday afternoons. They are currently knitting scarves to be given to the twenty young girls in Miss Bond's house. Donations of yarn would be appreciated.

Chapter 23

Let not thine heart envy sinners:
but be thou in the fear of the LORD
all the day long.

Proverbs 23:17

Sarah Biddle sat beside Jim Callaway and stared at the Braddock mansion in amazement. Behind them in the wagon were boxes filled with linens and kitchenware that had arrived the day before at the Burlington station. Jim had been in town to accompany Joseph to a livestock sale, and when he and Joseph had stopped by the railroad station and viewed the immense stack of crates, Jim had quickly offered to help Joseph do the hauling.

"I'd appreciate it, Jim—I surely would," Joseph had said with relief. "I hate to admit it, but since that accident, my strength just ain't what it used to be."

Sarah and Tom Biddle had been "given leave" to precede the Braddocks in returning to Lincoln. Abigail had charged Sarah with seeing to all the details of moving in, cleaning, and setting up the manse—with abundant instructions surreptitiously sent to Augusta in the event the task proved too monumental for Sarah.

Jim stared up at the mansion and whistled low. "I knew the Braddocks had money, but I sure never thought they had *this* much."

Sarah just sat, her heart beating rapidly, her blue eyes blinking in disbelief. "I didn't come over when I got back—the builder insisted I wait until he had it finished. Augusta and LisBeth never breathed a word. I certainly wasn't prepared for *this*."

The Braddock mansion was a massive, three-story conglomeration of porches, gingerbread, and gables. Above the porch trim, across the fascia of the house and along the roof line trailed a carved border of leaves and flowers. The porch wrapped around the north side of the house to a double wide portico where guests could be let out of their carriages protected from the weather. Stained and bevelled glass windows adorned the top portion of every window on the main floor. A stained-glass "B" was set into a small round window in the peak of the roof. The entire block the house stood on was surrounded by an ornate wrought-iron fence punctuated every few feet by brick pillars topped with coach lights.

Her hands shaking, Sarah reached into her reticule and withdrew a huge key. "Here's the key to the gate," she croaked. Jim hopped down, unlocked the gate, and swung it wide, then drove the team up the bricked path.

Sarah climbed down from the wagon and adjusted her pale gray suit. She stepped to the corner of the house to look about the grounds. Impeccable design was reflected in every aspect, from a small gazebo tucked under what would be a grape arbor, to the curving flower beds that stretched along the fence. Seedling trees had already been planted inside the fence. Behind the carriage house, a wide plot of earth had been left unplanted.

"That's my kitchen garden," Sarah explained.

Jim grinned. "*Your* kitchen garden, eh? Guess you already feel right at home, Miss Biddle."

Sarah blushed and turned to look at the back of the house. "Oh, no. I could never feel at *home* in such a grand place. All I want for my home is a little place in the country."

"Well, guess we'd better get this stuff inside." Jim led the team a few steps forward to give him better access to the kitchen entrance.

Sarah fumbled with the ring of keys the builder had dropped off that morning. "It'll take a minute." She was heading up the back steps when Jim said, "Why don't you go in the main door? Come around back and let me in." When Sarah looked doubtful, Jim urged her, "Go on in the main door, Sarah. I don't know much about females, but I do know you like fancy stuff. You can't tell me you won't enjoy pretending it all belongs to you, just once."

Sarah looked back at the massive oak door wistfully. "Go ahead," Jim urged. "Mrs. Braddock trusted you to set the place up for her. You aren't doing anything wrong."

"Will you go in with me?" came the question.

Shrugging his shoulders, Jim answered, "Sure, why not?"

At last, Sarah located the key to the huge door. Jim swung it open and they stepped inside. A short hall stretched before them. Etched glass panels in the double doors to their left revealed the library. To the right an arched doorway led into the front parlor. The walls were papered in deep red silk, and heavy velvet draperies hung at the windows. A Persian carpet in the middle of the room awaited the arrival of furniture to fill the empty space around it.

"The furniture will be coming soon. I'm to set up the kitchen now. Next comes Tom's room and mine, and then I'm to move in." Sarah's voice trailed off as the two walked through the parlor into the vast front entrance hall. A wide staircase led up and around, out of sight. A cozy window seat had been built on the landing where leaded bay windows jutted out to overlook what would be the rose garden.

Sarah and Jim headed down the hall toward the back of the house. To the right was the formal dining room. Behind it, a small breakfast room overlooked the side yard and opened onto the back porch.

When the two at last came to the kitchen, Sarah was overwhelmed. At the sight of the massive cookstove, the huge island for food preparation, the spotless white tile floor, she managed an, "Oh, my," and sat down abruptly.

Jim stared around the room with appreciation. "Well, Sarah, it looks like you've taken quite a step up in the world. Even a farmer can appreciate that this is one nice kitchen."

Sarah looked about her stupidly. "What will I ever *do* with all this space? I declare, if we had this kitchen over at the Hathaway House—"

Jim headed for the back door and turned briefly to say, "LisBeth'll be taking notes when she sees this and making a few suggestions to Mrs. Hathaway regarding needed improvements at Hathaway House"

"They've already had one of those meetings."

Jim raised one eyebrow. "Really?"

"When they got back from the Centennial, Augusta was really excited about what they'd seen. She's been sketching and drawing and talking to builders for months. I think she's given up on the idea of improving and decided to build a new hotel closer to the railway station. Mr. Braddock is going to invest in the project."

Jim frowned. "That Mr. Braddock sure gets around, doesn't he?"

Sarah ignored the tone in Jim's voice. "Yes, he's been real helpful. He helped Augusta with the plans and secured the option on the block he thought she should build on. I think he's fond of LisBeth. It just seemed like anything she was interested in, he tried to—"

"Guess I'd better get to unloading." Jim bent to prop open the door and clomped noisily down the steps, grabbing a crate and hauling it in. Just as he'd unloaded the last crate, a carriage rattled up the drive.

"Now who? I should have locked the gate," Sarah mumbled as she hurried outside and peeked around the edge of the house. LisBeth and Augusta were descending from a carriage. Tom had already jumped down and was running about the yard, whooping and exclaiming, "Great granny, Aunt Augusta. Look at the yard! Look at that porch!" He stopped on the steps under the portico. "Oh, I wonder where my room is? This place is so big!" Running back to the carriage house he rambled on, "They're going to have *three* teams of horses?"

Sarah laughed. "Tom, settle down. You'll have plenty of time to explore." Turning to Augusta and LisBeth she added, "Well, *you* two certainly kept a secret. You didn't tell me the Braddocks were building the biggest house in Lincoln!" She was suddenly serious. "I don't know if I'm up to running a show-place like this."

"Now, Sarah," Augusta demanded. "Don't sell yourself short. You ran the hotel single-handed when LisBeth and I were gone. And you learned a lot from that Mrs. Titus in Philadelphia. Abigail did nothing but brag on you in her letters. You'll do fine. You'll see."

Sarah wasn't quite so certain. "Who ever *heard* of a sixteen-year-old running a house like this?"

Jim interjected, "'Let no man despise thy youth,' Sarah. That's in the Bible. It doesn't matter if you're sixteen or sixty. You'll do fine."

Sarah's face glowed with pleasure at Jim's compliment.

LisBeth agreed. "You can't tell a book by its cover." Grinning mischievously she continued, "Why, just look at Jim Callaway, here. To look at him you'd think he's an aged mountain man, what with that white beard and all." She looked over at Jim, who began self-consciously pulling on his beard. "Who'd guess Jim's just starting out farming? Abigail Braddock thinks very highly of you, Sarah. She was very impressed with you while you were in Philadelphia. Even David said so in his letters."

At the mention of David, Jim jumped down from the back of the wagon where he had settled to watch LisBeth. "I better get this team back to the livery. Got a string of mares to get out to the homestead before sundown—promised Joseph I'd tend them over winter and break their foals." He clamped his hat back on his head and climbed up into the wagon box, walking the team slowly around the path that widened to circle a huge piece of statuary.

With orders to Tom to "stay out of trouble," Augusta and LisBeth hurried inside to tour the mansion and be properly amazed at the wealth displayed in its polished railings and floors, its Persian carpets, and lavish drapes. They went up-stairs and discovered Sarah's room, just across the hall from Abigail Braddock's.

As the three women inspected the manse, Tom tripped up and down the stairs, calling about every new discovery. He declared his own small room on the third floor "grand" and slid down the main bannister several times while Augusta unpacked crates, LisBeth washed dishes and cooking pots, and Sarah covered shelves with paper before arranging the new kitchen wares.

On his way back to the livery, Jim Callaway took a short detour by Tingley's Drug Store. The extra errand gave him a late start to the homestead, so it was well after dark before he had turned Joseph's string of mares into the corral and stabled his team. Still, he lit a lamp in the kitchen. Squinting into the foggy mirror that hung by the back door, he carefully shaved off his white beard.

CHAPTER 24

For the LORD seeth not as man seeth; for man looketh on the outward appearance, but the LORD looketh on the heart.

1 Samuel 16:7

In column three of the August 12, 1877, *Daily State Journal,* a simple announcement appeared:

Mr. David Braddock and Mrs. Abigail Braddock will return to our fair city to take up residence in their lovely new home within the week. Further reports will be printed following the reception to be hosted by the Braddocks this Friday evening.

For Augusta Hathaway, LisBeth King Baird, Sarah Biddle, and young Tom Biddle, those simple lines represented a major life change. Augusta realized that the time had come and wondered aloud how she and LisBeth would get along without Sarah and Tom. LisBeth read the announcement and thought of how she would miss Sarah's gentle ways. Sarah read it and left the kitchen abruptly, stifling tears. Tom stopped doing the sums assigned by Miss Griswall and wondered aloud if Mr. David would bring the new baseball and bat he had promised.

Augusta and LisBeth had already hired a new cook so that they could help Sarah and Tom move into the manse. Every day, Sarah had directed the placement of furniture, unpacked shipments from Philadelphia, and swept and cleaned as if the Braddocks had already taken up residence. Many afternoons she was assisted by LisBeth or Augusta. Most evenings, Sarah and Tom had taken their suppers at Hathaway House and returned to the familiar kitchen, helping LisBeth do the dishes, helping train the new kitchen help, and then being driven home by Joseph when the sun set.

Finally, the telegram came. The Braddocks were really coming. Sarah and Tom spent the last evening at the Hathaway House. When it was time to go, Augusta held Tom close and insisted on reading just one more story from a favorite book. As Augusta read, Sarah walked back to her former room.

LisBeth followed her down the hallway. Leaning against the doorway, she folded her arms and said, "I'm going to miss you, Sarah. It'll be odd not having you here to work with, and I'll miss having someone else to kid Aunt Augusta when she gets onto some political topic from the paper."

Sarah smiled wistfully. "That night that Joseph found Tom and I—me—in the loft of the livery—if you would have told me then that I'd soon be going to work for a fine lady in a mansion, that I'd have my own room and a good income. . . ." Sarah's chin began to quiver. She lowered her voice and whispered, "Sometimes I get scared thinking how good God has been to me." Looking up at LisBeth she added, "I can't figure why."

LisBeth shrugged her shoulders. "I can't answer that one. I've been reading Mama's Bible, trying to understand the way God works, and why he does the things he does. But I haven't found any answers yet."

LisBeth sighed and looked around the room. "It's hard to imagine this place being torn down and a new hotel. Aunt Augusta is even talking about building a house. The Centennial really got her going. And David encourages every plan she mentions. The two of them decided that if Aunt Augusta starts offering to take baggage to and from the depot free of charge, she'll attract more business. He thinks she can charge three dollars a day if she makes just a few improvements. It's nice of him to have taken such an interest in seeing her prosper."

Sarah smiled softly. "I think Mr. Braddock is interested in seeing Augusta *and* you prosper, LisBeth."

"Yes, he's been very kind," LisBeth said defensively.

Sarah looked about the room again before coming to the

door. "Guess I'd best get on over to the livery and ask Joseph for a ride to the manse." Suddenly, Sarah put her hand on LisBeth's arm and asked, "Pray for me tomorrow, will you, LisBeth? I've worked hard and I think I've got it all right, but I'm terribly nervous. Mrs. Braddock invited some pretty important people to her reception."

LisBeth patted Sarah's hand. "You'll do fine, Sarah. You're a wonderful cook and a good housekeeper, and Abigail is genuinely fond of you. You've nothing to worry about."

"I hope you're right."

"I know I'm right," LisBeth insisted.

"Whew!" Augusta exclaimed, falling into her rocker and unbuttoning her shoes. "Abigail Braddock certainly knows how to put on a lovely evening. But I'm glad to be home!" Augusta chuckled. "I was so proud of Sarah Biddle I thought I'd burst. Didn't she do a lovely job? Those dainty sandwiches—all the candy—she said she worked harder for that than she ever had at the hotel. But she was beaming with pride. And Tom sitting at the top of the stairs peeking through the banister. I think I counted thirty-five bonbons go into his mouth!"

LisBeth poured tea and settled next to Augusta.

"I've something to ask you about." LisBeth sat down and studied the floor while Augusta waited. Taking a deep breath, LisBeth launched her topic. "The ladies' society has finished our knitting. We have a scarf, hat, and mittens for each one of the twenty girls in Charity's house at the mission. When I get that last set of buttons sewed on that old coat Agnes brought in Monday, the mending will be finished and we'll have four trunks ready for the mission. I've been hearing from Charity regularly and I—well—I'd like to take the things up to the mission personally."

Augusta answered. "I should think David Braddock would be rather disappointed to have come all the way from Philadelphia and then to have you leave."

LisBeth fidgeted in her chair uncomfortably. "Does that mean you don't want me to go? I'll understand if you don't think you can do without me."

"That's not it at all, LisBeth. The two girls who answered the ad yesterday while you were at the Sunday school meeting can both start immediately. There's no reason you need to feel tied to the hotel. It's just that—"

"I can't stay here, Augusta. David . . ." LisBeth fidgeted again. After a long silence between the two women, she whispered, "I still love Mac. I can't stay here when David won't listen—"

Augusta's eyes flamed with anger. "What has he—?"

LisBeth hurried to answer. "He's been a perfect gentleman. It's just that he's always *there,* waiting. I don't *want* him waiting. I don't want *anyone* waiting. Why can't he be like Jim Callaway? I'm sure he's smitten with Sarah, but he's willing to wait and let her get a chance to try things out on her own for a while. He hasn't even been back to town since he helped her unpack that day."

Finally, Augusta said, "I don't approve of your running off, LisBeth. I've always been a person to stay and face things."

"I wouldn't be running away—exactly. I'm genuinely interested in the work at the mission. Charity Bond sounds so happy, so fulfilled, in her letters. She's changed so much. I'd like . . ." LisBeth stopped awkwardly again. "I'd like to know what it is that makes her so *content.*"

LisBeth looked up earnestly at Augusta. "I haven't said much about it, Aunt Augusta, but I think a lot about things—about Mama and Papa and the way things are going for the Sioux. I wonder about Soaring Eagle and Prairie Flower—where they are, if they're safe, if they're on a reservation somewhere. I know I can't do anything to help them, but somehow it feels good to be helping the Dakota children up at Santee. I'd like to go and see it for myself. I'd like to see if I can make any sense of everything that's happened.

"Mama kept it a secret about me being Lakota. I know she did it because she thought it best. But sometimes I wonder if

I should—own it." LisBeth stopped abruptly. "Mac knew and it didn't matter. I wonder what David Braddock would think, or do."

Augusta interrupted her. "LisBeth, I've always believed that there's only one color that matters. Red. The blood of our dear Savior. Your mother felt that way too. Not everyone does, I know. I wish I could give you certain advice." Augusta sighed. "Fact is, I'm not sure what I would do in your case, and I'm not certain what you should do, either. Just pray on it. God will tell you what's best."

LisBeth swallowed hard before saying, "You know what I wonder about sometimes? Right before Mac left with General Custer—right before they rode out—Mac leaned down to kiss me good-bye, and I took off that locket Mama had given me, the one with our pictures in it. I took it off and put in around his neck." Taking a deep breath, she continued, "Sometimes I lie awake at night and I picture the battle in my mind, and I see Mac dying, and—"

"Don't, dear, don't put yourself through this!" Augusta urged. But LisBeth kept talking.

"I see Mac, and he's . . . dead, and I remember what the paper said about how things were. I wonder if somewhere, right now, some Sioux brave is wearing my locket." LisBeth looked up at Augusta with wide eyes. "They do that, you know. They take trophies. Sometimes I lie awake at night and I picture a Sioux brave—like Papa—riding across the prairie, and he's put on his finest things, like Mama said Papa did when they got married, and he's wearing that locket." LisBeth studied the floor and said, almost in a whisper, "That means that in a way part of me is out there—with the Lakota."

Looking up abruptly, LisBeth changed the subject. "Anyway, I'd like to go up to the school to visit Charity and see what it's like there." She added earnestly, "Charity says they have a Christian Sioux *pastor* up there, Aunt Augusta. I'd like to meet a Christian Sioux. Then maybe I'd know a little about what Papa was like. Maybe I'd understand and know what I should do about *me.*"

Augusta said doubtfully, "If you feel you need to make this trip, I'll not stand in your way, LisBeth. When do you want to go?"

"I'd need to beat winter. I'd like to leave as soon as I could get word to Charity and make sure it's all right for me to come. Would you come too?"

"Goodness no, child! And if the weather is even the least bit threatening, I won't hear of you going yet, either. You'll have to ask Agnes to go." Augusta saw LisBeth's reaction. "You're visiting her daughter, LisBeth. You must at least ask her. Joseph is getting too old to haul heavy trunks about. I'll ask Jim Callaway to escort you to the mission. Jim Callaway's a good man, and he'll see to it that you get there and home safe." Anticipating a protest, Augusta held up her hand. "He can bring that string of mares and his team to Asa Green's. The rest of the homestead can be shut down for a short time. If I ask him to do it, he'll do it.

"And you mustn't run from David Braddock. It would break Abigail's heart. She's, well, we've both got our hearts set on the two of you—" Seeing LisBeth's reaction, Augusta hastened to go on. "Now listen here, LisBeth. Neither one of us old ladies is going to say or do one thing to push you into anything you don't want. I'm just not the type to be secretive about things, and you know it. So. You must give your heart a chance to heal. I understand that. But in the meantime, you must also give David Braddock a chance to become your friend."

LisBeth leaned her head against the back of the rocker and contemplated Augusta's demands. The two women rocked, filling the quiet room with a duet of creaking sounds. Then LisBeth said, "I wonder if David would still want to be my friend if he knew—"

She left the thought hanging in the air and returned to the subject of the trip. "You're right about Agnes," LisBeth agreed, "although I'll admit that I sincerely pray she'll say no."

"What about David Braddock?" Augusta wanted to know.

"I'll talk to David. I'll make him understand."

And she did.

"I understand, all right, LisBeth," David said angrily. "I understand that you're going on a two-week trip with Jim Callaway, and you won't even go to dinner at the Rialto with me." They were in the library at the mansion, and David turned his back on LisBeth. He walked over to a bookcase where he grasped the edge of a bookshelf and used all his willpower to keep from throwing a book through one of the leaded glass windows that looked out on the portico.

From the kitchen Sarah heard the anger in his voice and made a hasty retreat to Tom's room where she set to energetically checking his socks for holes that might need darning.

From her private sitting room, Abigail Braddock heard the anger in her son's voice and clucked sadly, "Oh, David. Be patient, David."

LisBeth felt strangely calm as she answered, "I want to take this trip, David. I want to see the work Charity is doing for myself. *It's important to me.*"

He kept his back to LisBeth as he retorted, "And *you're* important to *me.*"

"Then you should understand and let me go."

He wheeled about. "I'll take you."

"No."

"Why not?"

"You wouldn't understand."

"I *want* to understand, LisBeth. Can't you explain it to me so that I will understand?" His brown eyes softened as he pleaded. There was no longer anger in his voice, and LisBeth drew in a deep breath and relaxed.

"I don't think I can explain it. I'm not sure I understand it myself. I just need to see the mission and the work there. I've come to care deeply about the work there. I want to see it for myself."

David reached out to take LisBeth's hand. "I've come to care deeply for you. I'd like to take you there myself."

"You wouldn't be going for the right reasons. I'm going

because I'm genuinely interested in the work there and because I need to find my place in the scheme of things. My husband is dead, my mother is dead, and somehow I think that visiting that mission may help me find my place."

"But how could a visit to an Indian mission possibly help you with that?"

"By helping me to understand my past better, David. Maybe if I do, I'll be able to get on with the future."

"I still don't understand. How can a visit to an Indian mission help you understand your past?"

"Because, David, my father was Sioux. Because I have a half brother I've never met—somewhere—among the Lakota."

David blinked several times and dropped her hand.

"I want to know what they're like. I want to understand what it was that held my mother's love until the day she died. I want to know what it is that keeps Charity Bond at that mission. It's a blank space in my past that I want filled in, David. So that's why I'm going to the mission."

LisBeth reached for the bonnet she had set on a chair. As she tied it in place and stepped toward the door, she looked back at David and said quietly. "And I have to go without you, David, because just now, when I told you I'm half Sioux, you let go of my hand."

LisBeth left the library quickly and let herself out by the side door. She walked the mile back to Hathaway House and stopped in at Joseph's livery. She was going up and down the main row of stalls, scratching the ears of her favorite horses and singing softly to herself when Jim Callaway strode into the livery, looking down at the scribbled message Augusta had sent out to the homestead by way of Asa Green. He called Joseph's name and looked up to see LisBeth.

The old habit of pulling at his beard had not yet disappeared. He reached up to stroke his chin and smiled at LisBeth. Referring to the note in his hand, he said, "Says here a Mrs. LisBeth King Baird needs an escort for a trip north."

CHAPTER 25

Great peace have those who love
Your law, and nothing causes them
to stumble.

Psalm 119:165†

I can't abide Agnes Bond for two *minutes,* Augusta. How am I going to bear her for two *weeks?*" LisBeth moaned.

Augusta reminded her, "Agnes has had great difficulty accepting Charity's decision. Perhaps the trip will help her. And Agnes's presence as an escort will make it possible for you to go. Just keep those things in mind, and then pray for patience!"

Reluctantly, LisBeth agreed with Augusta. Reluctantly, she walked across town to do the inviting and miserably she walked back across town to inform Augusta that Agnes had agreed to go. "She fussed and fidgeted about it, but deep down I think she was pleased I'd asked."

"Charity is her only child, LisBeth, and complain as she will, Agnes misses her desperately. You're doing her a great kindness by putting up with her."

"Maybe," LisBeth replied, "but I wonder if I'm doing Charity any good—and heaven help poor Jim Callaway. I daresay Agnes will rattle even his calm and collected exterior."

The trio drove out of town the following Monday. Agnes groused and complained, fidgeted and fumed, but Jim didn't ruffle. When Agnes complained that the sun was hot, he jumped down to retrieve her parasol. When Agnes whined about the wind and thirst, he made a protected place for her in the wagon bed and took a detour to find fresh water. When

Agnes announced she hadn't slept a wink, Jim gave her his own thick blankets and slept on the ground, his head propped up on a roll of cloth.

Agnes feared snakes; Jim assured her he had an eagle eye and was a "dead shot." Agnes feared the horses would bolt; Jim explained that Joseph had insisted they take his best-broken team for the trip. Finally, Agnes began to share her heartbrokenness over losing her only daughter to the mission.

Jim offered, "When I worry about things, Mrs. Bond, there's a psalm that always comes to my mind that helps: *'When my anxious thoughts multiply within me, Thy consolations delight my soul.'* Now, I don't want to sound like a know-it-all, but there are some real comforting things in God's Word, ma'am." They were sitting around a campfire and Jim reached into his bedroll and pulled out his Bible. He handed it to Mrs. Bond. "Don't mind the writing in it. I like to underline things now and then so I can find ᵗhem later, when I need them."

Agnes opened the book and pursed her lips. "My, there's a lot underlined here."

Jim smiled gently. "Well, ma'am, there've been a lot of times when I've needed comfort."

Agnes looked up curiously, "Now, what's a fine-looking, healthy young man like you got to worry about? You've a good homestead and a bright future, I'd say. Of course, we need to get you a good wife." She looked pointedly at LisBeth, who was studying the finer details of the dirt at her feet while the two talked.

Jim chuckled, "Hold on, Mrs. Bond. You've already got a child to worry about. You don't need to be worrying yourself about me." He slid his hat down over his eyes and leaned back on his bedroll, calling an end to the conversation.

Agnes turned the pages of the Bible, and LisBeth got up to take a walk. From beneath his hat Jim cautioned, "Don't go too far, LisBeth. Rattlesnakes and wolves don't hand out calling cards."

"Why don't you walk with me, Jim?" LisBeth invited.

Jim sprung up and set his hat straight. Then, solicitously, he asked, "Mrs. Bond, will you be all right if LisBeth and I walk a bit?"

To LisBeth's amazement, Agnes Bond smiled kindly and, instead of whining, gave good-natured permission. "Run along, children. I'll be fine. It looks like the good Lord's about to give us a beautiful sunset."

LisBeth looked at Jim with surprise and got her shawl from the wagon box. The two walked along without talking for a while. When Jim broke the silence, it was to compliment LisBeth. "It's a fine thing you've done, LisBeth."

"I hope the children can use all the things that have been sent."

"Oh, I don't mean the clothes. I mean having Mrs. Bond come."

Lisbeth answered honestly, "Don't compliment me about that. There had to be a chaperone. But inside I kicked and screamed all the way across town to ask Agnes. I didn't think I could suffer her for this long." She looked up at Jim. "You've made it easy, though. How can you be so *patient* with her?"

"Oh, it doesn't take much patience, really. Once you look past the first layer, you see she's just another of God's children whose life hasn't gone the way she dreamed it would. She's frightened about what the future holds, and she tries to ignore it by getting into everybody else's business so she doesn't have to think about her own."

LisBeth retorted, "And how, may I ask, did you figure all that out?"

"Well, when Mrs. Hathaway asked me about driving you out, I said yes right away. Then I learned about Mrs. Bond, and I wasn't too keen on the idea."

LisBeth laughed. "I'll bet that's an understatement."

"But," Jim continued, "I just prayed about it, and finally I got peace about it. I read that verse that says, '*A man makes his plans, but the Lord directs his steps.*' I figured that God had a reason for sending Agnes Bond out here with us, and I decided I'd better go along with his plans. Things always go better when I go along with his plans and don't rush for my own wants."

"How do you know what his plans are?" LisBeth wanted to know.

"Sometimes I'm not sure. I just try to stay reading his Word, asking him to change me, and then I hope that what I end up wanting is in line with what he wants. I just go ahead and keep praying all the time that if it's not his plan, he'll slam a door shut."

"I wish I could trust *anyone* like that."

"LisBeth, the only One who deserves to be trusted that much is God."

Lisbeth frowned. "I thought I could trust him once. When I was little, we trusted God for everything from clothes to a place to stay. I tried to keep trusting him after I grew up. It didn't work out very well."

"LisBeth, can I ask you something personal?"

They had stopped walking and were standing on a small rise just as the sun set, casting one last golden glow over the prairie. LisBeth wrapped her arms about herself defensively. She looked up into Jim's serious, concerned, gray-green eyes and shrugged. Jim took it for permission to continue.

"When you talk about loving God and trusting God, it's always how much your *mama* loved him, how much your *mama* trusted him. I wonder, LisBeth, have you been trying to live on your mama's faith in God? Do you have any faith of your own?" He hurried to explain. "See, that's what happened to me. I grew up going to church and saying all the right things. Then, one day, when something . . . terrible happened, I found out something. I didn't have any of my own faith to fall back on. There was just this terrible, dark chasm. And I fell into it. It wasn't until I met Joseph and read that book I gave to Agnes that I finally got my own faith."

"Tell me, Jim, is that what's made the difference in you?" LisBeth clutched at the shawl that was slipping off one shoulder. Jim looked surprised. "Difference?"

"Yes, when you came to Lincoln you were so distant. Cold. Quiet. Like you were keeping yourself tucked away from everyone. Joseph said you weren't *living* life. You were just *endur-*

ing it. But something happened that changed you. That day you asked about buying the homestead—I noticed it then. There was something new about you, something new in your eyes." LisBeth blushed. "I don't know—it was like a light had come on inside you."

Jim smiled. "That's it, LisBeth. A light came on. God gave me a faith of my own, and it started healing the hurts inside."

"But what if something awful were to happen again? You don't know that everything is going to turn out the way you want it to. What if things just fall to pieces—you could lose the homestead or get hurt—what then?"

The answer was confident. "Well, now I've got something to fall back into instead of the dark chasm."

"What's that?"

"*'The eternal God is thy refuge, and underneath are the everlasting arms.'* I'll just fall back into 'the everlasting arms' and let Him carry me through."

"I could never do that."

"Why not?"

"I asked him to keep Mac safe. Mac died. I asked him to help me hold things together until I could get me home to Mama. Mama died. I'm not asking him for anything else. He didn't hear me."

"Maybe he heard you and said no. Maybe he has a plan for your life that meant you just had to go through those tough times."

LisBeth rejected the notion bitterly. "I don't think I care to learn about a plan for my life that involves so much pain."

Clearing his throat, Jim tried to answer. "I don't have all the answers for you. I can only tell you the things that have helped me." The sun dipped behind a hill and Jim took her arm. "It's getting late. We'd better get back to the campsite."

The two walked back across the prairie together and made preparations for their last night of camping out. Agnes turned in with only one small complaint about the fire not burning hot enough to make a really strong cup of coffee.

The campfire had burned low and Agnes was snoring softly

in the wagon box when LisBeth gave up trying to sleep and sat up. Wrapping herself in a quilt, she picked up a stick and began scrawling in the dust while her mind whirled between anger with Jim for having an answer for every one of her doubts and admiration for him for having gotten past his own dark time and going on with life.

She jumped at the sound of his voice saying quietly, "Don't fret, LisBeth. God loves you."

Jim resisted the impulse to say, "And so do I." Instead, he got up and set the coffee pot of water on the glowing coals. "I'll make you some coffee."

"Tell me about it, Jim," LisBeth demanded abruptly. She looked at him, her dark eyes pleading. "Tell me about that dark chasm you fell into. Tell me how you climbed out."

"I didn't climb out. I was *pulled* out. By the good Lord."

"I wish he'd pull *me* out of my dark chasm."

His voice was tender. "I think he will, LisBeth. I think he will."

Agnes snorted loudly and the two young people started at the sound, grinned at one another, and stifled laughter.

Jim poured two cups of coffee. "If you think it will help you, I'll tell you about my dark chasm and how God pulled me out. Joseph is the only living soul I ever thought I'd be able to tell about it, but if it will help you, I'll tell you." Settling next to LisBeth he began. "I never wanted anything out of life but to be a military man, like my father. I had great plans to rise to brigadier general someday and make my family proud." He told his story as briefly as he could. When he described Slim Buttes, LisBeth gasped, "Oh," and grabbed his hand impulsively. His voice shook momentarily, but he kept talking until he brought himself to Mac's homestead and to the night when he had found God's forgiveness.

"I can't explain the peace that flooded in, LisBeth. I have a feeling a person can't really understand that until he experiences it for himself. But it's real. And it doesn't go away—at least it hasn't gone away for me. Ever since that night in Joseph's room, I've had a desire to know more about God. I figure the best place to get to know him is just to read the book he wrote. So I keep reading."

Jim retrieved his Bible from the log where Agnes had laid it before retiring. "Now, there's some things in here I don't like much. But I figure they're true, and so I accept them. Here's one," he turned to a worn page and read aloud, *"'Whatever the Lord pleases He does, in heaven and in earth, in the seas and in all deep places.'* Now, that's pretty scary at first, but then I read, *'You were precious in my sight . . . and I have loved you'* and *'Even to your old age, shall be the same. And even to your graying years I shall bear you . . . and I shall deliver you.'"*

"But, Jim," LisBeth protested, focusing once again on herself. "God *didn't* pull me out of my dark chasm to show he loved me. He did it for you, and I'm glad for you. But he let awful things happen to me, and then he just left me to figure out how to handle it."

"You mean you feel like Job."

LisBeth remembered the name. "Isn't he the man who was so rich and then lost his whole family?"

"Right. Job lost everything, and he still worshiped God. But he also had plenty of questions about just why God let all that happen. The interesting thing to me is that God said he loved Job, but he didn't answer Job's question. God just said, 'where were you when I laid the foundations of the earth?' and 'Why do you contend with Him? For He does not give an accounting of any of His words?' He reminded Job that if he just gathered his spirit and his breath, all flesh would perish and man would return to dust. Job ended up saying, 'Behold, I am vile; what shall I answer Thee? I will lay mine hand upon my mouth.' It seems to me that there's really only one answer when we ask God why. It's not easy, but it's always the same answer: Trust and obey."

"That's *not* an answer."

"It's all the answer God gave. There are questions about life that we'll never have an answer for. But God's given me the faith to accept that 'the secret things belong unto the Lord our God.'"

Jim poured more coffee. "Can I ask you something?"

LisBeth nodded her head and sipped coffee. Expecting Jim to pursue the topic of religion, she was totally caught off guard when the question came. "Are you going to marry David Braddock?" Jim hurried to explain. "I don't have any right to ask, I know—I just—well, after what we've talked about to-night, I wouldn't want you to . . ." He started and stopped several times before finally finishing the question. "It'd be better if you had this thing about God solved before you made any life-changing decisions."

LisBeth answered him honestly. "Jim, I'm not going to marry *any* man in the near future. I don't know if I'll ever marry again. It's too soon, and I'm too confused about who I am—where I fit into everything, what I want to do with my life. It's all a muddle. I've been just carried along by life since a year ago July. Aunt Augusta whisked me off to the Centennial. Then when we came home I got involved in a lot of church meetings and civic things. Then the Braddocks came to visit and Sarah went home with them. We got caught up in watching the mansion built. Honestly, getting things ready for the mission is the first thing I've done that I thought of on my own. And it really brought joy back into my life. Now, I'm trying to sort things out." LisBeth set down her coffee cup and added, "Besides, I don't think David Braddock is really interested in me."

"He's interested." Jim said it so abruptly that LisBeth looked up at him in surprise.

"What makes you say that?"

He took a gulp of coffee. "I've watched him watching you. He's interested."

"That was before."

"Before what?"

"Before I told him that my father was Lakota Sioux. He didn't take the news too well." LisBeth watched Jim carefully. "You don't look nearly as surprised as David did."

Jim cleared his throat. "I already knew."

"And just *how* would you have known that?"

"Joseph and me are real close, LisBeth. He's been worried about you. He talks a lot about you."

LisBeth arched one eyebrow. "And what have you decided I should do?"

Jim looked at her tenderly. "LisBeth, I've got no right to tell you what you should do. All I can do is to say that I know God loves you, and I'll be praying that you find answers for your questions. You can't go on your mama's faith anymore, Lis-Beth. It was real, but it was *her* faith, and she's gone on to be with the Lord."

LisBeth wanted to prolong the conversation, but Jim brought it to an abrupt end by saying, "I'll keep praying for you. Maybe you'll find some answers at the mission." He poured out the remainder of his coffee, pulled his hat down over his eyes, and was asleep in what seemed like seconds. LisBeth sat up for a long while, going over all that had been said in the past few hours. When she finally slept, it was to dream about a Lakota brave riding across the prairie with her locket about his neck.

CHAPTER 26

There is no man that hath power
over the spirit to retain the spirit;
neither hath he power in the day of
death.

Ecclesiastes 8:8

The fall term at the Santee School had proved to be a challenging one. Students returning from their summer at home filled the residence halls. The field matrons were overwhelmed by the onslaught of work. Charity made out her first chore charts with the help of Rachel Brown, whom she had been assigned to help. She organized and cleaned, mended and cooked. She milked cows and tended bees, taught the girls hymns and studied Dakota. But most of all, Charity loved. From the moment she arrived at the Santee Mission, her heart felt at home.

All my life, she had confided to LisBeth in a letter, *I have concentrated on my own wants, my own pleasures. Now I am a slave to the wants and needs of others. It is strangely freeing. I fall into bed each night exhausted, but it is a wonderful feeling to have worn myself out on behalf of these dear girls. At times they frustrate me, but just when I am ready to throw up my hands in despair, one takes my hand and asks for a story or calls my attention to a row of buttons she has managed to sew on straight, and I am encouraged to go on. I know it sounds unbelievable, LisBeth, but I am at home here.*

The other matrons have been so helpful. There is one, Rachel Brown, who I am most anxious for you to meet. She has met with some tragedy in her life, but she is so gentle and kind with the girls that I strive to follow her example. We are all hoping that when you come, Rachel will take a much needed break. We are beginning to fear for her health. Her daughter Carrie is a dear child. . . .

Charity's letters were filled with hope and laughter. They were also filled with the needs that daily pressed on those who staffed the school. Reading the letters, LisBeth had been inclined to be jealous of Charity's newfound purpose in life. Now, rumbling north from Lincoln to deliver her wagon load of donated clothing, LisBeth reviewed Charity's letters in her mind, wondering if visiting the school would somehow help her to understand Charity's peace of mind.

Agnes Bond had also been the recipient of letters. Reading her daughter's letters, Agnes had snorted impatiently at the girl's romanticism. Now, rumbling north from Lincoln to deliver the wagon load of donated clothing, Agnes hoped that visiting the school would give her the opportunity to point out its bleakness and convince Charity to return home.

Jim Callaway had received no letters from the Santee Mission. He had been privy to a few of Charity's letters as they were retold by LisBeth. He heard, too, the longing behind Lisbeth's admiration to own a similar sense of purpose in life. Now, rumbling north from Lincoln, Jim prayed that LisBeth would find what she so desperately needed. *Help her, Lord, to drink from your fountain of living waters. Help her to know your love and the peace that passes all understanding.* He didn't actually put the rest of his prayer into words, but the hope was there nonetheless—the hope that in finding peace of mind and heart, LisBeth would find the ability to love again, and perhaps open her heart to a simple farmer who lived on a small homestead south of Lincoln.

She didn't want to, but Rachel Brown finally had to admit that she was breaking down. Once energetic and active, she had begun to drag herself out of bed every morning and trudge wearily through each day, falling into an exhausted and fitful sleep. Never feeling rested went from a minor annoyance to a condition that affected every part of her job as a field matron. When Mary Riggs first raised the topic of taking a leave of absence, Rachel rejected the notion. But in the few weeks since Charity Bond had been at the mission, Rachel had become more and more weary, and when Mary asked Charity to raise the subject, Rachel had become more receptive to the idea.

One morning as the two women struggled to take down the laundry that danced on a clothesline, Rachel reached for a sheet, and when it whipped up and out of her reach, she collapsed on the ground panting, "I love my girls, Charity, and I hate the thought of leaving them."

Charity folded the sheet before settling beside Rachel and taking her hand. "I know you do. Since I came here, I've so admired your care and patience with the girls." Charity collected her thoughts before adding, "But, Rachel, even the Lord himself took time away to rest and to pray. You'll do the mission no good at all if you work yourself to death."

Rachel withdrew her hand from Charity's and rubbed her crooked jaw, musing thoughtfully. "I've never really been as strong since this happened." Rachel stretched her hand out in front of her and flexed her crooked fingers.

"Here." Charity stood up and shoved an empty laundry basket toward Rachel. "I'll take it down, and you sit and fold it. That will be easier."

Rachel sighed. Then she began talking about the past. "It's just not in me to give up. It never has been. When I was hurt, they thought I would die for sure. We were hurrying to get to a new agency for Thanksgiving. Mr. Brown was to be an agent up at Yankton Reservation. I refused to leave all my wedding furniture behind . . . and so Mr. Brown managed to load it on. Then the wagon hit a deep rut hidden by the tall grass, and the entire thing tipped—wagon, furniture, and family. We all went tumbling end over end down a steep embankment. Mr. Brown was killed instantly. A few Dakota found Carrie wandering about crying." Rachel smiled ruefully. "They found me *under* my beloved wedding furniture. Mother's big dresser mirror had broken and cut my face—my jaw and hand were crushed. Inside, too, things still feel twisted. They didn't think I would live. But I did." There was no bitterness in Rachel's voice as she talked. She told about her crippling accident matter-of-factly as she folded laundry.

Charity whispered, "Oh, Rachel, I'm so sorry."

Rachel answered. "It took some time for me to come to terms with it. Almost everything I had valued was taken in that accident—my husband, my possessions, my physical beauty. But I still had Carrie. And God brought me here to the mission. Eventually I learned that I had gained more than I had lost. Here I found a new reason to live. A purpose."

Rachel sighed and stood up. With great effort, she tried to hoist the filled laundry basket. When she failed, she straightened up slowly and massaged her crooked hand. "I'm afraid, though, that Mary and Reverend Riggs are right. I'll be of little use if I force myself to stay on. And there's Carrie to think of. I suppose we will have to go back home for a rest."

The next day, Charity peeked into the kitchen of the Birds' Nest and called to Rachel. "Reverend Riggs was pleased you'd finally seen the necessity of a rest. We'll have to confirm it, of course, but plan on riding with LisBeth back to Lincoln and catching the train from there to St. Louis. It's all arranged."

From the table a small voice blurted out. "Oh no, it's *not* all arranged!" Carrie had been working on a little doll to be sent as a gift to a missionary child in China. She sat with needle and thread poised midair, listening to Carrie's announcement. Then she stabbed the doll emphatically and muttered, "It's *not* settled, and I *won't* go!"

Charity tried to soothe her. "But your Mama needs a rest, Carrie. Just for a little while. You two can go home to St. Louis and see your Grandma and Grandpa for Christmas. Then when the new year comes and your ma is rested, you can come back." Charity walked to the table and sat by Carrie, adding persuasively, "The girls and I will plan a welcome home party for you!"

Carrie would not be moved. She shook her head from side

to side until Rachel added wearily, "I'm afraid we must, Carrie."

"But Mama," Carrie protested, "I promised Mr. Soaring Eagle that I would show him all about Christmas." She looked up at her mother, her blue eyes shining, "He never *had* Christmas, Mama. If he sees Christmas, then he'll just *have* to love Jesus. He doesn't understand yet. I told him if he'd stay for Christmas, he'd understand."

"And what did he say to that?"

Carrie answered, "Well, he didn't exactly *say* anything. But I could tell he was thinking." Carrie looked from one face to the other. "I could tell he was thinking. And I got to be here so that when he comes for Christmas, I can explain it to him."

Charity patted Carrie's hand and reassured her. "Carrie, if you will go with your mama to St. Louis, I promise that I will make certain that when Mr. Soaring Eagle comes to our celebration, there is someone to explain it to him."

Carrie considered. Looking into her mother's weary face, she relented. "But I got to say good-bye to him and explain he should look for Miss Bond at the celebration. I got to make him promise he'll come." Her face brightened.

"In spring, when I see him again, he'll belong to Jesus and we can have a party!"

Not long after Rachel and Carrie became reconciled to being absent from the mission for the winter, John Thundercloud's congregation once again insisted that their hardworking pastor take a two-week sabbatical.

When John resisted the notion as unnecessary and foolish, James Red Wing insisted. "It's for your good. And ours. Even the Lord himself took time away. You will come back rested and ready to continue the battle. Go hunting, John." James paused momentarily and then added what he knew would convince John to go. "Take Soaring Eagle. He's been restless. His own people would be on their fall buffalo hunt."

"I haven't noticed a change in Soaring Eagle."

"I saw him yesterday," James answered, "just standing on the hill behind Dakota Home looking west. When Carrie Brown told him some visitors were coming to the mission, he grumbled something about more whites. Carrie was very upset. He talked to her later to say he was sorry." James concluded, "Hunting now would be very good for you, John. It would also be very good for Soaring Eagle."

As the two men talked, Soaring Eagle appeared, a different Dakota boy hanging off each arm and two more dragging at his legs. They were all laughing uproariously. The four boys finally won the struggle, dragging Soaring Eagle into the dust where he immediately sprang onto all fours and began charging here and there and spinning in circles. The boys shrieked with joy, shouting and pointing at the charging buffalo.

John looked at James. "So much for the white man's image of the stoic Indian."

Just then a bell rang and the melee around Soaring Eagle came to an abrupt halt. Boys ran in all directions, and Soaring Eagle dusted off his leggings and walked toward John and James with a somewhat embarrassed smile on his face.

"Those boys chased Rachel Brown's cow into her garden. They decided to wrestle with me instead."

John Thundercloud told him, "My church has said I must go hunting again, Soaring Eagle. Will you come?"

A glow of anticipation flickered in the dark eyes, and Soaring Eagle nodded.

CHAPTER 27

Where no wood is, there the fire
goeth out: so where there is no
talebearer, the strife ceaseth.

Proverbs 26:20

Charity Bond had said that she wanted to become
a missionary in order to "make a difference." The
day Jim Callaway finally drove the wagon up to the door of Dakota
Home, Charity was trying to make a difference in the mission's
fowl population. She had determined to cook an aged rooster
for supper. The rooster, however, refused to cooperate. The two
children who had been assigned to stalk the hapless creature had
called for Charity's help. As the wagon trundled up, the three
humans were in hot pursuit. The rooster darted across the
compound and under the icehouse. Charity and her two helpers
laughed and shrieked as the bird darted out from under the
icehouse and zigzagged its way across the compound and under
the church porch.

As Charity and the two hunters crashed in a heap on the front
porch of the church, Jim pulled the wagon to a halt and LisBeth
jumped down. The rooster charged out from under the porch
and was trapped by LisBeth's petticoats. She bent over to grab
the bird.

"This isn't exactly what I pictured as the life of a missionary,"
LisBeth laughed.

Charity retorted, "Oh, I know, LisBeth. We're all supposed
to be prim and proper and extremely serious." While the bird
squawked and flapped, Charity disappeared around the corner of the house calling back, "I'll be right back to give you a
proper greeting."

Jim helped Agnes down from the wagon, and they waited on the porch for only a few moments before Charity reappeared. She had put on a clean apron and was pinning her hair back up as she stepped briskly up onto the porch and said cheerily, "Welcome to the Santee Normal Training School!"

Shaking hands with Jim, she kissed LisBeth on the cheek and then gave Agnes such a sincere hug and kiss, that Agnes, who had decided she would hate the school and be miserable, found herself smiling and holding Charity close while she cried sincerely happy tears.

Charity wrapped Agnes's arm through her own and pointed. "That's the Birds' Nest over there. The little wing to the south is the living quarters. Rachel Brown and I share the apartment. The ladies will be staying with us." Turning to Jim she added, "Mr. Callaway, if you'll be so kind as to drive the wagon over there, we'll get LisBeth and Mother settled. Reverend Riggs and his wife, Mary, have asked to have you stay with them. "

Jim spread a quilt under a small tree and encouraged Agnes to rest while he got her a drink of water from the well. Agnes chattered, "This dear boy has just been so good to me. I don't know what LisBeth and I would have done—"

Jim interrupted her. "Thank you, Mrs. Bond. We'd better be unloading the wagon now." At Charity's direction, Jim hauled the trunks inside. "Mother will be in my room," Charity explained. "LisBeth, since Mrs. Brown already has her daughter, Carrie, in with her, we hoped you wouldn't mind sleeping upstairs with some of the girls. The trunks of donated clothing can be hauled up to the church. We'll have a group of women in tonight to sort things by size. Tomorrow we can hand them out." Charity was suddenly very serious. "You'll never know what a help this will be, LisBeth. What the government provides just isn't enough."

LisBeth blushed self-consciously. "It's nothing, Charity. Really. I'm glad to help."

Agnes offered, "You wouldn't believe what a tyrant she was,

Charity, insisting that each girl have a scarf *and* hat and mittens. It kept our needles flying!"

The next two hours were filled with introductions and greetings, tours and explanations of how the school operated. "We've a program all planned for you tomorrow evening," Charity explained. "I think you'll enjoy it."

Agnes went to her room to rest, and Jim took the team to be watered and bedded down. LisBeth followed Charity through her normal afternoon, plucking the rooster and peeling potatoes, sweeping the kitchen and setting the table.

LisBeth was full of questions and Charity answered them gladly. Agnes Bond woke from her rest and joined them in the kitchen to find Charity telling the story of a girl who had recently converted.

Charity's face shone with joy. "I used to think that marrying the handsomest and richest man in Omaha would be about the best thing I could accomplish," Charity shared shyly, "but, LisBeth, when Mary White Cloud said that she wanted to follow Jesus, I thought my heart would burst with joy. Being here is a prodigious amount of work, that's true. And some nights I'm so tired I don't think I'll be able to stand another day. Still, I know in my heart that as long as God can use me here, I will work and be happy doing it."

Agnes joined the two and Charity abruptly changed the subject. "Which brings me to another subject: Rachel Brown. She's been failing for some time, and we're all concerned. I've finally managed to convince her to take a leave of absence. But we're concerned about her traveling alone. Along the river she'd be susceptible to the ague. Could she and her daughter perhaps go back to Lincoln with you, LisBeth? They could catch the train in Lincoln and then ride nonstop to St. Louis. Rachel's parents would meet her there."

LisBeth didn't hesitate. "Of course they can come back to Lincoln with us."

Rachel and Carrie came in carrying a basket full of greens from a foray into the nearby field. Rachel smiled quietly and held out her crippled hand. "You must be LisBeth. And this is my daughter, Carrie."

Rachel turned to Carrie, who was standing quite still, staring at LisBeth in astonishment.

"Carrie," Rachel said gently, "come and meet Mrs. Baird, Charity's friend."

Carrie stepped forward mechanically and pumped Lis-Beth's outstretched hand. Then she looked at her mother and blurted out, "Mama—I seen her before. Remember, Mama? She's the pretty lady in the picture. The one in the locket Mr. Soaring Eagle lets me play with."

At first, LisBeth's mind didn't completely grasp what she heard. It latched onto the name Soaring Eagle and sent a chill through her body. Goose bumps prickled along her skin. In the silence that followed Carrie's announcement, LisBeth held her breath. When she finally inhaled, she took in air sharply and sat down abruptly at the kitchen table. Charity and Rachel looked at one another, not knowing what to say or do. Carrie crossed the kitchen and put her hand on LisBeth's arm.

"Mr. Soaring Eagle said that one lady was his mother and the other one—that's you—he thought was his sister. He said you wouldn't want to meet him, though."

LisBeth heard the words, but comprehension came in minute fragments. She couldn't link the words together. They came at her like shots from a rifle, in short bursts. *"His mother."* LisBeth tried to comprehend the notion that Jesse's lost son had perhaps been found. *"His sister."* Now everyone would learn that LisBeth was half Indian.

LisBeth put her head in her hands and tried to force herself to breathe evenly as she considered the revelation.

At LisBeth's response, Carrie grew immediately concerned. Looking up at Rachel she asked, her voice quavering, "Mama, did I do something wrong? I didn't mean to do anything wrong." Her brow wrinkled as she thought hard about the locket and Soaring Eagle. Rachel started to answer her daughter, but LisBeth spoke through her hands. "No, Carrie." Then she dropped her hands and looked at the child with a vacant smile. "You didn't do anything wrong. I just need to think about what you've said, that's all."

Looking at the two women who still stood near her, LisBeth spoke feebly. "I . . . knew I had a half brother . . . somewhere. I thought he might be dead." Tears coursed down her cheeks as she added softly, "Mac wore my locket into battle. I don't know why I did it. He leaned over to kiss me, and I just took it off and put it over his head." LisBeth shook her head in disbelief. "I've had nightmares about some Indian somewhere wearing that locket. I know they took trinkets . . . stripped the bodies."

She began to shake, and Charity came to her side. Wrapping her arms around LisBeth, she hugged her tightly. "Don't, LisBeth," Charity ordered. "Don't. It won't help. Don't think about those things. Think about," Charity hesitated, but then she knelt down beside LisBeth and looked into her eyes as she said, "think about the fact that you have been given the opportunity to meet your brother. You have a brother. You're not alone in the world, like you thought."

LisBeth was still shaking. "A brother. Yes, I have a brother. And it appears my brother . . . may have killed . . . my husband."

Jim Callaway had finished tending to the team and headed back for the house. He stepped into the kitchen just as the scene unfolded. LisBeth had collapsed into Charity's arms and began to moan softly, "My mother . . . Soaring Eagle . . . my brother . . ." Jim crossed the room and helped Charity guide her upstairs, where she lapsed into a fitful sleep.

Agnes Bond had heard it all. Every word. She had been privy to the best bit of gossip ever to come her way. She paced nervously in Charity's room, trying to fit all the details of the unbelievable story together. Agnes relished the next sewing circle when she would be able to report all the details.

A knock came at the door. Feigning sleep, Agnes sat down

on the bed and rumpled the covers before offering a feeble, "Yes?"

Charity came into the room and wasted no words. "Mother, I have something to say to you." Charity stood before her mother and her face was stern. "If you ever breathe one word of this to another living soul, you will *never*—do you hear me, Mother?—you will *never* hear from me again. LisBeth has just received a horrible shock. I don't know how she will decide to handle this news. But whatever she decides, she must not live in fear that she will be gossiped about."

"Charity! I must protest!" Agnes began. Charity interrupted.

"You are my mother, and I will honor you. But, Mother, you are also a gossip. We both know it. God forgive me, I know it because I participated in it. But that's past. God has forgiven me. He will forgive you, if you ask him. But that is not my concern at the moment. My concern is for LisBeth. You must go to her and promise her that for the first time in your life you will keep a confidence. You must convince her that she can trust you. How you will do that, I don't know. But you must think of a way."

Charity's words were serious, bitten off crisply in a short staccato that left no opportunity for Agnes to whine in self-defense. Agnes opened her mouth several times to protest. But when Charity had finished speaking, Agnes snapped her jaw shut. It began to quiver.

"No tears, Mother. Just a promise. You will go to LisBeth and you will promise discretion."

Agnes stood up. "Of course, dear."

"I have your promise?"

"I promise, dear."

"You understand that if you break this promise, you will lose your daughter?" Charity's blue eyes were cold. Agnes shivered and nodded, and the career of Lincoln's best-informed gossip was brought to an abrupt end.

While LisBeth slept, Charity, Rachel, and Jim discussed the situation. Carrie had been sworn to secrecy and sent off to play.

"Now remember, Carrie, not a word about this to anyone. We must decide what is best for LisBeth."

Carrie had added, "And for Mr. Soaring Eagle."

Carrie explained. "I asked him once why he didn't go find his sister and his mother. He seems so lonely. He said his mother is probably dead. He said his sister wouldn't want to see him. He looked awful sad when he said those things." Carrie frowned. "I'm *glad* I know who my family is. Mr. Soaring Eagle doesn't have *anybody*."

Rachel smiled at her daughter. "Yes, Carrie, you are right. We must try to understand what is best for Soaring Eagle, as well. So you go and play and keep this secret. All right?"

Carrie was serious. "I can keep a secret, Mama. I keep secrets good. I won't tell." Carrie tripped out the door and headed off to the garden, where Charity had set Agnes to weeding. In a few moments the two were working side by side, happily chattering away. Agnes finally had someone to fill her mind with new gossip, and she slowly gave up on the best gossip and replaced it with Carrie's stories to tell around the sewing circle when she got back home.

In the kitchen, LisBeth's friends each contributed what little they knew about her and Soaring Eagle. By the time all the notes had been compared, the three had a fairly accurate picture of the situation that confronted LisBeth. Still, not one had a glimmer of an idea about what could be done to ease the shock or pain.

Finally, when they had shared all they knew and still felt helpless to do anything to help, they did the one thing that would help the most. At Jim's bidding, they prayed.

CHAPTER 28

 Bless the LORD . . . who redeemeth thy life from destruction; who crowneth thee with lovingkindness and tender mercies.

Psalm 103:2, 4

LisBeth awoke feeling numb. Then she remembered and tried to make sense of it. But there was no sense to be made. The sounds of children's laughter caught her attention. She quickly scrubbed her face and arranged her hair, and then made her way carefully out of the family quarters and into the Birds' Nest. Supper was in process, and twenty young Dakota girls were eating and chattering and passing food. LisBeth wondered which platter held the hapless rooster. Charity sat at one end of the table, Rachel at the other. Jim Callaway had been invited to join them and had managed to fold his long legs under the table at Charity's right.

Conversation was held in a mixture of Dakota and English. Hesitating in the doorway, LisBeth noted with wonder that Jim was conversing in both languages with equal facility. Just as he reached over to serve more cornbread to the child sitting next to him, Jim noticed LisBeth. He was on his feet immediately and at her side, taking her elbow and guiding her to the table.

The group at the table maintained an awkward silence for a few moments, then Jim began telling a story and the meal was resumed with its usual clatter. The Dakota girls stole curious glances at LisBeth which she returned with a mechanical smile. She managed two bites of cornbread before her stomach warned her that further assaults would be refused. She turned to coffee and drank three cups, appreciating both the warmth and the stimulation the caffeine offered her dulled senses.

When the meal was over, the girls divided into teams and cleared the table, scraped the plates, and took over washing. One of the older girls politely encouraged "Miss Charity" and "Mrs. Rachel" to entertain their company and let the girls finish the evening chores. Charity and Rachel accepted the offer with relief and turned to LisBeth. Another uncomfortable silence ensued.

Agnes Bond spoke first. "LisBeth, dear," Agnes said, nervously dabbing at her upper lip with a napkin. "Charity and I have talked, and I feel that it is necessary for me to assure you that I—um—" Agnes cleared her throat nervously. "Well, dear, we both know that I have a reputation of—" Agnes paused again. "What I wanted to say, LisBeth, is, that any revelations about your past that have been made here at Santee will stay here at Santee. Only those things which you yourself decide to share with others will go beyond the reaches of this mission." Agnes blinked rapidly and looked over at Charity, who smiled and nodded with satisfaction. "And now, if you'll excuse me, I promised Carrie that I would help her finish weeding the beans." Agnes made her exit quickly.

LisBeth put her elbow on the table and leaned her head on her open palm. She stared at the scarred table and said to Jim, without looking up. "I didn't know you could speak Dakota, Jim."

Jim waited a minute before answering carefully, "You don't know a lot of things about me, LisBeth."

Charity interrupted, "LisBeth, we need to—"

LisBeth held up her hand and fairly barked, "No. I can't talk about it yet. I've got to sort it out, think it through." Jim reached for her. Taking her hand gently, he pulled her to her feet, wrapped her hand about his arm, and covered it with his own.

"May I request the honor of your presence on an evening walk, Mrs. Baird?"

With relief, LisBeth nodded and allowed herself to be led

through the door of the kitchen and along the road that led over a gentle rise. Jim held his hand over LisBeth's and didn't say a word as they walked along. Finally, LisBeth repeated, "I didn't know you spoke Dakota."

"Guess I left that part out the other night. It was part of my duty in the army. I speak Lakota, too, which is the language *you* should learn if you want to know about your people. Learn the language and you go a long way toward understanding— not just what they say, but the *way* they say it. Even the things they don't have words for."

Once again, they were quiet until LisBeth asked. "Can you tell me about it? About how you learned?"

Jim took a deep breath and stopped walking. He studied the dust and then raised his serious eyes to LisBeth's. Behind the gray-green, a light flickered. They had walked down the road and found the steep path that led down to the creek. Jim guided LisBeth down the path, and they settled by the creek. "After Slim Buttes, I was so full of bitterness and blind hatred— for life, for a God who would allow those things to happen, for men who do such things—and that included me. I groped through the miles and had decided to die when a bunch of Lakota found me. I told you about all that already."

Jim looked down at LisBeth. She was listening, fascinated. "But I didn't tell you the details about when I was in the village. One of them was called Soaring Eagle. He wore a locket and a cross and chain about his neck. He told me he had a white mother and a sister somewhere."

LisBeth gasped and clutched at his arm. Jim answered. "God only knows how he made his way this far east. He saved my life—even gave me a horse from his own herd. I rode it south until it gave out. Then I walked until I stumbled onto your homestead in the dead of night. You know the rest. Joseph found me and took care of all the things that haunted me. I got a new life."

LisBeth spoke low, "I wish I could find my way through the muddle, Jim. I wish there was someone to show me the way out."

"He's there, LisBeth," Jim said confidently. "He's there. You just have to ask."

"This—situation." LisBeth said. "What should I do? Where do I belong now? Everyone will know—"

"Do you want to meet Soaring Eagle?"

LisBeth frowned. "I don't know."

"If you don't, we can leave now. Tonight. I'll take you home."

"We can't do that. Agnes hasn't had any chance to visit with Charity. Rachel Brown needs time to pack, to take leave of the children. We promised to distribute the clothing personally."

"Then I'll find him and keep him away."

"Do you think he wants to meet me?"

"I can ask him."

LisBeth considered the idea. "Do you think he really killed Mac?"

"What if he did?"

LisBeth shook her head from side to side in bewilderment. "I can't quite fathom it. It's too bizarre to be believed."

"Unless there's a supernatural force at work."

"What do you mean?"

"I mean, maybe God is at work in both your lives. Maybe he's using all this craziness to work out some plan for your good."

LisBeth sighed. "I'm too tired for a theological discussion. I don't know how I feel about it. I wish I could be like you—get over it—get on with things."

"I had supernatural help." Jim put his hand on her shoulder. "LisBeth, you have a hole in your heart. Only God can fill it. I'll always have to come back to that until you've come to realize that only God has the answers to your questions."

LisBeth avoided the spiritual direction of the conversation. "I don't think I can bear to see him. I have this recurring dream of an Indian brave on horseback pounding at me, wearing that locket." LisBeth shivered. "I don't think I can bear to see him, even if he is my brother." LisBeth shivered again, and they got up to go. They had only taken a few steps when she stopped abruptly and looked up at him. "Does it make a difference to you that I'm half Lakota?"

"I thought we already settled that. Why do you ask?"

"Well, it seemed to bother David Braddock quite a lot when I told him."

Something flickered in the gray-green eyes. There was anger in his voice when he asked, "What did he say? Did he do something to hurt you?"

LisBeth shook her head and Jim relaxed. He took a deep breath, and said firmly, "It's a big responsibility, knowing another person's innermost hurts, LisBeth. I know some of yours because they've been made sort of public, whether you wanted it to happen or not. That kind of knowing forms a bond between folks, but sharing the *hidden* hurts, that forms a bond that's even stronger. I vowed I'd never let anybody know about my hidden hurts. But I've discovered that I can trust a few people.

"So when I tell you these hidden things about me, you got to realize that I'm saying something powerful about how I feel about things." His eyes sparkled as he looked at her. "I've shared some things with you, and now you own a piece of me that no other woman on earth owns. And I gave it to you knowing full well about who your brother is." Jim changed the subject abruptly. "We better be getting back."

The two walked back to Birds' Nest where Charity and Agnes, Rachel and Carrie waited anxiously. LisBeth bid Jim good night and went inside to face them.

Soaring Eagle was working James Red Wing's black mare when a stranger drove a wagon into the farmyard and stopped near the corral. Climbing down, the stranger walked slowly toward the corral and leaned lazily on the fence, watching Soaring Eagle as he taught the black mare to change leads in midair. The mare was feisty and swift, but she was also intelligent. The moment she understood what was expected of her, she went through a dazzling set of flying lead changes. Pulling her to a halt, Soaring Eagle dismounted and patted her neck, praising her and watching with amusement as she tried to ignore him.

"You think I believe that you are evil. But I see your ears turning to hear me. You do not wish to admit it, but you enjoy doing what pleases me."

The stranger shouted out. "Perhaps she is also one of a strange people, Soaring Eagle."

Soaring Eagle stared at the stranger carefully. Jim took off his hat and smiled. Slowly, recognition shone in Soaring Eagle's eyes. He smiled back. "She is *among* a strange people, Jim Callaway. How could she act any other way?" Soaring Eagle unbridled the mare, who trotted away, snorting and bucking playfully. As he walked to meet Jim, Soaring Eagle reached out to grasp his hand in friendship.

"I am glad to see that you have found your way back to life."

Jim nodded. "I, too, am glad to see that you have found a way to live."

Soaring Eagle shook his head. "I am not living yet, my friend. I am watching these people to see if they can show me the way to live. It is a hard thing."

Jim pointed to the locket. "You still wear your war trophies."

"They have become part of me."

Jim leaned on the fence and scratched the back of his neck. Soaring Eagle pressed him. "You must say whatever it is that makes your hand shake, Jim Callaway."

Jim grinned sheepishly and pointed to the locket. "One of the women you carry inside of that locket is here. I have brought her here. Your sister."

"How do you know it is my sister?"

"Carrie Brown told us. The minute she saw LisBeth—that's her name, LisBeth Baird—the minute she saw LisBeth, her eyes got big and she just blurted it out. Said she was the pretty lady in Mr. Soaring Eagle's locket."

Soaring Eagle pondered the revelation. He took the locket from around his neck and handed it to Jim. "You look."

Jim complied. Looking from the locket to Soaring Eagle he

nodded his head. "That's her. LisBeth King Baird. She was married to a soldier. MacKenzie Baird. She said he was killed at the Little Big Horn—the Greasy Grass. She said he had this locket on."

"She told you this?"

Jim nodded.

Soaring Eagle said sadly, "I am sorry I have brought pain to my sister."

"Her people brought much pain to you as well."

Soaring Eagle looked at Jim. "I would have killed them all if I could. Now I look for a better way to victory. They want to keep us all on the reservation. I will learn from them. Then I will leave the reservation and show them that the Lakota are men." Soaring Eagle learned against the fence and folded his arms. "I would like to know my sister."

"She's very confused about things right now."

Soaring Eagle turned to face Jim. "Tell my sister that I will not make her look upon my face." Jim nodded, and then Soaring Eagle added, "Wait." He trotted to the barn and came back clutching a yellowed quilt. "Tell her that I give her this to say that I grieve for what has caused her sorrow."

Jim asked, "What about what her people—my people—have done to *you*?"

Soaring Eagle looked at Jim and said slowly, "In my village there were bad Lakota. They did evil things. Here I have learned that there are villages where there are good whites. People who wish to help. What is happening to my people is bad, but not all the whites are bad. When you give this to my sister, you must tell her that what was done to her husband was a bad thing. But not all the Lakota are bad. Her father, Rides the Wind, was a good Lakota. Tell her that her brother, Soaring Eagle, is trying to be a good Lakota." Soaring Eagle ran his hand over the surface of the quilt.

"This was made by Walks the Fire. Jesse King. The story was told of this blanket, that when it was brought into our camp, Jesse King's friend, Prairie Flower, owned it. Prairie Flower kept it with her even after Jesse King left our people.

It has remained with us and we have remembered that not all the whites are bad. Now you give it to my sister and tell her that I wish her peace. I hope that she will live in peace."

Soaring Eagle walked back to the corral and whistled low. The black mare came trotting over. Soaring Eagle turned to Jim. "When this mare was wild, she kicked at me. But then I showed her that I was kind, and now she comes to me willingly. When I was wild, I kicked and fought the white man. But I have seen that the white man can be kind. And so I stay among them willingly to learn their ways. It is better than killing."

Jim nodded in agreement, and then smiled when Soaring Eagle added with a shrug. "There are too many of them. We cannot kill them all."

"Do you regret that, Soaring Eagle?"

Soaring Eagle smiled ruefully. "I have spent much time wishing that things were different. That way brought only unhappiness. Now I am trying to learn to live with the things that are different."

"And has that brought you happiness?"

He pondered the question before answering. "It makes my heart hurt less to stop hating. Sometimes I think that I will never be what you call happy. That is gone forever. But I am learning to live. I do not ask to be happy. I am from the old ways. The young ones who go to the mission—if they learn new ways, then happiness will be for them. That is good to watch. And I can live with the emptiness in my heart."

Soaring Eagle motioned to Jim. "You go back to my sister. Tell her that I am going hunting tomorrow with John Thundercloud. I give her this gift and I ask her to remember me without hatred."

Jim drove the wagon back to the mission alone, a yellowed quilt folded neatly beside him on the wagon seat.

CHAPTER 29

For he satisfieth the longing soul,
and filleth the hungry soul with
goodness.

Psalm 107:9

Carrie Brown sat beside Soaring Eagle and dangled her feet in the cool waters of the creek. Her lower lip quivered and from time to time she wiped a tear from her cheek. Soaring Eagle wrapped his arm about her thin shoulders, and she leaned against him and cried. After a bit, she pushed away and looked up at him. "Mama's sick, so I know we got to go. But I don't want to."

"You have said you will see your grandmother and grandfather. It will be a happy time, little Red Bird. When your mother is rested, you will come back to your friends. So why do you cry?"

Carrie sniffed loudly. "I'll miss Christmas."

"They do not have this Christmas in St. Louis?"

"Sure they do. Mama says we'll decorate a tree and have presents and everything." Carrie stifled a sob. "But my friends won't be there. *You* won't be there." Her young voice quavered again. "I promised I'd tell you all about it."

Soaring Eagle smiled kindly and patted Carrie's hand. "You must go with your mother, Carrie."

"You don't understand." Carrie took a deep breath and blurted out the burden of her young heart. "I promised you I'd tell you all about Jesus. At Christmas you'll understand— then you'll love Jesus too. You promised you would stay and come to Christmas. But if I go away, then you don't have to come to Christmas. You can run away. I heard Pastor Thundercloud and James Red Wing. They said you might go away. But you *can't* go away yet, Mr. Soaring Eagle. Not yet. You have to know about Jesus first."

Her young heart swelled with love and concern, and Carrie began to sob again.

Soaring Eagle looked at her with wonder. "You cry because of this?" The red braids shook as Carrie nodded her head vigorously. "Red Bird," Soaring Eagle said gently. "I will stay at the mission. I will go hunting with John Thundercloud, and then I will come back. When you are in St. Louis and you are celebrating this Christmas, I will go to the service. I will not run away."

Carrie smiled through her tears but still looked doubtful. "You promise?"

Seeing the tears stop so abruptly and the beloved young face brighten, Soaring Eagle reached up and took off the cross and chain he wore about his neck. "This belonged to my mother. I wear it to remember her." As he put the cross on Carrie, Soaring Eagle said, "You wear it for me now. With this gift I promise you that I will not run away while you are gone. I will go to Christmas and I will listen. I will be here to welcome you back when you return."

Carrie fingered the gold cross and then solemnly dropped it inside her pinafore where it would be hidden. "There," she said solemnly, "it's close to my heart." Standing up suddenly she dusted herself off. "Wait here!" she blurted out and darted up the path. Stopping at the top of the steep incline, she shouted, "I'll be right back!"

Carrie scampered back to the Birds' Nest.

"Carrie!" called Rachel. "Where have you been?"

Carrie shouted, "Be right back, Mama, got something to give to—" The name was lost as Carrie turned to run back down the path. Soaring Eagle was still there, waiting, and Carrie thrust Ida May into his hands. "I got nothing else to give you, Mr. Soaring Eagle. But you keep Ida May here—then you'll know I'm coming back. I wouldn't take *anything* for Ida May.

When I come back in the spring, I'll give you your Mama's necklace, and you can give Ida May back."

Soaring Eagle held the doll awkwardly. At the sight of the doll in his hands, Carrie was suddenly embarrassed. Hanging her head she muttered, "Never mind. It's just a dumb old doll—"

But Soaring Eagle interrupted her. Kneeling down to look into her face, he smiled gently and said, "I am honored that you trust me with Ida May, Carrie Brown. Do you remember when I told you that every Lakota keeps a parfleche, a box made of skins to hold those things he values most?"

Carrie nodded.

"When I left my people, I left everything behind except my parfleche. Ida May will sleep there while you are gone. And when you return in the spring, Ida May will be here to welcome you."

"And you?" Carrie insisted.

"And I will be here to welcome you, as well." Soaring Eagle tilted his head and said, "You must go. I hear Rachel Brown's voice calling you." Reluctantly Carrie trotted up to the top of the ravine. She turned and quickly signed "friend." Soaring Eagle returned the sign. When Carrie last saw him, he was standing by the creek, looking down at Ida May, the corncob doll.

Rachel Brown had been growing weaker as the days passed, and when LisBeth expressed concern to Jim and Agnes, they agreed that the trip to Lincoln must be accomplished as quickly as possible.

"We have to get her home to her folks, Jim. It would be terrible if . . ."

Agnes's eyes grew wide when she considered the import of LisBeth's concern. "Don't you be stopping to rest my old bones along the way," Agnes urged. "I'll have nothing but rest once I get home to that empty house of mine."

Thus, the clothing distribution was carried out hastily and

the Browns' things packed as quickly as possible. In only a few days, the small party was loaded and ready to head for Lincoln. LisBeth had been so busy for those few days that she had been able to stop thinking about Soaring Eagle for moments at a time. Still, she found herself watching every distant figure nervously and breathing a sigh of relief when strangers did not turn out to be Sioux braves.

Jim reassured her. "Relax, LisBeth. He promised he wouldn't come unless you wanted him. He may be a heathen by mission standards, but he's a man of his word."

LisBeth tried to calm herself and turn to the task of packing up Rachel and Carrie Brown. It proved to be a simple task, as they had few earthly possessions.

As the wagon rumbled away from Birds' Nest, Carrie tried to stifle her tears. Rachel reached out to hug her. "We'll be back before you know it, Carrie. You'll love it at Grandma and Grandpa's. St. Louis is where I grew up. I'll be able to show you so many things, and you can see where I went to school. You may even decide you want to go there yourself."

Carrie shoved away from her mother and shook her head stubbornly. "No. I want to come back here. I promised."

Rachel sighed wearily. "Perhaps the Lord's plans for us are different from our own."

Carrie smiled brightly. "Oh, I'm sure the Lord likes my plans."

Rachel and LisBeth smiled indulgently and LisBeth asked, "How can you be so sure?"

" 'Cause they're good plans. I'm gonna come back and make sure Mr. Soaring Eagle learns to love Jesus. We promised each other. We're gonna be friends forever. See?" Carrie reached inside her pinafore and pulled out the cross and chain. "Mr. Soaring Eagle said I should wear this until I come back. Then I can give it back!"

Rachel gasped. "Carrie! You should never have accepted that."

"Oh, it's all right, Mama. We traded. I gave him Ida May.

He's going to take care of her for me, and I'll take care of his cross and chain for him. He said it was *his* mama's."

LisBeth listened in disbelief and studied the horizon deliberately. She stole a glance at the gold cross and chain, smiling ruefully at the realization that even as she fled her living brother, his presence followed her in the form of a dirty white quilt hidden deep within one of the trunks and a gold cross displayed proudly by a child.

Peering over the edge of a hill, Soaring Eagle looked down on the small herd of deer and motioned to John Thundercloud to scramble up beside him. The two men motioned to one another and took aim. In a few minutes, they were working side by side, skinning two deer and loading their carcasses onto the backs of the string of mules they had brought with them on the hunt.

They had been away from the mission for two weeks. Their string of mules was loaded with meat, and as John tightened a strap he smiled. "The children will have a feast when we return."

Soaring Eagle nodded and lead the mules along an unseen path through the hills. In a short time, the two men were sitting by a fire roasting two prairie hens.

John Thundercloud broke the silence between them. "You have been quiet for days, Soaring Eagle."

Soaring Eagle took a bite of chicken before answering. He talked with his mouth half full. "All around us is open land. Emptiness." He stretched his hand out and motioned to the horizon. "I thought that when we came here, the darkness inside would be gone. I thought that hunting in the old way would bring back the light. But these hills are empty. My brothers are not just over there," he nodded toward a ridge, "skinning their own kills. Tonight there will be no celebration. No one waits to hear me tell of this hunt."

Thundercloud interrupted him. "There's everyone at the mission."

Soaring Eagle shook his head. "The people at the mission are good people. I see that." He struggled to find the words. "But they are not *my* people. Among my people, to be a man, we had to be good warriors and good hunters. I was a man." He nodded east. "I have been watching at Santee. You, John Thundercloud, are like our holy men. James Red Wing is trying to be what they call a farmer."

Soaring Eagle tossed his chicken bone into the fire and licked his fingers before continuing. "But I have not learned how *I* am to be a man there."

Soaring Eagle settled back and waited for John Thundercloud to answer him. With a prayer for wisdom, John said, "James and I both found our way in a new world by asking God to show us what to do."

Soaring Eagle considered and challenged. "Which god does a Lakota ask, John Thundercloud?"

"A Lakota should ask the God who answers—the God who says in his book, *'Whatsoever is under the whole heaven is Mine . . . every beast of the forest . . . the cattle upon a thousand hills . . . everything that moves in the field . . . the world is Mine, and the fulness thereof.'"*

"And this god you say owns the world, how do I know he will answer me?"

John Thundercloud replied earnestly. "Because he has promised to answer. He says, *'Call unto Me, and I will answer thee, and show thee great and mighty things, which thou knowest not.'* He says, *'If thou seek Him, He will be found of thee.'"*

Once again, the bitterness of the past rose up to block Soaring Eagle's vision of God. "If this god of yours owns all things, then why does he not care for them? Why does he let them be hurt? Why does he allow them to slaughter one another?"

Leaning forward, John Thundercloud answered. "I have pondered these questions for long hours into the night. All men wonder why God allows evil. In the end, we are not given the answer. We are asked to trust God and serve him. He promises that his purposes will be accomplished, even through the actions of evil men. He promises that in the end he will judge these evil things."

Sensing Soaring Eagle's rejection of this message, John Thundercloud held up his hand and begged, "Hear me, Soaring Eagle. Hear the end of the matter." Soaring Eagle settled again beside the fire, folding his arms to show his disagreement.

John Thundercloud continued. "It seems to me that your own life, Soaring Eagle, proves that God uses men's evil to accomplish what he wishes. It is wrong when the government breaks its treaties with the Lakota. It is wrong when the soldiers kill women and children. But did not God use those wrong things to bring you to us? Here you have heard again and again that God loves you and sent his Son Jesus to die for you. If you come to believe that, then you can have victory against all the wrong. If you come to believe that, you will have eternal life. Soldiers can come and kill your body, but you will go to be with God. The government can break its treaties and take your land, but you will still have your home in heaven. That is freedom, Soaring Eagle. Knowing that nothing men can do to you will change your future with God. *'If the Son therefore shall make you free, ye shall be free indeed.'* Jesus Christ died to set you free. He can help you live in a way that is right before God. He can help you live as a real man wherever you go."

John stopped for moment to allow Soaring Eagle to ponder the words. When no questions were forthcoming, John added, "Soaring Eagle, I am still trying to learn about God. For many years I have read his book. For many years I have tried to live for him. Still, I cannot answer all your questions. If I could know everything about God, he would not be God. You have said that there is a hole in your heart. You have said that darkness covers your life. I am only a man. I cannot answer all your questions about God. Open your heart to *him*. *He* will fill the hole in your heart. *He* will pierce your darkness with light. I can promise you this because He did this for me. And for James Red Wing. You see many Dakota coming to church on Sunday. They have had their homes taken away, just as the

Lakota. They have been killed and beaten and starved by soldiers. Still, they do not live in darkness. It is not that they are better men than you, Soaring Eagle. It is only that they have hearts that belong to God now. Ask God to show you what you must do. He will answer."

"This means I must give up the old ways."

"I think it means that you must stop clinging to what is past and embrace what is now—what you know to be true."

John Thundercloud's heart was beating rapidly as he anticipated yet another conversion among his people. But he was to be disappointed. Soaring Eagle grunted noncommittally and got up to check the hobbles on the mule train.

CHAPTER 30

Love covereth all sins.

Proverbs 10:12

By the time the wagon trundled into Lincoln, Rachel Brown was so weak that Jim had to carry her into the hotel. Augusta led him down the hall to Sarah Biddle's old room. Rachel smiled weakly and apologized for inconveniencing everyone.

"Don't be silly, Mrs. Brown," Augusta blustered. "You just rest up, and we'll have you on the train for home in no time. I'll telegraph your parents to let them know you're staying with us a few extra days. Don't worry, I'll say it just right so they won't fret. Carrie can sleep in the trundle bed, so she's right here with you." Augusta was still talking as she left the room and went off down the hall to direct the unloading of the wagon.

LisBeth leaned against the doorway to the room and chuckled. "I tried to tell you about Aunt Augusta, but sometimes you just have to experience her."

Rachel sighed. "Well, if a person can be willed to good health, Mrs. Hathaway will have me up and on the way home in no time."

Carrie came in pulling her small trunk behind her. She looked at her mother and her face clouded with concern. "You gonna be all right, Mama?"

Rachel forced a bright smile. "Of course I am, dear."

Jim hauled in another trunk. "Mrs. Brown, with your permission, I'll have Carrie ride along to take Mrs. Bond home.

Then she can help brush down the team when we're done. I'll introduce her to Joseph over at the livery, and she can explore the stables." Jim turned to Carrie and winked. "There's a grand loft to be explored, Carrie, and there's no telling when you might find a new litter of kittens tucked away in some corner up there."

With Rachel's relieved permission, Carrie went off with Jim. LisBeth turned to say something, but Rachel had fallen asleep, her traveling bonnet still on her head. She had not even had the energy to remove her gloves.

Out in the hotel kitchen, LisBeth encountered the handiwork of two new kitchen girls who had, since she had been gone, rearranged everything to suit them and scooted Jesse's and Augusta's rockers into a dark corner. Seeing LisBeth frown, Augusta drew her aside. "I've been reading my evening paper in my own parlor, dear. I think it best we move our activities there. The hotel is busier these days, and Cora and Odessa are proving to be excellent cooks and organizers. They don't speak English too well yet, but I think they're going to work out wonderfully. They're sisters. Answered my ad the day they got off the train. They've no family in Lincoln, and I'm amazed at their willingness to work. I don't want to lose them."

Just as Augusta finished, Cora and Odessa came in the back door together. The heavyset one, who turned out to be Cora, bobbed her head and blinked at LisBeth through thick glasses as she came forward with a boldly outstretched hand. She smiled and said through crooked teeth, "Cora Schlegelmilch," dipping into an awkward curtsy as she spoke. Odessa, the thin one, giggled and blushed as she followed her sister's example. Odessa, however, suffered from such painful shyness that she could only move her lips to form her name. Little sound came out. LisBeth reached for her offered hand and shook it solemnly. The sisters stood awkwardly staring at LisBeth. They looked at her shoes, then the hem of her dress, then her cameo, then, at last her eyes. When LisBeth smiled, the girls looked at one another, giggled again, and, grabbing for their aprons, hurried to work.

"Wait until you taste their dumplings," Augusta whispered. "Last night David Braddock brought John Cadman in for dinner and the old grouch ordered three helpings." Augusta chuckled. "He came to the back door when I was gone today and offered the girls twice my wages if they'd come to cook for Cadman House!"

"Twice?" LisBeth was incredulous. "Then why—?"

"Why are they still here?" Augusta asked as LisBeth nodded her head. "Cora just blinked at Cadman and said, 'Hataway House hires us. Pay ist gut. Ve like dat Miz Hataway. Ve stay.'"

Augusta smiled. "Of course, as soon as I got back, Cora told me all about it and asked for a raise. Which I gladly gave. We'll soon have to be charging fifty cents for a meal just to cover expenses if the salary war continues. I almost believe Lincolnites will *pay* twice the going rate if Cora and Odessa are cooking. Even David Braddock has been back, and he has Sarah cooking at the manse. Of course," Augusta added, "I think his interest in Hathaway House is connected with the personnel rather than the food."

LisBeth blushed. "I didn't think he and Mrs. Braddock were staying long."

"You've only been gone two weeks, LisBeth."

"It seems like a lifetime. Only a short ride north, really, but a lifetime away."

Augusta turned to talk to her new employees. "Cora, let's do lemon cake for dessert tonight, and can you make some of those dinner rolls you served with the roast on Tuesday?" Cora nodded energetically.

Augusta guided LisBeth out of the kitchen and into her private parlor where they settled to talk. "Tell me about it, LisBeth."

LisBeth told everything about the trip except the one thing that was perhaps the most important. She didn't mention Soaring Eagle. She described the school and Charity's work in glowing terms, expressing great admiration for the dedication of the workers and the progress of the students. She recounted Agnes Bond's whining and Jim Callaway's patience and every detail of the trip that she could remember, concluding by asking Augusta's opinion of Rachel Brown's health and what could be done to get her home to St. Louis.

"I'll have Dr. Gilbert check on her first thing tomorrow," Augusta offered. "Whatever can be done, we'll do. If it's within our power, we'll see that she gets to be at home for Christmas."

Augusta had just settled back to read the evening paper when the bell at the front desk rang, summoning her to check in new boarders. It was David Braddock.

"I saw Jim Callaway's rig at the livery," David explained. "I hope everything went well for LisBeth."

From behind Augusta, LisBeth called, "Everything went well, David, thank you." LisBeth came out of Augusta's parlor and leaned against the doorway.

David cleared his throat nervously. "Mother and I—we'd like to ask you to dinner, LisBeth. This evening." He turned to Augusta. "And we'd be most pleased if you'd come, too, Mrs. Hathaway."

Augusta declined. "Sorry, Mr. Braddock. But I've an ill boarder to care for. LisBeth brought back a Mrs. Rachel Brown and her daughter, Carrie. Mrs. Brown is on her way home to St. Louis for the winter. She's quite broken-down, poor thing. I'm determined to get her back on her feet and on a train for home as soon as possible. LisBeth, of course, is free to accept your invitation."

The door behind David opened and Jim Callaway stepped into the hotel, accompanied by Carrie Brown. Carrie was bubbling with enthusiasm, having actually discovered a litter of kittens in the loft of the livery, and anticipating a promised ride out to Jim's farm.

Jim interrupted Carrie's prattle. "Hope I didn't misspeak. I just thought Carrie would enjoy it," he lowered his voice as Carrie skipped through the dining room and disappeared into the kitchen to see if Rachel had awakened, "and it might take her mind off her mama."

LisBeth's eyes glowed. "It's a wonderful idea. Thank you."

Jim quickly removed his hat. "Of course, she'd probably

enjoy it more if you'd come along." He looked at Augusta and added hastily, "Unless, of course, Mrs. Hathaway needs you."

"I'd love to come along, Jim," LisBeth said, eyeing David coldly. "I'll pack a picnic lunch."

Carrie skipped back into the lobby with the happy news that Rachel had awakened and was hungry and might even get up for supper.

With a wicked gleam in her eye, LisBeth called Carrie over. "Carrie, dear, come show Mrs. Hathaway the lovely gift Soaring Eagle gave you before we left the mission." At the mention of the name, Augusta grunted with surprise. LisBeth hastened to explain. "It seems, Augusta, that by some miracle, my brother Soaring Eagle now resides at Santee Mission. I didn't actually get to meet him, but he gave Carrie this necklace. Can you believe it, Augusta? I remember mother telling us about this cross and chain, how it caused Rides the Wind to take her in, and how she gave it to her friend Prairie Flower. Prairie Flower must have given it to Soaring Eagle. And now, here it is, a living testimony to the love that can exist between nations." Every word that LisBeth said was carefully flung at David Braddock, and every word hit home. He blanched, and studied the floor while LisBeth spoke. She finished with bravado. "I didn't have the courage to meet him. But I'm going back in the spring, and if he'll agree to it, I'm going to meet him. I think families should support one another, don't you agree, David?"

David turned red and didn't reply. LisBeth pushed it further. "Thank you for your invitation to dinner this evening, but I'll be busy preparing our picnic lunch for tomorrow. I want to make sure that Carrie has a good time. And *you*, Jim Callaway," LisBeth said, patting his arm with great familiarity, "will be amazed to learn that I really can do something besides feel sorry for myself.

"Carrie, let's go see what we can make your mama for supper that will tempt her to eat until she's ready to burst!" LisBeth winked at Jim and disappeared into the kitchen with Carrie.

Jim Callaway and David Braddock stood in uncomfortable silence for a few seconds before Jim bid Augusta good-bye.

David turned to go, but Augusta stopped him. "I don't know what's gone on between the two of you, Mr. Braddock," Augusta said. "But I'll urge you to be patient with LisBeth, if you really care for her."

David put his silk top hat on his perfectly groomed head and answered slowly. "I earned that snub, Mrs. Hathaway. I've been stupid. I just hope to heaven it hasn't cost me the woman I want to marry." Tipping his hat to Augusta, David left the hotel and walked briskly to his carriage.

From beneath the brim of the hat he had pulled low over his eyes as he affected a nonchalant pose in the doorway of the livery, Jim Callaway watched Braddock climb into his carriage. As soon as the carriage was out of sight, Jim took off his hat and threw it in the air, letting out a whoop of joy that echoed into the livery and saved a mouse's life by causing it to leap straight up in the air just as the mother of the new litter of kittens pounced.

Roses. He sent red roses. LisBeth stared at them in disbelief and wondered how David had managed such a feat so late in the year. The card read simply, "Forgive me. D." LisBeth put the card aside to check on Rachel and was delighted to find her in the kitchen listening to Carrie prattle on about their day in the country.

"He's got a dog, too, Mama. He's named Jack and he's big and scary looking, but he's real friendly. He don't bite at all. We took a walk along the creek and had our picnic under a big cottonwood tree. We saw all Mr. Callaway's fields ready for crops next spring, and he told Mrs. Baird—she told me to call her LisBeth, though—he told LisBeth all about what he was going to plant and everything. And when we left, he pulled the very last blooms off his rosebush and gave them to LisBeth and me. See?" Carrie held up a drooping pink flower.

Rachel looked up when LisBeth came into the kitchen and noted the pink rose pinned to the bodice of her dress. Just then, a knock sounded at the back door. LisBeth opened it to find Mr. Miller's stock boy holding a bouquet of daisies. Again, a card said, "Forgive me. D."

By the time the supper hour came, Rachel was protesting Augusta's insistence that she rest and begging for a chance to help with something in the kitchen. "Absolutely not!" Augusta ordered. "Your one chore, young lady, is to get better so that you can catch a train to St. Louis in short order. If I hear you've been lifting a finger," Augusta shook her dish towel in Rachel's face, "I'll lock you in your room. Now, scoot!" Rachel relented, and with a copy of Mr. Dickens's latest novel in hand, retired to her room where she fell asleep long before completing even one page of the book.

LisBeth was helping set the tables in the dining room when another messenger boy arrived with a box of candy and another note begging forgiveness. Finally, David Braddock himself appeared at the hotel. He came to the back door, causing no small amount of fluster between the Schlegelmilch sisters.

"Vot a fine gentleman like dat doing coming to back door ov dis hotel, I like to know?" Cora whispered.

Odessa peeked over the rim of her glasses and whispered back. "He ask fur Mrs. Baird, dat vun." Giggling softly she added, "Is good-looking man, Cora!"

Cora shook a fork at Odessa. "You got no business about dat, Odessa Schlegelmilch. Now get dat lemon cake cut before Mrs. Hataway come out in dis kitchen for to see vat ve do!"

The two sisters stopped talking and began serving up lemon cake with renewed energy. David Braddock paced the floor waiting for LisBeth to appear. Finally, she came in from the dining room, balancing a tray full of dirty dishes with one hand and carrying a pitcher full of water in the other. David rushed to take the tray of dishes and shoved them at Cora.

"LisBeth, please forgive me."

LisBeth was cool. "You've already said that, David. Three times. Twice with flowers. Thank you. They are very nice. I put one bouquet in Mrs. Brown's room and took the other into the dining room. Once with candy. Thank you. Carrie will enjoy it, I'm sure. Now, if you'll excuse me, we have a larger than usual crowd." LisBeth turned to Cora and Odessa and said with a smile, "I think word is getting around town that we have the best cooks in Lincoln."

Cora and Odessa looked up briefly from their work and nodded their heads in appreciation.

David persisted. "LisBeth. Please. Say you'll come to dinner. Say you forgive me. I was a fool and I'm sorry. What more can I say? What can I do?" David was honestly distraught. LisBeth found it vaguely unattractive.

A voice from the dining room called for service, and LisBeth turned to go. "I don't know, David, I can't talk now. Come back later. No, come back tomorrow. After lunch. You can walk me to the sewing circle."

David answered humbly, "I'll be here tomorrow. Please don't leave without me."

When they met the next day, LisBeth's hurt feelings had been healed sufficiently through indulging in chocolates to give David a civil hearing. He apologized so profusely that LisBeth finally patted his arm and put a stop to it with an abrupt, "Come, come, David. Don't be so dramatic. You hurt my feelings. In a way, I'm glad it happened. Now everything is out in the open between us. Now we can be friends without any pretense. I haven't really known about my Sioux heritage for long. Mother only told me the year before she died."

David commiserated. "What a shock that must have been."

"A shock—yes. It was. There was so much I wanted to know. I still need to come to terms with it." They had reached the steps of the porch and LisBeth started up the stairs. She stopped on the second step, her eyes level with David's. "I was a coward not to face Soaring Eagle at Santee. Jim Callaway helped me see that. He didn't exactly call me a coward, but I can tell he thinks I should at least meet my brother. Then I can judge for myself what kind of people I came from. Jim thinks it might make things easier for me. I've been running from my past ever since Mac died. I just haven't been able to face it."

David answered doubtfully. "Some things are best left alone, LisBeth."

"Yes, some things are. But not this. Not for me. It will probably take all winter, but somehow I'm going to work up the courage to go back there and face him. Maybe when Rachel and Carrie Brown come back, maybe I'll go with them." LisBeth's eyes grew wistful. "I wonder what he's like."

"Are you sure you want to know? The papers are full of news of the Sioux, and the news is not very complimentary."

LisBeth's eyes narrowed. "You know, I once had a picture in my mind of rich people. I thought they were all terribly selfish and terribly conceited. Then I met you and your mother. You changed that. Jim Callaway said that Soaring Eagle saved his life. He said that he was respected and looked up to by others in his tribe. Carrie Brown says he's gentle and kind. I think I'll wait until I meet him before I blame him with some savagery likely exaggerated by reporters. I hope he'll do me the same courtesy."

David smiled indulgently. "Well, that can wait until spring. What are your plans until then?"

LisBeth retreated another few steps toward the church door. "To continue in the Ladies' Missionary Society work. We're going to sponsor two more students at the Santee school, and I've agreed to head up the committee to raise the additional funds. And I'll work at the hotel as much as Augusta will let me."

David interrupted her. "And will you come to Philadelphia for Christmas?" When LisBeth didn't answer, David continued. "Mother will have Sarah close up the house soon. We'll all be going back to Philadelphia. Tom too. We're hiring him a private tutor. Sarah's done well, but Mother wants her to be under Mrs. Titus's tutelage for a bit longer. I suspect the real reason is that Mother's so fond of Sarah and Tom she doesn't want to be away from them. When we next come to Lincoln, it will be spring. I don't want to be away from you that long, LisBeth. Will you come for Christmas?"

"David, I can't be gadding about the country. I have responsibilities. Augusta needs me at the hotel."

"Augusta is eager to see you get beyond working at the hotel. If it's a matter of concern, I'll personally provide funds to hire a replacement for you. I'll also provide the ticket to Philadelphia."

"It wouldn't be proper. People will talk."

"Not if you're my fiancée."

LisBeth retreated to the top of the church steps and opened the door. "Good day, David."

CHAPTER 31

And therefore will the LORD wait,
that he may be gracious unto you,
and therefore will he be exalted,
that he may have mercy upon you: for the LORD is
a God of judgment: blessed are all they that wait
for him.

Isaiah 30:18

Fall bit the leaves from every tree in Lincoln and sent them blowing past Rachel's window. With every day that went by, Rachel seemed to grow weaker. Dr. Gilbert came and prescribed tonics and diets, but nothing seemed to help. As Rachel grew weaker, Carrie grew more frightened.

Finally, Rachel gave up leaving her room. Dr. Gilbert shook his head when LisBeth and Augusta asked what could be done. Carrie grew quieter and more desperate, refusing Jim Callaway's enticements for rides out to the homestead and spending hours by her mother's bed, reading to her and working on a new doll she was making to replace Ida May.

The week that David and Abigail Braddock closed up the manse and left for Philadelphia, Sarah and Tom Biddle came for a farewell dinner at the hotel.

Augusta beamed with pride as she warned, "Don't you forget us here in Lincoln."

"Oh, Aunt Augusta," Sarah said softly. "Don't say such a thing. We'll miss you so. Both of you." Sarah looked at LisBeth. "I hope you'll accept Mr. David's invitation, LisBeth. He's said he's hoping you and Aunt Augusta will come to Philadelphia for Christmas. Please do."

Augusta turned to LisBeth. "What's this? You never said a word."

"I can't go to Philadelphia, Augusta. It's a ridiculous notion. I'm needed here."

Augusta protested. "LisBeth Baird, I'll not have you using me and this hotel as an excuse to turn down a lovely invitation. Of course you'll go to Philadelphia for Christmas. We'll both go." Turning to Sarah she enthused. "You tell David and Abigail Braddock that I'll be happy to escort LisBeth to Philadelphia."

Early the next morning, David pounded on the kitchen door, waking LisBeth and insisting breathlessly that she come to Philadelphia. "Sarah said that Augusta was delighted with the idea. I want to hear *you* say it, LisBeth. Please. Say you'll come. I won't press you about—anything. Just come for Christmas."

"All right. We'll come. But remember, you promised. You won't press me about—anything."

The joy in his face reminded LisBeth of a spoiled child suddenly given his way. Once again, something inside her was gently repulsed. Still, she found herself looking forward to Christmas in Philadelphia.

"I want to go home, LisBeth," Rachel said feebly. "I want so desperately to go home." She held the most recent letter from her parents and wept freely. LisBeth patted her hand and assured her that she would be stronger soon and be able to go home.

Rachel rubbed her crooked jaw and flexed her crippled hand. Slowly, deliberately she struggled to sit upright and looked squarely at LisBeth as she said firmly. "I'm dying." LisBeth started to protest, but Rachel held up her hand. "Please, don't humor me. It's too late. We both know it. Dr. Gilbert hasn't been able to help. Things inside me are just too—twisted—to work for much longer." She smiled wistfully as she added, "I'm glad I wore out working for God, though."

"I do wish Carrie could get to know her grandma and grandpa before . . ." She sighed and added quietly, "I would so like to die at home. The family plot is in a grand old cemetery with lots of shade trees. It's comforting, in a way."

LisBeth abruptly turned about. "Rachel, I'll take you home."

Rachel looked at her with wide eyes. "But how? I'm not strong enough."

"You're stronger than you'll be next week or next month. I'll take you home. We'll leave tomorrow."

Rachel's eyes took on an excited glow. "Do you mean it? I think I could manage to walk onto the train. We don't have to get off again, and Mother and Father would meet us there."

"We're going." LisBeth said firmly. "I'll tell Augusta, and we'll pack today. The train leaves early in the morning. If there are three tickets available, we'll be on it."

Three tickets were available, and Thursday morning found LisBeth King Baird helping Rachel Brown into a Pullman car for the journey home. Augusta blustered and waved and fought back tears as the train pulled out of the station. Carrie leaned out of the window, her red braids bobbing as the train picked up speed. Augusta's last memory of Rachel and Carrie was of Rachel's crooked half smile and Carrie blowing kisses. Behind them both, LisBeth's worried face appeared and she clasped her hands and looked to heaven, thereby imploring Augusta to pray for them all. Augusta nodded and waved, fighting back tears until the train was out of sight.

The Schlegelmilch sisters clucked in sympathy and presented Augusta with a cup of chamomile tea and a piece of sweet potato pie. "Ven you are vorried, a bit of tea and a bit of sweet, den a lots of prayers. Dat helps," Cora said as she presented the treat to Augusta. "Dat LisBet, she be all right. Dat Carrie girl, she be wit her Grandma und Grandpa. She be all right. And dat Rachel voman, she be wit her Gott. She be best of all."

LisBeth stayed in St. Louis longer than anyone had expected. Writing to Charity of Rachel's illness, LisBeth shared,

I don't really know why I have remained, except that Rachel seems comforted by my presence and Carrie seems to enjoy being able to remember about the mission with someone who has been there and seen

the things of which she speaks. As long as I can be a comfort, I will stay. I am daily amazed at Rachel's rich faith in God and her ability to accept this horrible thing that has befallen her. She seems to be totally trusting of God. It shames me, Charity. I have been so angry with God for taking things away from me. I am beginning to see, through Rachel's eyes, that perhaps God does allow things to happen so that we will learn to depend on him. That is what Rachel says, and when she speaks of it, I can see in her face that she truly has come to accept this illness as coming from God for a higher purpose. She does not know what it is, she says, but she repeatedly quotes Romans 8:28 to me. Have you read it? As I stand before her in a healthy state, I wouldn't presume to quote it to Rachel, but when she quotes it to me, it takes on a meaning and beauty that I can't explain. ". . . all things work together for good to them that love God, to them who are the called according to his purpose." Just imagine it, Charity, she is facing death, and she knows she will not see Carrie grow to womanhood, yet she simply gives it over to God and without any bitterness at all, she says sweetly, "The eternal God is my refuge and underneath are the everlasting arms." Oh for a faith like that!

Do share poor Rachel's condition with the children and have them pray for her. Perhaps God will yet work a miracle.

And if Soaring Eagle is yet there—and I pray he is—please tell him how very much it has meant for Carrie to have his gift with her. Tell him that his sister sends her greeting and she also thanks him for the gift of the quilt and wishes him peace.

Rachel Brown died not long after LisBeth wrote to Charity and was laid to rest in the family plot in the cemetery filled with trees in St. Louis, just as she had wished. She lived long enough to see Carrie form a strong bond with her grandparents and long enough to share her strong faith in God with LisBeth Baird.

Dear Jim,
Poor Rachel Brown was laid to rest today. Carrie is heartbroken, but she will find comfort in her dear grandparents, who truly cherish her and will give her a loving home.

I have written Charity at the mission to send her a copy of Rachel's memorial for the Word Carrier.

There is nothing else that I can do here, and so I will take my leave and be home soon.

Rachel has left me her Bible. I can see you smiling at this revelation, wondering if perhaps, having been given a second copy of the great book, I will at last read it. Rachel's Bible has a lovely inscription in the front. It says, "I want to master this Book so that the Master of this Book will master me." I think it is a lovely sentiment and yes, I will read Rachel's Bible. When I return to Lincoln, I also intend to pick up Mother's Bible once more and read the passages she has underlined.

I wanted to write to you, Jim, because you have expressed such a concern for me—not for any reason other than that you seem genuinely concerned for the person that is LisBeth. You seem to care that I find happiness and peace, and I appreciate that more than I can say. I still have a lot of questions, but being with Rachel during this time wiped away a lot of the bitterness. I have seen in this last year that so many others have suffered as much, if not more, than I have.

Perhaps without the bitterness standing in the way, I will be able to find my way to that peace that you own—what you called "the peace that passes understanding."

Pray that I will find it.

I will be in Lincoln for only a short while before Augusta and I depart for Philadelphia. The Braddocks have invited us, and Sarah and Tom insist that they will die of homesickness if we do not come. We will stay through Christmas.

Please keep watch over Joseph while we are gone, Jim. I fear that he is aging quickly, and I know he values your friendship, as do we all. If you are able to come into town before we leave, we would love to see you. If not, we will understand.

I remain your friend,
LisBeth King Baird

P.S. Psalm 55:22. I am trying to see if this works.

Jim Callaway found himself more than able to go into Lincoln to see LisBeth and Augusta before they left for Philadelphia. Indeed, he alighted on the doorstep of the Hathaway House Hotel the very next evening after LisBeth's homecoming. He found it necessary to stay in town for several days, joining Joseph for meals in the hotel kitchen and insisting on helping the Schlegelmilch sisters do the dishes.

"Vot you doin' vit your hands in my dishvater, eh?" Cora scolded.

"I'm helping wash dishes, Cora. That's what. Least I can do after you gave me that second piece of sweet potato pie."

Cora clucked and fussed. "You bachelors—you don't know nutting 'bout dem dishes. You git on out of my vay, and let me vork!"

Jim winked at Cora. "You come check my kitchen any time. Bet it's cleaner than yours!"

"Ya, and de moon is made ov green cheez too!"

Jim had joked and teased until the Schlegelmilch sisters finally accepted him. He was the recipient of a vast array of sweets and special teas.

Coming in from the dining room LisBeth teased, "You'd better watch out, Jim. They've set their eye on you and decided you're a good catch. They'll be tying you up until you promise to marry one of them if you aren't careful!"

"Who's promising to marry?" Augusta wanted to know as she came in the back door. "I declare, I leave you two for one bank meeting, and there's marriage and mayhem in my hotel!"

Augusta plopped down in the old rocker that still stood in the corner of the kitchen. Not waiting for an answer to her question, she offered a summary of the latest financial news and woes in Lincoln. "I pulled N. C. Sweet aside after the meeting and told him my plans for a new hotel nearer the railway station. He very nearly promised the bank would back me, so while we're in Philadelphia, LisBeth, I'll be visiting that architect David recommended to get some plans drawn up. I want a really fine building, one that will last into the next century—something to be a legacy for you to build on."

Jim asked abruptly, "When are you leaving?"

"We have tickets for Monday morning's train. Goodness!"

Augusta jumped up. "I've got to get the trim on my black suit replaced. I had Gladys over at Oppenheimer's lay aside a lovely new lace."

"I'll take the suit over for you, Aunt Augusta," LisBeth offered.

Jim grabbed his hat. "I'll walk you over, LisBeth." Augusta winked at LisBeth and Jim hastened to add, "Got some things I need to ask you about the homestead. I'd like to make sure you approve of what I'm doing out there. It's still your place, after all, until I finish paying for it."

LisBeth and Jim walked the four blocks to Oppenheimer's in silence, LisBeth waiting for Jim to share his plans and Jim wondering awkwardly how to say what he needed to say. LisBeth handed over Augusta's suit. As she and Jim left the store, she ran her hand lovingly over a bolt of turkey red calico that lay on the cutting table.

"Just in, Mrs. Baird," Gladys offered. "Can I save you a few yards?"

"No, thank you, Gladys. But it's lovely."

When they were outside, Jim offered, "I guess black does get old after a while, don't it?"

LisBeth nodded. "I feel guilty about wanting to dress fashionably again, but I can't help it. Sometimes I think wearing black just prolongs the agonies of grieving. There are moments when you can almost forget, when the hurting isn't so obvious. Then I reach for something and see all this black, and I remember." LisBeth sighed and looked back up the street toward Oppenheimer's. "It *was* lovely cloth." She brightened. "But then, there will be plenty of years in the future for the latest colors. Augusta wears black by choice. Perhaps I should follow suit and just pretend I'm wearing black because I think it's fashionable."

Jim chuckled. "It's good to hear you try to find a positive way to handle the things you don't like."

"I'm learning."

The two were near the livery before Jim spoke again. "Have

you seen the new mare Joseph brought in from the home-stead?"

"No. Is it the sorrel one you swore was worthless?"

Jim nodded his head. "Yep. And I was wrong. Joseph was right. She's going to look real stylish pulling the old carriage."

"We're almost back, Jim. What did you want to ask me about the homestead?"

Jim cleared his throat and began awkwardly. "Well, LisBeth. It's—" Impulsively he grabbed LisBeth's hand and pulled her into the livery. "It's personal," he blurted out. "I don't want anybody to hear it."

LisBeth sat on a hay bale inside the livery door and watched as Jim paced back and forth. Several times he stopped in front of her and opened his mouth. Then, he clamped it shut and paced again.

"For heaven's sake, Jim. What's the matter? Surely you know that I'm not going to object to anything you want to do out at the homestead."

"It's not what I want to do at the homestead, LisBeth." He sat down next to her and lowered his voice. "It's who I want to do it *with*."

LisBeth looked at him blankly.

"Will you pray with me?"

More confused than ever, LisBeth nodded.

Jim prayed and LisBeth tried to listen carefully, but her mind wandered as she tried to imagine why he was so upset. In the midst of her wondering, she realized that Jim had stopped talking.

"LisBeth, did you hear me? I'm . . . I'm asking you to be my wife."

He was looking at her intensely, his gray-green eyes smol-dering with feeling.

"What? I'm sorry, Jim. I didn't . . . hear you."

"Well, you're going off to Philadelphia, and I'm worried about what might happen there. I know you said you're going mostly because you're fond of Abigail and to see Sarah and Tom. But David Braddock's got his own ideas of what's going to happen at Christmas, LisBeth. I didn't want to say anything until I had the homestead free and clear," he jumped up and began pacing again, "but if I don't say something now, I'm going to lose you for sure. Not that I *have* you, still, if you don't know how I feel—"

LisBeth was staring up at Jim incredulously. "Jim, I had no idea."

He sat down beside her again. "LisBeth, I told you on the way to Santee that when I shared my past with you, you'd own a part of me that no other woman did. I don't mean to press myself on you." He laughed nervously. "I guess this is a pretty unromantic way to do this, after all . . . LisBeth, I love you. I'll never be rich, like David Braddock. I'll never be the kind of man that people in town look to for advice." Finally, Jim drew the courage to look at her. "LisBeth, everything I've done out at the homestead—it's been for you. It won't ever be fancy, but it could be *home*. We could raise a family—and serve God there—together." He took a deep breath. "I want to hold you when you cry, and make you forget all the terrible things that have happened to you. I want to be the one you talk to when you're angry with God, and I want to be there to laugh with you. I want to pray with you. I want to hold your babies and know they're mine. I want to hear my children call you *Mama,* and I want to be there when the children are grown and your hair turns gray." Jim stopped again, realizing he had blurted out much more than he had intended. He finished gently. "You don't have to say a thing now. I won't bring it up again. I just knew if I didn't say something before you went that maybe I'd lose you because I was too much of a coward."

LisBeth looked at him with wonder. "You just proposed to me, yet you expect I'll be going to Philadelphia?"

Jim nodded. "I want you to go, LisBeth."

"I don't understand."

"I want you to go and be with David Braddock and see where he lives. I want you to have a wonderful time."

"What if I don't come back? David *has* proposed."

Jim said quietly. "I thought he would have by now." He

looked at LisBeth evenly. "But you didn't accept, or you would never have let me say the things I've said just now."

"No, I didn't accept. But what if—"

He interrupted her. "What if you don't come back to me?" His voice shook with emotion. "Well, LisBeth, it's like this. If you said you'd marry me right now, I'd still tell you to go to Philadelphia."

At LisBeth's look of confusion, Jim tried to explain. "Homesteading is a hard life. I don't want to live with a woman who looks out the window and wishes she was someplace else—with the last name of Braddock. That's an amazing house David Braddock's built. If you want it, I guess it's yours." Jim took a deep breath. "But he'll never, with all his millions, be able to give you one drop of the love I can. He'll never stand at the window of that big fancy house and burst with joy at the sight of you coming up the drive the way I do every time you drive out to the homestead. He hasn't prayed for you—asked God for you—the way I have."

Jim took a deep breath and finally finished. "LisBeth, go to Philadelphia. See everything there is to see, and spend lots of time with David Braddock. I'll be here—believing that God meant it when He said, *'Trust in the LORD, and do good; so shalt thou dwell in the land, and verily shalt thou be fed. Delight thyself also in the LORD; and he shall give thee the desires of thine heart. Commit thy way unto the LORD; trust also in him; and he shall bring it to pass.'* I believe that God gave me the desire to ask you to be my wife. I think he'll honor it. If he doesn't want us together, then I'll have to let you go. I've been in places where God wasn't with me. I never want to go back to those places."

Finally, Jim reached for LisBeth's hand. She offered it willingly and realized that he was trembling as he bent to kiss the back of her hand. "God go with you, Lizzie Baird." He looked up at her and said earnestly. "Come back to me."

Before LisBeth could say anything, Jim Callaway jumped up and nearly ran out of the livery. She sat on the hay bale for a long time before returning to the hotel kitchen. Augusta looked up and her eyes narrowed as she asked, "What happened to Jim?"

LisBeth's voice trembled as she answered, "He had to get back to the homestead, I guess. Said he hopes we enjoy our time in Philadelphia." LisBeth made her way to her room where she spent the afternoon thumbing through her mother's worn Bible, wondering at Jim Callaway's odd proposal, and hungering to find the faith that enabled him to deliver it and trust God with the outcome.

CHAPTER 32

I bare you on eagles' wings, and
brought you unto myself.

Exodus 19:4

Solomon Yellow Hawk and Justin Spotted Bear
were tilling Rachel Brown's weedy garden when
John Thundercloud and Soaring Eagle returned from their
hunt. The two boys dropped their hoes and raced to the black-
smith shop. From there, four boys scattered to spread the word
that the hunters were back. By the time Thundercloud and
Soaring Eagle had reached the Riggs's cabin, half the school's
population had gathered to admire the success of the two men.

The next few moments were spent handing out a share of
their meat to every field matron present. Soaring Eagle's eyes
searched the small group until he located Charity. He gave her
a huge portion of one deer, and while he didn't say anything,
Charity sensed the question he wanted to ask.

"They are in Lincoln, Soaring Eagle. Rachel wrote to us that
she will rest there before going on to St. Louis. LisBeth is taking
care of her."

Once the meat was distributed, Soaring Eagle and John
Thundercloud were the recipients of many invitations to din-
ner. Soaring Eagle declined and headed for James and Martha
Red Wing's farm, having saved an entire deer carcass for them.
When he arrived at their farm house, he found Martha and
James working side by side in their own fields, picking up a
considerable crop of squash and pumpkins and piling them
in the back of their wagon.

Martha hurried away, leading the pony laden with the deer,

and promising the two men a hearty supper. Soaring Eagle set to working beside James. The two men worked for more than an hour before either one said much. Finally, the field was stripped of its fall crop and the wagon was driven near the barn where James had dug a cache pit. Lowering himself into the pit, he layered the vegetables with fresh straw as Soaring Eagle handed them down. When the pit was full, James covered it with more straw and stood up to survey his work with satisfaction.

"The hunt was good?" he asked at last.

"It was good." Soaring Eagle walked to the front of the wagon and lead the team to the barn. Surveying the corral, he commented. "Thomas Yellow Hawk has come. Did he buy many ponies?"

James nodded. "Yes. He was very pleased with our ponies, Soaring Eagle. It was obvious that they had been trained by one who knew much about horses. I thank you for your work."

A shrill whinny split the air and a black mare stuck her finely shaped head out of one stall. Soaring Eagle looked at the black mare with surprise. "Thomas Yellow Hawk praised your herd, yet he left the best horse behind?"

James smiled. "The black mare is for you, Soaring Eagle. When she foals in the spring you will have the beginnings of a fine herd again. I only hope that you will not use her to leave us."

Raking through the black mare's tangled mane with his fingers, Soaring Eagle pondered James's words. "Hear me, James Red Wing, for this is not the time to tell a lie. When I first came here, I hated the white man for what he did to my people. But now I have begun to walk a new road. I do not know yet where it will take me. But I know I cannot go back to the old ways. There is no longer hatred in my heart for the white man." Turning to face James Red Wing, Soaring Eagle said solemnly, "I am trying to learn how to be a man here. It is a different way. Thank you for giving me the black mare. Now you must tell me what to do to help you here and to help at the mission."

Soaring Eagle stayed at the Santee school through the fall. Through Martha he learned of Rachel Brown's worsening illness. Each Sunday as he sat, his arms folded, on the back pew of the church wishing, that Carrie's big blue eyes would peer down the center aisle and smile at him. He wrestled with the boys and continued to go to classes with the adults. His English became ever more fluent, and when the last killing frost ended gardening, he began to learn to set type in the print shop.

As he set type, he read the articles that appeared in the *Word Carrier,* forming opinions on the topics discussed therein and challenging James Red Wing and John Thundercloud on various issues. "John Thundercloud—I read where they say 'Why do not the Indians till the ground and live as we do?' May we not ask why the white people do not hunt and live as we do?"

"Be careful, my friend," came the response. "If you begin to sound too able in these matters, Reverend Riggs will be asking you to go back east with him to convince his supporters to send more money our way."

Soaring Eagle snorted. "I do not think that Reverend Riggs would want to travel with a wild Indian." The prospect made him laugh aloud.

James laughed with him, but when he walked away, he broached the topic with Martha. "The school always needs money, Martha. The sight of Soaring Eagle—the 'wild Lakota'—tamed and living a civilized life would do much to help the work of the school. You've heard him tell stories to the school children. He holds them spellbound. God could use such a talent to further the work here."

Martha shook her head. "Soaring Eagle has changed a lot since he came to us, but he's not converted, and he may never be. He's singularly repelled by the notion that there is only one way to heaven and that it didn't come through a Lakota."

"We don't have to save him. God will do that."

The Red Wings dropped the subject, but separately, each one began to pray more earnestly for the soul of Soaring Eagle. Fall melted into winter, and word came that Rachel Brown was weakening. Soaring Eagle worried about his friends and wished for spring. While he was perfectly capable of writing to Carrie, he didn't. Somehow he sensed that in this new world, such a communication would be unacceptable. There was no tangible communication between the two, and yet the friendship remained strong. Soaring Eagle carried thoughts of Carrie with him, and Carrie prayed often for her friend.

In Santee, as Christmas approached, the children became more and more excited about their seasonal party. A dinner was planned, and Martha Red Wing deftly organized six committees: food and money solicitation, bread baking, cake making, pie making, chicken plucking, and general management.

James teased Martha about the last committee. "General management sounds like the committee left over for the bad cooks."

Martha smiled wisely. "There is always a place at Santee for everyone, no matter their talents—or lack of them."

Christmas Day dawned clear and cold. Before noon it was snowing and the children began to fear that their families might not be able to attend the celebration. As the afternoon shadows lengthened and families began arriving, the snow grew thicker. Charity organized another committee to gather extra quilts and blankets for those who would no doubt want to spend the night at the mission. By the time the hour for the program had come, a dangerously cold wind rattled the window panes.

"Of course we're having Christmas," Charity retorted when one of her charges fearfully asked about the program. "Nearly everyone is here already, and the storm can't last long. It's not a blizzard. It's just snow."

The Red Wings had been at the school all day, having entrusted the feeding of the stock to Soaring Eagle, who said that he would come to the program. "I promised Carrie Brown I would not miss Christmas," he explained simply.

Far away in St. Louis that Christmas Day, Carrie Brown sat beside her grandparents in their church in St. Louis, fighting back tears of loneliness. She snuggled against her grandmother and wondered if Mr. Soaring Eagle would ever learn to love Jesus. The thought that he might not brought more tears, and she finally succumbed to sobs of fear and sadness while her grandmother held her close and whispered comfort.

Had she been at Santee, Carrie would have known even more comfort, for just as the Christmas program was beginning, a solitary figure stepped quietly through the church door. Not finding a seat, he stood at the back of the church, his fur-lined moccasins crusted with ice. As Jim Callaway had once said, Soaring Eagle "might be a heathen but he's a man of his word." He had trudged through waist high drifts to keep his promise to Carrie Brown. Soaring Eagle was present for Christmas at Santee.

The small church was decorated with evergreen boughs at the end of every pew and along the altar. Candles set the room ablaze with a golden glow. At the front of the church, a tree had been hung with small presents and the berries collected by the children before the storm began. Soaring Eagle looked at the strange decorations and was unable to hide his amazement.

The evening program began with the boys singing,

> *Maa duidi adi*
> *Jesus di ki dits adi*
> *Heesame di tawts*
> *Adu dita makadats*
> *Di ki dit a haawa*
> *Mi idits seekuha.*

When John Thundercloud rose to give his sermon, the room grew so quiet that he could have whispered and every word would have been easily heard.

"We are glad that you have come this evening to honor and exalt our Lord Jesus Christ. It may seem strange, my friends, that our young men have sung the hymn that is known among our white sister churches as 'Rock of Ages.' In truth, it is I who requested it, because it reminds us that while on this day we celebrate the birth of Jesus, it is his death that gives meaning to his birth.

"The message of the birth of Jesus Christ is one that is totally unique from the message of any other birth. The apostle Paul summarizes the purpose of the coming to earth of Jesus Christ. He says, *'This is a faithful saying, and worthy of all acceptation, that Christ Jesus came into the world to save sinners.'* That is an aspect of the celebrating of the birth of Christ that we must not overlook. Why did Jesus Christ come into the world? God says that his Son came into the world for the express purpose of saving sinners.

"The message of Christmas goes all the way back to the beginning of time, when God made a man and a woman and placed them in a garden. The man and the woman rebelled against him. Immediately they were consumed with guilt. They tried to cover themselves with garments made of leaves. God had warned them that the penalty for sin would be death. They were experiencing that in that their fear had already separated them from God. But God loved them. He gave them garments made out of animal skins. And there the point is driven home that *'without shedding of blood, [there] is no remission'*—no forgiveness of sins.

"You and I are sinners. Guilty and condemned before God. That is the starting point of understanding the significance of the birth of Jesus Christ.

"Most people are offended when holy God says, *'There is none righteous, no, not one'* or *'All have sinned, and come short of the glory of God.'* Most people are offended when God says that all our righteous deeds are like filthy, polluted rags in his sight—unacceptable. He says that by our works no human being will become righteous in his sight.

"Most people are offended when they are told that, because they are sure that by doing the best they can that God will accept them. God says no. The message of Christmas is that God says no. He must intervene on our behalf. He must provide the sacrifice that can take care of our sins.

"So the eternal God—the One who lived in eternity—became a man born at Bethlehem. I don't understand it, but it's true because God says it is. He did it for the purpose of living on this earth and going to the cross to be crucified. Why? Because *'the wages of sin is death.'* The penalty for sin is death. Jesus Christ was crucified to pay the penalty for sin. God in his grace had intervened on our behalf. Jesus Christ was raised from the dead. Why? Because he had accomplished righteousness for us.

"The message of Christmas is not complete unless you understand the background for it. Humanity has fallen into sin. God has promised to step down from the throne of glory and become a man in the person of his Son so that he might go to the cross and bear in his body on the cross our sin and then offer to a fallen humanity the free gift of eternal life by believing in him."

Pastor Thundercloud paused for a moment and looked about the crowded room. Picking up his Bible, he held it in one hand as he continued, "Let me read again the statement of the apostle Paul. *'This is a faithful saying, and worthy of all acceptation, that Christ Jesus came into the world to save sinners.'* You see, you must come to grips with the reality that you are a wretched, vile, condemned sinner. And a holy God says that you will spend an eternity in hell unless you receive the free gift that he has provided for you through the death of his Son, Jesus Christ.

"The message of Christmas is one of great celebration, if you understand what it is about. God is condemning sin. At the same time he is providing a way of forgiveness from sin.

"The question is, what does Christmas mean to you? Do you understand who Jesus Christ is? Do you understand why the Lord of glory, the sovereign of all, would step out of eternity and into time to be born as a human being so that he could be crucified on a cross? He did it because there's no hope for you or me apart from him. The message of Christmas is a message of hope. There is a free gift offered to all who will turn from their sin and believe in Jesus Christ as their Savior."

Closing his Bible and stepping down from the platform,

Pastor Thundercloud bowed his head and concluded his message with a quiet, "Let us pray."

When John Thundercloud had begun his Christmas message, Soaring Eagle stood at the back of the room, his arms folded in his characteristic I-am-here-but-I-do-not-agree manner. As the words swept over the small congregation, however, something supernatural took place. John Thundercloud would later say that he could almost see Soaring Eagle's heart breaking. Thundercloud sent out arrows painted with the blood of the cross, and each one hit its mark. Guided by the Holy Spirit, the arrows split the shell of bitterness and questions that surrounded Soaring Eagle's heart.

At the conclusion of the service, everyone present received a gift made by the school children. Soaring Eagle was amazed when Charity Bond pressed a tiny package wrapped in brown paper into his hand. Amid the bedlam of childish cries of delight, she leaned close to whisper, "Carrie said that if you kept your promise, I was to give you this gift." Soaring Eagle unwrapped the package to find a small paper cross. On one side, Carrie had printed carefully, "Jesus Loves Soaring Eagle."

Soaring Eagle made a hasty exit. He fought his way through the drifting snow back to James Red Wing's barn, where he dug a fire pit and started a small fire. The black mare poked her head over her stall door and whickered quietly. Soaring Eagle patted her gently as he passed her on his way to the ladder that led to the loft. From his parfleche, he took a small bundle wrapped in white skins and carefully unwrapped the Bible that he had heard read so many times around the campfire in his youth. Setting the Bible aside momentarily, he used the skins to wrap up Ida May, the corncob doll. He took the Bible back down the ladder and settled by the fire.

He turned the pages slowly, looking for Walks the Fire's marks. She had used Rides the Wind's paints to smudge along the margins on many pages. Soaring Eagle read,

Who hath measured the waters in the hollow of his hand, and meted out heaven with the span, and comprehended the dust of the earth in

a measure, and weighed the mountains in scales? . . . Behold, the nations are as a drop of a bucket, and are counted as the small dust of a balance. . . . Have ye not known? have ye not heard? . . . It is he that sitteth upon the circle of the earth, . . . that bringeth the princes to nothing. . . . Lift up your eyes on high, and behold who hath created these things . . . he calleth them all by names. . . . Even the youths shall faint and be weary, and the young men shall utterly fall: but they that wait upon the LORD shall renew their strength; they shall mount up with wings as eagles; they shall run, and not be weary; and they shall walk, and not faint.

Fascinated, he continued to feed the small fire and read the book. He flipped page after page, reading where Walks the Fire had marked. *"Hope in the LORD: for with the LORD there is mercy, and with him is plenteous redemption."* Finally he came to one of the gospels and read the complete story of the Jesus that Carrie Brown had insisted he come to love. He had heard the story often at the mission church. But this night, as he sat by the fire, it was as if he had never heard it. He was perplexed when men hated Christ and angry when they killed him. He rejoiced when Christ was found alive again. Soaring Eagle read through the night.

James and Martha Red Wing stayed at the mission, worrying and wondering why he had left and hoping that he had not finally gotten his fill of the white man's religious ceremonies and taken to the hills.

But Soaring Eagle would never get his fill of the faith that had been introduced to him by the whites. As he read and pondered, he believed. As he believed, he read more. Suddenly it was dawn, and the fire had burned out, and the black mare was stomping and snorting and demanding her breakfast.

Soaring Eagle got up stiffly to tend the stock. The snow shone whiter than he had ever seen. The sky was a deeper blue than he remembered it ever being. As he tended to the livestock, Soaring Eagle began to sing an old Lakota song. He was surprised to realize that it brought him no pain. He looked back on his youth without bitterness. He remembered Walks the Fire and Rides the Wind with joy.

It would be some time before Soaring Eagle could articulate what had happened. In that night, he had come to realize the truth that Carrie Brown had written so carefully on a small paper cross: "Jesus Loves Soaring Eagle." It was a simple message, but it filled the hole in Soaring Eagle's heart and turned him away from the bitterness of the past.

CHAPTER 33

If riches increase, set not your
heart upon them.

Psalm 62:10

Early in December, Augusta and LisBeth were greeted at the train station in Philadelphia by Sarah Biddle. The station had been decorated for the holiday in a grand fashion, with festoons and greenery everywhere.

At seventeen, Sarah had the mature bearing of a young woman. Her blue eyes shone with pleasure as Augusta commented favorably on her snow-white waist and linsey-woolsey skirt. Skipping along at her side, young Tom whooped with delight and pounced on LisBeth and Augusta with such energy that the two women were momentarily the center of attention in Philadelphia's railway station.

"Tom! Do calm down," Sarah pleaded, but her smile encouraged him. "What will all these people think of this racket?"

Tom answered readily. "They'll think we really love Aunt LisBeth and Aunt Augusta!"

Sarah laughed. "And they'd be right." Sarah surprised both LisBeth and Augusta by offering a shy hug and saying earnestly, "I'm so *glad* you've come! Mr. Braddock hasn't given us a moment's peace getting the house ready for you."

They walked briskly through the railway station and were duly impressed by the four-horse team that drew an elegant carriage sporting a holiday wreath on its polished black door. Their arrival at the Braddock mansion caused no small stir. As Abigail deftly ordered each trunk to its destination—by way of the *back* stairs—and escorted Augusta and LisBeth into the parlor for tea, LisBeth looked about her in wonder. She had only seen the music room and the veranda on their brief visit during the Centennial. Now she was introduced to the rest of the manse, which was so vast that it made the house built in Lincoln truly resemble a summer cottage. When they finally were escorted upstairs to freshen up, LisBeth was happy to learn that she and Augusta would have adjoining rooms. Actually, they had their own small wing of the house and shared an elegant private parlor. Just off LisBeth's room, there was a small maid's room.

When Grace, the maid, presented herself to help LisBeth unpack, LisBeth fled to find Abigail, who was giving orders to the cook about supper.

"What is it, dear?" she asked kindly.

"Mrs. Braddock, I can't . . . I mean . . ." LisBeth blushed. "I can't have Grace, Mrs. Braddock. I'm just not used to it. I know you mean well, and I hope you can forgive me for being so common, but, really, I'll unpack my own clothes and things. Could Grace just go back to doing whatever she does when you don't have guests?" LisBeth turned redder with embarrassment.

Abigail patted her hand. "I told David it was a ridiculous idea, dear. But sometimes he just won't listen. He just doesn't understand that all his generosity is sometimes—well—misplaced."

"I hope he won't be offended."

"Of course he won't." Abigail smiled. "He'll just be embarrassed when I get to say 'I told you so.' I'll love it." Turning to the cook's helper, Abigail said, "Jenson, please inform Grace that she won't be required to tend our guests. Tell her they are from the independent west, and they are used to doing things for themselves."

David had been previously committed to a business meeting, so he didn't join them for supper. LisBeth and Augusta got reacquainted with Abigail in her Philadelphia role as a grand hostess and were delighted to learn that the Abigail Braddock of Philadelphia was no different from the Abigail they knew from Lincoln. She handled a number of servants with ease, and she was obviously accustomed to three forks and as many spoons at every meal. Still, she was the same warm and loving person who had stayed at Hathaway House.

Sarah flitted between being a friend of the guests and her role as housekeeper-in-training with amazing ease. She relaxed into familiarity when she could and maintained an appropriate deference in the presence of other servants.

The first evening, Augusta and LisBeth retired early. LisBeth heard hoofbeats on the street below and went into the private parlor where she could look out a window onto the street. She saw David emerge from a fine carriage.

With a start she realized that Augusta was watching her watch David. Settling into an overstuffed chair, Augusta offered, "I'm sure he'll be disappointed that you've already retired, LisBeth."

LisBeth sat down and sighed. "I'm glad we came up early, Augusta. All this is just a bit too—grand. I'm homesick. And I've a knot in my stomach just thinking about the balls and dinners Abigail has planned. I don't know the first thing about such grand living."

"Just be yourself." Augusta advised. "You'll make some mistakes, but if you're honest, those that are worth their salt will appreciate you and like you. The ones that raise their eyebrows and 'tut-tut' your frontier ways aren't worth worrying about."

"I just don't want to do anything wrong to embarrass David."

"David won't be embarrassed by you, LisBeth," Augusta said with conviction before adding, "and *I'm* pleased to see that you're getting on with your life, dear."

LisBeth sighed. "I'm trying, Augusta."

A soft knock came at the door. Augusta answered it and brought in a huge bouquet of red roses. "Delivered by another servant—I don't remember seeing this one before. How many do you suppose they have?"

LisBeth retrieved the card from the flowers and read aloud, "Welcome to the ladies from Lincoln. D." Turning to Augusta she smiled. "I guess David has his own servant too. Since I sent mine away, and I have to do the abominable task of turning down my bed myself, I think I'll get started!" She laughed and tossed the card on a small table that sat by the doorway.

The Christmas season in Philadelphia was an extravaganza of sights and smells and tastes. The mansion was decked with splendor. Evergreen bows and great red velvet ribbons wrapped the banisters of the staircase and spilled over every mantle in the house. A few days before Christmas a ten-foot blue spruce was hauled into the parlor. LisBeth and Sarah were joined by Abigail and Augusta, and the four women spent the entire day cutting elaborate paper ornaments and tying ribbons and feathers and dried roses to every branch.

Tom presented them with an enormous gold-foil angel for the top. "The wing's torn, but it'll still be all right, won't it?" Tom said with concern.

David had just come in to admire the tree, and he hoisted Tom up to place the angel in its rightful place at the top of the tree. "It's *more* than just all right, Tom," he insisted. "It's the best angel this house has ever had. Wait until you see this tree on Christmas morning," David added. "We'll have every branch tipped with a lighted candle."

"Will we have presents too?"

"Tom!" Sarah implored, embarrassed.

David laughed. "You bet we'll have presents, Tom! Mother and I can't wait for Christmas this year. It's going to be wonderful!"

Augusta and LisBeth went with the Braddocks to balls and the opera, to church and concerts. Every morning LisBeth and Augusta slept until a fashionable hour, recovering from the previous late evening. They awoke to tea and toast served on silver trays by Sarah, who they usually convinced to sit down and eat with them. The breakfast hour was followed by reading and writing letters. David had somehow arranged for the Lincoln paper to be mailed to Augusta, "The dear boy," Augusta enthused, as she scanned the papers and fretted over an increase in business at the Cadman House.

At lunch, Tom Biddle usually bounded into the room and recited his morning lessons. He was enthusiastic about his upcoming holiday break from school and loudly critical of his strict tutor, Mr. Powers.

Every afternoon Abigail went calling or was called upon. Augusta and LisBeth sometimes accompanied her, but Augusta spent many days in the library with David, planning and replanning her new hotel. While they talked, LisBeth read. She ran her hands lovingly over the shelves of leather-bound books and despaired of enough time to enjoy them all.

David Braddock was charming and attentive without being overbearing. He made suggestions for the hotel with honest humility and respect for Augusta's business acumen. The new hotel was to have sixty-two rooms. Augusta and David planned every detail, including the advertisement to be placed in the *Daily State Journal* announcing its opening.

The new Hathaway House Hotel
The most select hotel in the city.
Augusta Hathaway & LisBeth Baird, Proprietors

New Brick Building—Steam Heating—All Modern Conveniences—Everything Genuinely First-Class—Rates, $3.00 Per Day—Special Rates Available to Parties Stopping Several Days and to Regular Boarders—Corner 8th & P Streets—Only One Block from the Depot—Free Baggage Handling for Our Guests.

Augusta had plans for Joseph's livery, as well. "Of course we'll move it. I want him right next to me, as always. I bought enough land for it. I want to offer my customers the best stabling in town." And so, another ad was prepared, to be adorned by a drawing of a fine horse.

Joseph Freeman,
Owner of Freeman's Barn,
Livery, Feed, and Boarding Stables.
Dealer in Fancy Horses.

Turns Out the Most Stylish Single or Double Rigs in the West.
The Prices Are Made So Reasonable That It Is Cheaper to
Hire from Freeman Than to Keep a Rig of Your Own.

LisBeth read the ads and commented, "What's this about Joseph being a dealer in fancy horses, Augusta? He won't like that. It promises something he can't deliver."

David answered. "Well, LisBeth, it seems that Augusta has an interest in bringing some new bloodlines to Nebraska. We're going to work out a plan where I'll bring out my stallion in the spring when Mother and I come to open up the house. I'll stable him at Joseph's livery and—" David blushed at the frank talk and didn't finish the sentence.

"You'll have to take the stallion out to Jim Callaway's, David. Joseph keeps his best mares out there. He's been trying to improve his stock already with Jim's help." LisBeth smiled primly and apologized. "I'm sorry if I've shocked you with my open conversation about such private matters, Mr. Braddock. You must realize that we frontier women don't have the same sensibilities as your refined ladies here in the city."

David laughed heartily and LisBeth decided that she liked him immensely. She began looking forward to his return from business luncheons. She especially enjoyed the afternoons in the library when he invariably ended up discussing business and politics with Augusta.

One afternoon when Augusta went shopping with Abigail, David went into his library to find LisBeth curled up in a chair reading. He flushed with pleasure and immediately sat down across from her. "I hope you'll enjoy the ball at the Grants' this evening, LisBeth."

LisBeth laid her book aside and looked out the window with a sigh. "I'm sure it will be fine."

"Just fine? Don't you *like* social evenings?"

"Oh, I'm just homesick, I guess." LisBeth brightened. "I must sound like an ungrateful brat to you, David. I'm sorry. We've had a lovely visit, and I thank you for outdoing yourself to see that we were properly feted. It's just," LisBeth hesitated, "all a bit grand for me—that's all. We settlers don't really fit into grand Philadelphia society—Augusta with her booming voice and opinions." LisBeth chuckled. "I thought Rebecca Braxton was going to faint last evening when Augusta began to talk to the *men* about politics. I'm sure that just isn't done here in Philadelphia."

David smiled indulgently. "Perhaps it should be."

LisBeth smiled back. "Perhaps it should. But I don't think Augusta will be the one to convince your friends of that." She got up and walked to the window to look out into the darkening street.

"What else, LisBeth? What about *you*? Has someone done something to make you feel that you're not welcome?"

LisBeth shook her head. "Oh, no. Everyone's been very gracious, really." She turned her back to the window. "As soon as they learned that I was a military widow, when they heard about Mac being at Little Big Horn," LisBeth smiled wistfully, "well, it rather romanticizes the shabby black dress."

"You're not shabby, LisBeth."

LisBeth smiled again. "By comparison to Rebecca Braxton and all your elegant friends, I'm quite shabby, David. Now if *they* were widows, they'd have the latest fashions made up in black silk, trimmed with black jet buttons and beads. I don't mean they'd be insincere. They're all just very—different. They've been raised by two parents in surroundings very different from mine. It shows. I'm not saying they are better than we Lincolnites, but face it, I'm not exactly *fashionable*."

David moved closer to her. "I don't care if you're fashionable or not. You're a fine woman. You've been through a lot, and you deserve every good thing that comes your way."

LisBeth looked out the window and was quiet for a long time. When David spoke up again, she jumped. He reached out to turn her face toward him. "Where did you go? What are you thinking?"

"I was just trying to picture what Mama would say about this grand life I've been living these past few weeks. She would be wondering what all these fine people do to make a difference.

And can't you just imagine Jim Callaway at one of your dinners introducing himself? 'Yes, ma'am—I'm Jim Callaway—no ma'am, just plain Jim Callaway—call me Jim.'"

David was careful with the new topic. "Jim might be out of place here, but he's a good man. People would eventually see past 'plain Jim,' and they'd like him."

"Yes, they would," LisBeth agreed.

A servant quietly knocked, opened the door, and announced that dinner was served. After the main course, LisBeth rose abruptly and excused herself. "I hope you won't take offense, Mrs. Braddock, but I don't think I'm up to a social evening. I'd just like to rest if that's all right." LisBeth went upstairs and changed into her nightgown. She turned out the gaslight in her room and sat by the window looking out at the golden circles of light cast by the gas streetlights on the cobblestones below.

It was Christmas Eve, and Lisbeth found herself longing for the narrow streets of Lincoln. She smiled at the memory of Agnes Bond's weak soprano voice trying to sing the descant she attempted at every Christmas Eve service at the Congregational Church in Lincoln. Closing her eyes, LisBeth imagined the candlelit church and the scent of evergreen. Folks would crowd into the pews, and if it had snowed, the aroma of the evergreen would soon by challenged by the smell of wet wool and leather.

Pastor Copeland would be climbing into the pulpit about now to retell the story of shepherds and angels. And maybe a tall, redheaded farmer would have found his way into town to slide into the back pew.

Christmas morning began with a boy's loud whoop just outside LisBeth's door and a "Ssshhhhh" from what LisBeth knew must be Sarah. LisBeth jumped out of bed, pulled on her wrapper, and ran to her door. Peeking out into the hallway she whispered at Sarah, who was already dressed and motioned her and Tom into her room. Her eyes sparkling, she presented each with a small package.

"This is a secret, you two—from me, to you. It's not much."

Tom was already tearing into the paper and exclaiming over a small stack of gigantic feathers.

"Jim Callaway assured me that they're honest-to-goodness eagle feathers, Tom."

Sarah had already opened her package and was fingering a small beaded pouch. "The children at the mission made it, Sarah. I thought you might be able to use it on your chatelaine." Looking at the ornate chatelaine that was clipped onto Sarah's waist, LisBeth said doubtfully, "I didn't realize that you'd be dressing so fancy. You have a *silver* one."

"It's beautiful, LisBeth," Sarah said, tying the small pouch through an opening in the silver filigree. "And a perfect size for my thimble. Thank you."

Sarah and Tom grinned simultaneously and Tom demanded, "Can I go get it *now*, Sarah?" Sarah nodded and Tom was out the door.

When he returned, he was carrying a small package that proved to be a new Bible. LisBeth chuckled as she fingered the pages. "I think *someone* is trying to tell me something! This is the *third* Bible I've been given in the last two years." Then looking at Sarah and Tom she hastened to add, "But it's the first one that's *just mine*. Thank you. And Merry Christmas!"

Their private celebration was over, and Sarah hastened downstairs to begin preparing her first elaborate Christmas morning breakfast. Tom followed her into the kitchen. In no time he had folded newspaper into a hat into which he stuck the eagle feathers. When the Braddocks and their guests descended for breakfast, Tom was running up and down the drive, pretending to be an Indian.

The grand entrance into the parlor after breakfast presented a breathtaking sight of the tree ablaze with candles, just as David had promised. For the next hour, gifts were given and received with appropriate Philadelphian restraint, until LisBeth opened her gift from Abigail and David

Braddock. Abigail presented the gift with an apology. "I hope you won't think us too familiar, dear, but—" Not knowing what else to say, she sat down and watched while LisBeth unwrapped the most elegant black gown she had ever seen. Everything was there—the yards of silk, the black jet buttons, the heavy beading—everything she had described to David that day in the library. Her eyes shone with pleasure and then clouded with tears as she remembered just why the dress had to be black. Still, there was no bitterness in the tears, and LisBeth realized at that moment that time was, indeed, healing the wounds of the past.

Every gift had been opened and breakfast served when the doorbell rang. David had given his butler the day off and answered the bell himself. A very hurried delivery boy tipped his hat and charged up the street without waiting for a tip.

David brought the package to the table. "It's for you, Lis-Beth."

LisBeth saw the return address and excused herself, leaving everyone at the table to wonder. Retreating to the library, she sat down and carefully unwrapped it. When David opened the door to check on her, she was absentmindedly looking out the window. In her lap was a mound of calico. Turkey red calico. Just a few yards.

Chapter 34

Cleave unto the LORD your God, as
ye have done unto this day.

Joshua 23:8

On Christmas Eve day, a half-frozen farmer rode into Lincoln and climbed stiffly down from his horse in front of Freeman's Livery. He slid back the main door of the stable and made himself at home, unsaddling his horse and rubbing him down before walking to the back of the stable and pounding on Joseph Freeman's door. When there was no answer, Jim Callaway went in and stoked the fire in the small stove in the corner of the room. Removing his boots, he sat on a chair and stretched out his legs, wriggling his toes and waiting for his socks to dry before he pulled his boots back on and went out to break the ice in the water buckets that hung in each stall.

As Jim got to the last water bucket, a familiar voice called from the back door, "You the new stable hand?"

Jim turned around and grinned at Joseph. "Hey, Joseph. Merry Christmas."

Joseph shivered. "Saw the smoke from the stove. Thought Asa Green done got sick of his Mama raggin' at him and come back to work. I gave him today and tomorrow off 'cause I don't expect much business. Things are slow in town."

Jim picked up a pitchfork and began to muck out an empty stall. "I just came in to check on things." He deliberately turned his back on Joseph and tried to ask nonchalantly, "Anything new in town?"

"She ain't wrote since she left. Haven't heard a thing, Jim. Guess that means there's no engagement—leastways, not yet."

The knot in Jim's stomach relaxed a little, and he grinned at Joseph. "All right, I confess. I couldn't stand it out at the homestead—alone—thinking—"

"Trust in the Lord, Jim, trust in the Lord."

"I'm trying. I know the right verses to read, and I've been reading them too—at all hours of the night, since I'm not sleeping too well." Jim took a deep breath and stabbed at the straw at his feet. "It's hard to trust the Lord about some things. I can trust him fine about the crops and the animals and even about the finances for the homestead. But trusting him to bring LisBeth back to me after she's seen all that fancy living," Jim shook his head, "there's not a woman alive wouldn't want a life like that."

"There's not a woman alive wouldn't want a fine man like you to share her life with, son," Joseph reassured him. " *'Trust in the LORD with all thine heart, and lean not unto thine own understanding.'* "

"I'm trying, Joseph."

Joseph smiled wisely. "You know, the Bible says that *'the just shall live by faith.'* Look at it this way. The Lord is just giving you a chance to live by faith. He's growing you up a little while he makes you wait."

"Then I got some powerful growing pains. I haven't been able to eat a decent meal since the day she left. I made a grand speech about how I wanted her to go, how I wanted her to have no regrets."

"And now?"

"Now I wish I'd run to that train the day they left and made a fool of myself begging her to stay here."

Joseph laughed. "You got it bad, boy."

Jim smiled. "You got that right."

"Well, come on back here and let's get out the checkerboard. You can blabber on about it as much as you like—as long as you let me beat you a few times."

The two men retreated to Joseph's room where they played

checkers until hunger rumbled in the quiet room. Joseph brought out the fixings for a supper of cold cheese sandwiches and beans. When the church bells began ringing to announce the Christmas Eve services, Jim looked up and asked, "You goin' to church tonight, Joseph?"

"I thought about it."

Jim asked, "Mind if I come along?"

"To *my* church? Why don't you go on over to the Congregational Church with the other white folks."

"That mean you don't want me in your church?"

Joseph shook his head. "'Course not, Jim. It just ain't usual, that's all. Truth is, there ain't *never* been a white man inside, unless you count Joe Heiner, the undertaker. He come in once to claim old Keefer Douglas—dropped cold stone dead one morning while he was takin' the offering. Caused quite a stir."

The two men shared a hearty laugh before Jim sobered up and said, "Well, Joseph, it's like this. It just seems like I ought to be in church tonight. And if Lizzie and Mrs. Hathaway were here, I'd be right beside them over there at the Congregational Church. But I came into town to get away from being alone."

"Then come on, son." Joseph slapped Jim on the back and shook his head. "Gonna be some heads turnin' at the A.M.E. Church tonight." Joseph chuckled. "Can't wait to see Reverend Field's face!"

The service at the Congregational Church that night was just as LisBeth pictured it from Philadelphia. There were candles aglow, and evergreen boughs, and Agnes Bond's uncertain soprano voice sounding above the choir in a sincere but decidedly off-pitch descant. However, her vision of Jim sliding into the back pew didn't come true. Jim Callaway was at the A.M.E. Church a few blocks away, standing in a pew with Joseph Freeman. The A.M.E. choir members sang familiar carols in unfamiliar rhythms. Jim watched them, fascinated. They in turn kept an eye on the white boy who stood next to Joseph, self-consciously trying to join in the service. When Reverend Field rose to give his Christmas message, he invited the congregation to rise and join him in prayer. Jim closed his eyes and began to pray for his Lizzie. All around him sounded "Yes, Lord" and "Amen." He heard the voices praising God and, in his loneliness, was comforted.

Christmas, 1877, was especially significant for three people.

Jim Callaway realized that the fellowship of believers could reach over the artificial barriers that society created and soothe a man's soul.

LisBeth King Baird realized that an uncut piece of turkey red cotton meant more to her than a finely tailored silk dress.

And a wild Lakota named Soaring Eagle realized that what Carrie Brown had said was true—Jesus loved him.

CHAPTER 35

O LORD, Thou art my God; I will exalt thee, I will praise thy name; for thou hast done wonderful things; thy counsels of old are faithfulness and truth.

Isaiah 25:1

David Braddock kept his promise. The entire time that LisBeth and Augusta were guests at the Braddock mansion in Philadelphia, he didn't press LisBeth about marriage. He wisely resisted the urge to put an expensive ring under the Christmas tree and waited until his guests' trunks were packed and being loaded into a wagon to be trundled to the railroad station.

Only when Sarah and Tom Biddle had said their good-byes and stepped onto the porch to hug Augusta did he finally catch LisBeth by the hand and lead her into the library.

LisBeth was wearing the exquisite black gown Abigail Braddock had had made for her.

"You look lovely, LisBeth. I'm going to miss you."

"Thank you, David."

"Will you miss me?"

"Abigail said you'd be coming early in the spring to open the house in Lincoln."

"Will you miss me?"

"I hope you'll stay in touch. Please write."

"That's not what I asked you, LisBeth. Will you miss me?"

LisBeth looked down at clenched hands and whispered, "Yes. I will miss you."

There was relief in his voice. "I promised not to press you."

"Yes, you did. Please keep that promise."

"I just wanted to make sure that you know I haven't said anything because of that promise, not because I've changed. Nothing's changed, LisBeth. I still want the same things I mentioned before."

LisBeth blushed and took a deep breath as David hurried to finish. "May I kiss you good-bye?"

LisBeth raised her eyes to David's and wished they were gray-green. Quickly she kissed him on the cheek. "Good-bye, David," she whispered and fled.

Augusta and LisBeth had arranged to spend a few days in St. Louis before returning to Lincoln. David Braddock had recommended an architect there who specialized in hotel design, and LisBeth was eager to visit Carrie Brown. The two women easily made their way through the melee in Union Station and arrived at the Choteau Hotel with time and energy for a walk along the riverfront.

Augusta had arranged for a meeting with Davisson Kennedy at his office the very next day. In spite of the cold, LisBeth hired an open carriage and admired the old cathedral and other fine buildings along the waterfront as the carriage made its way to Carrie's new home.

As the door to the Jennings's modest home opened, two bright blue eyes peeked out from behind her grandmother's skirts and smiled a welcome. At sight of LisBeth, Carrie stepped from behind her grandmother and held out her hand solemnly. "Thank you for coming, LisBeth." Carrie turned immediately to her grandmother. "Mrs. Baird told me to call her LisBeth a long time ago, Grandmother. It's still all right, isn't it?"

Lucy Jennings nodded her head. "Of course it is, Carrie." Turning to LisBeth she added, "Thank you for taking time to see Carrie, Mrs. Baird. She's talked of nothing else since you wrote to say you would come."

Carrie wasted no time in pursuing her agenda. "Well. It's like this, LisBeth. God called my Mama to heaven, so I can't go back to Santee now. I have to finish school first. *Then* I'll go back." Carrie reached up and removed the cross and chain from about her neck. She held it out to LisBeth. "Now I have to grow up before I go back, and I promised Mr. Soaring Eagle that I'd give this back to him in the spring. Since I can't go back yet, I need a grown-up to take this back to him. I promised. Mama said we always have to keep our promises."

LisBeth fingered the cross and chain and said, "Yes, Carrie. We do have to keep our promises."

"Now, Mr. Soaring Eagle has Ida May. And you can tell him to keep her for me. Ida May's a prairie doll, and she might not like it here in St. Louis. I figure if I tell Mr. Soaring Eagle to keep Ida May until I come back, then he'll know I'm going to keep my promise and come back. But I'm just a little girl. I shouldn't keep his gold necklace, do you think?"

LisBeth thought for a moment. "Well, Carrie, I think that if you kept it, Soaring Eagle would understand. But if you want me to give it back to him, I will. I told Miss Charity that I would come back with more clothing for the children in the spring. As soon as the weather breaks, I'm going to do that."

"Are you going to see Mr. Soaring Eagle, then?"

"Yes, Carrie, I am, if he will see me."

"Is he really your brother, LisBeth?"

"Yes, I think so." Then LisBeth asked, "Are you certain that it's my picture in that locket he wears?"

"It sure is."

"Did he say he took it from my husband himself?"

"Yes, ma'am. He said it like he was real sad about it."

LisBeth took a deep breath and looked at Lucy Jennings, who was inspecting her ceiling in a vain attempt to hide the amazement at the conversation she was hearing.

"What is Soaring Eagle like?"

"Well, at first he acted mean—no, that's not right—he was just real serious and *quiet,* and all the grown-ups thought he was mean. But I knew he wasn't."

"How did you know?"

"Oh," Carrie shrugged her shoulders, "I don't know. I saw

him look at me, and when I just walked up and said hello, his eyes smiled. He didn't smile on the outside, but I could see that he was smiling inside. I decided he wasn't mean. He was just lonesome. Sometimes when folks are quiet, other folks get scared. Especially when it's an Indian. Reverend Riggs says that people will always think the Indians are savages as long as they dress like Indians. That's why they have to cut their hair and wear uniforms at the school—so folks will pay attention to what they say and do and not always think they are savages. Well, anyway—Soaring Eagle is quiet and he still dresses like an Indian. But he's pretty, LisBeth, like you. There's feathers and beads—he's got a whole row of thimbles hanging from the fringe across his shirt. And locks of hair. But he said they aren't scalps. He said it's hair from people he loves. Even from his favorite horses."

"What else has he told you about?"

"Gosh. There's lots of things. Can you stay for lunch?"

LisBeth hesitated, but Lucy Jennings was not about to miss out on the unbelievable story unfolding before her. "Please, Mrs. Baird. Stay. We'd be happy to have you."

Carrie willingly chattered the afternoon away, telling Lis-Beth everything she could remember about Soaring Eagle. LisBeth drank in every detail and asked questions until even Carrie was worn out. Finally, late in the afternoon, LisBeth reached over to pat Carrie's hand and said with emotion, "Carrie, I don't know how I will ever thank you for the gift you have given me today. You may not understand this now, but someday you will. My mama died last year and my husband too. I thought I was all alone in the world. I knew I had a brother named Soaring Eagle somewhere, but I thought it was impossible that I would ever know him. Now, you have given me my brother." LisBeth paused before asking, "Do you think he is at all like me?"

Carrie thought hard. "I think he's confused about things." Her face brightened. "But he'll be okay by springtime. I been praying for him, and once he knows about Jesus, I think he'll be okay. *Then* he'll be like you. As long as you know Jesus too."

Carrie looked up at LisBeth. "You *do* know Jesus, don't you, LisBeth?"

Lucy broke in. "Carrie Brown—what a question!"

Carrie was unabashed. "Well, Grandma, if she don't know Jesus, then she ought to go with us to hear Mr. Moody preach. You been inviting all sorts of people. Why don't you invite LisBeth?"

Lucy Jennings laughed and shook her head, turning to LisBeth to apologize. "Walter and I have been helping in one of the inquiry rooms at the meetings. Have you heard Mr. Moody speak, Mrs. Baird?"

When LisBeth said no, Lucy explained briefly. "He's a great evangelist, and he's been here in St. Louis conducting meetings for a few weeks. The results have been wonderful. God has truly blessed. Walter and I have often regretted that we did not give ourselves to mission work in our youth. Although it surprised us, Rachel's commitment was always something we rejoiced in. Now we have had an opportunity to serve the Lord right here in our own city. If you would be at all interested, we'd be honored to have you go with us this evening."

LisBeth accepted. "I'd love to go, Mrs. Jennings. Thank you so much for inviting me. I'm sure Augusta will want to go as well. She never misses an opportunity for a new experience. Is this the same Mr. Moody who conducted services in Philadelphia before the Centennial? The gentleman that even President Grant and his cabinet made time to hear?"

"The same. He conducts a very dignified service. There have been amazing results, but he allows none of the hysteria that sometimes accompanies revival meetings. He's a most powerful speaker, quite eloquent. And yet, the subject—which is always the gospel—quite covers up the speaker. I think you'll find it to be one of the happiest meetings you have ever attended. There is warmth and, well, a feeling of sunlight in every meeting. The preaching begins at eight o'clock. We'll be around for you and Mrs. Hathaway about seven o'clock—every chair in the hall is usually filled by half past seven."

Carrie interrupted. "You won't forget about taking the necklace back to Mr. Soaring Eagle, will you, LisBeth?"

LisBeth knelt down and clutched the necklace over her heart. "I won't forget, Carrie. I promise you that if Soaring Eagle will see me, the very first thing that I will do will be to give him back this necklace. And if he doesn't want to see me, I'll leave it with Charity Bond."

"He'll want to see you, LisBeth."

"How can you be so certain?"

Carrie looked at LisBeth as if she were a simpleton. "'Cause you're his *sister*. You're *family*. When Mother told me I would be living with Gram and Gramps, she explained it. Families ought to be *together*."

LisBeth and Augusta rode with the Jennings to Moody's meeting and were astounded by the turnout. Augusta commented, "I haven't seen an acre of people in one place since the Centennial!"

The meeting was held in an unfinished warehouse that seemed to LisBeth to be larger than Union Station. A choir directed by Moody's well-known partner, Ira Sankey, filled the air with the sounds of familiar hymns as people crowded onto benches. When sufficient numbers had arrived, Sankey directed the crowd to several hymns in the tiny Gospel Hymns booklets that had been placed on every chair in the hall.

Promptly at eight o'clock, Mr. Moody stepped out and, planting his hands on the rail that ran along the front of the platform, began to speak. He was only about 5'6" tall, solid, and stout, with a full black beard and thick, luxuriant hair. Augusta leaned over and whispered, "He looks like a man of business—not at all what I imagined."

"Friends," he began, "The title of my message this evening is simply 'The Gospel.' I read from First Corinthians, chapter fifteen, verse one. *'I declare unto you the gospel which I preached unto you, which also ye have received, and wherein ye stand.'* I do not think there is a word in the English language so little understood as the word *gospel.* We hear it every day, and we have heard it from our earliest childhood, yet there are many people, and even as many Christians, who do not really know what it means. The word *gospel* means good news. When the angels came down to proclaim the tidings, what did they say to those shepherds on the plains of Bethlehem? *'Behold I bring you* sad *tidings?'* No! *'Behold, I bring you* bad *news?'* No! *'Behold, I bring you* good *tidings of great joy, which shall be to all people.'*

Moody spoke with earnestness and simplicity. LisBeth listened, longing for joy in her own heart.

"Before I was converted, I used to look on death as a terrible monster. He used to throw his dark shadow across my path."

LisBeth remembered getting the news of Little Big Horn and getting off the train to find that her mother was gone. Yes, she had also looked on death as a terrible monster.

Moody continued, "I felt a coward then. I thought of the cold hand of death feeling for the cords of life. But that is changed now. The grave has lost its terror."

LisBeth wondered and wished that the grave held no terror for her.

"As I go on toward heaven I can shout, *'O death! where is thy sting?'* That last enemy has been overcome, and I can look on death as a crushed victim. All that death can get now is this old Adam, and I do not care how quickly I get rid of it. I shall get a glorified body, a resurrection body, a body much better than this. The gospel has made an enemy a friend. What a glorious thought, that when you die you but sink into the arms of Jesus, to be borne to the land of everlasting rest! *'To die,'* the apostle says, *'is gain.'*"

As she listened to Moody describe how his own view of death had changed, LisBeth was reminded of the joy that Augusta had said lit Jesse's face when she was discovered, dead, in her bed. Augusta had once said that it was the very same smile that they saw when Jesse talked about Rides the Wind.

Moody was continuing, "Another terrible enemy was sin. The gospel tells me my sins are all put away in Christ. Out of love to me, He has taken all my sins and cast them behind His back."

LisBeth thought about Jim Callaway and the joy in his face when he described the night he had realized that his past was forgiven. Jim Callaway viewed God as his friend. LisBeth longed to know God as her friend. Was there sin standing in the way? *I've been so angry at God. So rebellious. So bitter.* LisBeth was convicted that perhaps she had hung onto the bitterness and the anger for so long that they had, indeed, become sin.

"There is another enemy that used to trouble me a great deal—judgment. I used to look forward to the terrible day when I should be summoned before God. I could not tell whether I should hear the voice of Christ saying, *'Depart from Me, ye cursed,'* or whether it would be, *'Enter thou into the joy of thy Lord.'* The gospel tells me that is already settled. *'There is therefore now no condemnation to them which are in Christ Jesus.'* I am not coming into judgment for sin. God's Word has settled it. Christ was judged for me, and died in my stead, and I go free."

Moody spoke with compassion and his message pierced LisBeth's heart. She wanted her inner enemies to be conquered. She wanted the inner peace that she'd seen in the lives of Jesse King and Jim Callaway, the kind of peace that Mr. Moody was talking about. She wanted to know that she belonged to God. She decided that that meant she had to give up the bitterness and the anger.

"Sinner, would you be safe tonight? Would you be free from the condemnation of the sins that are past, from the power of the temptations that are to come? Then take your stand on the Rock of Ages. Let death, let the grave, let the judgment come. The victory is Christ's and yours through him."

Victory. LisBeth pondered the word and thought, *Yes, God, I want victory. I want the struggle inside to be finished. I need help to get through it. I want to know You. I want to know that You will help me just like You helped Mama and Jim.* Wondering if he would forgive her, LisBeth held up her anger and her bitterness to

God. Then, she turned her attention to the great evangelist as he offered God's answer to her unspoken prayer.

"It is a free gospel; any one may have it. If you would like Christ's own Word for it, come with me to that scene in Jerusalem where the disciples are bidding him farewell. Calvary with all its horrors is behind him; Gethsemane is over and Pilate's judgment hall. He has passed the grave and is about to take his place at the right hand of the Father. The hour of parting has come. Is he thinking about himself in these closing moments? No, he is thinking of you. You imagined he would think of those who loved him? No, sinner, he thought of you then. He thought of his enemies, those who shunned him, those who despised him, those who killed him.

"He gives His disciples His farewell charge, *'Go ye into* all *the world, and preach the gospel to* every *creature.'* I can imagine Peter saying, 'Lord, do you really mean that we shall preach the gospel to *every* creature?'

"'Yes, Peter.'

"'Shall we go back to Jerusalem and preach the gospel to those Jerusalem sinners who murdered you?'

"'Yes, Peter, go back and tarry there until you are endued with power from on high. Offer the gospel to them first. Go search out that man who spat in my face and tell him I forgive him; there is nothing in my heart but love for him. Go search out the man who put that cruel crown of thorns on my brow; tell him I will have a crown ready for him in my kingdom, if he will accept salvation; there shall not be a thorn in it, and he shall wear it for ever and ever in the kingdom of his Redeemer. Find that man who took the reed from my hand, and smote my head, driving the thorns deeper into my brow. If he will accept salvation as a gift, I will give him a scepter, and he shall sway it over the nations of the earth. Yes, I will give him to sit with Me upon my throne. Go seek that man who struck Me with the palm of his hand; find him and preach the gospel to him; tell him that the blood of Jesus Christ cleanseth him from all sin, and my blood was shed for him freely. Go seek out that poor soldier who drove the spear into my side; tell him that there is a nearer way to my heart than that. Tell him that I forgive him freely; and tell him I will make him a soldier of the cross, and my banner over him is love.'"

As the great evangelist drew his word picture, LisBeth pictured the beloved soldier in her past and the battle where he was killed and the brother who was involved. The message of forgiveness spilled over her. For the first time she considered the Christ who had been so badly mutilated and yet had asked God to forgive his tormentors. LisBeth was weeping as the great evangelist came to the end of his message. Augusta gripped her hand and felt her tremble as Moody finished his sermon.

"I thank God I can preach the gospel. I thank God for the 'whosoevers' of the invitation of Christ. *'God so loved the world that He gave His only begotten Son, that* whosoever *believeth on him should not perish, but have everlasting life,'* and 'whosoever *will, let him take the water of life freely.'"*

The last remnant of LisBeth King Baird's doubting fell away. The final bits of bitterness and anger were cast out of her life. They were replaced by a flood of peace and joy. Finally, she was able to believe and to take the water of life. In later years, LisBeth would look back on the service and say, "That night, the Lord satisfied my thirsty soul and filled it with what is good."

When the meeting concluded, LisBeth and Augusta bid the Jennings good night and rode back to the hotel in silence. LisBeth looked up at the clear, star-filled sky and was suddenly filled with such joy that she thought her heart might burst. She tried to explain it to Augusta but found that she could not.

"I'm just so *happy,* Augusta. I don't feel bitter or angry anymore. I really think that God will be my friend now, and it's *good* to be alive. I can't wait to get home to tell Jim about it."

The moment she heard herself speak Jim Callaway's name, she stopped abruptly and looked at Augusta with amazement.

"What is it, dear?"

"I just realized it. It's been there all along, but I didn't want to see it."

"Yes?"

"And I think it's all right, Augusta. Somehow, I know it's all right with Mac."

"*What* is all right with Mac, LisBeth?"

"That I love Jim Callaway." LisBeth smiled broadly and repeated it. "I love Jim Callaway!"

The morning after her conversion, LisBeth Baird called on Lucy Jennings to request the name of a good dressmaker. Lucy provided the name, and LisBeth took a few yards of turkey red calico to her shop and convinced the young woman to make an exception and promise a finished dress in only a few days. Augusta and LisBeth spent a few extra days in St. Louis, and then LisBeth sent a telegram to Joseph Freeman in Lincoln, Nebraska.

When the train pulled into Lincoln, LisBeth tried not to look. She took great care to arrange the pleats of her skirt and beat at the dust that had collected on the hem of her turkey red calico dress. As Augusta descended from the car behind her, LisBeth bent to pick up her satchel. The tips of two scarred boots came into view. They were trail worn and hadn't been polished.

LisBeth stood up abruptly, her eyes following the line of the rumpled denim work pants, up each button of the blue flannel work shirt, to the slightly cleft chin, the aristocratic nose, and finally, the gray-green eyes. She waited, but Jim didn't speak. His eyes were serious and cool, and they held the flicker of a question.

Standing on tiptoe, LisBeth leaned towards the broad chest and whispered, "You may not be rich, and you may just be a simple farmer, but you're my Jim. You love me, and you love my Lord, and that's all I'll ever want. I've come home, Jim." To the shock of passersby, she kissed him on the cheek.

It was all Jim needed. The question went out of his gray-green eyes. They were flooded with warmth as he bent low to whisper something back. What he whispered was just for LisBeth's ears. But he called her Lizzie, and she loved the sound of it.

CHAPTER 36

Thou hast turned for me my mourning into dancing.

Psalm 30:11

It was after Christmas before the news of Rachel Brown's death reached the Santee Normal Training School. Charity told James and Martha Red Wing, who told John Thundercloud, expressing grave concern for Soaring Eagle.

"What will he do now, John? He seems to have found faith, but this is just one more loss for him. He'll never see little Carrie again. I know that our God knows what is best, but sometimes in my own human weakness, I look on things like this and wonder about it. It seems that God could have given Soaring Eagle some happiness before testing his faith."

"May I borrow one of your horses, James?" John wanted to know. "I'll find him and tell him."

John nodded. "He headed north along the creek."

"Pray for us. Pray that I'll say the right things." John leaped onto the borrowed horse and easily caught up with Soaring Eagle. The two rode side by side for a while, until Soaring Eagle said, "You must say what you have come to say, John. I know you have bad news. You try to act as if you are only on a ride, but the horse has been running hard, you hold the reins too tightly, and it is James Red Wing's horse."

With a silent prayer, John Thundercloud said, "Rachel Brown died just before Christmas, Soaring Eagle."

Soaring Eagle pulled his black mare up sharply and asked sadly, "And what will become of the little Red Bird?"

"She'll stay with her grandparents in St. Louis. It is said that they are good people and that they are happy to have her with them. She will have a good home."

Soaring Eagle looked at the horizon and took another deep breath. John Thundercloud watched him closely, and tried to offer comfort. "Rachel was happy to have made it home, Soaring Eagle. They said she just went away—like the snow melting in the spring. I am sorry I had to bring you this news. I know she was a good friend to you. I don't know why God lets these things happen. Sometimes there just don't seem to be any answers except that He is working things out for the good of those He loves. I don't know if that offers you any comfort, but I know that it's true."

The two dismounted and began to walk, and the black mare nuzzled Soaring Eagle's shoulder affectionately. He stopped to run his hands through her mane and began to talk.

"When I was a boy, my father died. In the way of my people, I cut off my hair and wailed with grief. There was an emptiness that no one could fill.

"When I was young, Walks the Fire was taken from among the people. I thought she was dead. Once again, I cut off my hair in grief. I slashed my arms and the emptiness inside me grew.

"When I was a man, my people were scattered. There was nothing to do but come here. I filled the emptiness inside with bitterness and anger."

Soaring Eagle looked at John Thundercloud and a faint smile came to his face. "I was filled with bitterness and anger. But Carrie Brown put her hand in mine and was my friend. Rachel Brown told me that God loved me. Now they are gone. I will wail and mourn. But I am not empty, John Thundercloud."

Soaring Eagle's eyes misted over. "You have said that Jesus promises that his children will see those that we love again. I will see Rachel and Carrie Brown again."

Thundercloulld responded, "I came here filled with advice for you, Soaring Eagle, thinking that I would have to encourage you to overcome bitterness and anger toward God. God's

Word says that *'if any man be in Christ, he is a new creature: old things are passed away; behold, all things are become new.'* When I look at you, I see a new creature."

Soaring Eagle agreed. "Yes, that is it. That is how I feel. Inside, there is something new." Leaping astride his mare, Soaring Eagle challenged, "Come, I will race you back to James Red Wing's. You will see how this little mare can run." And he was off, clinging to the sides of his pony as she darted across the prairie.

LisBeth spent the first two weeks of January writing letters. She sent them off with no small amount of prayer and waited nervously for replies.

January 15, 1878

Dear David,

Duplicity is not something I relish being accused of, and so I will make this letter a straightforward one. Jim Callaway has asked me to be his wife. He actually made his proposal before Augusta and I came to Philadelphia for the holidays. However, he forbad me to give an answer before I had spent the holiday with you and your mother. He wanted me to have every chance to experience the kind of life I was giving up if I accepted him.

David, please believe me when I tell you that I did not come to Philadelphia under pretense. I did not hold you up for comparison to someone else. I shall always think of you and your mother with great affection.

I know that you would prefer no detailed explanations of how my heart was turned to another. It would pain you and, not being an educated woman, I fear that my powers of communication would fall woefully short of expressing it all accurately.

It was after hearing the famous Mr. Moody preach in St. Louis that many things were brought to closure for me.

I hope that God will enable you to rejoice for me, David. I am finally, fully happy again after a long season of grief.

Please remember me to your mother with my fondest regards. Per-

haps it is a naivete on my part, but I will continue to hope that we will have the pleasure of both her and your company again when you are in Lincoln.

David, I wish you the greatest happiness. If this letter brings you sorrow, please know that I have written it with the best intentions. I truly believe that I am following God's will for my life. Since I believe that, I also believe that it would not have been his best for either one of us had I accepted your proposal. Believing those things, we must both conclude that He has a better plan for you, David. I will pray that He will hasten to reveal the better way to you, and that He will grant you wisdom and great happiness in the future.

Your sincere and devoted friend,

LisBeth King Baird

January 15, 1878

Dear Sarah,

This is a letter that pains me because I fear it may cause you pain, but I will pray that God will explain to your heart what I cannot and enable us to continue through life as the devoted sisters that we have become.

Sarah, you above all others know how very confused and lost I have been this past year and a half. MacKenzie and Mother's deaths set me afloat. It has taken a year and a half of love from those around me and love from God to finally and completely anchor me to the Rock of Ages.

When Augusta and I stopped in St. Louis to see poor little Carrie Brown, we found a happy child who was simply trusting Jesus for the future. That played a part in what was to occur. With Carrie's grandparents, we attended a service of the great evangelist D. L. Moody, and at that service all the things that Mother ever taught me finally made sense—for me.

Jim Callaway has often told me that my problems were centered on the fact that I was trying to live on my mother's faith. He said that I needed a faith of my own. Well, thanks to the grace of God at work through D. L. Moody, I have got a faith of my own, and now I know, I really know what Mother was talking about all those years. My own faith is a new one, and not so great as hers, but I think it is genuine, *and I am seeing differences every day in the way I respond to life. I am finally, fully at peace.*

God has not answered all the why's I have been asking, but He has given me the ability to accept that "all things work together for good," whether LisBeth King Baird understands the details or not. Jim says that I have finally understood what he meant when he talked about the "peace that passes understanding."

Already in my letter I have made two references to Jim Callaway, and now I must refer to him again, and I do it with a trembling hand. Sarah, I truly love you as my sister, and I pray that you believe me when I tell you that I don't mean to cause you pain. Jim Callaway has asked me to be his wife.

I hope that when you come in the spring you will allow me to tell you all about it. Paper and pen provide such an artificial means of communicating the greatest life experiences. I wanted to come and tell you this in person, but we are hurrying to get another donation ready for the mission, and I have promised Charity that it will be there as soon as the snows melt and travel is possible. Some of the children and families are in dire circumstances.

Sarah, can you forgive me? I know this news causes you pain. You have grown to be a woman since you first saw Jim Callaway. I am hoping that what you have felt for him was what we call a "crush." I am also hoping that God will enable you to be happy for us, and that this news will not separate you and me. Please, Sarah, write to me at once. I need to hear from you.

Your loving sister,
LisBeth

January 19, 1878

Dear Charity,

The ladies and I are working hard to collect another wagon full of clothing for your children. As soon as the weather will hold, we will start out.

I am looking forward to seeing you and to telling you all that has happened since we were at the mission last fall.

The greatest of these is that I have finally come to a fuller, more personal relationship with God. I will tell you the details when I see you, but now I believe I understand what it is that has motivated you to serve at the mission. The same faith has brought me comfort and started me on the road to a better life than I had hoped possible.

The other news is that Jim Callaway and I are to be married. That will require one evening of visiting in itself. I have confided in your mother. Does that surprise you? Really, Charity, she has become such a dear friend. Who would have thought it possible? Thank God for his working in our lives.

Last, I am writing to ask you to play a role in what I hope will be more great news for some future letter or diary page. Charity, could you ask Soaring Eagle if he would want to meet his sister in the spring? I don't know what the proper channels would be for such a meeting, or how it could be arranged. Perhaps Pastor Thundercloud could advise us? I have enclosed a note to Soaring Eagle. Please ask Pastor Thundercloud to read it and, if he thinks it appropriate, to give it to my brother as a preparation for our meeting.

I await your response with a hopeful heart, Charity.

In the Love of the Lamb,
LisBeth King Baird

January 19, 1878

Dear Soaring Eagle,

I have just written the three words that open this letter, and I find my hand trembling and I must wait and pray before adding more. To think that I am writing a letter to my Lakota brother is almost too strange to be believed. It is certainly a testimony to the fact that "God works in mysterious ways, his wonders to perform."

I am writing in hopes that God will perform yet another wonder, and that it will be a wonder for us both. I am coming to Santee as soon as the weather allows to distribute more clothing for the children at the school. It is a sincere effort, Soaring Eagle, but there is another and greater reason for my coming. I am hoping that you and I may at last meet. Last fall when I was at the mission and learned of your presence, I simply could not emotionally handle the revelation. In my selfishness, I didn't stop to even consider what the news of my presence must have meant for you. If you can forgive my selfishness and my weakness, I trust you and Pastor Thundercloud to arrange an appropriate time and place for us to meet.

I will most certainly be trembling with fear and emotion at that meeting, so I write to assure you that my emotions bear no trace of resentment toward you, Soaring Eagle. God has enabled me to forget those things that lay behind. I am trying to reach forward to those things that are ahead and I would like to do that with my brother at my side. If that is possible, please communicate through Charity Bond.

If you do not wish to see me, Soaring Eagle, I will understand. You did not choose to be raised by a white woman, and you did not choose the pain and confusion that that has no doubt brought into your own life. If you want to leave it behind you, I accept that. You owe me nothing. Go in peace, knowing that your sister will pray for you always.

Your sister,
LisBeth King Baird

Almost immediately LisBeth received a telegram from Charity Bond telling her that Soaring Eagle and Pastor Thundercloud would meet her in the spring.

It was a few weeks before LisBeth heard from Sarah. When Sarah's letter finally arrived, LisBeth went to her room and opened it with shaking hands.

Dearest LisBeth,

Of course I was surprised when you wrote, and, yes, somewhat shocked at the revelation of your engagement. But, LisBeth, how could you think that I would be anything but delighted? I admit to some attraction to Jim Callaway—he is, after all, a most attractive man. But working for the Braddocks and living in Philadelphia has presented new possibilities in life. I think you are right—I had a girlish crush on Jim Callaway. Now that I've matured I can thank God that He has given happiness to two of the people I care most about in life.

LisBeth, nothing will ever come between you and me—not if I can help it. I know there are girls who would let silly jealousies destroy their friendship, but please think better of me. I wish you and Jim nothing but the best. I am so glad to know that you are once again smiling

*and living instead of just enduring life, as Joseph Freeman used to say
of you and Jim.*

*I assume that you also wrote to Mr. Braddock although he would
of course not speak of it to me. He has been rather remote of late.*

*Mrs. Braddock only says, "David has had a disappointment,
Sarah. We must be especially kind to him. I'm certain he'll be his old
self in due time." She seems truly happy for you, LisBeth. She plans on
returning to Lincoln in the spring.*

*I regret that it took me so long to answer your letter. I'm certain it
caused you some concern. It took some thinking for me to sort through
things so that I could write you a letter that was open and honest and
reflected how I truly feel, rather than how I should feel.*

*This letter reflects my true heart. There is no duplicity in the words
when I say that I will be one of the happiest people in the church when
you make your way down the aisle to become Mrs. James Callaway.*

*Mrs. Braddock has said that we will open the house in Lincoln on
April 1. She wants to be there in time to direct more plantings on the
grounds, and I know that an invitation to your wedding would be welcomed. She is much too kind a lady to want anything but the best for
you, and she is genuinely fond of you.*

With loving regards, your sister-in-heart,
Sarah Biddle

CHAPTER 37

Tomorrow the LORD will do wonders among you.

Joshua 3:5

It was a spring evening at the Santee Normal Training School. LisBeth, along with Jim Callaway and Agnes Bond, had arrived at the mission earlier in the day. As the sun set, Agnes and Charity lighted a lamp and moved into the parlor at the Birds' Nest, taking with them a laundry basket full of mending. LisBeth sat on the front porch, tapping her toe nervously as she watched Jim ride away. He was headed to tell Soaring Eagle that LisBeth was there. Charity had already told LisBeth that Soaring Eagle and Pastor John Thundercloud had said they would ride up to the church early the morning after the travelers arrived.

As she watched Jim ride away, LisBeth sat down at the edge of the rough-hewn porch. She looked about her at each building of the campus and tried to picture Soaring Eagle participating in the activities there. She thought back to every story her mother had ever told about Soaring Eagle's boyhood. Finally, LisBeth jumped up and headed down the path that led to the spot where Soaring Eagle had saved Carrie and Rachel Brown from a rattlesnake. Carrie had told her the story, and now, as LisBeth sat alone on the creek bank, she tried to imagine her brother standing just on the other side of the creek. She tried to decide what she would say, but words failed her, so she sat quietly, listening to the sounds of water spilling over the rocks and birds twittering in the low brush.

When an owl hooted, LisBeth got up and made her way back

to the Birds' Nest, where Agnes and Charity sat, still mending. The two looked up when LisBeth joined them, taking up a needle and thread and beginning to sew a button on. The women worked together in silence for several minutes before anyone spoke. Finally, Charity laid aside her mending, took up a book, and began to read aloud. After only a few pages, she laid it aside, picking up her Bible instead. She began reading, *"The Lord is my shepherd, I shall not want. . . ."* When she had finished the psalm, Charity said, "LisBeth, there's really nothing I can say to help you through tonight and tomorrow. But I'll be praying for you. Really praying."

With that, Charity patted LisBeth's hand, stood up, and said, "Mother, I think we should retire and give LisBeth some time to think." Agnes laid down her mending and the two women left LisBeth sitting in a chair, watching the shadows from the lighted lamp play on the walls. In only a few moments, she blew out the lamp and retired.

LisBeth tossed and turned and prayed through the long night. She dressed at dawn the next morning and hurried out to the kitchen of the Birds' Nest. Jim was already there, waiting with a cup of strong coffee in his hand. As LisBeth drank, the cup shook. Jim took the cup from her and set it on the table. He was seated across from her, and he took both her hands in his own. "Soaring Eagle is just as nervous as you are, LisBeth. It's going to be fine. Let's pray."

Jim waited for LisBeth to pray, but she looked up at him with shining eyes and said quietly, "I think God is just going to have to read my heart, Jim. I can't find the words."

"Then we'll just open our hearts to him and be quiet before him for a minute."

Jim prayed, "Lord, LisBeth doesn't have the words, and neither do I. We're just going to be quiet here with You for a minute and ask You to go before us and make the way straight." He waited for a few minutes before squeezing LisBeth's hands tightly and murmuring, "Amen."

LisBeth got up shakily and Jim wrapped his arm around her as they walked to the church. Soaring Eagle and John Thundercloud had already arrived, and their hobbled ponies grazed not far away. The two men had lit a lamp, whose light spilled out of the church door and cast a warm glow across the porch.

Taking a deep breath, LisBeth stepped inside.

He was sitting at the front of the church, in the same pew where Carrie Brown had reached out to put her hand in his. He heard LisBeth's footsteps on the porch. When he heard the footsteps coming up the aisle, he stood up and turned around. He had risen shortly after midnight to prepare for this meeting, and he was dressed in every piece of finery he had saved from the old days. His hair was clean and shining, braided into two thick braids wrapped with red calico and decorated with beads and feathers. Gold rings hung from each pierced ear. The five eagle feathers earned in battle hung down the back of his neck from his scalp lock. A fringed and decorated scalp shirt hung almost to his knees. The heavily beaded moccasins and leggings fashioned by Prairie Flower's loving hands completed the wardrobe.

He started to walk toward LisBeth, but when he saw her hesitate, he stopped, too, and stood in front of the pulpit in the small church looking at her. John Thundercloud and Jim Callaway stood quietly, not daring to move or speak.

LisBeth looked at her regally adorned brother and was amazed. Taking a deep breath, she stared at Soaring Eagle and realized that she had seen this face all her life, for it was her own face, molded into more masculine features and hardened by outdoor living.

Soaring Eagle looked upon his sister and saw his father's eyes in the face of a woman. He saw Rides the Wind's cleft chin—even his hairline. Soaring Eagle's eyes smiled with recognition.

One would have expected Soaring Eagle or LisBeth to say something that would be forever quoted by their descendants as they retold the story. But Soaring Eagle was content to stand and take in every detail of the face before him without saying a word, and LisBeth was too nervous to remember what she had planned to say. She finally broke the silence with, "I wish

Carrie Brown were here, Soaring Eagle. She would know what to say."

At the mention of Carrie, LisBeth reached into her pocket and withdrew the golden cross. With a trembling hand, she reached out to Soaring Eagle. "She sent this back to you."

When she opened her hand and Soaring Eagle saw the cross, he slowly reached up to pull the locket from beneath his shirt. As he moved, the thimbles woven into the fringe across the shirt jingled.

He took the locket from around his neck and walked toward LisBeth. "This has traveled a long road of sorrow. I return it to you, my sister, in hopes that now it will make a way of joy between us."

LisBeth opened her hand and Soaring Eagle took the cross and chain, replacing it with the locket. When he touched LisBeth's ice-cold hands, he said quietly, "Walks the Fire's hands were this way when she tended my wounds long ago." His eyes searched LisBeth's, and he went on. "When I look into your face, I see the face of our father, Rides the Wind. He would have rejoiced to see you, LisBeth King Baird. I wish that both our father and our mother could be here now to see that God has ended our wandering and brought us together."

Soaring Eagle had pondered this meeting for a long time. He had prayed for God to show him a way to get across all the barriers between him and his sister. Prayer had reassured him, but he had been given no revelation of what he should say or how he should act in her presence.

However, the God of all grace was there that spring morning in Santee, Nebraska. One testimony to that fact was what Soaring Eagle did after he took the cross and chain from LisBeth's outstretched hand. John Thundercloud would later testify that any doubt he had of the reality of Soaring Eagle's being a new creature in Christ was washed away by his next action.

Soaring Eagle, Lakota warrior, raised to show little emotion in the presence of strangers—Soaring Eagle, great hunter, raised to maintain a stoic bearing in every situation, no matter how painful—Soaring Eagle, man of God—knelt before a white woman and with a voice that broke with emotion said softly, "I come to you this day, my sister, with a broken heart, knowing that I have done things that caused you pain. I ask you to understand that these things were done to defend my village. Even so, my heart is heavy knowing that I caused my sister to mourn. We shared the same father on this earth. We both knew the care of the same woman. But greater than these things is this—God is our Father. Please, *Tanke*—my sister —I ask you to hear what I say and to forgive me."

LisBeth Baird didn't have the knowledge of Lakota society to appreciate fully what was happening. Jim explained it to her later. But LisBeth didn't need knowledge of Lakota society to do the right thing. And she did it.

Kneeling down in front of her brother she reached out to take the cross and chain from his hand. Putting it around his neck she said softly, "Soaring Eagle, *my* people have done things to cause *you* much pain. My heart is also heavy. We shared the same father on this earth. We knew the care of the same woman. And, yes, God is our Father. Please, my brother, I ask you to hear *me* and to forgive us all."

There was more to be said, but it would have to wait. Neither Soaring Eagle nor LisBeth could manage more words. Dawn sent a faint light streaming in the windows and doorway of the little mission church. It illuminated a scene that neither John Thundercloud nor Jim Callaway would ever forget. Kneeling in the aisle of the little church were a Lakota brave named Soaring Eagle and his sister, LisBeth King Baird—holding hands and weeping.

> But they that wait upon the LORD shall renew their strength;
> they shall mount up with wings as eagles;
> they shall run, and not be weary;
> and they shall walk, and not faint.
> Isaiah 40:31

ABOUT THE AUTHOR

Stephanie Grace Whitson was born in East St. Louis, Illinois, and received her B.A. in French from Southern Illinois University in Edwardsville, Illinois. A full-time homemaker, Stephanie has been married to her husband, RTW, who shares Rides the Wind's initials, for twenty years. They homeschool their four children and operate a home-based inspirational gift company called Prairie Pieceworks, Inc. Stephanie is an avid quilter and, with a partner, markets an original line of sewing-related jewelry through their company Mulberry Lane, Inc.

For the past six years the Whitsons have lived on ten and a half secluded acres in rural Nebraska. The story of Jesse King and her descendants was inspired by the lives of pioneers laid to rest in an abandoned cemetery adjacent to the Whitson property.

To receive information about future works by Stephanie, write to her at:

Stephanie Grace Whitson
3800 Old Cheney Road #101-178
Lincoln, NE 68516

An excerpt from Book 3
in the Prairie Winds Series

As Jim tore out of the farmyard on Buck, Sarah rushed to heat water and ready clean linen for the doctor. But before the water was even lukewarm, LisBeth staggered into the kitchen. Her dark eyes wide with terror, she blurted out, "No—time—Sarah. There's no time for the doctor." She managed the last word and then was overcome by the contraction that left her pale and breathless, her knuckles whitening as she grasped the back of a chair.

As soon as LisBeth's grip on the chair relaxed, Sarah helped her back to her bed. She barely had the quilts pulled back before Lisbeth was struggling again. As LisBeth fought against the next contraction, Sarah ran back to the kitchen for a knife and the kettle of water. She noted with dismay that she sloshed some of the water on LisBeth's new wool rug as she hurried through the parlor.

But LisBeth was calling for her, and Sarah hurried back to her side. Setting the kettle on the floor, she dampened a cloth. Then she turned LisBeth's face toward her and looked into her terrified eyes. Tenderly laying the cool cloth over LisBeth's forehead, Sarah said, "LisBeth—listen to me. There's nothing to be afraid of. I know what to do. I helped my mother birth my baby sister Emma. There's nothing to be afraid of, do you hear?"

LisBeth stopped moaning and a glimmer of hope came into her eyes.

"Do you hear me, LisBeth? We can do this." Sarah paused and consciously forced confidence into her voice. "With God's help, we can do it. You're young and healthy, and there's nothing to birthing a baby. Just stay calm, and hold my hand.

I'm right here. I'm not going anywhere. There's nothing to it." Even as she spoke, Sarah prayed, *Dear God, let it be true. Let the baby come easy. Please, God, help me know what to do, help me remember what Mama said.*

There was no more time to pray, for even as trust shone in LisBeth's eyes and a faint smile played about her lips, another contraction came, and she and Sarah were carried into the world where birth and the valley of the shadow of death were often the same thing.

Bookstore Journal Bestseller!

Walks The Fire

The first in a trilogy. *Walks The Fire* tells the story of Jesse, a pioneer woman who falls in love with and marries a Christian Sioux Indian. When Jesse's husband and child are killed on the trek across the Nebraska prairie, she is taken in by a village of Sioux Indians. When she learns to love a Sioux brave, Rides the Wind, Jesse discovers that leaving the whole world behind brings unexpected gifts from God.

0-7852-7981-4 • Trade Paperback • 312 pages